THE GORGE

By Scott Nicholson

Originally published as THEY HUNGER

Copyright ©2007 Scott Nicholson
Haunted Computer Books
ISBN: 978-1-62647-959-3

Haunted Computer Books
P.O. Box 135
Todd, NC 28684 USA
www.AuthorScottNicholson.com

CHAPTER ONE

Shoulda ditched the bitch back in Marietta.

Ace Goodall was tempted to open his fist and let her tumble down the ravine. She was dead weight, dragging him down, same as any woman. That's all they were good for, except on those cold nights when they opened their legs and gave up their heat the way God intended. It was September, and the nights had definitely taken a turn toward chilly in the Southern Appalachian Mountains. So she might be worth keeping for a little while, despite being a bitch.

He pulled, wrapping his other arm around a maple sapling for balance. She barely weighed a hundred pounds, though she was nearly as tall as he was. Five feet five inches, not much rump to speak of, knockers the size of peaches but not nearly as fuzzy. Her hair was black and stringy, but considering she hadn't bathed since the last rain a week ago, she looked pretty good. Plus she was rich, or had been once. Not that money was much use out here in the wilderness.

He squeezed her wrist a little harder than needed as she scrambled for purchase on the leaf-covered loam. *Clara Bannister. An uppity fucking name if there ever was one.*

"You think they saw us?" she whispered.

"No, but they sure as hell are going to hear us if you don't shut that trap."

She couldn't. Figured. Anyway, the river throbbed in the background with a white wash of sound, so they weren't likely to be heard.

"Was it some of *them*?"

"Don't rightly know. It's not like they wore dark suits and sunglasses like the spooks on TV."

"Who else would be way out here on a weekday?"

Ace wondered that himself. They'd encountered a few serious hikers, and those were pretty easy to spot with their worn leather boots, sweaty bandannas, and oily hair. Most had fancy backpacks with aluminum framework, far superior to the ratty Army-surplus canvas jobs that he and Clara carried. He'd been tempted to pull out his Colt Python and ask politely if one of the Greenpeace freaks cared to trade, but then he'd probably end up shooting somebody. Word would get around, and the peaceful back-to-nature bit would go all to hell.

Hikers were no trouble, because even if they knew about Ace Goodall's track record, they would never expect to meet him face-to-face, especially thirty miles from the closest convenience store. Normal people had a hard time believing Ace's kind existed, and probably slept better that way. They didn't understand that Ace was toiling on their behalf, doing The Lord's dirty work himself because they lacked the balls and faith and outrage. No, hikers wouldn't give him a second glance.

These last two had been different. Sure, they packed all the right brand-name gear, sported a touch of stubble, and bore that gritty-eyed look of men who had recently slept under the stars. But something wasn't right. Maybe their steel-toed Timberlands weren't scuffed enough, or their gaits were too precise, like soldiers on a field exercise. They didn't droop. They stood upright, alert, as if paying close attention to their surroundings. More like hunters than hikers.

If Ace and Clara hadn't been resting on a slight rise, under the shade of a lightning-charred oak, they probably would have bumped into the pair on the trail. Ace trusted his instincts, what he called his "little messages from above," and his gut reaction had been that these guys were trouble. Not trouble like Ace, who could cut you open and count your ribs from the inside before your heart stopped beating, but trouble of the long-armed-law variety.

"Something ain't right about them," he said, wiping sweat from the back of his neck. Though the nights had hinted at frost, it was still Indian summer during the day. The woods were rich with the smell of goldenrod, daisies, and ironweed, as well as the ripe odor of rotting leaves.

"They didn't see us, though." Clara gave him a smile, and those neat white teeth irritated him, a reminder of his own upbringing. His family couldn't afford dental care. Though Ace had just crossed that hallowed ground into his thirties, he'd already lost three adult teeth, only one of them from a fistfight. Some of the others were black, and a cavity in his bottom left molar had hit the roots and tongued him with hellfire.

"I told you, The Lord's looking after us. It's holy work."

"I believe you."

"Sometimes I feel like I could drive right up to the biggest police station in the South, park right out front in a handicapped spot, wave my pecker around, and they'd never even give me a ticket." Ace forgot to keep his voice down. A prison chaplain had once explained to him about "religious mania," but though Ace had a fondness for crazy people, he didn't cotton much to maniacs. Besides, the two hikers were probably a mile away by now.

"What do we do now?" Clara asked. "If we go back to the trail, we might run into them."

"We got an hour or so before sundown." Ace squinted through the sparse foliage of the treetops to the smeared patch of purple sunset in the west. "Let's just stick to the ridge and then set up camp when we find a flat spot."

He turned and walked between the towering hardwoods, knowing she would follow without question. The river pulsed with a constant dull roar below them, a white noise that washed over the sounds of birds and small animals. The force of the river made the ridge vibrate. Ace could dig that raw power. Like the bombs in his knapsack. Ace wasn't much of a nature freak, but he'd learned the best way to evade attention was to go where no one else bothered. If that meant hiding out for a while in the ass end of Possum Paradise, then so be it.

They had been following the Unegama for three days, though the trail sometimes meandered away from the river's course because of the steepness of the grade. Ace had seen the foaming brown-green water and, even from a safe distance, he could visualize it churning around rocks and making its mad dash for the Atlantic Ocean.

He bent, kicked up a fist-sized stone, and hurled it into the gorge. If he had bigger balls, he'd stand on the rocky ledge and take a piss. Nothing like heights to make a man want to arc a yellow rainbow. But he figured water made its way downhill no matter what, and eventually it all ended up in the same place.

They came to a group of jagged gray stones protruding from the black dirt like the fingers of a premature burial victim. A fine, chilly spray added weight to the air. The trees thinned and Ace could make out the walls of the gorge. Off-white rock plunged eighty feet down, worn smooth by eons of running water that had probably started as a ridgetop trickle and then cut its way deep into the skin of the Earth. The rock bore the stubble of twisted, stunted balsams, and veins of quartz crystal glittered in the dying daylight. Though they were fifty feet from the ledge, Ace got vertigo from the yawning space of the gorge.

A section of the ledge had recently given way, judging by the dirt clinging to the upturned roots. The rocks were different, too, not worn and splotched with gray moss like those across the rest of the ridge. Clara had told him the Appalachian chain was the oldest stretch of mountains in the world, which Ace thought was dumb, because the Book of Genesis set down the creation date of the heavens and Earth as all at once.

So how could one mountain be older than another? At any rate, Ace didn't like the thought of standing anywhere near that ledge. The walls of the gorge looked like so many stacked pieces of rock, anyway, and if a piece kicked out somewhere near the bottom, the whole ridge might tumble down.

He moved away from the ledge, heading into the woods. It would be time to camp soon. Clara stood a moment longer, looking out over the ripples of soil and trees that spread as far as the eye could see before vanishing into a soft, blue haze on the horizon. Ace waited for her footsteps in the leaves behind him.

"Haircuts," he shouted, loudly enough to be heard over the river.

"Huh?" Clara's pretty pink mouth was hanging open. If

he were a violent man, he'd backhand her for looking like an idiotic mouth-breather.

"Haircuts. That's what was wrong with them. Trimmed above the ears, the kind that don't need no comb."

She nodded, finally closing her mouth. Ace unclenched his fists and rubbed a palm over his own greasy, tangled scalp.

"Think of the people we've seen out here," he said. "None of them looked like they been in spitting distance of a bar of soap. Pretty much, most of them looked like they had fleas."

Clara scratched her underarm, as if remembering some of their sleazy lodgings of the few weeks. "Those guys looked clean, like something out of the Ivy League," she said.

Ace didn't know diddly shit about the Ivy League. Sounded like soccer, or some other foreign sport. "Or maybe Quantico," he said.

"Good thing they didn't see us, then."

Ace smiled, curling his tongue in the gap of a missing canine. "Told ya, it's God's doing," he said. Just like God had helped him rig the time-delay fuses on those bombs in Birmingham and Tupelo. A little fire and brimstone for the baby butchers.

He waved toward a small clearing away from the ledge. "Come on, let's make camp before dark."

CHAPTER TWO

The thrill is gone.

B.B. King sang it as a bluesy lament about lost love. Bowie Whitlock applied the sentiment equally to his dead wife, his profession, and his unfortunate and unwanted habit of drawing the next breath. The breaths were coming a bit short now, and he wondered if his legendary endurance had faded a little with time, rust, and indifference.

A mile deep in the Unegama Wilderness Area and he already felt used up, a wet nurse with a dry tit who had a half-dozen snapping, hungry mouths to feed. The real journey still lay ahead, all thirteen miles of it, not counting the half-day hike to the launch point. Wednesday had broken at forty degrees and died at seventy, Indian summer in the mountains. All of them would be sweating by the time they reached their campsite at the headwaters.

The thrill is gone and still you walk. Alone.

Bowie was in the lead, and the group had fallen into a single-file march, though the trail was several feet wide. This part of the trail was clearly marked, with little change in elevation, and there was no practical need for Bowie to take point. He'd done it as a psychological tactic, wanting the group to know who was in charge.

Even if the trip went smoothly, a time would inevitably come for quick decisions. Probably not of the life-and-death variety, despite Farrengalli's blowhard attitude and big chin, but the remote heart of the wilderness was no place to debate the pecking order. Farrengalli had fallen to the rear of the group, probably fantasizing about all the Vietnam War movies he'd watched.

ProVentures' patsies, Bowie had taken to calling the members of the group. Like him, they each had a reason for being there, mostly having to do with a mixture of moxie, money, and a little bit of madness. Vincent Farrengalli, a loudmouthed Italian from the Bronx, had immediately set Bowie's pulse two degrees above where it needed to be. Farrengalli was trouble, mostly because he was the least qualified to be on the trip. ProVentures and *Back2Nature Magazine* wanted him for his dark looks and brashness, which amounted to handsome publicity whether the trip was a success or failure.

Bowie gave an extra tug on his belt. He'd poked a third notch in the leather during the summer, a tribute to the two hundred daily sit-ups and his vegetarian diet. Obsessive routine served him well. One more rep, one more step. Prevented him from thinking, dwelling, remembering. Memory was a thing to be obliterated at any cost, be it through pain, pride, or the simple joy of loathing the jackasses who had hired him.

At least those jackasses paid well. If Bowie survived this gig, he'd be set for a few more years of solitude. Attitude was everything, and a little mystique helped with the hype. Bowie had a reputation, all right, though he only cared when the bean counters made a big deal of it. He knew he was on the downhill slide and soon reputation would be all he had left. But that was just as well. The thrill, after all, was gone for good.

Nothing left but the next step, the next rep.

The next breath.

For perennial Tour Du France champion Lance Armstrong, it had been all about the bike. For Bowie, it was all about the boots. He'd logged two thousand miles in the personally designed Timberlands that hugged his feet like twin sets of spooning lovers. In the group orientation meeting, Bowie had advised everyone to buy either a waterproof boot or else apply waterproofing themselves. He'd even recommended SealSkinz socks, though he wasn't getting any sponsorship kickbacks from the company. But he didn't think anyone had followed his advice. They'd probably survive, but he wouldn't mind if they were visited with blisters, bunions, athlete's foot fungus, and the odd hangnail thrown in for good measure.

"Yo, how much farther?" said someone a couple of places back. Bowie had to slow his breathing and divert his cynical musings to come up with the name.

Initials.

Something with initials.

Rhymes with "hay."

Okay.

A-okay.

Okay McKay.

C.A. McKay, the golden boy, the next Lance Armstrong. Finished sixth at the Giro del Capo, fourth at the Stazio Criterium, and, with Armstrong's retirement, was expected to soon move to the head of the United States bicycling class. Bowie suspected that if the sponsors had decided on a mountain bike expedition instead of a white-water trip, McKay would be point and Bowie would be watching the sun and moon track the big sky above his cabin near the

Missouri Breaks in Montana. Bowie almost wished he were in that remote and personal world, lost in thought, except he knew thoughts would lead to that dark hole, a place his mind sought as persistently as a tongue probed a lost tooth.

Biker boy.

C.A. "Okay" McKay.

The type of catchy name you need.

Nabbed the latest cover of Cycling News, *gets laid more than George Clooney, but on* this *trip, he's middle of the pack. I'm first.*

"A mile and a half," Bowie said. The distance to the Unegama headwaters where they would make camp was more like a mile and two thousand feet, but he wasn't sure his fellow travelers would appreciate the distinction. And he didn't want to waste breath explaining. Truth be told (not that he'd ever admit the truth—no use changing old habits now), his lungs were working a bit harder than expected.

"Mile and half," McKay passed along, so much louder than necessary in the hush of the forest that Bowie suspected he, too, was sucking for oxygen. "With wheels, I could do that in ten minutes."

"Well, next time get your bike company to put up the money, and we'll do it the easy way," Bowie said. "This time we're doing it the ProVentures way."

"The best way," said the man behind Bowie and in front of McKay. Bowie had forgotten the man's name. All Bowie knew was his checks were signed by the outdoor adventure company, which had been started by two stoners with a love for the great outdoors, but now mostly employed computer geeks and business majors. The two founding stoners had made their fortune on a sleeping bag with a "most excellent" logo, one designed to appeal to daybreak rollers, High Noon huffers, teatime puffers, and midnight tokers. The logo featured an infamous five-fingered plant in bold green beneath a jagged red slash. "Just Say Maybe," read that original logo.

Over the years, as the rebel teen customers became soft in the belly and no longer lit up before board meetings, the ProVentures logo had transformed first to a five-branched green tree, then an upended peace sign; then the red slash went away, and for the last five years the company was widely recognized for its slanted P logo with a lesser-green image of the globe behind it.

"The best way," Bowie parroted without looking back. Point never looked back, unless there was an emergency.

"The ProVentures way," the company man said, almost as if a cheer were expected.

"Pro-fuckin'-*Ventures*," Farrengalli shouted from the rear. "You guys fucking rock."

Fuckin' A, Bowie thought. *The dude's going to say "Fuckin' A" any second now, because he watched* Apocalypse Now *ten times.*

"It's only natural," the company man said, spouting the slogan the company had adopted after the stock split four ways.

"O-o-o-o-o-nly   FUCKIN'   NATURALLLLL!!!!!" Farrengalli bellowed in a voice that drowned out the first few whistling birds and scuffling ground animals Bowie had heard since the start of the hike. He wanted to tell the greaseball to eat a dirty root. Because the quiet had been nice. Almost too nice.

Every point walks alone.

In the quiet, they look for things to confess.

They look for things right in front of their faces.

The Unegama Wilderness Area compared neither in size nor reputation to some of the Midwestern regions that had been preserved by early and optimistic Congresses. But this forest appealed to Bowie. It was old, diverse, and strange. The hardwoods rose up to the sun, the evergreens crowded the waterways, and a thousand low-growth species sprouted from the black loam of the ancient hills. This was an ancient world, a secret world, no matter how many feet had marked these trails.

He'd memorized the maps, because such mental exercise took his mind from the dark hole. He'd been raised in the region, and had cut his teeth as a white-water guide on the lower stretch of the river. The mid-level kayakers hit the Unegama on the lower three miles, where the few challenging rapids were broken by gentle and scenic runs and the river emptied out on a lake. Bowie had even led a few advanced runs on the middle stretch, but he'd known of few paddlers crazy or suicidal enough to try the upper waters.

"Natural," muttered the man behind Bowie. Travis Lane, the ProVentures rep.

Natural. It's only natural. The company's successful slogan had contributed to the inevitable gutting of the word. Nothing was natural these days. Nature itself was a commodity, bought and sold by power companies. Air reduced to profit.

Breathe.

Bowie hated his lungs. They were two hot bricks. He could have hiked this trail without a second thought eight years ago. Now, second thoughts were all he had.

And thoughts of the woman in the group, who should

never have taken the assignment. For personal reasons. Very personal reasons.

Breathe, step, breathe.

"Only natural," Bowie said under his breath, which was the only way he could say it at the moment.

Farrengalli opened his loud mouth from the curve of the trail. "Hey, Okay, how's the view?"

"Looks pretty *super*natural to me, if you believe all the bullshit stories," McKay said. That drew a laugh from the whole group, with the exception of Bowie. He sucked a snicker back up into his nose.

"It's only fuckin' *NAAAAAAA*tural," Farrengalli rumbled, startling a raven that had been watching the group from the high perch of a sycamore. It took wing, and Bowie saw the bird framed briefly against the sinking sun before it disappeared over the treetops.

The low clouds were bruised and troubled. The forecast had called for clear skies, but the escarpment and the altitude led to unpredictable weather in the wilderness area. If conditions turned wet, they'd be doing a lot more hiking than rafting. The Unegama was treacherous in the best of times. At its worst, it could drink a man like a tornado swallowed a gnat.

And then there were the legends. About something else that could drink a man.

"Hey, Bowie, how's the view from up there?" Farrengalli bellowed.

Bowie wished the clouds would collide long enough to piss on the jerk's parade.

CHAPTER THREE

As Clara cleared away branches and stones to make a flat space to camp, Ace ran a fine strand of trip wire around nearby trees. The booby trap circled the perimeter of the camp. He placed detonators in three sections, with the pull triggers set for a three-second delay. The detonators were each attached to two pounds of C-4 plastic explosive, the same kind he'd used on those abortion clinics. Ace kept one bomb, because the Free Militia taught him to keep something in reserve at all times.

Ace returned to the campsite, pulled the sleeping bag from his backpack, and tucked the plastic explosive among the dirty clothes. The sleeping bag stank of old sweat, though he could barely smell it over the odor of his own body. They shared the sleeping bag, which cut down on the weight they carried, but sometimes Clara's birdlike bones poked into his side or thigh and it got a little too cramped. She'd complained about his snoring once, but only once, by God. He rolled out the nylon-filled bag and sat on it.

"Should we risk a fire?" Clara pulled some tin cans from her pack, along with a plastic water bottle. They'd been drinking from springs, but the water seemed safe enough. The way Ace figured, the government probably hadn't gotten around to dumping its shitty chemicals in the mountains yet.

"It ought to be safe this close to the river," Ace said. "The way the breeze kicks up over the gorge, the smoke will spread out fast. We can keep the flames low and snuff it before full dark."

Ace gathered some twigs and dry needles from the surrounding balsams. He scooped out a hollow in the dark soil. After spreading the tinder around, he ignited it with his Bic. Clara used a little field can opener to open some pork and beans, which she slopped into a black-bottomed aluminum pan. Ace angled a few rocks around the fire, adding some larger sticks until they caught and crackled, then sat back while Clara cooked. Ace longed for a burger and fries, something gut-clogging that would slow the runs he'd endured for the last few days. He was sick of beef jerky, canned beans, and that sweetened horseshit Clara called "energy bars."

They'd been wandering the Unegama Gorge Wilderness Area for a couple of weeks, ever since the last close call back at that motel in Cullowhee. He'd looked out the window and seen a County Mountie idling in the parking lot and talking into a handset, no doubt running the plates on the stolen car. Ace put an Atlanta Braves baseball cap low over his forehead, sent Clara out, and told her to meet him at the Dumpster in five minutes. She wore a sweatshirt and a baggy-assed hippie skirt, so no cop in his right mind would take her for a killer at first glance. A doper, maybe, but she was too fresh-faced to be linked to a half-dozen homicides. Give or take a few. Ace had lost count, and he'd never learned to read well enough to follow the newspaper accounts, though he sometimes clipped the stories.

From the Dumpster, they'd slipped into the woods, walked a half mile, and thumbed a ride in a pickup. Clara sat up front, Ace in the bed, and Ace figured she did the driver a slobbery favor, because he went ten miles out of his way to drop them near the Appalachian Trail. Ace had a map of the wilderness area, figuring sooner or later he'd have to take to the woods. He hadn't counted on company, but here Clara was, and here he was, and beans sat steaming in the pan, a soft, soapy lump of fat floating in the sugary sauce.

"Do you really believe it was the FBI?" Clara asked. The idea seemed to excite her, because her eyes brightened. Or maybe it was the firelight dancing off her pupils.

"Probably not. Haircuts or no haircuts, they got no reason to look for us out here."

"If they traced that stolen car—"

"They don't know it was me that stole it. Could have been anybody. Cars get swiped every day in this country. They don't call it 'the land of opportunity' for nothing. Course, they also call it 'The Land of the Free,' and that's a goddamned laugh."

She stirred the beans with a pocketknife. "Do you want sardines or potted meat with this?"

"The stink-ass fish." Ace had a sudden ache for the good old days, right after the first bomb when he'd been something of a folk hero among his peers. He'd parlayed his notoriety into a modern-day Underground Railroad without the niggers, finding food and shelter among various militia groups and fellow freedom fighters.

Those were days of hamburger and Pabst Blue Ribbon, high spirits and big plans. But one by one his allies turned their backs, because the feds had brought heat down on all of them as a result. After the second bombing, Ace had pretty much become an outcast among outcasts after two women and a child had died in the blast. As if it were Ace's fault that that the baby-killing bitch brought her kid along when she visited the clinic. Those abortionist sluts were always looking for someone to blame besides themselves.

He had been working his way north when Clara stumbled into his life, ten miles outside Atlanta. She was hitching in the rain, and he pulled over to lecture her on the murderers and rapists and spics and other trash that prowled America's highways, preying on the innocent. She said she was heading north, but in no hurry. Three days later, they'd killed their first victim together.

Well, Ace did the killing, but she was there. She loved him extra special that night.

Clara was still a long way from Virginia, but at least she was safe now, Ace thought. Even if she couldn't cook worth a damn. Nuts and berries would taste better than the shit she served up.

"How long do you think we can hide out in the gorge?" she asked.

"Be too cold by Thanksgiving. You ain't got enough meat on your bones to get me through a winter night and I sure as hell wasn't born no polar bear. I guess I'll be heading back to Alabama then."

"I thought we were going north."

"You ain't supposed to think. And who said anything about *you*, anyway?"

Clara stirred the beans with the fork attachment of a Swiss Army knife, and then drained the sardine oil onto the fire, causing it to spit. Amid the sizzle, Ace heard the snapping of a stick, a sound less brittle than that of the flames. He was going to ask in a low voice if Clara had heard it, but she'd probably blurt out, "Hear what?" and every bear, cop, and mugger in a ten-mile radius would know their location.

Instead, Ace reached into his jacket and put his hand on the Python. "I got to take a dump," he said, rising from the log and heading toward the trees from where the sound had come. The sun had sunk further behind the mountains, bruising the sky and causing shadows to rise from the forest floor.

"You forgot the toilet paper," Clara said.

"Worry about your own ass," he whispered to himself.

Probably wasn't those two haircut guys they'd seen, the two dudes who probably weren't Feds. But Ace didn't take stock in a whole lot of "probablies." Besides, they'd seen enough hippies in the gorge, and Ace trusted them about as much as he trusted the Internal Revenue Service. He wouldn't be surprised if one raided their camp just to see if they had any dope. Ace would only use the gun as a last resort, but last resorts were like probablies—they had a way of coming along a little too often.

And he'd rather not have them trigger the C-4. He didn't have much experience with open-air explosions and he wasn't certain about the shrapnel and explosive force. Plus, since he'd been forced underground, the shit was hard to come by.

On this side of the ridge, away from the river, the slopes were less rocky. Ace pressed himself against the trunk of a massive oak, gray moss tickling his cheek. From his vantage point, he could see most of the valley. A rhododendron thicket lay in a little depression below. In the dying light, the ripples of the distant ridges looked like giant ocean waves, a soft fog settling in the valleys. It was peaceful out here, with nothing but the birds and squirrels to bother him. A man could think in the mountains, if left alone. Sort things out, make sense of the world, get his shit together. Shut out the white noise of modern life.

To hell with it. This *was* modern life, where women flushed their babies while the goddamned Republicans turned up their noses and Democrats rolled over and took it up the ass. A life where the cops wanted to slap him in irons when they should have been pinning medals on his chest. A life where the innocent had no rights and those who fought for the innocent were guilty. A life where—

Something moved in a stand of sugar maples to his right.

Sun dappled the ground through the red leaves, but the wind had momentarily died, so it couldn't have been swaying branches. Ace exhaled with his mouth open, letting his lungs empty so he could hear better. Leaves scuffled with sudden movement. A man stepped into a gap between trees, bent low as if sneaking. Ace recognized the gray flannel shirt, the brown vest, and the haircut.

One of the Quantico boys.

The agent (and Ace was certain now the pair had been FBI agents, he'd just been lying to himself as usual) crouched in the cover of a fallen tree, and then worked his way up the slope. He was forty yards away from Ace, out of pistol range, even a Python's. Ace wouldn't risk a shot anyway, not until he'd located both agents. The noise would give away his position, and the element of surprise would shift again. Right now, the Feds thought they were on the hunt, closing in, but it was Ace who held all the cards.

The agents were probably going by the book, closing in on them from each flank. They had probably seen the fire.

So it was Clara's fault. He'd tried to talk her out of it, but could you tell a woman anything? No, their heads were harder than the goddamned granite that lined the walls of the gorge.

Ace wondered if the FBI agents were trained military. If so, they might know how to detect trip wires and avoid them.

It would serve Clara right if he just waited for the agent to reach the ridge, then head down the slope himself and leave her to catch all the heat. Without the backpack and supplies, he might be in for a few rough days, but that beat trial in a federal court. United States prosecutors would probably go for the death penalty, and though Ace wasn't afraid of dying, he couldn't bear the humiliation of being called "guilty."

A trial would give him a chance to take the stand and explain just who was guilty (all those long-haired hippie women who let murderers vacuum babies out of their bellies) and who was innocent, but true justice was not only blind, it had a sock in its mouth and cotton in both ears. The only judgment that mattered would be handed down by Him Above. And Ace imagined a mighty big pat on the back was coming, and a soft chair, and a heavenly fridge that never ran out of beer.

The agent was now in decent range, fifty-fifty chance that Ace could take the top of his skull off, but the second agent hadn't put in an appearance. Darkness had a deeper grip on the woods now, and the agent's flannel shirt blended into the undergrowth. But his skin was as white as a pearl, making his progress easy to track. He must be the desk jockey of the pair; Ace knew the FBI often teamed a shrink with a piss-and-vinegar guy. While the piss-and-vinegar guy would be the most dangerous, you better not misunderestimate anybody who'd made it through Quantico. They were usually good men who just happened to work on the wrong side of good and evil.

Ace's palm sweated around the Python's grip. He hadn't shifted so much as a finger since drawing his weapon. The bark of the oak was digging into his cheek, but the tree's mass gave him comfort. The Fed had his pistol out, probably a high-caliber Glock, but no way could those bullets cut through a tree. If only Ace could locate Piss-and-Vinegar, he'd feel like the odds were even.

Clara called Ace's name.

The agent lifted his head from concealment, looking in the direction of the camp. Ace could have pegged him like that critter in the Whac-A-Mole game, but the situation might play out even better now. Because, from the ruckus Clara was raising, Ace had a good idea where the second agent was.

Haircut Number One broke into a run, leaving the thick evergreen undergrowth for the easier route between the large trees. Ace could have made his escape then. But if they took Clara, they'd learn a lot about Ace, plus the Feds would swarm the area like flies on fresh shit. The best strategy was to take them both down. Besides, he'd be doing the country a favor by knocking a couple of moochers off the taxpayers' tit.

Ace followed Haircut Number One, who slung his pack to the ground and jogged, bent low with a small, two-way radio to his ear. "Suspect in sight?" the agent said into the mouthpiece.

A static cackle was the only reply, the words washed out by the noise of leaves crunching beneath the agent's boots. They were getting near the clearing. And the trip wire.

The campfire threw throbbing waves of light against the trees. Ace ran in a simian gait, relaxed and confident. He played the scene out in his mind, the two agents grilling Clara, asking about her companion, scaring her into a confession. He'd peg Piss-and-Vinegar with the first shot, then drop Haircut Number One before the sound of the first shot died away. Then he'd walk out of the trees, tuck his gun in his pants, and ask Clara if the beans were ready.

Except the game didn't follow the rules.

The dusk roared, the trees shook, and the explosion's concussion cast a warm wind across his face.

CHAPTER FOUR

Jim Castle (the man Ace had dubbed "Piss-and-Vinegar") was full of only piss at the moment. Mostly he was pissed at himself. Eight years in the Navy SEALs; another six as a special agent in the FBI's Hostage Rescue Team, or the "Super SWAT guys," as they were called in house; 14 months assigned to the Goodall case, mostly as a sideline observer with a too-clean desk; then, three glorious weeks sleeping in the woods and eating what tasted like chipped horsemeat and Kennel Rations, riding shotgun on The Rook (whom Ace had dubbed "Haircut") as they searched the gorge. All that time and effort building to the biggest moment of his career, and now he was stuck in the Appalachian equivalent of the Black Hole of Calcutta.

"Jim...." Derek Samford's voice came from the handheld radio somewhere below him. The radio had slipped from his belt when he'd fallen—or more precisely, when the earth had moved.

If Castle could have reached the radio, he would have told The Rook to stay on point, to take Goodall down first and then worry about his partner. They needed a nail in the Bama Bomber. That's the only way this ending would be happy. Because Castle had screwed the pooch big-time, the kind of boondoggle that would make them howl with laughter back in DC.

But only after Goodall was locked away, of course. No

one would laugh before then, especially the older veterans, who would see their own decline mirrored in Jim Castle's bad judgment. Not the fresh faces, the new agents who thought scars and kills were the measure of a man. And certainly not the higher-ups, who were getting reamed by Southern Congressmen and the press over their continued inability to nab a fugitive with a recorded IQ of ninety-five.

Castle moved his legs. Nothing broken, though his hips were jammed tight between two molars of granite. He had some nasty scrapes along his thighs, and a tickling sensation down his shin signaled a line of oozing blood from his knee. He arched his neck and looked at the diminishing funnel of daylight ten feet above. The opening in the earth was raw and jagged, and pale roots poked from the soil like sick snakes. Specks of dirt sprinkled down and bounced off Jim's face and shoulders. A piece of grit lodged in the corner of his left eye, and he blinked it to mud.

The sides of the opening didn't appear in immediate danger of collapse, so Castle figured suffocation wasn't the biggest danger.

No, friend, suffocation is not your biggest danger. Your biggest danger is Robert Wayne "Ace" Goodall walking up to the edge of the hole, whipping out his baby-maker, and showering you with a tender stream of golden humiliation. Just before capping your ass and bringing the Bama Bomber back into the national headlines.

Good agents avoided headlines, even those like him who were scrambling down the final rungs on the FBI ladder. They didn't wear dark glasses just for vanity. Speak to the media only when necessary, and only when higher ranks were dodging the microphone.

He'd wanted one of those doors to open that led into the

Puzzle Palace, the field agents' fond nickname for DC headquarters. But he was far too old already, and this wasn't a good time to get his name in the papers. No matter how you cut it, showing up as a casualty in the first paragraph wasn't such a hot career move.

He had a .357-caliber Glock in his shoulder holster, but his upper torso was too contorted to reach the pistol. He was in no shape for a shoot-out.

"What's your 10-20?" came The Rook's modulated voice. Though the broadcast was muffled, the words somehow echoed, as if a small cave yawned below him. That was just wonderful. If he managed to wriggle free of his rocky vise grip and slide down, he had no idea how far the drop would be. Another ten feet, no problem, maybe a twisted ankle. Twenty feet, in that kind of terrain, meant broken bones, deep contusions, and the real possibility of head trauma.

Then relying on The Rook to find him and drag him to safety.

Derek Samford wasn't technically a rookie, and wasn't all that much younger than Castle. He'd put in three years as an Army officer, aced his courses at Quantico, and then eased into the unit known as Behavioral Sciences. He was more cerebral than hard ass, more Jodie Foster than Edward G. Robinson, but The Rook had endured twenty-two-and-three-quarter days in the backwoods without a complaint and only a slight case of butt-crack rash. He consulted his wrist compass a little too often, tracking the sun's path and acting the part of Nature Boy, though the wristband was of the blaze-orange variety that warned hunters not to shoot because a two-legged hairless monkey was on the other end. Castle could forgive him for the silly instrument because his partner knew north from south.

The Rook would make the grade one day, keeping his hair groomed to whatever standard the FBI brass decreed, working overtime in exchange for having a life, and succeeding whether or not he lost a partner along the way. So Castle's probable death meant nothing to the outcome of the case.

Death? Assuming Goodall doesn't blow your brains to scrambled eggs, you'll probably live hours. Long enough to regret it.

Castle's decision to outflank Goodall and his companion had seemed like a solid strategy. The book on the Bama Bomber was "armed and extremely dangerous and likely to take a busload of nuns with him." In a showdown, Goodall would use the woman as a shield, or kill her on the spot. While Castle and The Rook would be limited in their gunplay because of an innocent bystander, Goodall had nothing to lose. Rampant homicide was a blank check.

Not that Castle believed the woman was truly innocent. Everybody was guilty of something, and then it was just a question of degree.

A stone the size of his fist bounced within inches of his shoulder. The opening above him shivered again, as if bracing for the onslaught of winter. But the ground wasn't cold yet, so it shifted and settled. A runnel of dirt sloughed down from his left, adding another few inches of weight against his waist.

Suffocation was the most likely outcome, for sure. If Goodall didn't come back to finish the job first.

Castle had been edging up to the camp, guided by the thin thread of smoke from the fire. He'd gone from tree to tree, moving the way they'd taught in Hogan's Alley. But shooting at cutout targets was a little different than shooting a breathing human being. Even when this particular human being deserved it, if "human" even applied to someone who taken at least four lives. Five if you counted the fetus.

Castle had gone over every possible detail with The Rook before they made the approach. Every detail except the possibility of a booby trap. The plan was to capture Goodall alive if at all possible (though they both knew no one would question a kill), make sure the woman didn't take one for posterity, cut off any escape routes, and use the cliff edge to block Goodall's retreat. Castle from the left, with the sun at his back, and The Rook closing in from the east, aided by his hunter's compass. No way could Castle have foreseen a trip wire.

No way, because the brass hadn't expected Ace Goodall to actually be in the Unegama. Otherwise, why would they have sent me?

A bomb that matched the previous attacks had detonated in San Antonio a month ago, shifting the manhunt from the Southern states to Texas. The tip placing Goodall in the Southern Appalachians was one of those believed to be a complete waste of time, but one that had to be followed up nonetheless. Since experienced, knowledgeable agents were in short supply and needed for the primary investigation, mop-up was left to burnouts like Castle. The FBI hadn't bothered to set up a regional command center or a communications post, and their radio batteries were all but dead.

This was one mission he'd been stuck with, for sure. Castle was wedged tighter than a cork in a parakeet's ass.

"10-20?"

The Rook. On the radio. Probably hunkered down behind a tree somewhere, analyzing the situation, measuring Goodall's probable reaction with the blunt instruments of psychology and guesswork. No shots fired, so the situation was still under control. That was the book, and The Rook went by the book. Under control.

"Control" was a military word, the delusion of a former officer. Over the past three weeks, The Rook had taught Castle plenty about Robert Wayne Goodall. The personality assessment was crafted from bits of the Unabomber, Eric Rudolph, Timothy McVeigh, and—

Imaginary cases and boondoggles.

Something tugged on his boot, somewhere in that numb space below.

Must be a loose rock falling, putting more pressure on him. That meant the little cavern was shifting. Another palm's worth of dirt sprinkled onto his shoulders from above. So the bomb-spawned earthquake hadn't finished its business yet. The mountain hadn't settled. God still wanted to play with his latest plaything, like a cat batting a crippled mouse.

The tug came again.

"Jim."

Castle heard The Rook both above him and on the radio's speaker below him. "Down here."

The Rook's head appeared in the opening, silhouetted against the dusk. "Are you hurt?"

"Not yet. Where's Goodall?"

"I didn't see him."

Castle wiggled, kicking his foot, trying to free it from whatever had it snagged. "Take him down. I'll be fine."

"I can't leave you."

"Take him down, damn it."

"I lost him. What the hell happened?"

"Trip wire. I blew it."

"Hey, we all make mistakes."

Castle grimaced. His mistakes were getting to be pretty frequent. But this might be his latest and greatest. This might be his last.

The Rook lay on his belly and stretched an arm into the gap. Castle reached up, the shoulder muscle complaining, but a good two feet separated their fingertips. "I'll have to find a branch or something to pull you out," The Rook said.

"Watch your ass. Goodall's got to be around here somewhere."

"The camp was empty."

"I heard the woman scream."

"No shots, though. Maybe he took her. Hold on. I'll check the camp."

Castle could hold on, all right. Not like he had anything better to do. Though the tugging on his boot had grown more insistent. Castle remembered the *Jaws* craze, when TV and newspapers were filled with shark frenzy. Bite victims often described their initial attacks as painless yanks, but then looked down to find the stub of a limb gushing blood.

Attack. He wondered why that word had entered his mind. What did he suspect, that a giant mutant groundhog was chomping on his shoe leather, trying to get at the flesh inside?

Something swooped over the opening, a fleeting shadow that strained against the dusk. Castle's perspective was skewed due to the narrowness of the opening, but the thing appeared to flutter its wings like a bat. Except these wings hadn't been frantic, guided by a blind pilot.

They had moved as slowly as a crippled vulture's, a bird that only needed a few strokes to lift its body and glide on the wind currents. The vultures couldn't have found him already, could they? If so, he'd damn well show them he was far from carrion.

Or maybe the vulture was after something else. Maybe Goodall had left a victim in the vicinity, either the girl or some unlucky hiker. Or maybe the Bama Bomber had been killed by his own shrapnel.

No, God never dished out such fair justice. If justice is blind, then God is nearsighted.

The bird swooped overhead again. Castle saw now that it wasn't a vulture after all. Freshwater herons might live near the river, or some other large fisher, but this creature flew without purpose. This thing didn't even seem to have real wings.

It was red and wrinkled and hideously ugly, almost as large as a man.

Sort of like the creature under his childhood bed might have looked. But Castle didn't want to think about that. Besides, the bed was far, far away. But night was getting closer by the second.

CHAPTER FIVE

One of the bombs must have had a faulty trigger, because it had detonated a couple of seconds after the first two. Ace hadn't expected the wire to set off all three bombs. The sulfuric stench of explosives filled the air, along with shredded bits of leaves. After Ace picked himself off the ground, it took a second to get oriented.

Haircut Number One was prone on the ground, yelling into the radio. "Castle! You down?"

A voice, most likely that of Piss-and-Vinegar, broke through the static and burst from the speaker. No words came out, only an angry moan.

"What's your 10-20?" Haircut said into his mouthpiece, rising and circling below the clearing, nearly disappearing into the gloom. In the silence that followed the explosion, Ace hustled to keep up. If Piss-and-Vinegar was down, then Ace could nail Haircut during the rescue attempt. Cops and soldiers had those stupid codes of honor that required them to risk their own lives for their fallen buddies.

"Ace?" Clara called from the camp.

Haircut, hearing her voice, headed toward the ledge that opened up onto the gorge. Piss-and-Vinegar must have tried to sneak up on the camp from that side, figuring to hide among the rocks. Haircut stopped, set aside his radio, and sprawled on his belly in the jumble of granite slabs.

The bombs had triggered a landslide.

He shouted down into an opening in the rocks. The roar of the river kept his words from reaching Ace, who gripped a dead tree at the edge of the clearing. Though the deepening darkness disguised the sheer expanse of the gorge, Ace could feel it in his gut, and vertigo turned his knees to jelly.

Damn. He would have loved a two-fer, getting headlines in big type, but he wasn't quite ready for the last hurrah. A cop killing would pretty much guarantee his own execution, and he wanted his death to mean something. The Lord had told him that life was sacred, even if that life was still in its mother's belly. But all life wasn't created equal. Ace scrambled away from the agent, glad to put some distance between him and the ledge. He doubled back to the campsite, expecting to find Clara there.

The beans had turned black in the pan, the fire had burned low, and Clara was nowhere in sight. Damned high-toned bitch. Let the Feds have her. She couldn't tell them much they didn't already know, and by noon tomorrow the sky above the gorge would be filled with swarms of helicopters. SWAT teams would be jogging behind bloodhounds, and tens of thousands of acres of wilderness would be about as good a hiding place as a cop's bedroom closet. Come to think of it, killing the two Feds might buy him a day or two, but he couldn't force himself to face that black gulf beyond the ledge.

He rolled up the sleeping bag and headed along the ridge, going upriver because the terrain was easier. As darkness gripped the forest, Ace had to feel his way through the trees, one arm raised in front of him to ward off branches. The roar of the river provided the only guide, and even its thundering steadiness was unreliable. He came to a clearing and paused, listening, wondering if the Feds had somehow found his trail.

At the edge of the clearing stood a form that blended with the surrounding murk.

Hunched like a monkey, too short and wiry to be Clara.

Friggin' Feds had tracked him.

Ace reacted the only way he knew, fueled by the anger of being outsmarted. The gun was in his palm before he even thought about it, and three explosions echoed against the trees before he was aware he'd pulled the trigger. From twenty feet away, the slugs should have punched the Fed to the ground. Instead, the form lifted slowly, like a scarecrow on a wire, and drifted through the treetops.

The fucker is FLYING, Ace thought.

Unless secret agents had come up with Buck Rogers backpacks while Ace had been laying low, then something was seriously wrong. Ace fired one more time as the figure cleared a gap in the trees.

Its outline was plain against the mottled sunset clouds. It was shaped liked a human, no doubt about that, but it was smaller, knotted up, its arms spread out to reveal short, ragged wings and legs trailing out behind. A keening wail arose from the creature, a cross between the hoot of a gut-shot owl and scream of a gang-raped wildcat.

Ace turned and ran blindly into the woods. *Wrong angel*, he told himself.

Ace kept pushing the possibility to the bottom of his mind, the way you'd drown a pesky kitten. When you did the Lord's work, you automatically made enemies. Most of those enemies wore sheep's clothing and hid behind the cross themselves, hypocrites who shunned Ace's kind

"Step it up," Farrengalli shouted from the rear. "There's a bonus if we reach the falls before dark."

Raintree wondered how Farrengalli would have fared on these trails three centuries ago, when buffalo and elk still made their seasonal passes and wildcats and red wolves stalked easy meat. He somehow believed even the hungriest of predators would find the man's flesh distasteful.

Equally annoying was the man in front of Raintree, who peppered his dialogue with corporate slogans. The group had been chosen with care, but the company man was a tenderfoot. Raintree couldn't claim any true outdoor experience, but at least he was in shape. He'd won a bronze in the 2000 Olympics, wrestling in the middleweight class, and had gained a few weeks of notoriety as sportswriters worked the "noble savage" and "the last pure American" angles. He was dream copy, and it didn't hurt that he had raven-black hair, piercing dark eyes, and the type of chest muscles that led to a few seminude appearances in high-brow magazines marketed to frustrated females.

Raintree parlayed the fleeting fame into a fitness gym in Oklahoma, and his clients included a handful of minor Hollywood stars known more for their builds than their brains. Raintree expanded his network so that it now included six gyms, and ProVentures had partnered with him in developing a line of personal workout equipment. In truth, Raintree had offered little input, merely letting the company use his face and facsimile signature on the products. In exchange, he signed the checks and smiled for Dove Krueger, the company's official photographer. Like him, Dove had also been recruited on this trip, though he suspected his motives were far different from hers.

Ahead, Bowie Whitlock stopped and stood aside while the company man passed and took the lead.

"Keep walking," Bowie said to the ProVentures rep. He didn't speak to Raintree, but their eyes met in mutual sympathy. Raintree noticed the guide was panting a little. Probably could have used the ProVentures Raintree Regimen, where "you measure your chest by the size of your heart." Trademarked, copyrighted, satisfaction guaranteed, and your money back if you didn't notice results within thirty days. Of course, most men were embarrassed to admit that they had failed a manly challenge of any kind, so refunds were few.

The woods had a rich, earthy smell, almost that of a corpse. The smell had grown stronger and more primal the further up the steep trail they'd hiked. The group had debarked at a popular scenic overlook, where rubbers and beer cans were the most significant signs of wildlife, but they hadn't met any fellow hikers in the last two hours. The casual outdoors enthusiasts rarely ventured into this kind of terrain, which had made it all the more appealing to the ProVentures marketing department.

"We'll be at the falls in an hour," Bowie said, not shouting but in a firm enough voice that everyone could hear, even Farrengalli. "Don't worry about bonuses. We'll all do fine once we make it out of here alive."

Raintree smiled. The guide had said "once" instead of "if." Raintree didn't really expect anyone to die, but he knew ProVentures wanted to play the whole thing up like some kind of reality show, where a team of rugged individualists had to work together while simultaneously competing to see who was strongest. The company would be disappointed if there wasn't at least a broken leg out of the trip, though they also wanted to prove the safety of their new inflatable rafts.

Raintree had drawn short straw and a $2,000 bonus for being one of two lucky "contestants" to carry the raft. The Muskrat was surprisingly light, weighing only four pounds, and was made of a synthetic rubber blend that ProVentures claimed was "the ultimate evolution of the kayak."

Slogans, catchphrases, sucker language. This trip was all about the hype, and if Raintree had to play the "noble savage" yet one more time, that was okay, because this time he had his own agenda.

He touched the medicine bag at his side. White magic, white medicine.

He was only half Cherokee, but his father's side was about as genetically pure as possible, given the tribe's long and civilized association with the white settlers before President Jackson declared war. Most of the Cherokee that once populated the North Carolina, western Georgia, and eastern Tennessee regions had been rounded up and driven west in an infamous forced march fraught with disease, exhaustion, and death. The Trail of Tears led to a reservation in Oklahoma, which the Cherokee shared with a handful of other Native American tribes.

The Cherokee were among the smartest and most adaptable tribes, the first to form a written language in an attempt to negotiate with the federal government. Wisdom and diplomacy didn't fare well against the U.S. Army's rifles, yet more proof that the pen was never mightier than the sword. However, not all were relocated, and scattered members of the tribe that called itself Aniyunwiya, "the real human beings," managed to survive the settlement push.

Over a century and a half later, the Cherokee still clung to a tiny reservation in western North Carolina, the debt for the tragedy paid in the form of a sparkling gambling casino. Raintree wasn't bitter about such things. History had rolled over millions of victims, the human tide swept on, and the best one could hope for was to find personal peace. Which was his mission now.

His Cherokee ancestors had trekked these mountains, had hunted the ridges in the summer, setting up seasonal camps along the river. For a young man, the trip was a challenge of courage, journeying alone for days at a time on a vision quest. Hunger and exhaustion may have contributed to the effect, but the male didn't return until he had encountered the animal that would serve as his spirit guide. Raintree might never be a warrior, and he was already approaching middle age, but this trip offered him a final chance to follow the distant footsteps of his forefathers.

Even if he walked with palefaces.

"Pick up the pace, you guys," Farrengalli shouted. Raintree hoped the Italian's own vision quest included a rabid skunk.

Or those legendary creatures his ancestors had said would swoop down from the rocks in troubled times.

"We're ahead of schedule," Bowie said, now some thirty feet behind Raintree but moving again. Dove Krueger was in front of Farrengalli, and Raintree figured the loudmouth was ogling her ass.

"I want to get camp set up so I can munch some of these *dee*-licious ProVentures N-R-Gee Bars," Farrengalli said.

"'Nature's tasty boost,'" said the company man at the head of the group, quoting a television commercial that ran on a series of MTV extreme sports shows.

"Plenty of time for a campfire, Farrengalli," Bowie said. "Don't get your Lycra in a twist."

Raintree walked on, wishing he were wearing moccasins instead of five-hundred-dollar custom boots.

Something was out here, he knew. Call it his medicine, his vision, his destiny. In this forest that was older than his people, older than all people, something waited.

CHAPTER SEVEN

The Rook returned minutes, or maybe centuries, later and knelt at the lip of the opening. "Here. I found this at Goodall's campsite."

He tossed a rope into the hole and it bounced off Castle's shoulder. The rope was about the thickness of a clothesline, but made of threaded nylon and strong. The Rook belayed the rope against a nearby tree trunk and said, "Get a grip, partner."

Castle wrapped the rope a couple of times around his palms. At the first tug, the rope tightened and burned his flesh. Castle bit back a grunt of pain. Samford dug his heels into the ground and yanked again. This time Castle wriggled his waist and felt the soil and rocks loosen around him. He slid up a few inches, but more dirt trickled down from the raw slope above. Castle wasn't sure whether Samford could pull him free before the whole rim of the opening collapsed.

His boot was hung. He kicked it free, wondering if a tree root had fallen in the hole before he had. He pictured his bootlaces tangled in the wormy white roots. Samford tugged the line again, and hot curls of pain peeled from Castle's shoulder sockets. This time, he moved upward a good six inches, and now he could move his hips enough to wriggle free.

"You're getting there, Rook," Castle said. Above him,

Samford tied off the distance he'd gained, then dug in again and leaned back. Castle eased upward, incongruously imagining he was being squirted from the womb. Only this womb was the cold belly of the Earth, and its progeny was thirty-five years old, a sick sack of blood, bone, and skin. Not old enough yet for day diapers, too young to walk on its own.

Castle felt himself drop as the rope suddenly went slack. He popped back into his previous position like a cork rammed into the neck of a wine bottle.

"Damn," Samford said. "Did you see that?"

Castle's breath stalled between his lungs and throat. "Goodall?"

"Some kind of giant bird. Red fucker, skinny as a flying monkey."

"Well, get me out of here and maybe we can roast its ass for dinner."

Samford restored the tension on the rope and once again worked Castle free. A stone the size of a fist tumbled down and bounced off Castle's chest, dinging the edge of a rib bone. Darkness had taken a bigger bite of the sky, and the air seemed heavier with the deepening night.

Castle shivered, wishing he was sitting around the campfire and talking shop with The Rook, going over Goodall's assessment, planning strategy. Once a deal started going down, even the most carefully arranged plan gave way to improvisation. That meant instinct and cunning always trumped intelligence, which was probably why Goodall had managed to escape capture so long.

We'll see about that, once I get my sorry ass out of this bottleneck.

Castle's thighs emerged from the narrow gap that had

attempted to suck him underground. He fought to find purchase with his feet, the rope cutting into the soft meat above his wrists. He got one knee out and lodged himself against the moist soil so he wouldn't slip back into the hole.

"Keep an eye out for Goodall," Castle said. "He might be waiting around to put another couple of scalps on his belt."

"He's gone," Samford said. "I cleared the perimeter when I got the rope."

"You're the profile guy. You know he's slicker than owl shit."

"The assessment says he's megalomaniacal but he's not reckless. Hell, he's a survivor. He'd rather laugh at us tomorrow than risk a showdown today. Every day he avoids capture is another day he achieves cult status in the eyes of his anarchist buddies."

"They're not anarchists anymore. We call them 'terrorists,' remember?"

"Yeah. That damned Bin Laden. He's given a bad name to mass murderers. Now let's get you out of there and regroup."

Samford drew the line taut and Castle tried to draw his other leg from its subterranean snare.

"I'm hung up," Castle said. He was more annoyed than worried, though he desperately wanted to be out of the hole by full dark. Crickets and other night insects had started their sonorous clicking and chirruping, a sound that was comforting when heard from the back porch, but oddly disturbing in the deep wilderness. And he kept imagining the flapping of those ragged red wings. Castle could probably reach his Glock if needed, but he'd have to free his right hand first.

"Let me tie off and maybe I can slide down and help," Samford said.

"You'll bring a load of loose dirt down on the way. Better let me work it out myself."

"Okay. I'll do a quick recon."

The Rook was Behavioral Sciences all the way, and though he'd undergone the same new agent training as Castle, he was not HRT-tested. Sure, he'd been in a talk-through in a couple of crisis situations, had worked mop-up on serial killer cases, and put in a couple of years twiddling his thumbs in the Department of Homeland Security's clownfest. But he'd never drawn fire and had never pulled the trigger.

Castle, a SEALs vet, had gained a grudging respect for The Rook over the last few weeks. Enough respect that he didn't want his partner to face Goodall alone. If The Rook died because Castle was nailed like a cheerleader on prom night, tripped up by his own stupid feet and carelessness, then it would add yet another shingle to Castle's spot on the Quantico Wall of Shame.

"I'll be free in a second," Castle said. "I'm not sure everything works right, so you better stick around."

"I thought you said you weren't hurt."

"What did you expect me to say?"

"That you love me."

"Hey, pard, this ain't Brokeback Mountain."

"Man, you got no sense of humor anymore."

"My second wife took it in the divorce settlement."

"Okay, take your time. Goodall's long gone, I'm telling you. Fits the assessment. Live to fight again another day."

"Or to get another headline. Three hundred and twenty days and counting. Or is it twenty-one? I lost track."

Castle rotated his ankle. Though more loose dirt and rocks had fallen in his attempt to scramble up the bank, there was space around his thigh. He couldn't see into the inky darkness below. Whatever had snagged his boot still clung to it. He thought he heard faint scratching sounds against the leather heel.

The night plays strange tricks on the mind. Even the cavemen knew that. Why else would they huddle around the fire and tell stories? Because the monsters in their heads were worse than the real monsters outside, the ones that only wanted to eat them.

Castle flashed to one of his childhood memories, one so persistent it had outlasted the face of the first girl he'd ever kissed, the aluminum ding of his first tee-ball base hit, the smell of popcorn at the Titusville drive-in theater. The thing under the bed that scratched the dusty mattress frame, claw tips working idly back and forth. The thing, with arms as long as fire hoses. The thing, breath rasping as it chuckled, sausage-chub tongue playing over sharp, yellow teeth. The kind of teeth that ate little boys for a midnight snack, once those arms reached up, probed under the blankets, and clamped onto the nearest boy ankle. The kind of—

The boy may have cowered into the wee hours, balled so tightly in the blankets that even a flea would have found a meal difficult, but Jim Castle had put away childish things. A bout with testicular cancer, three bad marriages, a stint in the Navy SEALs, and an assignment with the FBI's Hostage Rescue Team had made sure of that.

Faith and imagination had no more room on the stage. This wasn't a world where monsters slithered out from shadowy crevices; in the twenty-first century, the monsters packed themselves with explosives and walked into a crowded market, carried automatic weapons into a post office, or put a torch to churches. Some of the worst monsters were fixtures on the nightly news, spewing their brand of poison as political ideology, letting others carry out their bloody work.

So the thing that had his foot wasn't a monster. Though he and the Rook had ditched their backpacks while closing in on Goodall, Castle hadn't forsaken all his gear. The small hatchet still hung in a leather holster on his hip. He disengaged his right hand from the rope, unsnapped the button, and freed the hatchet.

The hole through which his leg dangled was too dark and cramped for him to hack blindly at whatever held his boot. At best, he could use the thick blade to probe around and maybe pry himself free. He rammed the hatchet head down beside his calf. It struck something soft and meaty.

From beneath him, a bleat arose, or maybe a chuckle— *the kind of sound that rolls off a sausage-chub tongue—*

No, that was likely the last gasp of the radio he'd dropped, running down its NiCad battery in the dark. They'd limited communication to preserve batteries, and the FBI had not bothered to set up a command post in the area.

Because Goodall wasn't supposed to be here.

He poked again, working the blunt blade around his boot. The chuckle turned into a slithering hiss, like that of an animal in pain. Castle pulled the blade up and in the gloaming half-light saw the edge was coated with a viscous liquid. Not blood, exactly, though the liquid was dark....

Castle yanked his foot with all the desperation of a five-year-old boy bundling blankets against the monster under the bed. This time it came free, accompanied by what sounded like fingernails on leather and a moan of disappointment.

"Pull me the hell out of here," Castle yelled, flinging the hatchet into the hole.

Samford gave no response, but Castle found now that his legs were free, he could scramble up the embankment with no problem. He gouged his boots into the loose dirt, sending rocks skittering down the slope. Castle hoped his actions would trigger enough of a landslide to bury whatever lay coiled in the deep recesses of the Earth—

with its long fire-hose arms—

as he worked the rope hand over hand, the slack curling around his legs. Dusk had gained a deeper hold, as if the hole below, now uncorked, had spilled its ink into the sky. He reached the raw lip of the bank, wondering why The Rook had gone silent, and hooked a knee up and planted it on solid ground. Then he wriggled his waist over, feeling more dirt give way below him in a damp avalanche.

"Samford," he grunted, angry and a little scared. What if Ace Goodall had taken advantage of the shadows and crept up on his partner? He'd heard no gunfire, but Ace no doubt carried a hunting knife. Castle fumbled for his Glock as he wriggled the lower part of his body onto *terra firma.* He rolled, the pistol in his hand, forcing himself not to look down into the hole at the creature lurking inside—

Not a creature, just an old root, not a set of long, curling claws but a brittle branch—

The high-pitched squeal ripped the fabric of the night. It came from Castle's left, maybe twenty feet away. At first Castle thought the sound had come from the woman believed to accompany Goodall.

Then: *SkeeEEEEeeek.*

The shriek phased in an arc overhead, like the

stereophonic knob twiddling of a stoned-out rock guitarist or the rusty creaking of a giant coffin lid. Castle lifted the Glock and tracked the sound with the barrel, as if it were another Hogan's Alley test in Quantico. At the FBI academy in Virginia, trainees were taught the basics of hostage negotiation, trigger jitters, and the kill shot. But Castle couldn't recall any of those field exercises that had gone airborne.

Against the black sails of the sky, the shape was tangled and awkward, like a broken biplane. Or, he realized, an oversized bird with a healthy hunk of prey.

Like the freaky red monkey-bird he'd seen earlier.

Too large, too obscene, too out of place in this ancient but hushed wilderness.

A sick, soaring thing.

On clumsy, stunted wings, as if learning to fly.

The soft moon on the mountaintops gave the creature a silhouette, and Castle's finger tightened on the trigger. Not enough to squeeze off nine rounds, but enough to scare him. He'd almost broken the Hogan's Alley code. Don't shoot until you identified the target.

Because Castle recognized something in the disappearing jumble of wings, limbs, and limp meat.

The Rook's wrist compass, blaze orange, torn and bobbing in the light of the quarter moon.

CHAPTER EIGHT

Gotta find the stupid bitch before the Feds do.

Ace Goodall plowed through the underbrush, all five-foot-six inches of him, as the branches and brambles plucked at his camo jacket. He figured the highfalutin bitch had turned on him, somehow signaled the agents and given away his position. Thinking back, he realized that bit with the campfire was obvious. She had probably been plotting against him for weeks, just waiting for her chance to betray him. Eve, Delilah, Jezebel. The Bible warned against such things. But God had put a little nub of weakness between each man's legs.

But God in his infinite wisdom and mercy had also sent help from above. As Ace had watched from the shadows of the forest, debating whether or not to throw down on the pair of Haircuts, the fucked-up bat-thing had come to the rescue, swept down and scooped up the younger one, dragging it across the sky. Ace could have sworn a soft rain of blood had trailed from the struggling agent as the broken angel fluttered against the dusk. Ace could have easily taken the other one, the one who had fallen into the hole, but Ace figured maybe that was part of God's plan, too. As if the Guy Upstairs had opened up the Earth to drag the Haircut straight to hell.

Proof that God was a patriot and approved of Ace's holy work.

But Ace knew that God never took care of all the details. God only issued the commands, and left it to the foot soldiers to carry out orders. God might have steadied Ace's hand while he built the bombs, but it was Ace himself who cooked up the nitromethane and mixed it with a gel of gunpowder and ammonium nitrate. Ace, who had dropped out of school in the seventh grade and never made it to basic algebra, much less chemistry, had learned from the best in a Dakota compound. He'd learned to wire an electric relay with a simple timer, stuff you could get at Radio Shack for less than ten bucks. The hardest part had been to pretend to be one of *them*, one of the baby-killing heathens in the human chop shops known as abortion clinics.

The first had been easy. He'd posed as a Birmingham municipal worker, gone in with his tool kit and a clipboard, clean blue coveralls, and no one had questioned him. In America, despite the post-9/11 fear of terrorism, a white male with a confident walk was never challenged. He'd set the bomb in a bathroom stall right next to the administrative office, figuring on luck and a little help from God. The blast the next morning had been spectacular, sending ceramic shards into the temple of the clinic's top doctor, taking the murderous life of a nurse practitioner who'd just happened to be washing his hands (like Pilate) at the bathroom sink, and shutting down the clinic for three weeks.

The next two bombings were tougher, because security got tighter, and he wasn't helped at all when some copycat amateur botched a mission in Los Angeles, the land of fags and liberals, where there were more baby-killers than bad actors. The La-La-Land bomber had hit a free clinic serving

Hispanic immigrants, and while Ace figured there were enough illegal spics swarming the country, that was a mission for a later generation. The copycat had blown himself to bits while trying to plant the bomb, causing no other casualties and launching a week of media speculation over whether the Bama Bomber had met his end two thousand miles from home turf. The Feds knew better, though, because the MOs were different, as well as the chemical composition of the bombs, so the manhunt had scarcely eased.

Then Ace had picked up the bitch outside Atlanta and his luck had changed for the worse.

She had to pay, or at least get on her knees and beg forgiveness.

Just after the angel had delivered Ace from the Feds, Ace had stopped by the camp, retrieved his backpack—*only one goddamned bomb left*—and begun his hunt for Clara Bannister. Her disappearance had been too convenient, too coincidental. She should have yelled a better warning. Sure, she had screamed, but the scream was probably an act to give away their position. Same as the campfire. She'd insisted on the campfire. A hot meal, she'd said. The smoke would lay low, she'd said.

As if the bitch knew the first thing about survival training.

Ace jogged on, holding one forearm up to shield off the branches and slapping leaves. He'd left the trail, figuring he could head off Clara. She'd stick to the gentler switchbacks that had been cut first by animals and then maintained by hikers who liked their recreation a little bit on the raw side. Predictable, right down to the treacherous little slit between her legs.

He'd show her. He'd show her good.

In the fading daylight, he'd lost his fear of the great, open gorge below. The night was God's protective tent, a church of hush and solace. Some people feared the dark, but to Ace, it was a place where God filled all the cracks of the world. The river was a gentle wash of sound far below, and that's where the bitch would flee. Water flowed downhill, and so did blood, and so did the weight of sin. Clara had sinned, and she knew it.

Not by spreading her legs and taking his seed night after night. No, that was her duty, his right. Her sin had been that of Delilah, of seeking to lay him low before the enemy, of making him weak. Though the Book of Judges set down that Samson had been captured and blinded, in the end God restored Samson's strength and allowed him to drag down a heathen temple on the heads of the Philistines. That was a clear sign to Ace that, though he'd been tricked and seduced by beauty, he still had a final destiny to fulfill. A bomb that would bring down the house.

And she could repent by helping.

He'd been thinking about it for days, and now that they'd given the Haircuts the slip, it was time to work their way out of the wilderness and continue the mission. It was simple, really, so obvious that he wondered why God had shrouded it in secrecy for so long. He'd brought Clara to him for a purpose, and even though the darkness now pressed against him like a liquid, the vision was a beacon that propelled his feet down the slick, leaf-carpeted slopes.

They would enter the clinic together, she as the pregnant young girl with an accidental burden, he as the concerned and supportive partner. The slight bulge of her belly would not be a four-month-old fetus, however; it would be a girdle of C-4 or TNT, the detonator tucked just under her breasts. By the grace of God, they'd take down a half dozen of the modern-day Philistines and their vile priests, bringing down the roof on their false idols and strange gods, the butcher shop of their wicked beliefs.

Grinning, he sped on, toward the rushing water below.

CHAPTER NINE

They'd made the foot of the falls just before dark, right on schedule. The group had unpacked and set up their tents (from the ProVentures Pup series), started a fire, and gathered around for a meal of energy bars, instant coffee, soy jerky, and banana chips.

Bowie checked their faces as the flames danced in their eyes. They showed no signs of exhaustion, except for Travis Lane, the ProVentures rep. Bowie made a note to keep an eye on him. Chances were good the marketing whiz's creativity was limited to tricky words and behavioral psychology, and didn't extend into the skills necessary for backwoods endurance.

Lane had removed his boots and was busy rubbing his feet.

"What's wrong?" Farrengalli said to him. "They sold you on the wrong pair of footwear?"

"The ProVentures line is perfectly suitable for this type of hiking," Lane said. "Add a little fur and an extra lining, and you could hike the Antarctica with these."

Farrengalli had produced a silver flask from somewhere, and it glinted with firelight as he tilted it against his lips. He wiped his lush Italian lips and said, "That sounds like a good gimmick for next year. You gotta cut me in on that action." He glanced at Bowie and flashed those big incisors that could probably cut his leg out of a steel trap if necessary. "Maybe even let me lead it."

Bowie didn't rise to the bait. The embers were deep, orange, and hypnotic. Soothing, the way he imagined hell might be after you got used to it. He'd probably find out one day, but not too soon. He still had a lot of misery to endure, a lot of memories of Connie, a lot of years left to waste.

"Sounds like a job for snowshoes," C.A. McKay said. He looked unfazed by the evening's exercise, as if compared to pedaling an uphill stretch in the French Pyrenees, the long hike was the equivalent of a kid's second week on training wheels.

"It would be a good opportunity to promote the Igloo outfit," Lane said, not knowing when to clock out. "Insulated with goose down, double-layered with an advanced synthetic blend, guaranteed at twenty below."

"Let's worry about tonight, not next year," Bowie said, noting that all five faces turned toward him when he spoke. Even that beautiful one that made his eyes hurt.

"What's the worry?" Farrengalli said, voice louder than necessary even given the roar of the falls. A fine spray filled the air, adding an extra chill to the September night. The fire did a good job killing the moisture, but Bowie knew they would all wake up damp and stay that way until they reached the end of the run.

"Maybe 'worry' isn't the right word," Bowie said. "Maybe it's 'concern.'"

"Look, we got the best equipment money can buy, except we got it all for free, we're getting paid, we're going to have our pictures in a national ad campaign—" Farrengalli paused, gave his gleaming grin to Dove Krueger, and said, "Hey, sweets, don't forget to make this mug the poster child of the trip."

Krueger, who'd carried the added burden of eight pounds of advanced photography equipment, winced at Farrengalli's crude endearment. Like Bowie, she didn't acknowledge the man's attempts at irritation. She reminded Bowie of his wife, and—

No, he couldn't go there now. Wait until the safety of the sleeping bag, the disturbed dreams, the persistent image of her hand reaching through the snow—

"The Muskrat may be new, but the principles of river rafting are pretty well established," Bowie said.

"Come on, we went through all this in orientation," Farrengalli said, hitting the flask again. The liquor, or whatever was in the container, had flushed his face. But it could have been excitement, or maybe the warmth of the fire. Farrengalli displayed an easy familiarity with the flask, as if they had ridden the same currents for years.

"That was on paper," Bowie said, keeping his voice steady, letting the tumble of water over the rocks add its backing beat. "The river isn't paper."

"The rapids range from Class V to Class III," McKay said. "Big deal. We can take it like a rubber ducky takes a bathtub."

Easy for McKay to say, but McKay had trained with world-class athletes. White-water courses were rated on a scale of difficulty ranging from one to six, with Class I being the easiest, the water so gentle that you could almost walk it faster, assuming the depth wasn't too great. Class VI carried the real risk of death.

"Thirteen miles, with an altitude drop of two thousand feet over the entire run," Bowie said. "The most difficult hair run in the eastern United States. We have long stretches of portage where the river spreads out into shallows, and when we're not carrying gear to the next put-in, we'll be bouncing around on short falls, eddies, undercuts, and troughs. You already see the hiking is no cakewalk. The rafting is even worse, and a paddle won't make much difference if you get caught in a sinkhole. Assuming the equipment holds up, we'll be tested to the limits."

"The equipment is fine," Travis Lane said. "The Muskrat's been on the drawing board for four years already. It's undergone every laboratory test in the book."

"This isn't the laboratory," Bowie said.

"ProVentures has a lot riding on the expedition," Lane said. He was the closest one to the fire, stooped over and rubbing his hands as if wanting to pocket the heat for later.

"Not as much as we do," Bowie said. "ProVentures would pay with a tax write-off. We'd pay with our lives."

"Ooh," Farrengalli said. "Major drama. Did you write that down, sweet stuff?"

Krueger, who had been taking notes by firelight, wrinkled her nose as if smelling a skunk. She was examining the climbing gear, coiled ropes and steel pitons that glinted orange.

"We wanted a difficult launch to prove a point," Lane said. "An outer shell of polyurethane-coated nylon. A single-chamber inflatable exterior, resistant to abrasion, stitched seams reinforced with the most advanced epoxy. The interior layer features a series of separate chambers so that the raft functions even after a puncture. Screw caps with a hand-pump accessory means you can break it down and pump it up again in about two minutes."

"I bet I can pump it in thirty seconds," Farrengalli said,

curling his arm and showing biceps the size of a swollen grapefruit.

"I'll bet you can pump a lot of things in thirty seconds," Krueger said. "But I bet you never last a minute."

Farrengalli's eyebrows, which actually ran together in a single furry strand, rose on his forehead. His mouth rounded into an idiotic O, as if he couldn't decide whether he was being ridiculed.

McKay laughed and gave Krueger an affectionate slap on the shoulder. He was sitting closer to her than necessary. Bowie wondered if the cyclist would cause trouble of a different kind. Farrengalli was an obvious prick, but McKay might be a subtler one. And Krueger was attractive by any standard, even his, perhaps made more so by the fact she was the lone pussycat in a pride of lions.

Having only one woman in the group had been a bad choice. Dove as that one woman was even worse.

"Breakdown will be easy," Lane continued. The lack of confidence he'd displayed when confronted by the wilderness had fallen away now that he was in his element. "Maximum weight capacity of one thousand pounds, yet deflates to a carrying weight of five pounds. Telescoping paddles weigh another four pounds, and when you throw in the hand pump at five pounds, you get a package that can carry four of us downstream but fits into the space of a loaf of bread."

Robert Raintree, who had been sitting on a fallen maple at the edge of the clearing, finally spoke. "We have two rafts," he said. "How do we split up?"

"Like we planned," Bowie said. "The rafts have a maximum capacity of four people, but we'll be running three per."

"*Menage a trois,*" McKay said, leaning toward Krueger. "How does that sound, *ma cherie?*"

"You might be a stud when pedaling in France, but that lousy accent wouldn't get you in anybody's pants," Krueger said. "Much less two pairs at a time."

Bowie grinned. Maybe he wouldn't have to worry about her after all. She was capable of handling herself, and her outdoors credentials were as solid as his. After all, while he'd been out of the game in self-imposed exile, she'd been mountain climbing, wind sailing, hang gliding, and ice-floe snowshoeing, much of the time with a laptop and camera. Besides, he knew a little more about her, and her stamina, than any of them.

"McKay, you and Lane will ride with me in the lead raft," Bowie said. He'd originally wanted McKay and Farrengalli together, but based on their behavior, he thought their egos might lead to dangerous differences of opinion. On Class V waters, there was room for only one battle of wills: human versus nature, not man against man.

"Righteous," Farrengalli said. "I get to ride with the two quiet ones."

"I don't think there will be much time for talking," Bowie said. "Maybe at midday we'll switch off, but if things are going smoothly, we'll probably stick with what works."

It usually took an hour or two for rafters to coordinate their paddling and work as a team. Bowie again regretted the company's tactic, making a cold run with no rehearsal. ProVentures scripted everything else, so why not manipulate the Muskrat field test so it looked great for the cameras? Why risk so much for a product in which the company had obviously invested thousands of development hours?

Because it was a pure publicity stunt. In fact, Farrengalli had been selected in the equivalent of a reality TV show, a competition in the Arizona desert that had been featured on the outdoors cable series *Wild Life with Natalie,* featuring a buxom aerobics queen who alternately taunted and coaxed the competitors. According to rumor, Farrengalli had bagged Natalie in the star's trailer one night, just before a final elimination round. Farrengalli subsequently won an obstacle course race that featured a hundred-foot-pole climb to a rocky plateau, a thousand-foot wade through waist-deep quicksand that was actually colored oatmeal, a reckless rappel down the side of a butte, and two barefoot miles across the scorching sand with nothing but a wineskin full of cactus juice for sustenance. Whether Farrengalli's bedding of the show's host contributed to the victory, no one was willing to say, but Bowie would bet all the sponsors were smiling.

The series had been augmented with a feature story in *Back2Nature,* with Dove Krueger providing the photographs and copy. Krueger already knew Farrengalli, Lane, and Raintree through her work with ProVentures. Bowie hadn't known any of them until the ProVentures vultures had tracked him to Montana, made an unannounced helicopter landing on his ranch, and laid their obscene offer on his chipped plywood table. As much as Bowie could fool himself into believing he was the right man for such a job, in his heart he was as much of a prostitute as any of them. This tour would keep him in dried beans, bait, and ammunition for the rest of his days, which meant he'd never have to leave Big Sky Country again.

But his remote cabin was nearly three thousand miles away, and the solitude he craved would have to wait for his sleeping bag. For now, he needed to take charge and plant the idea that if there was any trouble, the group would turn to him for a decision.

"The river's low," McKay said. "Maybe we should check for portage trails in the morning."

"No," Bowie said, knowing Lane was listening. "We do this by the book as much as possible."

"Looks to be running around two feet," McKay said. The group had gathered at the water's edge before making camp, and though much of the seventy-foot waterfall was hidden in shadow, the weak moon caught enough of the silver spray to suggest its glory. Even a distance away from the falls, the ground vibrated with its thunder.

"It'll look different in daylight," Bowie said, standing. "We should all get some rest. Let's make an early start tomorrow. Breakfast at six, launch at dawn."

They had lined their pup tents around the clearing, and Bowie didn't wait for the others to follow his command as he headed for his. He imagined Farrengalli would finish his flask first, and McKay would probably wait a few minutes in order to appear independent. Lane was already yawning, probably the sorest among them. Krueger would be eager to escape the unwanted male companionship. Robert Raintree—

The two had scarcely spoken since the trip began. Bowie sensed the man harbored no unnecessary rebellion, nor did he seem overly interested in the adventure ahead. Though his eyes were open, his head was still as if he were meditating, or listening to the forest beyond the roar of the water. Bowie gave a brief nod and wriggled into his tent.

He undressed in the cramped space and slid into his sleeping bag, his calves and thighs aching more than he had expected. Tomorrow, his shoulders would get a workout from using the paddle, and when he next lay down, his entire body would be throbbing like the root of a rotted tooth.

Closing his eyes, he was assaulted by the same familiar sight, one that hadn't lessened in intensity over the past five years.

They had been cross-country skiing, in a fairly treacherous but popular valley in Jackson Hole, Wyoming. The sunlight sparkled off the snow, the air temperature was forty degrees, and the wind was mild. A perfect day, even when viewed through shaded goggles. Bowie was a hundred feet ahead, figuring to blaze a trail so his wife's passage would be easier.

Bowie thought the first rumble came from his stomach, it had been so gentle. The second was accompanied by a small spray of loose snow, and then the massive wall of white clinging to the mountain above had let loose, thundering down like the cavalry of the Apocalypse.

By the time Bowie had flailed the long skis around, the bulk of the avalanche had swept past, tossing a few chunks against his shins and coating him with powder, but otherwise leaving him unscathed.

Connie was gone.

The silence that followed in the wake of the avalanche was a mockery of the noise with which it had broken loose from its winter-long moorings. Bowie stripped his gloves, knelt, and removed his fastenings, cursing his clumsy fingers. By the time he propelled himself into the settled trough of snow, precious seconds had passed. Avalanche victims didn't die of broken bones, shock, or exposure. They died of suffocation.

After a fifteen-minute search, he finally spotted a patch of blue against the glistening white. Her stiff and gloveless hand, the fingers lifted as if waving good-bye.

Or reaching for him.

The diamonds in her wedding band gleaming in the reflected light.

He rolled over in his sleeping bag, but there was no direction where that hand wasn't waiting, waving, beckoning, curling at last into an angry fist. He should have died with her. By now, instant death held no appeal. His punishment was to linger for an excruciatingly long time, to share his endless nights with the memory, to taste the cold air of his failure.

As always, the sun could not come soon enough.

CHAPTER TEN

He caught up with her a couple of hours after sundown.

Clara had youth on him, and she was no stranger to the woods, but Ace Goodall had a manic energy that both attracted and repelled her. Back at the camp, when he'd gone after the agents, Clara decided enough was enough. She understood his mission of bombing abortion clinics. That was clearly a fight on the side of right, and appealed to her self-destructive nature, but killing people in cold blood just because they were cops didn't seem Christian.

Oh, she would probably face the death penalty if she were ever dragged to trial, but she had planned over the past couple of months to die by Ace's side, going out in a blaze of glory. Whether it came from police bullets or a double suicide, she'd not feared it, and almost welcomed it.

Still, when she had a chance, she had fled. Not to escape arrest; no Earthly court could trump the higher law, as Ace had said. She had fled because of something inside her that screamed for life. She was too young to die. God must have given her a purpose separate from helping Ace.

Not that running had done much good. So deep in the wilderness area, the trails were few, and the darkness slowed her, too. She'd left her backpack at the camp, and she was tired and hungry. She'd found a little creek and drunk water from it, figuring there was no pollution or sewage since the wilderness area was protected from development. The water had refreshed her, but she needed sleep. She curled in a ball on top of a damp bed of leaves, and was just drowsing off when the boot nudged her side.

She opened her eyes to see him standing over her, his silhouette dark against the broken canopy.

"You run away," Ace said.

"I was scared," she said, thinking fast, wondering which lie he would believe. Though he was cunning, he didn't seem too experienced with women. She'd used that to her advantage while letting him believe she was of Old Testament stripe, subjugating herself to her man. All the while, she was feeding off his anger and his dangerous streak.

He flipped on a flashlight, blinding her in its sudden golden circle. "You ought not be scared if you're living right."

She sat up, squinting, her eyes burning. "Did you kill them?"

"I didn't. The Lord took care of that."

"The Lord?" Ace gave the Lord credit for each bomb that successfully exploded, each time he gave law enforcement the slip, each newspaper headline that spread the word to others who might join in the holy work. "What I meant was did you shoot them? Like that man in Atlanta?"

"I told you, He sent a wrong angel. My hands are clean."

True, she hadn't heard any shots, but she might have been out of range if he had stalked the agents for long. And Ace was given to visions. They were probably the hallucinations of the schizophrenic. She understood that on an intellectual level. She'd been majoring in psychology, spicing it up with some philosophy and religion courses, at Radford University in Virginia. She was no dummy.

"Your hands are clean and your soul is white," she said, repeating the line he'd used the first time he'd told her about his work.

"I don't like it that you run away."

"I can't help it, Ace. I'm not as brave as you."

"Well, get up off the ground. We got to get out of here now. The Feds will be swarming these woods in a couple of days, once the Haircuts don't check in on schedule."

Clara stood, brushing the wet leaves from her clothes. The chill had seeped into her skin. "It will take a week to hike out of here."

"We'll go down to the river. Maybe we can find a boat or something."

"You saw the river. It's too dangerous for a boat."

"Don't be talking to me about danger. We're going to be fine."

Clara wanted to ask, *Then why are we running?* But she didn't want to risk a slap. Violence begat violence, that was the way of the world, and a vile tongue was just as bad as an angry right arm.

"I'm glad you found me," she said. "I might have been lost." She meant it in the physical sense, but knew Ace would pick up on the spiritual aspect, too. He might not have had a formal education, but he was wise in the dark ways of the human heart.

"Well, like I said, heaven sent a sign."

Ace was big on signs. He'd picked his bombing targets through a process that involved a map, a red magic marker, and deep prayer. Behavioral psychologists would say Ace was engaging in antisocial acts to atone for his upbringing at the hands of a drunken trucker and a mother who had run away with a Mexican landscaper. Clara didn't quite buy that herself. After all, she had been raised in an Ohio trailer park and had not only kept her virginity until high school, she'd been an honor-roll student and had eliminated the word "ain't" from her vocabulary.

"What was the sign?" she asked.

"An angel come down from the sky. Like I said."

The forest was quiet around them, the river issuing a gentle whisper half a mile below. "What does it mean?" she asked, knowing it could only mean one thing.

"The Lord's shining on us."

"Did you bring any food?"

"The Lord will provide."

Clara was a believer, but she was also a pragmatist. She didn't think manna would fall from the skies or fish would jump out of the river into their hands. The Lord helped those that helped themselves, her father had often said. He was about as honest as a minister could be, and besides his one weakness, had been a great leader and kept the commandments. Nowhere in the Good Book did it say not to drink, Preacher Floyd Bannister always said. His flock wasn't always as convinced, but few of his sheep had actually read the Bible all the way through, and besides, hangovers kept the Sunday morning sermons short.

Ace started down the trail. An owl hooted somewhere in the woods above them. She wondered what Ace's "angel" had actually been. Maybe a crow, maybe a bald eagle, maybe a strangely shaped cloud. She allowed him a respectful lead of about ten paces, then followed, alert to the sounds of the night.

She wondered if she should tell Ace her secret. It would

probably just make him angry. Besides, there would be time later, once they were safe in a dry motel room, where she could take a hot shower and make him a warm, loving bed. Let him plan his next act of holy war. That would be the right time for conspiratorial whispers.

CHAPTER ELEVEN

Whitlock is pretty much a pussy. What kind of name is "Bowie," anyway? Reminds me of that faggoty British rock star.

Vincent Farrengalli shook his flask. Maybe an inch of Tullemore Irish Whiskey left. Good fuel to warm somebody up on a chilly September night. Especially since the hot chick, Dove, had shot down his advances. Well, let her stew. She was probably in her tent right now, fingering herself off while thinking of him. She probably just didn't want to make the others jealous. She seemed like the type who'd be considerate and upfront, all that type of shit.

Or a dyke. Probably a damn rug-muncher.

He and the cyclist, C.A. McKay, were the last two survivors. The rest of them had turned in. Farrengalli was a little sleepy himself, but no way was he going to let some California golden boy outlast him. Besides, he wanted to finish the Tullemore.

"So, what do you think of the dish?" Farrengalli said.

"Dish?"

Farrengalli tilted his head toward Dove Krueger's tent, which was off by itself as if wilderness protocol required gender segregation. "What was up with those shorts? Legs like that, she had to know she was working the crowd. The tops of her socks rolled down. Cute."

"I'd say she was going for comfort," McKay said. He rummaged in his fanny pack, and Farrengalli thought the guy was going to break out a joint, some of that Mexicali red bud that had you singing Eagles and Tom Petty ballads until dawn. Instead, the cyclist drew out a harmonica.

"What's your trip?" Farrengalli took another dose of whiskey. Alcohol never failed to get better the deeper it sank into his belly.

"I'm not on a trip," McKay said.

"Sure you are. Don't tell me you came on this treasure hunt because you needed the money. You got more sponsor stickers on your ass than a NASCAR driver."

"This is a different game for me." McKay put the harmonica to his pursed lips, licked the length of the instrument, and gave an experimental blow. A low note wended through the night, full of vibrato and a suggestive sensuality.

"Well, I got to be honest with you," Farrengalli said, though he had absolutely no intention of doing so. "I'm here for the gear."

McKay tilted the harmonica so that the silver casing reflected the firelight against the nearby treetops. "The gear?"

"Yeah, the free stuff. Sleeping bags, boots, tent. I figure they'll give us a year's supply of N-R-Gee Bars and propane as a consolation prize. And don't forget a subscription to *Back2Nature Magazine*."

McKay glanced at his watch, and Farrengalli could picture the fag pumping away on his stationary bike, measuring his pulse, counting the revolutions per minute, analyzing his calories, and generally doing all the sissy workout stuff that cyclists did. They all seemed to enjoy raising their snug rears up just a little too much when they went into a hard stretch. They loved their chamois inserts, their lubricants, their stiff leather seats. A bunch of candy-assed fags.

"There's no such thing as a free ride," the cyclist said.

"Tell me. What did they pay you for this gig? I got to confess, they didn't exactly go deep inside their jackets for me, if you know what I mean."

"My agent handled the negotiations, and my accountant dealt with the contracts. I think I signed something a few months ago. Who has time for that kind of thing?"

"Agent, huh? Where do you get one of those?"

California Boy grinned, and Farrengalli didn't like those even, sparkling teeth. They were the kind of teeth that, back in the Bronx, he would want to put a fist—

"I thought you were on television already," McKay said. "I saw one of the network commercials."

"Yeah, they put me on TV. Wasn't so bad. Catered meals from McDonald's during the breaks."

"McDonald's, huh?" McKay put the harmonica to his lips again, this time teasing out a couple of high notes.

Farrengalli licked at the rim of the flask, numbing his tongue with the dregs. "Three meals a day. Same as a prisoner."

McKay leaned toward the dying campfire and blew into the harmonica. He played an up-and-down scale that had a country-bluegrass flavor, the volume baffled so as not to wake the campers. The melody was familiar, but one you had to hear a couple of times to place.

Farrengalli lowered the flask and blinked, wood smoke in his eyes. "Hey, I know that song."

McKay waited through the four beats of silence and repeated the riff.

Farrengalli snapped his fingers and joined in on the last

few notes in an off-key bass. "Wha-wha-wha. Like in the movie."

Deliverance. The Burt Reynolds movie where the guys on the canoe trip get stalked by hillbillies. And Ned Beatty takes it up the rear while squealing like a pig. No wonder Biker Boy liked the song so much. And, Farrengalli had to admit, it was kind of clever, since McKay was on a white-water trip, too.

You got a purty mouth, Farrengalli wanted to say. *But your teeth are too sharp.*

McKay did his own call-and-answer on the harmonica, while Farrengalli stomped his foot against a log. The harmonica now pierced the night, and Farrengalli looked into the surrounding woods, wondering what might be out there watching them. Even a hillbilly wouldn't be stupid enough to hang out in the middle of nowhere without a good reason. There were easier places to hunt and fish, and the pickings were slim if all you wanted was some corn-hole action. One thing for sure, McKay wouldn't be any competition for Dove Krueger's sweet spot, though the woman had probably gone ga-ga over those blue eyes. Girls always fell for the fags, for all the good it did them.

McKay was in the middle of the tune, the point where a bluegrass band would be rollicking along on banjo, guitar, and stand-up bass, when Bowie stuck his head out of his tent. "Hey!"

McKay stopped playing, and the sudden stillness was a stark contrast, with only the steady rumble of the falls to break the silence.

"I don't care if you guys want to stay up all night, but let the rest of us sleep,' Bowie said. "Somebody's got to be worth a damn tomorrow, or we won't make the first head wall."

"Okay, Chief," McKay said. "Whatever you say."

Farrengalli didn't even look at the guide, keeping his face to the fire. After Bowie ducked back inside, McKay returned the harmonica to his fanny pack.

"What do you make of him?" Farrengalli asked.

"He acts like he knows what he's doing."

"Comes off like a hard ass to me. The kind of pushy that hides being afraid."

"He has a good reputation, and he used to run this river when he was younger."

"That's what I'm saying. He's not so young anymore. He's got at least eight and maybe ten years on the rest of us."

McKay shrugged, a swishy, effeminate gesture that didn't fit his muscular shoulders. "Experience takes time. At least one of us knows what he's doing."

"Sure, but I'm going to keep on eye on him. I don't trust him. I got the feeling he'll fold when the pressure's on."

"Maybe there won't be any pressure."

Farrengalli tapped a drumroll on his flask. "Oh, there's going to be pressure, all right. From inside and outside."

"What's that supposed to mean?"

"Don't worry about it, Golden Boy. Just watch your own neck, that's what I'm saying. When it comes down to it, we're all on our own."

McKay stood and kicked a smoldering log into the deep red embers. "Yeah, whatever. This isn't a reality show, man. This *is* reality. See you in the morning."

Farrengalli shook the empty flask as McKay left the fire, wishing there was enough whiskey to slosh around. A final swallow would have set his head right. He'd wondered if the fag would hit on him. His kind sometimes did, and Farrengalli never got upset about it. It was kind of flattering, in a way. Why wouldn't they dig the same thing the chicks did?

No big deal. The important thing was that Vincent Stefano Farrengalli had outlasted McKay and the others. He would perform better than them, and on less sleep. He would finish first no matter what. He stared into the deep red eye of the fire for a few minutes before turning in himself.

CHAPTER TWELVE

Jim Castle was completely lost. The trails had turned him around, and though he could hear the water rushing through the deep groove of the gorge, he wasn't sure how he could reach it. Once, he'd broken into a clearing that had turned out to be the stone face of a cliff edge. The Unegama River ran a hundred feet below, winding a silvery path toward an eventual, unseen ocean.

At that point, the gorge was the length of two football fields across. According to Derek Samford's maps, this western side of the river was wilder, steeper, rockier, and more dangerous. There were only a few main trails, and they were so rarely traveled that it was easy to branch off into an animal path or a washed-out section that suggested an established route. Especially when walking by the light of a quarter moon that was often veiled by low gray clouds.

Castle was afraid to use the flashlight. He told himself it was because Goodall would see his approach and either sneak into the woods until Castle passed or else ambush him. But, in truth, he was afraid of attracting the thing that had taken Samford.

It wasn't a thing. It wasn't a bird-beast or a man-bat or an escaped extra from the set of Hellraiser. *It was a hallucination, clear as day.*

If Samford were still around—*if it* was *a hallucination, how do you explain what happened to your partner?*—he would undoubtedly have attributed Castle's delusion to exhaustion, stress, and the trauma of having nearly been blown to bits or buried alive. That's exactly how Samford would size it up, including the tricky little part where Samford himself was dangled in the air like frankfurters on a string. The Rook was a behavioral psychologist—or had been—and could make sense of such perverted stimuli. Castle, though, could only pretend it hadn't happened.

While knowing it had.

And the rustling in the treetops can't be just the wind.

The sound seemed to follow him, though he was constantly changing pace, one moment dragging his feet, the next breaking into a half jog, hoping to put more distance between himself and the hole in the ground, where the mountain had given way and opened onto a dark, cold space that might have been sealed off for eons. He thought of his feet dangling in that emptiness, of the soft scratching against his boots. Maybe the thing that took The Rook had been released from some primal prison by the bomb blast.

A species that was probably blind and at home in the eternal dark. But that made no sense, either. Nature wouldn't have given such a creature wings, and what kind of food would it have found?

A hallucination was much more comforting than its possible reality. Castle could accept a crack-up. Like taking a bullet for the team, it was an occupational hazard. More than one agent had been released from active duty and turned out to pasture at the funny farm after a harrowing hostage situation or a shoot-out. All the training in the world couldn't totally remove the vulnerability that was hidden inside all humans.

A branch broke overhead. Here the trail was narrower,

the canopy nearly unbroken, and in the quiet of the night, the sound was like a pistol shot.

Castle paused, ears filled with the roar of blood and his own breathing. One of the things was up there—*yes, THINGS, plural, because one was trying to tug him down into the hole while the other had flown away with The Rook. No telling how many of them had crawled from that nightmare orifice*—and even though he was positive they didn't exist, he was equally sure that a wizened, leathery, gray-skinned creature was hovering in the treetops, marking him, drooling and hungry.

The handle of the Glock was slick with his sweat. In these conditions, with poor light and close quarters, the stalker had the advantage. But .40-caliber bullets had a way of equalizing affairs in a hurry. Assuming the creature was made of flesh and blood and not fairy dust.

You're over the edge, Castle. You don't know what happened back there, but you figure a bullet's going to solve the problem. Three bullets. One for the master, one for the dame, and one for the little boy who hides under sheets.

He wasn't going to let any creature rip him from this world before he found the Bama Bomber. He'd made this vow to The Rook's soul, though he believed in souls about as much as he believed in the Great Pumpkin. Or, for that matter, flying, man-eating backwoods monkey-birds.

"Come out with your hands up," Castle said, the words sounding foolish even as they left his lips.

The only answer was the fluttering, dying leaves of the hardwoods. Castle scanned the trees, eyes straining to penetrate the deep shadows. No doubt the Appalachians were home to nocturnal birds such as owls, and other occasionally airborne mammals such as bats and flying squirrels.

The Rook would know. He'd become an armchair expert on the region during their week of preparation. But maybe you never knew everything. Remote places, lost, harsh corners of the world, wild lands like the Appalachians, maybe they kept a few secrets.

After a couple of minutes, Castle's heartbeat slowed. His mind was playing tricks, and was still the same mind that harbored little Jimmy's dark bedroom fantasies. The mind was more cluttered with trivia and memories now, shaped by training and experience, but it, too, still kept a few secrets. The monsters were no longer under the bed. They were here, around him, scuttling in the dark.

He wanted to laugh. No monster could be as bad as Ace Goodall, a man who would probably kill again and again until he was caught. Capturing Goodall was the only mission here, the only mystery. He could sort out the rest later, after The Rook's body was found and the forensics people went to work.

Sure, he was lost, but dawn was only about four hours away. Tomorrow, he'd be able to figure out where he was. He began walking again, and a hundred yards later, he came to a break in the trees. He walked out onto a granite shelf that was spotted with lichen. The gorge opened before him, and the moon was at its apex, limning the chalky cliff walls and throwing a gentle blue light over the wilderness.

Against the sky were the silhouettes of three flying creatures. Castle couldn't gauge their size because he had no point of reference, but if he had to guess, they were about the size of the thing that had carried away The Rook.

The creatures rode the high wind, frayed wings unsteady. They drifted aimlessly, their flights uncoordinated. Two of them nearly collided. They made no sound, though Castle imagined the rush of the water below might be their voices.

He didn't believe in them, but that didn't stop him from easing back into the cover of the forest.

CHAPTER THIRTEEN

Derek Samford hadn't died instantly, as his partner believed.

He'd been keeping an eye out for Ace Goodall, tightening the rope as Castle climbed out of the hole. He wasn't sure what type of explosion had triggered the landslide, because earthquakes were rare in the Appalachians. The mountain range was so ancient that some believed it had existed before the continental drift and ran beneath the Atlantic Ocean. The far end of the chain wasn't in Maine, but Scotland. Those rounded hills amid the misty lochs shared a lot of geologic characteristics with these rocky, worn ridges. That much was in the research Samford had absorbed when he'd first gotten the assignment.

He had a week's notice, and he'd met Castle only three days before they were dropped off at the border of the wilderness area. He'd heard of Special Agent Jim Castle, of course. Castle was the kind that fellow agents admired but the brass tried to bury. Funny that it turned out the Earth itself had tried to bury Castle.

And the sky had yanked Samford away.

Samford blinked against the darkness. It was complete, as solid against his skin as water. He was lying on a cool, hard surface that wasn't quite flat. The air was stale and held a faint stench of fur and decay, like the den of a hibernating animal.

He couldn't remember what had happened after the vicious jerk to his shoulder. His first thought had been that Goodall had crept up on him and grazed him with a bullet. Though Samford had never been shot before, he knew a bullet would have delivered a more powerful punch, shredding meat and bone. This wound had been cleaner, colder.

He reached to touch it now, his arm heavy and slow, and felt the soggy fabric of his insulated vest. He eased a pinkie tip into the gash. It didn't hurt. Not much, anyway. He wondered if shock were setting in, or something worse.

He couldn't trust his senses, and the total blackness disoriented him. He squeezed his eyes shut so hard his cheeks quivered, and then flicked his eyelids wide open. Still dark. He tried to rise, but his chest and head were sandbags. Sleep tugged at him from somewhere in the base of his skull and he found himself smiling.

Death in the line of duty. That wasn't so bad.

Except Goodall had nothing to do with his current situation. Samford had been plucked from the ground like a trout on the hook end of a fishing line. Fighting the drowsiness, he searched the muddy avenues of his memory. Images fell against each other like a domino game played with funhouse mirrors:

The spurt of blood arcing from his shoulder.

The rush of air up his windpipe, his own scream taking forever to reach his ears.

Scabbed, gnarled fingers making a noose around his ankle.

The world going upside down.

The rake of branches across his face as he was lifted.

Down in the hole, the pale and confused oval of Castle's upturned face.

The sweep of wind as he rose higher.

The river far below, cutting a silver thread between the rocky cliffs.

Then, his vision clotting to gray.

Waking up here.

Or maybe not awake.

Maybe he was dead. That would explain some things. But his chest rose and fell, his fingers moved, his eyes opened and closed. The numbness of the wound had worn off, and though the pain still wasn't great, it was enough to remind him that his nerves still functioned. And, apparently, his blood still flowed.

Something clicked to his right, a distance of maybe ten feet away, maybe twenty. The acoustics were strange, the sound eliciting a single muffled echo, suggesting he was in an enclosed space. He held his breath for a few seconds, listening. When the sound wasn't repeated, he exhaled though his nostrils. He was in a cave. That explained the stale air.

But he would have to be deep in the Earth to be without light. Even the gloomiest, most overcast night held the faint gray of obscured stars. Maybe he'd fallen into the hole while helping Castle and had been hit on the head, and a landslide had sealed him up like a pharaoh tucked under a pyramid. Goodall could have rigged some type of follow-up bomb. That would explain Samford's lack of consciousness, but it didn't explain those disturbing memories. He reached for his face, felt the smile still frozen on his lips, and ran his fingers over his scalp and around his skull. No lumps, no other wounds.

Besides the gouge in his shoulder and a little exhaustion, he was fine. Nothing to do but wait it out and recover his strength, then get up and explore. In the meantime, he could play over Goodall's assessment and guess the bomber's next move, because Castle would want to resume the hunt once they were both—

The clicking sound came again, closer. Five feet, maybe. He thought again of hibernating animals. Animals didn't hibernate in the fall. This was the season they spent growing fat, packing on pounds for the long winter ahead.

Samford willed his lungs to work steadily, though his heart banged against his rib cage like a meth junkie in a jail cell. Quantico didn't train for sensory deprivation. Being held captive in a mountain cave wasn't one of the scenarios designed by the FBI theorists. But was he really captive?

If he weren't so tired, he would find out.

The click again, and behind it, a sinister rasp.

A click to his left, above him. The cave must be larger than he'd first thought. Enough headroom to stand.

Another click, and farther away, another. A soft flutter, then another, erupting into flapping.

Wings.

Bats.

Samford relaxed a little. Of course there would be bats in a cave. The winged mammals were as ubiquitous as mice, and, unless they were infected with rabies, were utterly harmless. Their sonar would detect Samford's movements and inform the creatures that Samford was much too large to serve as prey.

The flapping grew more agitated, and was strong enough to stir the fetid air of the chamber. Perhaps full dark was coming on outside and the brood of bats was preparing to alight as one, to sweep out of the cave's opening in that iconic and primordial image that launched a hundred spooky movies. But those images had always been accompanied by frantic squeaking. Why were these so silent?

The next click, like fingernail on bone, was so close to his wounded shoulder that he felt its vibration.

The flapping became frenetic, and a leathery wing brushed his face. The fluttering hovered nearer, and there must have been dozens of them. He tried to picture their faces, those wrinkled slits where eyes should be, their moist gray noses, tiny teeth behind black lips. The image didn't comfort him.

It was touching his shoulder now, not with a finger, but with something softer. Even with the numbness, he could feel its velvety texture, with just enough abrasion to tickle him. It was the moist, sandpapery flesh of a tongue, one much too large to belong to a bat.

The tongue played around his wound as if wielded by a lover in the early stages of oral sex. Samford, despite the horrifyingly pleasant sensation, would have slapped it away, but his arms had become as heavy as his head. The drowsiness returned, and his groin flooded with warmth. He had an erection.

The tongue teased, and there was something doubly disturbing about it. There was no breath behind it. Whether a bear, a fox, or an oversize bat, it should be panting as it licked.

A memory rushed up, the image of the thing that had borne him aloft and carried him to this chamber that would serve as his sepulcher.

The tongue found the heart of the wound and entered.

It grew more vigorous, wiggling as it found the nourishment it sought. Lips smacked with sticky residue. Another tongue joined the first, the flapping became a percussive rattling, the air of the chamber buzzed with clicking, slithery movement.

Through it all, Samford kept smiling, even as he screamed.

CHAPTER FOURTEEN

Bowie had slept maybe three hours total, but he'd only dreamt of Connie once. In the rest of his dreams, he'd been running a kayak down the Unegama in a Class III stretch popularly known as "Beaver's Lick." Class III waters were challenging for a beginner, and even carried a slight risk of injury or death, but such a run was nothing to an experienced paddler. In the dream, however, everything went wrong. Bowie's paddle acted as if it were stirring molasses, the kayak took on water, and he found himself broadsiding boulders and getting caught in ripples. Worse, it had begun to rain, and Bowie couldn't seem to make shore.

He awoke before dark, more tired than rested, his legs and lower back sore from the hike. The best way to get loose was to get moving, so he rolled up his sleeping bag and carried his clothes into the woods. The first birds were mouthing off about the start of another great day in the wonderful world, and nocturnal animals scuffed leaves as they returned to their daytime hiding holes. Bowie stripped nude and was about to wriggle into his water-resistant SealSkinz when a twig snapped behind him.

He turned, squinting into the underbrush, instinctively dropping the loose clothing in front of his crotch. "Hello?"

Dove Krueger laughed. "Your ass is so white, I thought it was a full moon."

"Very funny. What are you doing out here?

"When nature calls, there's only one answer."

"It's a half hour before sunup. Why don't you get some more sleep?"

"I'm not sleepy," she said, her voice closer now. The forest was expectant with the coming day, right on the threshold of full life, but for the moment, the world hung in that eerie half light between night and morning.

She stepped out of the shadows into the lesser gray, moved his hands away, and felt for him. Her breath was warm on his cheek, and though he couldn't quite make out her face, he could picture it as plainly as a photograph. She had washed, and smelled earthy, like chamomile and mint.

"An early riser, like always," she murmured with approval.

"Dove. We're done with that, remember?"

"Feels like we're just starting." She grabbed his right wrist and guided his hand to the front of her sheer cotton gown. Her nipples were bare and hard beneath the fabric.

"We're done with that," he said, though the words almost stuck in his throat.

She didn't slow her stroking, and he didn't pull his hand away, though he kept it still. Her lips touched his neck and her hair fell soft against the skin of his shoulder. The contrast of her heat against the morning chill raised gooseflesh along his back.

"Dove," he whispered, and it took all of his willpower to step away. The first hint of red painted the sky in the east, and he thought of that old nautical saying, "Red sky at morning, sailors taking warning." The birds were louder now, and the muted music of the falls provided a peaceful backdrop. This, the moment before true dawn, was one of the points where the fabric of reality was the thinnest, when order was at its most vulnerable, when reason fled.

He could see the outline of her body now. The cotton, damp from the night river air, clung to her form, her black hair loose and tangled around her face. "You'd better get back to camp before the others wake up," he said.

"Because they'll talk, and maybe lose respect for you, and the test run will be compromised," she said. "The mission comes first. Duty calls, and all that other macho horseshit."

"It's not that. It's—"

"She's dead. You told me that yourself, even if you don't believe it yet. I can't make you believe it, either. That's something inside you. But you don't have to suffer forever because of it."

"You promised never to bring that up."

"I'm a woman. What's a promise when it stands between me and what I want?"

She was right. He knew, once he'd told her about his loss, she'd eventually find a way to use it against him. He'd suffered a moment of weakness, and any outdoor adventurer knew it was those moments of weakness that killed. He feared another such moment now.

"I don't regret what we did in the Adirondacks," he said, speaking faster now, fearing the yawning power of the timeless and frozen dawn. "But it's done. We met at a bad time for both of us and—"

"Shut up," she said. "It was only the right time."

She was on him again, and this time he didn't fight it. His body was taking over, tricking him, and his hands roamed over her curves, then lifted the gown up and over her head. It fell to the ground, and she lowered herself, kneeling on the fabric. The distant, gentle throb of the falls provided a primitive sound track to her action as she took him in her mouth. Unbidden, Farrengalli's bellow entered his head: *It's only fuckin' naturalllll....*

"Dove, stop," he said, though his hands betrayed him by reaching for her hair and urging her head forward.

After ten seconds of sweet torture, she backed off and said, "Stop now?"

"Damn you."

In the dimness of approaching morning, he saw the gleam of her grin. Then her mouth was busy again, but Bowie had other ideas. He pressed her shoulders and eased down beside her until they were lying side-by-side on their discarded clothes. Leaves scratched at his bare skin, but he scarcely noticed. His senses were consumed by the heat at the center of her body, the seat of her soul, the moist, inviting tunnel that demanded exploration. He tongued and caressed her until she mewled; then she gouged her fingernails into his back and pulled him on top of her. She rubbed his aching hardness against her damp opening, then guided him inside. It fit like always, like new. She arched her back, throwing herself up to meet his slow penetration.

"I don't love you," he whispered, biting her ear.

She timed her words with his thrusts. "I ...never... wanted... you... to."

"Good." Her neck was slightly salty and her hair smelled of wood smoke, with a hint of rosemary and mint. He tasted it again just to be sure.

"You've gotten better. Have you been practicing?"

"Does my hand count?"

"I want this to last."

"Three days."

"No, I mean you. This."

He shut her up by putting his tongue in her mouth. She hadn't brushed her teeth, but neither had he. Nature didn't care. Nature didn't even notice.

She rolled him over and sat astride his hips. The light was better now and he gazed into her half-lidded eyes. He wondered what she was thinking about, figured nothing, and decided he didn't want to think, either. He moved with her, against her, around, and she leaned down so her nipples brushed against his as she rocked back and forth.

"The others can't know about this," Bowie said.

She stopped moving. "Stop now?"

He pushed up against her. His back was no longer sore. His back had never been better. His legs were fine, too. Other things were improving by the minute.

He reached for her hips so he could control her movements, but he didn't need force. They were already in synch, grinding out a rhythm as old as the river. Their sweat sprang against the September air, enhancing the slickness between them.

From the camp came Farrengalli's voice, calling out for Bowie. He wondered if anyone would come this way to heed the call of nature. He smiled. He didn't give a fuck. Well, he only gave *one* fuck at the moment.

"Are you close?" she whispered, slowing until her motion was almost imperceptible, a blissful Sisyphus stone pushed to the mountain peak.

"You wanted this to last."

"We've got a river to run."

"The river will still be there."

"Do you love me yet?"

"Never, bitch."

"Finish me, asshole," she whispered, and her words harmonized with the sibilant wash of the Unegama.

Her movements became more urgent, and Bowie was all too familiar with the quickened breath, the slitted, almost reptilian eyes, and the pinking of her cheeks. Her climax coincided with the splintered arrival of the sun, and she bit his shoulder to keep from crying out. The pain turned strange in Bowie's brain, combining with the rush of primal joy that coursed up from his toes. She sensed his approach and writhed away in silent passion, whimpers squeezing between the teeth that sank deeper into his flesh. His entire body became a giant, throbbing organ and he exploded like the dawn.

Dove collapsed on top of him in a twin pounding of hearts. She relaxed her mouth and let her head drop against his shoulder. Wetness tickled the skin under his arm and her breath made a soft breeze against his neck. His hands slid from her hips to the small of her back. At the volcanic center where they were joined, Bowie couldn't tell where he ended and she began. Like always.

"I lied," he said when the treetops stopped spinning.

"I know," she said. She lifted her face to look at him. Her mouth was smeared with his blood.

"Hungry?"

"Not anymore."

The leaves scratched his back and his legs. One of his feet was planted against a stump. An ant crawled along his hip and he twitched, causing Dove's breasts to wiggle against his chest.

"Again already?" she asked with a grin. She licked the blood from her lips.

"They'll be wondering where we are."

"Let them."

He took her by the arms, rolled her to the side, and reached for his SealSkinz. "Let me go first. You come in two minutes."

She giggled. "I may be easy but I'm not that fast."

"Very funny. Sorry I called you a 'bitch.'" He wrestled his legs into the tight, water-resistant SealSkinz.

"I'm used to it." She had her own waterproof outfit, an older model that was scuffed and frayed, sky blue with a broad yellow stripe down the middle. "By the way, which lie did you tell this time?"

"Does it matter?" He adjusted his crotch inside the SealSkinz and rolled the single piece the rest of the way up his torso, stretching the rubberized fabric. He'd only been with one woman since the last time with Dove. During his marriage, he'd averaged ten times a week. Now, he realized with dismay, he was lucky to get lucky once a year. He apologized to his penis for the hibernation, though it was fairly content and dreaming at the moment.

"See you at launch," he said, walking the perimeter of the clearing so he and Dove wouldn't exit from the same point and arouse suspicion.

CHAPTER FIFTEEN

In many ways, losing a partner was worse than taking a bullet yourself.

In addition to the shame of letting Ace Goodall slip away, Jim Castle now had a permanent black mark on his record. Assuming The Rook was actually dead. Castle didn't quite accept the image of the winged creature carrying a grown man into the sky as easily as a hawk might rip a mouse aloft. But The Rook's yell of pain had been real, and against the small, still sounds of the night and the susurrant river, it seemed to echo off the trees and around the hard shell of Castle's skull.

Agents accepted the possibility of dying in the line of duty. That was part of the excitement of the job. The rush of adrenaline came with the territory, and premature and eternal retirement was an occupational hazard. But just as airline pilots believed their next flights wouldn't be that one-in-a-million with an unhappy ending, in the back of their minds, all agents believed it wouldn't happen to them.

And if you lost a partner, you expected it to happen by the book: a car crash during a high-speed chase, a shoot-out in a hostage situation, or an explosion during a security detail. Maybe even through someone else's goof, like the failure to see a trip wire. You didn't expect some deformed bird of prey to pluck your partner from the sky and dangle it like a rag doll.

Castle had moved away from the collapsed section of hillside. He wanted to be as far away from the scene of the attack as possible. He'd collected their backpacks and gone to Goodall's camp, figuring to wait out the night, collect what clues he could find in the morning, and hike back to civilization.

Once there, assuming he could make it without The Rook's compass and memory, he'd file a report, turn in his badge, and check himself into an orderly brick building with daisies bordering the porch and grass that stayed green year round. A clean, well-lighted place, with bars over the windows through which no giant monkey-birds could crash.

The forest at night had taken on a menacing quality. A skein of clouds filtered the quarter moon, and the tall branches were like wicked arms twisted by a thousand winds. Leaves rattled in the underbrush, and each new scraping sound heralded the stealthy approach of the bird-beasts. He found a rough trail, one not marked on any map and likely the path of both prey and predator, and followed it along the ridge.

His backpack held a flashlight, but he was afraid to use it. The light might summon the creature—or *creatures*, if the thing in the hole had been of the same species as the flyby nightmare—and with the night closing in, his years of training failed him and he became the lost boy in the big, cold bed, the shadows holding terrible monsters.

Only this time, he didn't have a mother who would come running when he called. Not that he'd called her often. Even then, he'd had a deep streak of pride that battled his fear. Here in the Unegama wilderness, there was no one to peek into the dark spaces and declare them safe.

He wondered how much he would fudge the report. The Rook was relatively young and had never married. No kids. That should have been a comfort, but somehow the lack of survivors made his death (and Castle couldn't accept any other outcome) all the more empty, as if his genetic soup had poured into the ground and been lost forever.

Yes, the report would be fiction. It had to be. The Rook would fall from a cliff, in hot pursuit of Goodall. That might earn him posthumous recognition and save Castle some shame. It would also send extra personnel into the area as they looked for a fallen hero along with the mass murderer who had caused The Rook's death.

Except they couldn't save Castle. Whether he made it through dead or alive.

The rough animal trail turned into a rippled wash of soil, the erosion of centuries creating a series of natural steps down an embankment. Water flowed downhill, and the river eventually joined up with Lake Chotoa. The lakeside was densely developed, though mostly for summer homes. Few people would be there this time of year, but Castle would get help. There were probably even cell phone towers there.

With the radio batteries dead, the cell phone was his only means of communication. But the phone had been rendered useless here in the gorge, blocked from signals and isolated from other systems. Reaching the lake might again connect him with the real world and its sane, solid angles. A world without man-sized, man-eating birds.

Castle scrambled down the wash, senses tuned to the crunching leaves beneath his boots. The hair on the back of his neck stood up, and his ears strained against the soft roar

of the river for any odd sound—
Like the flap of giant wings—
Such as Ace Goodall's footsteps.

The wash bottomed out on a wider section of trail, one that was still primitive but passable. If Goodall and the girl were reunited, they'd be moving slowly. Like him, they were probably headed for the river, wanting to take the fastest possible route to escape now that their whereabouts were known. Perhaps Castle could catch up with them and take down Goodall. No one would blame him for killing the subject. Goodall was wanted dead or alive, with a $100,000 bounty out for information leading to his arrest and conviction. Killing the murderer would maybe ease some of the acid that roiled in Castle's gut, the juice of failure and fear.

Forget the bird-beast. Forget The Rook. Forget little Jimmy Castle, the kid who shivered under the blankets. This one's for law and order.

Yeah, sure. Let's fall back on that one. Duty.

Because you know what's under the bed, and you're too afraid to peek.

Castle drew his Glock and jogged silently through the murk of night, not buying his own line of bullshit.

CHAPTER SIXTEEN

The hell she thinks we are, beavers? Why did I let her talk me into coming down to water? We'da been better off hiking out the way we came in and taking our chances thumbing south.

Up close, the river was both faster and deeper than it had appeared from the high ridges. A few big boulders jutted up wet and gray, the current beating froth between them. Ace Goodall couldn't swim, and his fear of the water was almost as bad as his fear of heights. No way would he let on to Clara, though.

After all, this was all her fault. If she hadn't fucked up when the agents came snooping around, Ace would be waking up to instant coffee and a packet of instant oatmeal. Instead, he was forced to lie on his belly and scoop river water into his mouth. No telling how much fish piss he was drinking.

Clara knelt beside him, splashing cold water on her face. They had slept for an hour or so, Ace leaning against her so he'd wake up if she tried to run away again. Even though God was on his side, God didn't do much to cut out the loneliness.

The joy of setting off those clinic bombs had faded and left him hollow, and even the newspaper clippings didn't quite cheer him up. Sure, his mission was important, but it wasn't until he met Clara that he found true pride in his work. In her, he had a partner, but most importantly, he had someone who admired him and appreciated the role God had given him. Even though she was still a dumb, highfalutin bitch.

"What now?" he asked, raising his voice over the water.

"I guess we follow the river," she said. "It ought to come out somewhere."

"Sure. It comes out at the ocean. What other bright ideas do you have? Want me to gnaw some damned trees in two so we can build a raft?"

"Ace, don't get mad. We got away, didn't we?"

"Thanks to the angels. But I don't see them nowheres now. Looks like we're on our own."

He squinted toward the east, where the sun rose like an egg yolk sliding up a greasy griddle. The river was loud and the tinkling, splashing, and gurgling hurt his ears and set him on edge. Sharp, high-pitched sounds had always bothered him. Maybe because his dad had worked him in the sawmill at the age of six, when Ace's job had been to carry away the scrap bark. The rusty blade was as tall as Ace, with teeth as big as those in a shark's grin.

Ace had been there the day his dad had lost three fingers to the mill. Not in the saw, but in the great fan belt hooked to the gasoline engine that drove the blade. The fingers had kicked out and bounced off a pile of wood chips at Ace's feet. He'd looked down at them, thinking how they didn't look like fingers once they were no longer attached to a hand. More than anything, they resembled fat, pale grubs that had swollen and popped.

A good lesson. When you take something out of its rightful place, it don't belong no more. His dad had wrapped a dirty handkerchief around the maimed limb and met the day's quota. The fingers lay where they were until the sawdust and wood chips covered them.

"About how far do you think it is?" Clara asked. For an uppity rich bitch with an uppity name, she looked like hell. Watery, purple pouches bulged under her bloodshot eyes, her hair was oily and tangled, and her clothes were damp and dirty. She was way too scrawny, and Ace wondered not for the first time if she was the kind who threw up after eating. He heard some of those uppity rich bitches did that sort of thing.

He wondered if Eve had thrown up after the first bite of the apple, once she knew the thing was poisoned with sin and forbidden knowledge. Hell, no. Of course not. The natural thing to do, the *woman* thing, was to poison Adam.

"I reckon three or four miles," he said, pulling a guess out of the air. Lying had never been a problem for him. "At least if we stick to the river, we know we're going downhill."

"Think the police will know about the agents yet?"

"Don't hardly see how. They ain't been dead long enough to go missing. Of course, there might be other ones already in the woods that we ain't seen yet."

"What will they do to you for killing them?"

He sighed, but the sound was lost in the sweeping roar of the river. "How many times I got to tell you? It was the angel that killed them, not me."

"Yeah, but you're the one they'll blame."

Ace had to agree with that. The law had always nailed his ass for the least little infraction. Every time someone tossed a rock through a school window, little Robert Wayne Goodall took the fall. When the neighbor's cat turned up skinned and hanging from a tree branch, Bobby Wayne's ass was also swinging in the wind. When a fire took down the new Sunday school wing of the Beulaville Baptist Church, Goodall drew his first stretch, a three-month cakewalk in a juvenile detention center in Mobile.

That's where he earned the nickname "Ace," partly for his skill at poker and partly because he'd fought off a big German goon who'd wanted Bobby Wayne to swallow his one-eyed bratwurst. The German had eventually found another sweetheart and befriended Ace, and they'd spent their sentences swapping out cigarettes, lies, and survival tips.

Bouncing from juvie to high school had been a case of frying pan to fire. The probation officer was on him like a green fly on shit, and Ace could hardly score a joint without the crew-cut motherfucker reading him the riot act. Home life was hell, his mom lost in the Bible and Dad a hopeless workaholic who couldn't understand why his little Bobby Wayne couldn't straighten up and follow in his footsteps. After all, Dad may have lost a few fingers, but he still had ten toes and they all pointed toward God's golden stairway.

Ace took to staying out all night, sometimes balling some skank welfare slut in the trailer park, sometimes just sleeping out in the woods under a blanket propped up on sticks. It was in the Alabama pine forest where he first felt at peace. Alone, he felt everything made sense, and when he first heard the Voice, he thought it was just another too-loud radio blaring from an open window on the freeway. But the Voice didn't fade with distance. It stayed right there until it made itself heard. Probably like Jesus did when God sent Him out to wander the wilderness.

"Ya gotta carry your own cross when the time comes,"

his mom was fond of saying.

He didn't know about no cross, but when he started carrying around a Bible, the probation officer suddenly became all smiles, his teachers cut him enough slack that he didn't drop out until he reached legal age, and he wasn't an automatic suspect every time a Coke machine was jimmied or a motorbike turned up missing. That was when Ace finally appreciated the power of the Lord: Go to church of a Wednesday night and twice on Sunday, and you could pull the wool over the eyes of a lot of sheep.

With their blind faith, Ace turned seriously cruel instead of just being casual about it.

"Ya gotta carry your own cross when the time comes," he said now to Clara.

"What does that mean?"

"Nothing. It's just words."

"We're out of toilet paper."

He nodded, wondering what Jesus used to wipe his ass when out wandering in the wilderness. Probably, the Devil had popped up and offered the Lord a roll of Charmin hot off the presses, saying, "Sit on my porcelain throne and be king of all thou survey." Jesus would never take the soft wipe, the easy way. No, He'd rather tough it out, ass rash or no.

"Let's get walking," Ace said.

Clara nodded, waited for him to take the lead, and he wanted to slap her silly straight teeth down her throat. Just because Eve was beyond his reach.

Instead, he pointed downriver. "That way."

Clara nodded again, like she knew it all along, then gathered her macramé shawl about her shoulders and sought a flat path near the shore.

Uppity bitch. Ace followed her, pausing first to spit into the churning river.

CHAPTER SEVENTEEN

"What the fuck, Raintree?"

Robert Raintree looked up from his stump. Beside him was his backpack. He'd broken down his tent, tucked it and his sleeping bag away, and had rekindled the campfire for breakfast. He'd dipped into the medicine bag and found peace, as he had on so many mornings.

He'd been sitting on the stump for two hours. He'd seen Bowie Whitlock slip into the woods, then Dove Krueger following him a few minutes later. A distant woodpecker nailed a staccato breakfast, the wilderness equivalent of a barnyard rooster. After that, he'd lapsed into meditation, the way he imagined his ancestors had done before their vision quests.

But Farrengalli was now in his face, loud, asinine, raw as nature and twice as ugly.

"Excuse me?" Raintree said.

"You're, like, up with the birds, dude."

"I thought we were getting an early start."

Farrengalli blinked at the ragged, red dawn. "Yeah. Where's that asshole Whitlock, anyway?"

The way Farrengalli had been drinking from his flask last night, Raintree was surprised to see the man had no sign of a hangover. If anything, flushed cheeks and a pained expression seemed to fit Farrengalli, as if waking up in anger were the only reason to bother opening his eyes at all.

"Got any extra water?" Farrengalli said. "I'm thirsty as a mother whore."

"Whitlock said to ration."

"Well, the river looks clean enough."

The river was probably clean enough two hundred years ago, when his ancestors had hunted the watering holes for elk and deer. No, not all his ancestors. He was only half Cherokee, and he was pretty sure his bloodline had been tainted with Choctaw and Shawnee, other tribes that had been driven West and lumped together. "I wouldn't advise it, unless you're going to boil it first."

"Hey, Red Man, afraid to drink a little bear piss? Probably put some hair on your pecker. Or you rather drink'um firewater?"

So much for peace. Raintree closed his eyes and concentrated on the whisper of soft feathers through his central nervous system. Good medicine.

Farrengalli spat a dry chunk of mucus into the fire. "I'm making coffee. Might as well get the old blood system jumpstarted while I'm waiting around for these clowns. Hey, where's the chick?" Farrengalli undulated his hands in the shape of feminine curves. "You know, the hot squaw?"

Raintree said nothing. He listened again to the birds and their timeless songs of morning, wondering what messages they were sharing. At the edge of the clearing, Travis Lane and C.A. McKay were busy breaking down their tents. Dove Krueger's tent stood with its front flap open, empty. Whitlock's gear was already packed, except for one of the Muskrats, which lay in a sleek bundle near the campfire.

"You don't talk much, do you?"

You more than make up for the two of us, he wanted to say, but Farrengalli was right. Raintree spread out the raft he'd been carrying, attaching the hand-operated air pump to the outer valve. Travis Lane hurried over, already sweating though the air was not humid.

"Do you know how to connect it?" Lane said. "Make sure you inflate the inner and outer layers to the same pressure."

"Him smart Injun," Farrengalli said.

Raintree screwed the pump to the valve stem and began working the handle. The raft swelled like a blister. The outer layer was blue, the inner canary yellow. There were no seats, just three sets of nylon belts lined on the rubberized deck. A series of hardened vinyl loops ran along the outer rim of the raft, and held nylon cord that could be used for tying off the raft and securing gear. Raintree had inflated the raft during the orientation session, but in its intended habitat, he could better appreciate the ingenuity of the design.

"Thirty-two pounds," Lane said, excited for the first time since the journey began. "Now fill the inner layer."

Raintree was connecting the pump to the second stem when Whitlock emerged from the woods and approached them.

"Where you been?" Farrengalli said, glancing at an imaginary wristwatch. "The fish are biting and your friends here were about to shove off without you."

"I was reconnoitering downstream," Whitlock said. "Only a fool launches without knowing what's waiting ahead."

"You look like a fairy in that wet suit," Farrengalli said.

"Hey, Farrengalli, don't knock the SealSkinz," Lane

said. "That's space-age design right there. Remember, you're on ProVentures's dime right now."

"Right, Boss." He turned to Raintree. "I got a feeling this is going to be a case of 'Too many chiefs and not enough Injuns.' *Har-haw-haw.*"

Raintree winced at the man's braying, exaggerated laugh, but kept his attention on the pump's pressure gauge. When the pressure levels of the two chambers matched, Raintree packed away the pump while Lane tested the raft with his boot. Whitlock brought out the paddles and extended and tightened the telescoping handles.

"Hey, sweetmeat, where you been?" Farrengalli hollered.

C.A. McKay, now wearing his SealSkinz and backpack, hollered back, "I know I'm pretty sweet, but this is strictly for the ladies."

"Get over it, Golden Boy. I wasn't talking to you."

"And the ladies don't want it, anyway," Dove Krueger said.

Farrengalli let out his braying laugh again, silencing the birds.

Dove's hair was wet and she had obviously washed it. She, too, was dressed in a SealSkinz, and Raintree had to admit it did wonderful things for her figure. Like the others, she had worn sparse, loose clothing while hiking, and lightweight fabrics were the smart choice when you had to pack them back out at the end of the run. Her SealSkinz left delicious little to the imagination, and it was the kind of little that was the most fun. Raintree wouldn't be surprised if she were the cover model in the *Back2Nature Magazine* when the special Muskrat edition hit the stands. In a bikini, holding a paddle in a suggestive manner, sitting astride the Muskrat with her tanned legs spread.

She's not your vision. Keep your mind clean and open or you'll miss the sign when it flies in front of your face.

He wondered why the word "flies" had popped into his head. Ravens, he knew, were the largest of the crow family and a common ceremonial symbol among the Cherokee. The tribe even had a legend of the Raven Mocker, a spirit that changed forms and deceived people. Eagles, hawks, falcons, herons, owls, and other birds of prey had found their place in tribal lore, though many of the species were now extinct in the Appalachians.

His vision was just as likely to be of a bear, fox, or maybe even a mountain lion. Though there was no reason for the creature to be of either air or Earth. Perhaps it would be a trout, a frog, maybe even a salamander. No reason to think his spirit mirror, what some Northwestern tribes called the "totem," would be a noble one.

"Let's get this show on the road, folks," Whitlock said, pumping up the second raft. "We should make it to Babel Tower by late afternoon and we can set up camp there."

Babel Tower. A sacred site for the Cherokee, which they had called Attacoa. How like the White Man to impose its own religious name on the mountain.

"We're not going to stop on the way?" McKay said.

"What do you think this is, a ride at Disneyland?" Farrengalli said. "You're a long way from California. And *Paree*, too."

"Fuck off, Farrengalli. I've had enough of your mouth."

Farrengalli dropped his backpack and leaped across the fire to McKay, moving so swiftly that Raintree barely had time to register the action before Farrengalli had McKay by the shoulders, shaking the cyclist so hard his head wobbled. Whitlock moved almost as fast as Farrengalli, stepping between the two struggling men and driving his forearms against their chests. "Cool it," the tour guide said.

McKay backed away, but Farrengalli lunged at him, throwing Whitlock off balance. "I don't have to take that shit from a sweet boy like you."

Whitlock got Farrengalli in a bear hug. "Easy, easy."

Raintree debated helping Whitlock, but decided it was too early in the game to choose sides. Travis Lane stood with clenched fists, anguish curdling his face. Farrengalli jerked free of the restraint hold and spun, squaring off with Whitlock.

"Bring it on," Farrengalli shouted, spittle flying from his lips as his eyes danced from face to face. "Any of you. *All* of you."

Whitlock raised his arms and showed his open palms in a gesture of surrender. "Don't blow it, Vincent. We've all got a lot riding on this, especially you."

"You don't know what the fuck's riding what."

"Mr. Farrengalli, the company won't be pleased if this test run fails before the Muskrat even gets wet," Lane said. "Don't forget the bonuses."

Dove Krueger approached him, calm, her mouth twisted. "Remember what we talked about before?" she said to him, just loud enough that Raintree could hear. "You're the real story."

Farrengalli rubbed at his face, then stepped toward the fire and kicked one of the smoldering logs. "Just everybody stay off my back, okay?" He stormed off to collect his gear.

McKay's shoulders sagged. "Honeymoon's over, I guess."

"We're still on schedule," Lane said. "We all knew this

would be stressful. We're in good hands, right, Mr. Whitlock?"

Whitlock ignored him. He said to Dove, "What did you mean, he's the real story?"

"An ego thing. Nothing you'd understand."

Whitlock blinked, muttered something under his breath that Raintree couldn't hear over the hissing rush of water. Raintree finished inflating the raft, listening to the harsh gasp of the hand pump.

"Okay, people," Bowie shouted. "Let's rock 'n' roll. Dove, kill the fire. McKay, finish pumping up the second raft. Lane, secure the gear in Raintree's raft. Farrengalli ..."

The Italian turned his back, fumbled with the front of his shorts, and moments later his urine arced into the dying campfire. "Hey, Dove, you heard the man," he said as stinking steam arose with a hiss. "Come give me a hand with this hose."

"You know where you can stick it, jerk," she replied.

Farrengalli's laughter echoed off the trees and boulders. Raintree figured the man's mood swings would lead to a few more confrontations before the trip was over. But that was Whitlock's problem. Raintree had only one problem, the one inside his head, where the medicine swam, where crows flew and deer raced and mice scurried and snakes slithered, and nowhere, nowhere in the only-fuckin'-natural world, was there a place for him.

CHAPTER EIGHTEEN

Castle found the discarded backpack just after sunrise. It lay about ten yards off the trail amid scuffled leaves. The backpack held an empty cardboard toilet paper tube, a quart-sized zip lock baggie that held some granola crumbs, and a dog-eared novel by somebody named Charlaine Harris. Judging from the pastel colors on the cover, Castle figured the book belonged to the girl. He couldn't imagine Goodall reading much of anything besides survival manuals and the Bible.

Except his own headlines, he heard The Rook's voice say in his head.

The zippered section of the backpack contained a sealed condom, a can opener, and a pack of matches from the Bull's Eye Bar & Grill in Stone Mountain, Georgia. Goodall had been careful in his first bomb attack, leaving few clues despite the heavy concentration of agents assigned to the case. Some believed if Goodall had been content with that one blow for perceived justice and had slipped back into the remote wilds of the upper Midwest, his identity would still be a mystery. Instead, he had grown increasingly reckless, and now that he'd been discovered, he had nothing to lose.

He never had nothing to lose in the first place, said The Rook's voice.

"Look," Castle said, feeling stupid for talking to himself.

"He left this here for me to find. He doesn't care that I'm after him."

Oh, he does care. Remember the assessment. Everything's a cry for attention with him.

"Oh, yeah, if you're so smart, why did your ass get hauled off by some weird bat-winged creature that doesn't exist?"

I respect your experience, partner, and you're about the squarest man I've ever met. If I were your shrink, I'd lie down on the couch and let you *do the analyzing, then gladly pay the bill later. But right now you can't trust your own head. You haven't had a wink of sleep, you're delirious, you're hungry, and three weeks in the wilderness can do strange things to anybody.*

Above, the treetops veered in an autumnal spin of rust, gold, and dying green.

"Damn," Castle said. "I'm talking to myself."

It's okay to talk to yourself, came The Rook's voice—that same combination of sidekick pep and college-professor smugness that plagued some behavior science guys and pissed off the SWAT types. *After all, this is your show.*

"That doesn't bother me so much," Castle said. "The thing that bothers me is you're probably dead."

You're probably right.

"What the hell happened to you?"

You know as much as I do.

"That's a stretch. You've got three degrees, as you like to keep reminding me. I'm just a dummy with a narrow set of skills that happen to come in handy if you ever need to kill a man. Oh, and I have clumsy feet."

They didn't teach about monsters in college.

"I don't believe in monsters."

Audible sigh here. You can't lie to me. I'm inside your head, remember?

"Reckon so."

You've always believed in monsters.

"What on Earth would the Bama Bomber be doing with a condom?"

Maybe he likes to make funny animal balloon shapes. I'll bet he does a great poodle.

"You're not taking this seriously."

Why should I? I'm probably dead, remember?

Castle peered down the trail. He couldn't see the river, but he could hear it and sense its power behind the wall of trees. He tossed down the backpack. "I'm talking to myself."

I don't know, just postulating a theory here, but I'm betting the monsters only come out at night. So you can relax a little. You have about eleven good hours of daylight left.

"I'll get him for you."

No, you'll get him for you. *I'm just a figment of your imagination and therefore have no influence on your behavior.*

"Whatever. Just shut the hell up, will you?"

Castle scolded his tired legs into action and descended to the river.

CHAPTER NINETEEN

"My feet are tired, Ace."

Ace's feet were kind of tired, too, and it didn't help that his boots had gotten wet. He could picture his toes, pale and shriveled as maggots on a griddle, skin peeling from his heels. As a member of the Dakota Sons of the Cross, he'd camped in the sub-zero winters of the Grand Tetons. The number-one rule of survival was to keep your socks dry.

Food was no problem, not when you could stomach bark, leaves, and berries. You could melt snow in the mountains, or built an igloo, or dig into a stump and find sleeping grubs. You could always eat the corpses of your traveling companions if necessary. God wouldn't hold a grudge over a thing like that.

Wet and tired feet were another matter altogether. But that didn't mean you had to bitch about it. "We just rested a half hour ago," he said.

"You said they were dead. They can't catch us."

"But their buddies will be swarming before you know it." He squinted at the sun, which was now clear of the horizon and slanting through the golden treetops. Light glinted off the river, liquid diamonds, kicking up foam like Schlitz from a shaken keg tap.

"What will we do when we get there?"

Ace didn't know where "there" was, but he wasn't for a

second going to let on. "The river empties out onto a lake, and where there's a lake, there's rich people. We can steal a boat or hot-wire a car, head north."

"North where?"

"Anywhere the heat's off."

"Like Virginia?"

Damned women, always asking too many questions. Always yammering. Couldn't shut up and appreciate the fine music of the outdoors. Couldn't appreciate silence. Didn't want peace, and didn't want any man around them to have it, either. It's a miracle God didn't make Eve choke on that apple when the serpent passed it on down to her.

Eve was to blame. Original sin, eating of the tree of knowledge, the curse of reproduction. Got Adam drove out of the garden. Brought death to the world. Ace figured the serpent did a whole lot more to Eve than just feed her the piece of forbidden fruit. Knowing her, knowing all women, she most likely had the thing curled around her legs, moaning for joy while good old Adam was out tending to business.

As if they hadn't caused enough trouble, they wanted to take the choice of life or death into their own hands and out of God's. Ace couldn't understand why God would even create such a nasty creature in the first place. Come to think of it, give him a snake any day. The odds of being poisoned were a lot lower.

"Maybe Virginia, for a start." His feet burned, and he was sure he had a blister on his left big toe. Nothing rubbed raw like a damp sock. "Okay, let's rest a minute."

They sat on a flat rock the size of a double bed. "The river's gotten faster," she said.

"Deeper, too. Wish I had a pole." He glanced upstream,

where water squeezed between piled boulders like spit between crooked teeth. He grinned and nodded his head. Sometimes, you didn't even have to offer up prayers to get them answered. Sometimes, God knew what you would ask for before you even thought of it yourself. "Fisherman's fucking luck," he said, giving Clara a smile more sinister than that of any reptile.

Clara's eyes followed his gaze. Two people were heading toward the boulders in a canoe, the sun dancing off their white helmets. They both furiously worked paddles, flailing arms protruding from thick orange vests. One of them shouted, but the rush of water swallowed the words. The canoe twisted sideways and they beat at the water with their paddles, trying to orient the watercraft.

"They won't make it past those boulders," Clara said, as calm as a spectator at a golf match. She had her tennis shoes off and was rubbing her feet.

"Damn right they won't." Ace retrieved the backpack and rummaged inside. He brought out the Python and let his shooting hand rest in his lap.

"They're trying to make shore."

"Yep." The couple had lost control of the canoe, so it was a toss-up whether they would land on Ace's and Clara's side of the river. Though the current was swift, Ace was willing to ford the river if necessary. After all, God had sent along the canoe, and who was Ace to insult God by not taking advantage of opportunity?

Their features were difficult to discern due to the distance and the soft morning haze that hung over the water. The couple wore goggles that masked their faces and combined with their slick helmets to give them the appearance of insects. The canoe hit a swell and dipped, tossing a thin geyser off the bow. The paddler in front pitched forward and the craft spun out of control, bouncing off a protruding boulder. The person in the rear dug a paddle against the rock and pushed off, propelling the canoe into a shallow, milder eddy. The one in front jumped overboard into knee-deep water and led the canoe toward shore.

Toward Ace. Sometimes, God made things easy.

"Get your stuff," he said to Clara. "We got a boat to catch."

By the time the two people had wrestled the canoe onto dry land, Ace had nearly reached them. He hid behind the bleached bones of a fallen tree and tucked the gun in the back pocket of his camouflage pants, not wanting to scare the couple. They knelt, gasping and heaving, trying to catch their breaths, exhausted from their fight against the current. One of them peeled off goggles and shook her head, freeing damp and curly locks of brown hair.

"Jesus, Pete," she said. "Didn't you see the rock?"

"I was port and you were starboard, remember?" said Pete. "You have to stroke on the opposite side of the direction you want to go."

New Joy-zee. Probably Jews to boot. Ace hated Yankees on general principles, not just because he'd been born in a slave state. He hated Jews because he was supposed to, though he never understood that part about Jesus being a Jew. *How could you hate Jews but worship Jesus?*

As Ace watched from his hidden vantage point, Pete unsnapped the chin strap that held his helmet in place. The helmet fell away, revealing a balding head. Pete appeared to be about forty, pink-faced, with a longshoreman's belly and a stock broker's upper arms. His companion, probably a wife or girlfriend, was having none of his explanations, though Pete made perfect sense to Ace. The bitch slammed her paddle against the wet rocks.

"Getting in touch with nature, my ass," she said. "Why couldn't we have done Atlantic City like I wanted? Fresh seafood, slot machines, gin and tonics, you could have gone fishing on the dock if you wanted to get wet."

"Please, Jenny," Pete said. "We're doing fine. Let's just rest a minute."

The bitch called Jenny sat on a rock, removing her orange padded vest. She had nice tits. Used them to get her way more often than not, most likely. It's a wonder Pete had talked her out of Atlantic City. "What now, Cap'n Ahab?" she said.

"We're only a mile from the falls. We can eat lunch there."

"We just started," Jenny-bitch whined. "We'll never get back to the car at this rate."

Ace felt sorry for poor old Pete. He hoped Jenny was good in the sack, at least. She had to have something going for her, besides the tits or else why would Pete put up with her? Except, for some guys, tits was reason enough.

Ace would have probably backhanded the bitch by now. He glanced back at Clara, who was still busy gathering the clothes she'd put out on the rock to dry.

"Mother Mary on a crutch," Pete said. "Canoe's dented. They'll probably keep my deposit."

"Two hundred bucks. I could have stretched that into three days at the slots."

"There's life outside New Jersey, you know."

Give her hell, Ace cheered silently. *Let her know who's boss. Woman was made slave to man. No shame in it. That's just the way God set it up.*

"Like, this is life?" Jenny's voice grew shrill, tits shaking in her excitement. "This is *life*? This is a backache and wet clothes and mosquitoes and we could have gotten killed out there while you played Ranger Rick with a three-inch dick."

She was pouring it on, and Pete didn't have the balls to rise to the occasion. *Pussy-whipped or worse. She probably had the biggest dick in this couple. Old Pete probably bent over for her.*

Pete looked at the canoe, which sported a bushel-sized dent near the bow. "You're right, honeybunch. What do you want to do? Break for lunch? You can have a dry pair of socks if you want."

Ace's blood pressure jumped. First, he'd felt bad for Pete, hooking up with such a bitch. But now he felt anger, because Pete was letting her walk all over him. Enough was fucking enough. He needed a boat, but even worse, he needed to show these people what was what.

Ace stepped over the fallen tree. "Howdy, folks," he said, trying to be polite, though his voice quivered just a little. Yankees expected Southerners to be polite.

"Hey," Pete said, instantly wary. Jenny drew up, folding her arms across her chest.

"Looks like you had a little trouble."

"Yeah." Pete gave a weak attempt at a laugh. "Water's up this morning."

Ace nodded. "Running hard, all right. Not usually so wild this time of year."

"We're not from around here, you know."

"Never would have figured it."

Jenny-bitch was letting Pete do all the talking now, for

probably the first time ever. Pete's eyes shifted from side to side. "Are you canoeing it? Or kayaking?"

"I flew in from heaven on the red-eye."

"Listen, are you going to mug us? This isn't Central Park, and...."

Pete glanced at the backpacks strapped in the canoe, no doubt wondering if they contained any valuables that weren't insured against theft. Ace smiled, letting his dark, chipped teeth make the answer.

"We don't have any money," Jenny said, the bitchiness gone from her tone, now just another scared cunt as she edged over to hide behind Pete. "Honest. We're on vacation."

Remember that, Petey, next time you're giving it to her hard and dry and hurting. Remember she deserves it.

"I don't want no money," Ace said. He was many things, but he was only a liar when necessary, and right now it wasn't necessary. "What good is money out here in the sticks?"

"Jesus," said Jenny under her breath before shifting into what could only be a high-pitched mockery of Pete. "'Appalachian Mountains,' he says. 'Get in touch with nature.' Nature, my fanny. Like this is some dreamland. Like you don't touch anything but yourself these days."

Pete defensively raised the paddle and aimed it toward Ace, playing hero, keyboard-honed muscles already straining. "We're registered with the Park Service. They have my driver's license."

Ace looked around, made a big show of a shrug. "Who needs a driver's license out here? And I don't see no Park Service."

"Look, we don't want any trouble."

"Don't matter what you want," Ace said, enjoying this a little more than he thought he would. "Trouble found you anyway."

Clara came out of the thick hedge of underbrush that skirted the branch-cluttered shore. "Ace, what are you doing?"

"These nice folks here said we could borrow their boat," he said. "Once I explained to them about your sick aunt, o' course, and how we had to get there before the hospital turned off the machines."

"I don't have a sick aunt," Clara said.

Ace made another big shrug. He sure knew how to pick them. Well, between her and Jenny and a dozen other women, put them all together and maybe you'd get enough brains to do a three-piece jigsaw puzzle.

Screw it. Time's a-wasting.

He pulled out the Colt revolver.

"Mother Mary," Pete said, no longer pink-faced.

"I knew it," Jenny wailed. "He's going to rape me."

"I don't do nothing to a woman against her will," Ace said. "Just ask my sweetheart."

"He won't hurt you unless he has to," Clara concurred.

"You don't have to," Jenny said, a little too eagerly.

"We just want the boat, okay?" Ace didn't need any extra drama. He had plenty enough already. Jenny was Pete's problem, and God grant him the strength to deal with it. "Our feet are tired and it's a long way to the end of the river."

"But we'll get lost," Pete said, his Northern whine now in perfect pitch with Jenny's, as if the two had been practicing together for years. "We don't know the trails."

"You'll learn 'em." He waved the revolver like a bank

robber in a movie, the piece heavy in his hand. "Leave the paddles. You can take your backpacks."

"He's not going to rape me," Jenny said. Ace couldn't tell whether she was relieved or disappointed. Maybe she had a little seed of submission in her, as God intended. She sounded like a woman who could be put in her place at the hands of the right man. With this Pete clown, fat fucking chance.

The couple took their belongings out of the canoe, and Clara tied her backpack to the steel support bar that ran across the middle of the boat. "How do you work this thing?" Ace asked Pete, hefting the paddle and testing its weight.

Pete was all too anxious to get Ace downriver. "Row on the opposite side of the boat from the direction you want to go. Say you wanted to go left, and hard. Then both of you will paddle on the right."

"You're not going to shoot us, are you?" Jenny asked, still standing behind Pete, still Yankee, still ninety-nine-percent bitch.

"They might identify us," Clara said.

"Mercy is as mercy does," Ace said. "We'll be long gone by the time they hike out of these woods and get back to the world. Let's get this piece of shit in the water and make like ducks. Besides, the angels ought to take care of them."

Ace dragged the canoe to the edge of the river, keeping the Colt where the couple could see it. Not that he expected Pete to make a play, but he'd seen plenty of men screw up at the hands of a woman, and Jenny might be the type who got off on recklessness. As long as she didn't risk nothing herself. And she wouldn't. She was a woman. Some things were as sure as the sun of a new day and the eternal love of the Lord.

The canoe sat a little askew in the water, probably because of the dent. Ace climbed in front, pushed against the sandy bottom with his paddle, and eased the canoe toward the white water.

"Hey, wait for me," Clara said, running after him, splashing to reach the boat and clamber into the back, nearly tipping it in the process. Ace grinned. He hadn't considered leaving her behind at all. He'd forgotten all about her.

Maybe I'm getting sentimental in my old age.

"Thanks for the canoe," Ace hollered at Pete and Jenny, the New Jersey couple who would probably sell the story of this encounter to some magazine. Make money so Jenny-bitch could spend it on games of chance.

Then the current caught the boat and he found himself fighting it, the paddle jerking in his arms, the rocks approaching too fast. Clara wasn't much help on her end, and the boat jerked and plunged in the water, threatening to spill them at any moment. They had gone a hundred feet backwards, squirting down a thin waterfall that splashed Ace's neck and shoulders, before he finally got the hang of it and pointed the canoe downstream.

His arms were noodles. But, Ace had to admit, the rush was decent, and riding the rapids sure beat the hell out of hoofing it.

CHAPTER TWENTY

Bowie saw immediately that his decision to group Farrengalli, Raintree, and Dove was a good one, though he didn't like putting Dove at the Italian loudmouth's mercy. She'd handled herself well so far, despite her moment of weakness in the predawn mist. But that had been his weakness, too. Doubly so, since he was the leader, and the best leaders knew when to deprive themselves for the good of the group.

Bullshit. He couldn't lead himself out of a paper bag, much less guide this bunch of losers to a healthy payday. Matter of fact, a paper bag fit just right, because Farrengalli's flask had aroused a thirst he hadn't felt in four years, not since he'd picked up a white chip at a meeting of Alcoholics Anonymous and dropped the liquid amnesia he'd relied on in the aftermath of Connie's death.

While Raintree's craft made good headway after launch, Bowie's crew was flailing and flagging, already a couple of hundred feet behind. Bowie had mentally dubbed Raintree second in command, though not through any overt show of favoritism. Raintree had taken position in the rear of the craft upon launch. On big water, a pilot sat far above the waterline, just before midship. In white water, the paddler in rear had the most responsibility, using the paddle as a rudder to guide the vessel.

They had been on the water less than an hour. Lane,

sitting in front of Bowie, was left handed, and would have made a good complement to his two right-handed partners if he had more stamina. ProVentures' corporate ringer was clearly worn out from the previous day's hike, and apparently a night's sleep on the hard ground had done little to recharge his batteries. So much for his company's sleeping bag with its space-age polymers and annoying name of "Hibern8."

Lane was what was known as a "lilly-dipper" in boating vernacular. Though Bowie and McKay were strong enough to compensate for Lane's futile flailing, there would come a time when three oars would be needed. Ahead, Raintree's raft skidded through a rooster tail, with the craft leaping up and hanging free of the water for a full two seconds before smacking back into the foaming rapids.

"See that?" Lane shouted above the roar of the water. "Awesome."

"Hang on," Bowie said. "Curler coming up river right."

While the first part of the run had been relatively calm, with rocky shorelines broken up by occasional sandbars, the channel now narrowed, with one side of the gorge marked by a thirty-foot granite wall and topped by desperate scrub pines. The right side of the river was pocked with large boulders, and Bowie wasn't sure the raft would hold up against full-speed contact. A vicious slab of wet, sparkling stone, its edge like a hatchet, appeared off the starboard bow.

Bowie's warning of a curler had come too late to prepare. The current had accelerated over the last fifty feet, the water deceptive because the whitecaps had disappeared. Instead, the surface of the water was ribbed, as if preparing to bottom out like bathwater rushing down a drain. Bowie could sense the pull of the water drawing them toward some hidden threat ahead, either a hole or haystacks, a standing series of high waves.

First, though, he had to fend off the blunt-edged shelf of rock. He thrust out his paddle and jammed it against the rock like a jousting lance, expecting the telescoping handle to shatter. Instead, the impact jarred his forearms and caused the raft to turn sideways.

"Left, left, left," Bowie shouted, thrusting his paddle off the port bow. Lane, who hadn't had time to change sides, still worked the opposite side, but McKay hesitated, unsure of the proper reaction. By the time he stabbed his oar in the water, the boat had turned another ninety degrees and they faced upstream as the raft bucked and rubbed over a series of submerged stones.

"Shit," Bowie said. "Hold off, McKay, and let me turn it."

Bowie flipped his paddle and dug it hard off starboard, bracing his legs against the yielding, inflated walls of the watercraft. The resistance caused the raft to spin, and they were once again heading sideways down the river. An aberrant current pushed them toward the cliff on the left side, despite Bowie's desire to stay on the swifter but smoother side of the river.

"Hang on," Bowie shouted as the raft smacked against the head wall and stuck, caught by the raging current that sought to shove the rubberized craft and its occupants through the unforgiving granite. Water spurted over the side of the raft, pooling in the bottom, chilling Bowie's legs despite the SealSkinz. The Muskrat was designed to stay afloat even if fully flooded, but its handling ability would be severely diminished.

"Shove off from the wall," Bowie commanded. McKay dropped his paddle on the deck and pushed with his hands. Lane sat petrified, watching the white-tipped waves boiling over the rim of the boat. Bowie spied a crevice in the granite wall and wedged the tip of his paddle handle into the dark cleft. He used the paddle like a fulcrum, easing the boat downstream.

His effort, combined with McKay's, caused the boat to grate against the rough head wall, but it was moving. One more yank of the paddle and the Muskrat lurched free, still drifting sideways, half-submerged, but no longer being crushed between an insistent force and an unyielding mountain.

Bowie let out a whoop of exhilaration. *The thrill may be gone, baby, but the juice is still pumping.*

Then he remembered the trough that undoubtedly lay ahead, and knew they were in trouble after taking on so many gallons of water. Bowie drew little comfort knowing Raintree's raft had made it past the treacherous channel. Raintree, with a keen sense of anticipation, had managed to direct his crew to keep right, skipping down a series of softer stairs to a gentle eddy a hundred yards downstream. Raintree, Dove, and Farrengalli pulled onto a sandbar and grounded out, waiting to see how the other raft fared.

"Hair ahead," Bowie shouted, using the slang for a "hair-raising" or "hairy" stretch of water. He didn't have time to instruct Travis Lane on negotiating the trough, but he hoped McKay had enough experience and tenacity to hold the rear. Bowie would have had little trouble negotiating the rapids in a solo kayak, complete with spray skirt and double-paddled oar, but in truth, the Muskrat didn't handle all that well.

While an improvement over other white-water rafts, in the end the shortcoming was that it required experienced crew members who knew each other's strengths and weaknesses. Bowie hadn't been given time to mold the two crews into smoothly functioning units.

The raft pulled to the left and Bowie jammed his paddle off starboard, braking by holding it still and letting the current push the end of the raft around. Too late, he noticed McKay was violently stroking on the port side, canceling out Bowie's maneuver and sending the boat sideways again.

"Damn," Bowie said. Lane had dropped his paddle in the flooded bottom of the boat and held onto the grab loops on each side.

"Lean left, lean left," Bowie said, hoping the combined weight of their upper bodies would help kill the spin. Bowie and McKay leaned until their shoulders touched the bow, but Lane sat upright, hunched and shivering. They hit the heart of the trough, rocks piling up on both sides of the boat.

"Look out," McKay said, but Bowie wasn't sure which hazard he meant. Several awaited them, and all were dangerous.

The raft banged sideways off a rounded gray rock, and Bowie noted a seam of crystal quartz scarring the length of the granite. The morning sun sparkled there like wet fire; then the raft was past the rock and riding a set of haystacks, water pushed over barely submerged rocks that created a deep sine wave of ripples. The raft leaped over the haystacks, briefly catching air despite the extra weight of the flooded deck. The raft set down each time with a shuddering splat before launching over the next stack.

"Hole," Bowie shouted. "Big motherloving hole."

He glanced downstream, and saw Raintree watching with interest, Dove wading toward them—wading toward *him*—and Farrengalli standing on shore lighting a cigar.

Bowie knew this hole, but the current had changed since his last run here eleven years ago. He cursed himself for his overconfidence. Rule number one was "Know the river." Rule number two was copped from Clint Eastwood: *A man's got to know his limitations.*

Bowie had broken both rules. The hole lay at the bottom of a shelf of rock, but an eight-foot drop awaited first. The last haystack led to a short run of quiet but fast river as the current squirted them toward the waterfall. "Hold onto your asses, gentleman," Bowie said, as calm as any *Titanic* officer.

"Only fucking natural," McKay said in mockery of Farrengalli.

"Shit," was all Lane said as the raft slid over the slick rock and dumped itself toward the hole. Bowie had released his paddle and Lane's caught water, flipped up, and banged off Bowie's helmet. He sucked in a moist piece of air and braced himself for impact. They were airborne for what seemed like full seconds, and the spray dancing in the sun was like a rain of soft jewels. Then all was tumble and roar as the bow met the spinning current below and pulled the craft and its occupants underwater.

Once submerged, Bowie let go of the grab loop. The cold punched him like a hundred fists of ice. Millions of years of erosion had cut a deep groove at the base of the waterfall, causing the current to swirl like a washing machine's spin cycle. With luck, it would kick them all out to the quieter water, but it could just as easily suck them down and continue drumming thousands of gallons of water onto them.

Despite his PFD, Bowie felt as if were wearing cement clothes. He opened his eyes and saw the dim gleam of the sun on the surface of the river six feet above. Not much in a swimming pool, maybe, but the river was hungry today.

One foot touched bottom and he used the contact to push off, this time cupping his hands and stroking. Against the pressure of a river, a swimmer's stroke was nearly useless. Bowie was determined not to go gentle into the river's belly. But now he needed air. His lungs were hot bricks in the oven of his chest. The book on river suction was to relax your body and let the current push you to safety instead of trying to fight it. But instinct required a struggle.

Eyes closed, he touched something soft and yielding, realized it was the raft, and felt along the bow for the grab loop. He should have held onto the raft in the first place, but he hadn't yet developed faith in the Muskrat. He doubted even Lane would bet his life on the latest ProVentures design if it came down to it.

Finally, his head broke surface and he drew in a breath that tasted of pine, fish, and mud. Farrengalli shouted something from the shore, but Bowie couldn't make it out because of the foam crackling in his ears. He shook his wet hair from his eyes. Lane bobbed ten feet away, head hanging limply to one side. McKay was nowhere in sight.

Go down for McKay or check on Lane? Triage—who's in the most immediate danger?

Though McKay was fit and had some white-water experience, he might have underestimated the suction of the hole.

No, YOU'RE the one that did the underestimating, asshole. Already trying to duck responsibility?

Raintree swam toward Lane, with Dove right behind him, so Bowie fought around the lip of the hole, where the current was less powerful, until he was upstream of the waterfall. Then he eased along the base of the rock shelf until he was under the wet sheet of water. The filtered light gave the cavelike space a gray, funereal quality.

McKay clung to the rock face, grinning. He shouted over the continuous liquid thunder. "Some ride, huh, Captain?"

"This isn't a game. I thought you were under."

"I've had worse."

"You'll probably get worse, before this one's over."

"I just thought I'd rest here a second. Too much peace and quiet will drive you batty."

"Lane may be hurt."

"Screw him. Leave him for the buzzards. What do you think of Dove Krueger? I think Farrengalli's working her."

"I hadn't noticed. Come on. We've got to regroup."

McKay smirked. "Aye, aye, Captain. It's only fucking natural."

"Look, you want to play kissy-face with death, go for it. Just don't do it on my time." Bowie hugged the base of the rock a moment, then dog-paddled along the edge of the current into the sunshine.

CHAPTER TWENTY-ONE

According to the maps that Jim Castle had recovered from The Rook's backpack, only one major trail wound along the northern shore of the Unegama River. With daylight, he was better able to orient himself, and upon reaching the river's edge he was faced with a decision. Ace Goodall and his companion either had forded the river to reach the trail system on the other side, or had followed the water downstream.

If they had crossed, Castle would have little chance of finding them, because the trails branched off toward a number of peaks and scenic overlooks. The pair (and he now fully believed Ace had a partner, willing or not—after all, why else would he carry a condom?) could evade detection for days or weeks on the south side of the river.

Castle placed his bet on Goodall's desperation. No doubt The Rook would have said desperation didn't fit the assessment, not after all the cold-blooded attacks the man had committed. But The Rook's education and behavioral interpretations hadn't done him a bit of good.

After all, The Rook had been plucked into the sky by a creature that Freud wouldn't have acknowledged in any mortal nightmare, much less in the real world. Castle was coming to believe the real world no longer existed; in his exhaustion, the Unegama and the surrounding cliffs and forest had become an illusory landscape that had little use for humans and their philosophy.

Goodall would head downstream, seeking the straightest and surest escape route. Despite the Biblical clues the mass murderer had dropped during his eighteen-month reign of terror, the Bama Bomber wasn't seeking persecution, and clearly wasn't ready to lie down spread-eagled and allow the nails to be driven into his palms and feet. No, Goodall's survival instinct was as strong as that of any rodent or cockroach. The Rook's textbooks had no chapters that spoke in plain language, but Castle was sure the bomber was as shallow as the lowest car thief or child molester.

Take the easier, softer way, the path of least resistance.

Shit, Castle had been doing it for years. He could have been a senior agent by now, behind a desk somewhere and building political capital, remaining neutral until a group from either political party got a hammerlock. Then he could have slid into their envelope, turned up in the right filing cabinet, and then sat around polishing his brass and assigning blame for the rest of his career.

Now, he had no one to blame but himself, because Goodall had tricked him and nature had yanked his underwear into the crack of his ass, he had a hangover without the benefit of Scotch, and he was pulling a blind tail on one of the country's ten most wanted.

"Hello?"

Castle was so deep into his own ruminations that he thought at first the voice was that of The Rook, who had been a disconcerting presence in his head for the last few hours. "Shut up, Rook."

"Oh, no. He's one of *them*, Pete."

The Rook speaking in a female voice? Castle looked up from the damp, stone-pocked sand of the shore. A man and a woman stood among the gold-dappled shrubs of the forest edge. Castle had his Glock raised before he realized the man wasn't Goodall.

"Hey," the man, Pete, said. "Don't shoot. We don't have anything to steal."

Castle gave them a subtle, trained scrutiny. The man was paunchy and balding, not the kind to be in the wilderness at all, much less parked by the river with no gear. The woman was clearly annoyed at something. Probably a number of things. Castle had a stock appraisal of women with tiny upper lips and pinched eyes, and his decision to avoid them had so far always been proven correct. Sometimes belatedly. She reminded him of his first wife.

He hadn't realized he'd been carrying the Glock in his fist. Too late to pretend to be just another hiker, but no need to blow his cover yet. He tucked his weapon behind his back. "You folks okay?"

Pete kept his eye on the arm that held the gun. "So far. But we have nothing left to steal."

"Who would be dumb enough to rob people in the middle of nowhere?"

Pete and Jenny exchanged glances. "You're not with *them*?" the woman asked.

"I'm not with anybody." *Because a mythical monster carried off my partner last night.*

"We'd feel better if you put that away," Pete said. "If you don't mind, that is."

"What is it with hikers and guns?" the woman whined. "Christ, it's not like there's anything to shoot out here besides squirrels."

"Seen anything strange?" *Like maybe a man-sized flying thing that had no wings?*

Pete opened his mouth but the woman beat him to it. "If by 'strange,' you mean having a gun stuck in our faces and our canoe taken away, yeah. If that doesn't count, then we're just sitting here waiting for the bus."

"Will you stop with the mouth a minute?" Pete said to her. "If he wanted to hurt us, he would have done it already."

Which wasn't necessarily true. Castle had worked support on a California case in which the killer had befriended a family at a campground, spent several days sightseeing with them, shared a barbecue of hot wings, and then had cleaved the four of them into pieces with a hatchet. Most psychos didn't want to kill strangers. That wasn't much fun. Exceptions like Ace were driven by other motives, and The Rook could have recited a laundry list of them if he were still around. But he wasn't.

Castle eased the gun under his armpit, into the shoulder holster. "Didn't mean to scare you. It pays to be paranoid, that's all."

"You're looking for him, aren't you?" Jenny said.

Castle nodded. "Who was with him?"

"A girl," Pete said. "A looker. Lean legs, decent tan, like she was on spring break from college."

"She wasn't that pretty," Jenny said. "You didn't look above her chest."

"Stop with the mouth. This man's a cop. I can smell them a mile away."

"Why were you scared, then? He's a little closer than a mile and you stink so bad you can't smell nothing much."

"Stop with it."

Jenny was reminding Castle more and more of his ex-wife. He cut in. "You said he took the canoe?"

"About an hour ago."

Castle glanced at his wristwatch. It was nearly 11 a.m. If Goodall and his companion had any paddling skill at all, they were probably two or three miles downriver by now. "Do you have a trail map?"

"No," Pete said. "We thought we were sticking to the river."

He didn't have much chance of catching up with Goodall. Guiding the couple to safety would take the rest of the day, but at least it would be a form of public service. He hadn't served much of anybody since entering the Unegama Wilderness Area, and had one big red mark in his ledger. And he should probably warn them that a weird gray flying monster might grab them.

But monsters aren't real. They're just shadows under the bed. And it looks like they're plenty scared enough already.

Castle set down his backpack, knelt, and rummaged until he found one of the maps. He gave it to Pete, but Jenny promptly snatched it away. "You couldn't find your ass with both hands and a flashlight," she said.

"There's only one major trail on the north side," Castle said, looking at a point between them, where a large balsam pine towered over the rocky outcropping, its gnarled roots gripping the soil of the bank as if afraid of being set adrift. "Do you have a compass?"

Pete shook his head, and Jenny ran out her lower lip as if wondering what else he'd forgotten. She unfolded the map and said, "Straight north on foot and we'll be in Atlantic City just in time to retire."

"You can't miss the trail. The sun's heading west, so

stay ninety degrees from its path across the sky and you'll be okay."

Pete cast a dubious glance overhead. "But the sun's nearly   straight   up."

Castle pointed north. "Just go that way, then."

"'Go that way,' he says, Mr. Big Shot Cop," Jenny said. "And if we don't, are you going to write us a ticket?"

"Stop with it," Pete said.

"I'm sorry, but I have to go," Castle said. It was always possible that Goodall could have had an accident or spilled the canoe. If his traveling companion were a fraction as annoying as Jenny, then the Bama Bomber might have a short fuse already. Or had pushed her overboard.

"Thanks for the map," Pete said. "This guy who robbed us? Is he big trouble?"

"Let's just say, with any luck, you might be called as a witness in one of the biggest federal trials since the DC snipers. Assuming we all make it out of here alive."

"The man's an optimist," Jenny said to Pete. "You should pay attention, you might learn something."

Castle was already heading downstream, following the shore, watching the slick, wet stones at his feet, when he wondered if he should warn the couple about giant flying creatures with dishrag wings that could swoop down and carry them away. Nope. That was nuts.

Not "nuts," said The Rook, who was apparently determined to ride mental shotgun for the duration of the journey. *You're just a person of psychological difference. A momentary case of schism, a delusional-disorder poster child, a shrink's wet dream. Nothing to worry about.*

"I'm beginning to worry about *you*," Castle replied aloud. "Because you sound crazier than I am. And you're probably dead."

Why would you go and hold a little thing like that against me?

"Because I have a feeling I might be joining you soon."

No shit, Sherlock.

Behind Castle, Pete and Jenny were arguing over the map, and Jenny appeared to be winning. Castle hoped, if those weird, bloodthirsty nightmare creatures really existed, they would find her. She probably tasted bad, but at least Pete would get the pleasure of watching her being dragged away across the sky. If he lived long enough to enjoy being a widower.

CHAPTER TWENTY-TWO

The Rook wasn't quite dead, though the distinction made little difference to him.

In the pitch darkness, he couldn't tell how many of the creatures had put their faces to his neck and chest. It could have been a dozen, or it could have been two or three repeating the act. It wasn't the soft sipping sounds they made that was most disturbing; it was the lack of their breath on his skin, the coldness of the lips that nipped at his upper body, the occasional teasing of lazy teeth.

He was completely immobile. Not paralyzed, for he still had some feeling in his limbs and still sensed some motor control, though his lack of action was giving the lie to that belief. A deeper, more primal part of him was enjoying the surrender, perhaps in the same way a rabbit's brain released relaxing chemicals when the animal was caught in the fox's jaws. His erection hadn't faded in the slightest during his fourteen hours of captivity, though it had long since stopped affording him any pleasure. Now it ached, persistent, throbbing, and promising no release.

He'd tried to speak a couple of times, wondering if the creatures were intelligent. As far as he could tell, he'd been conscious the entire time, though parts of the last few hours had taken on a surreal quality that pushed aside the initial shock. Perhaps, he was simply losing his mind, the most likely and most acceptable conclusion. During his master's program in behavioral psychology at Stanford, he'd arrived at a personal rule: If you wondered if you were insane, then you *were* insane. All that remained was the elimination of any lingering doubts.

In the program, his specialty had been aberrant behavior. Like any kid growing up with Stephen King and bad horror movies, he knew all about vampire myths, with the living dead arising from their graves at night to suck the blood of innocents, in turn changing the victims into like-minded, eternally thirsty monsters. And like most sane (or formerly sane) people, he found them a bit laughable, though the psychology behind the public's attraction to the myth was fascinating. It seemed anybody could stamp a pale, pointy-toothed European bisexual on a paperback novel cover or a movie poster and the product would achieve success, however little deserved.

Even more fascinating than the eternal appeal of these fictional tropes were the actual, flesh-and-blood people who believed themselves vampires. They drank blood as a ritual and slept during the day, fearing they might turn to ashes upon exposure to the sun. Some even managed to induce a conversion reaction that caused them to break out in hives or boils if presented with the Christian cross, garlic, or sterling silver, all weapons used against the vampires of popular lore.

To Derek Samford's trained and modern mind, such behavior was as explainable and legitimate as the religious hysteric who spontaneously bled from palms and feet in a sympathetic imitation of Jesus Christ. Aberrant, certainly, but not necessarily harmful.

So vampires were out of the question, and these cold-blooded creatures that were using him as a sacrament couldn't be aberrant humans, given their lack of breath. But rational explanations had failed him long ago, shortly after he had been dangled upside down like a side of beef on a slaughterhouse hook and whisked away to this hidden hole in the world.

Samford's exposure to the so-called "hard sciences" was limited. He'd been through basic chemistry and physics, but preferred a realm where the rules were more flexible, thus ensuring that no theory or opinion could ever be completely wrong. Or at least not *proven* wrong.

But he doubted if even a PhD in biology would have allowed him to stamp a name or genus on these creatures. Through the long night of susurrant licks and soft scratching sounds, Samford had attempted to distract himself with speculative ruminations.

Anything to keep himself from thinking about—

—the blood on his shoulder, wounds still wet and oozing, wounds that weren't allowed to crust and dry because moist tongues kept at them—

—the probability that he was dying, a fuel tank being drained to the dregs, liquid sand pouring through the tight tube of an hourglass, hours shrinking to minutes and eventually seconds and finally to a full forever.

Samford, an agnostic since the age of seven, wished he had a potential afterlife from which to draw comfort. Heaven, purgatory, or reincarnation held no special appeal to him, but at the moment, he would prefer even the most fiery and punishing Baptist hell over the possibility that he might return from the dead, as depraved and unnatural as the beasts that now took turns with his flesh.

If he could have belatedly summoned faith, he would have prayed hardest of all for some higher power to wipe the rigid smile from his lips.

Instead, he waited, and he served.

One of them pulled away from his shoulder, and despite the general numbness that infected his entire body with the exception of his penis and the open sores on his torso and neck, he was glad for the respite, because for the space of a heartbeat (and a tiny gush of blood that pulsed out along with it), he could pretend the whole encounter had been a bad dream caused by the hard ground beneath his sleeping bag, that he'd soon awaken, make coffee, and discuss with Jim Castle whether or not they were really going to capture Robert Wayne Goodall and what it might mean for their careers.

Then another tongue laid into him, with gentle teeth around it, and he knew there was no more career, no bad dream, nothing but the juice of his soul seeping away into the everlasting night.

CHAPTER TWENTY-THREE

"Could be worse," Pete said.

"Yeah?" Jenny sat on a stump, rubbing one of her bare feet. It was pale and wrinkled, fungal skin flaking. "How could it be worse? Like maybe your mother was with us? And it's going to rain?"

"Stop with it. If I'm reading this map right, we're only about four miles from the ranger station."

"One, you couldn't read a map unless it was leading you to a strip joint, and two, the ranger station's only open in the summer, remember?"

"Well, might be a pay phone there. And maybe a shelter we can sleep under."

Jenny let out an exaggerated, wet sigh. "No pay phones, dummy. No electricity. No plumbing. Nothing. You wanted to get away from it all, and we sure as Christ did."

"Hey, if we make it out of here, we'll have this to look back on. We pulled through together when times were tough."

"Like when you lost your job? Six months of Scotch pulled you through that one. My miscarriage? You were busy banging that slut dental hygienist. We know all about getting through tough times."

"Do we have to go into all that? You can't give it a rest, can you?"

"Not when my feet are killing me and my belly's

growling and I'm stuck out here in the middle of nowhere with a wannabe Daniel Boone."

They had walked maybe two miles so far, most of it uphill, and Pete had only the slightest idea where they were. They had passed a couple of trail intersections marked with signposts, so Pete guessed they were going in the right direction, but judging from the scale of the map, the ranger station was at least six miles away, not four. He was trying to keep Jenny's spirits up, but was struggling to keep from slapping her.

He'd only struck her once, when she'd found out about the dental hygienist. He'd never had to hit her again, because she didn't know about the daycare teacher down the block, the bank teller with the D cups, or her own sister Lillian, who had first seduced Pete at a family reunion and had made it a regular feature of their Thanksgiving holidays thereafter. Not that Pete considered himself a stud or anything. He'd been popping Viagra since it had first arrived on the market, and sex with Jenny happened about as often as the coming of an Ice Age, with about as much warmth.

He'd been hoping the trip to the North Carolina wilderness would awaken her primal instincts, because despite his philandering, he thought of himself as a loyal and supportive husband. When he'd said, "For better or for worse, until death do us part," he'd meant it, though he occasionally regretted it. This had turned into one of those occasions.

"We can go for days without food," Pete said. "Water's our main concern."

"We just left a bunch of water. Why didn't you think to drink some of it?"

"Bacteria. You want diarrhea for the next three weeks, go ahead."

"Looked clean to me. No houses means no toilets. No civilization, remember? That's what you kept telling me. Like it was a *good* thing."

"At least you'll have a story to tell your bridge club. About how I let us get our canoe stolen at gunpoint. And we how ran into a real-life FBI agent. And we—"

"—and we died on a dirt trail in the land of the hillbillies."

Jenny was always one for melodrama. Never happy unless things were at their absolute worst. Pete was no Mr. Sunshine, but he'd learned to play devil's advocate to give their relationship some talking points. "Okay, we make it back, get to the rental car by tomorrow, catch the first flight out of Charlotte, boom, back in Jersey before you know it."

"Slots in Atlantic City?"

"Whatever you say, babe."

Funny how surrender was the only path to victory in a marriage. Pete was just about to say the ranger station was maybe only three miles away when he heard a peculiar whining sound. Thinking a mosquito was orbiting his ear, he swatted, but the sound grew louder. He wondered if they had somehow stirred up a nest of bees.

Jenny screamed, bees for sure, she was allergic to them, and if they ever made it out alive, he'd never hear the end of it—

Her scream blended with the heightening whine, her face was fixed on a point behind him, and her eyes were wide and he noticed the irises were brown, funny how you could live with somebody for fifteen years and not know the color of her eyes.

Pete was about to turn when the sky dropped on him, hammering him into the loam of the forest floor. He tried to stand, but his legs were sodden stumps. Jenny was still screaming, and somehow the noise was out of place in the previously hushed wilderness. His shoulder hurt, and his arms, and a steel band of agony girded his chest.

He looked down and saw gray hands gripping his upper torso, long, knotty fingers tapering to sharp talons. The fingernails sank into his flesh, one above the other, exploring the gap that divided his rib cage. The hands tugged and the talons sank deeper, spawning a gush of blood.

Pete, swaying on his hands and knees, could only stare with fascination at his torn skin, struggling to stay upright against the weight on his back. Jenny screamed. He wished she would shut up.

Animal attack. Bear, mountain lion, something. Except he knew better. Those hands and the cruel, sinewy fingers belonged to a creature that had no place on this Earth.

Buzzing in his ear. The papery rattle of a dry tongue. A tug at his neck.

Numb. Fading to black. Blood warm on the inside of his shirt.

Shit. Talk about melodrama. He was dying and didn't know how.

He collapsed as the teeth gained a better purchase on his neck and the gap in his chest widened. He opened one eye and saw Jenny running. Maybe Jenny would make it.

The ranger station was only a million miles away.

Just like he was.

Going.

Shit.

Just before he went under, as his life fluids leaked into the ancient Appalachian soil, he felt the weight lift and heard the shrieking scream as the creature went after Jenny. Pete grinned, broken leaves sticking to his lips.

CHAPTER TWENTY-FOUR

"Maytagged their asses," Farrengalli said, looming over Raintree as he and Dove checked Travis Lane's condition. "Put the bastards through the spin cycle."

Raintree gave the idiot a cold look, but Farrengalli kept on. "Hey, where's Whitlock and the Golden Boy? Making out under the waterfall?"

"If you don't want to help, at least shut up and stay out of the way," Dove said. Farrengalli glowered and shoved his boot against the beached raft, sending it skidding across the mud. Then he went to the water's edge and squatted, waiting for the foundered second raft to make its way downriver.

"How is he?" Raintree asked Dove. Lane had been unconscious when they'd pulled him from the water. He appeared to be breathing regularly, though when Dove peeled back his eyelids, his pupils were tiny dots of ink against the gray irises.

"I don't think it's a concussion. Pupils are the same size. Pulse is normal. No shock." Dove moved with knowledge and experience, checking Lane's scalp for trauma.

"Should I get the first-aid kit?"

"Want my armchair diagnosis?"

"Sure."

"He passed out from fright."

Raintree was glad Farrengalli hadn't overheard, or he

would have ridden Lane for the duration of the trip. "Well, if he wet his pants, at least it won't show."

Dove grinned, but only for a second before her eyebrows arched with concern. She looked upriver at the waterfall that had dumped the raft. "Bowie, where are you?" she said, half to herself.

She's worried about him. And not just as a team leader.

Raintree felt a twinge of jealousy, and it annoyed him. He touched her wrist, and was about to tell her not to worry when Bowie emerged from the rock shelf and gave out a shout. "Get the raft!"

Farrengalli waded in until the water was above his knees, and then swam toward the half-submerged raft with smooth strokes. He caught it fifty yards downstream and guided it toward shore, pushing it before him, hanging onto the grab loop with one hand.

Bowie and McKay climbed the rock face beside the waterfall, finding a natural shelf and edging along it until they reached the shore. By the time they reached Lane, the man was sitting up, spitting brackish phlegm and cussing.

"Passed with flying colors," Bowie said.

"It didn't burst," Lane said.

"Took on water too easy."

"It's a field test." Lane gave a wet hack. "We can take all the information back to the lab. ProVentures wants us to reach takeout in one piece, and we're still in one piece."

"Another incident like that and we're walking out, bonus or no bonus."

"Don't worry about it, Bowie," Dove said. "We could use a break anyway. Early lunch?"

Raintree was impressed with the way Dove Krueger handled both Whitlock and Farrengalli, as well as her calm approach in treating Lane. He knew little about her, only that she was a highly regarded journalist known for her coverage of extreme sports and outdoor adventures. She and Bowie exhibited a familiarity with one another that made it seem like they'd worked together before. None of his business, though. His spirit was already troubled enough without speculating on the affairs of others. He touched the medicine bag for comfort.

McKay helped Farrengalli wrestle the second raft ashore, tipping the water out and dragging it beside the first. Lane stood on shaky legs and inspected it. "See, no damage at all. Built to withstand the worst that nature has to offer."

"Is that the ad copy or did you improvise?" Bowie asked.

"Maytagged your asses," Farrengalli said.

Lane ignored Farrengalli's taunt. "I have complete faith in our products, or I wouldn't bet my life on them."

"But what about betting *our* lives?" Bowie asked.

"Hey, there's no such thing as bad publicity," Farrengalli said. "If a couple of you clowns buy the farm, then there's more glory for me."

"Hey, man, this isn't a canned episode of *Wild Life with Natalie*," McKay countered. "This is reality. I'd like to see you handle that spill."

"No sweat, Golden Boy." Farrengalli puffed out his chest, as if expecting another physical confrontation. Raintree stepped between them, sensing Dove would do so if he didn't. "Let's eat, gentlemen. According to the map, we're about halfway to Babel Tower. Two more hours on the water and we should reach our campsite."

Farrengalli glared at Bowie. "You going to let Geronimo

here give the orders from now on?"

"That wasn't an order," Bowie responded. "Let's give Mr. Lane a chance to recuperate, and we could all stand some refreshment. If you don't mind, that is."

"Bush-league bullshit," Farrengalli said, stalking off toward the edge of the woods.

"He's going to be trouble before the trip's over," Dove said to Bowie.

"He was trouble before it even started. Okay, folks, crackers and dried fruit; then it's time to catch some serious hair."

Raintree gathered his backpack, noticing Dove and Bowie sat down together to share their rations. He went into the woods away from Farrengalli, wondering if the sylvan glade would offer up the vision he sought. A large part of him felt foolish. Vision quests were archaic, lost in the early nineteenth century, vanished like the buffalo and elk.

Nowadays, vision quests were offered as vacation retreats, a week in the desert or the high mountains with a self-proclaimed "spirit guide" who accepted cash, traveler's checks, or credit cards. Like the sad old men who made their living posing in ceremonial headdress for tourist photographs, Raintree was just another sellout. He'd traded on his image and heritage as much as anybody, a cigar-store Indian with good teeth and muscle frame, blessed with a lithe form that might in another time have wrestled grizzly bears and cougars.

Farrengalli clearly hoped someone would die on the journey. Raintree didn't care. He didn't know which was worse.

But he wanted to succeed. He would do it for his

people, though the Cherokee had changed along with the rest of the civilized world. The White Man took their lands but later made good by granting gambling casinos. The Great Spirit had abandoned its people yet again, but then rolled sevens after they had given up all faith.

He rummaged in the medicine bag. A couple of the black, a white, and maybe one of the yellows for good measure. Raintree looked toward the sky, up where one of the White Man's gods was supposed to dwell on a golden throne. He saw no sign of such a god, but a few clouds had drifted from the northwest, high cumulus with swelling, gray underbellies. All part of the Great Spirit, along with the forest, the river, the rocks, and—

"Where the *fuck* is everybody?"

Farrengalli. A force of nature unto himself.

Raintree was about to return to the others along the riverbank when he saw a creature drifting high off the cliffs, perhaps a half mile away.

A hawk? A feathered brother that would fulfill his quest and provide him with strength and knowledge?

No, its wings were too awkward for that of a hawk, its flight uncertain. This creature angled against the wind as if it had been thrown off the rocky heights and expected to fly or drop like a stone. It flew as if it had no direction, no purpose.

Raintree squinted against the veiled sun, trying to make out the winged form. Even from this distance, the creature projected a non-avian aspect. Its lower body was dense, not built for aerodynamic grace. It appeared to be gliding, its wing-like projections held out stiffly from its trunk. It cut a slow, lazy ellipse, a darker speck against the clouds, and then it disappeared among the distant treetops.

Seconds later, Raintree realized what he had witnessed, but could only smile to himself. The Great Spirit played tricks when delivering visions, and those who sought too hard often engaged in flights of fancy.

The thing had been a man.

Flying without a plane, hang glider, or parachute.

Raintree touched his medicine bag. Psychedelic mushrooms, jimson weed, foxglove, and belladonna were natural paths to visions. But Raintree didn't want the natural path. He craved the finest that modern drug companies had to offer, in clean, easily digestible pill form. He had been saving the best stuff for some unforeseen sacred moment. Maybe visions came when least expected, and made so little sense the seeker had to dream on them for weeks or months or even years to understand their meaning.

Or, perhaps, he had imagined the whole thing.

Raintree unfolded himself, rose, and headed back to the rafts, anxious to finish the journey, no longer so curious to suffer sacred visions.

CHAPTER TWENTY-FIVE

Despite what Ace thought, Clara Bannister wasn't from old Yankee money and she wasn't an uppity bitch. She'd been raised in a mobile home in Cleveland, Ohio. Her father had been an automotive mechanic as well as a preacher, and had briefly been on the pit crew of Indy 500 champ Al Unser. In between sermons, he ran his own garage and raced the dirt tracks.

Her mother worked the counter at the Dairy Queen, attending night school at the local community college, taking five years to get a two-year degree in physical therapy. Not enough money to make it out of the trailer park, but they had instilled a strong work ethic and a passion for success. And a whole severe slate of morals.

Sometimes, she wondered if her overachieving nature related to those roots. Such a beginning wasn't humbling. It was embarrassing. In junior high, once she was old enough to know better, she loathed catching the school bus with the dirty-kneed, runny-nosed brats from the neighboring trailers. She deserved better.

In her off-the-rack Kmart jeans and thrift store blouses, she was always four years behind the trends, but the real cruelty was that she'd been granted just enough intelligence to be painfully aware of her condition. She didn't fit, even though she pursued the usual outsider fields of band, theater, and art. Even among the losers, she came up lacking.

But there was one area where genetics paid off: rides. When the other juniors were sporting about in pre-owned Hummers and Toyotas, her dad put her behind the wheel of a lovingly restored 1969 Camaro. Such cars were the fuckmobiles of their era, and Clara did her best to uphold that reputation. Clara had never derived as much self-esteem and satisfaction as she did when chauffeuring some boy around the downtown square a few times before parking in the alley and rutting with him in the backseat, leaving him spent but her bright-eyed and eager for the next pickup.

Determination (and a timely sexual encounter with the high school counselor) had won her a scholarship to Radford University in Virginia. She did well her first semester, but made the mistake of falling for an anthropology professor who turned her on to the pleasures of hallucinogens, feminism, and radical politics. When she should have been studying for finals, the nights were spent instead with sagging candles, oversized pupils, and debates about the "eternal struggle."

The sex was lousy, but the discussion was exhilarating. Such stuff was as far removed from her childhood trailer park as she could imagine, and nothing could have made her happier. Clara roved from Green Party to Marxism to Taoism to Maoism and, despite a brief love affair with the chairman of the Radford Young Republicans, she began exploring the extreme libertarian fringes. Out there where left and right collided in a conflicting ideology of legalized drugs and Fourth Amendment fever.

The sophomore Clara had grown bored with acid, as even the most ardent hippies eventually did, because once you'd visited *there* a few times, it wasn't so revolutionary or appealing. Instead, she was drawn to a new form of excitement, one she would never have thought possible and one that no doubt would have sent her father toward his third and probably fatal heart attack. She found she enjoyed pain.

At first, it had come in fleeting electric brushes, such as a boy who bit her nipples a bit too hard through inexperience. Then the Young Republican had taken delight in twisting them between his thumbs and fingers until she yelped in a surprise that he took as delight. A Buddhist old enough to be her father had picked her up in a bar and taken her to a motel room, tied her to the bed, and left her there for two hours until she wet the sheets.

He then proceeded to remove his leather boot strings and lash them across her bare legs, back, and buttocks for an additional two hours. Sometimes cruelly slapping, sometimes teasing the laces across the welts. He entered her at dawn and, raw and tingling and confused, she experienced the first orgasm of her life.

From pain, she evolved toward danger. Still an honor-roll student during daylight, Clara became a denizen of the wee hours, cruising closing times and only talking to the most drunken and abusive men, occasionally bedding them if they weren't too intoxicated to perform. Sexual stimulation became as boring as the Lucy-in-the-Sky cosmic trip of LSD, but the possibility that she might be harmed or even killed gave her a deep satisfaction. Educated enough to recognize her perversion, she couldn't find an answer in the writings of Freud, Jung, Skinner, Nietzsche, or Friedan. She dared not visit a shrink.

During a golden autumn day, she'd awoken in

Moultrie, Georgia. She vaguely recalled a road trip for a rock concert (she sensed it had involved one of the Grateful Dead's surviving members), but didn't remember her traveling companions. She'd lost her purse, her pockets were empty, and her clothes disheveled. She probably could have gotten a wire transfer for a plane ticket from one of her lovers or abusers, but the thought of hitchhiking appealed to her.

Only crazy people hitchhiked, and only crazy people stopped to pick them up, but a young woman never had to wait long on the side of America's highways. When Ace Goodall pulled into the emergency lane in his rusty Ford pickup and rolled down the passenger's-side window, she almost told him to forget it, she'd wait for a Cadillac. Ace told her to get in the goddamned truck right this fucking second, what was she trying to do, get picked up by a goddamned peckerhead pervert or something and get raped?

When he first told her he was a murderer, she glanced at him out of the corners of her eyes and grinned. When he insisted, she nodded, staring through the windshield at the highway ahead and wondering how much damage she'd suffer if she rolled onto the pavement at sixty-five miles per hour.

Then he told her about the bombs, and she remembered seeing something on the news about them, abortion clinics, a few doctors and patients killed, a nationwide manhunt, no description of the killer but FBI experts agreed the guy knew his stuff. He was widely believed to be an American terrorist, though the word "terrorist" was rarely used for white killers, even mass murderers like Timothy McVeigh and the Unabomber.

It was Ace's knowledge of the details of the bombings, as well as his glee in sharing them, that had convinced her. Fifty miles north of Athens, she had given up the idea of escape and instead warmed to a new fever. Traveling with a soon-to-be-famous maniac offered a strange, romantic beauty. A higher purpose. A reason to live and probably die.

Life on the run was occasionally more exhausting than exciting, though, and now was one of those times. Her shoulders ached from paddling, the current had bumped and rocked the canoe until she thought her bones would come apart, and thirst had turned her throat into a tunnel of sand and gravel.

"Can't we take a break, Ace? Nobody's on to us."

Ace, kneeling in the stern and watching for rocks, didn't answer for a half minute, so she repeated the question. He pushed off against a sodden log, driving the canoe toward the middle of the river. Then he turned around. "You hear that?"

"Hear what?" The constant wash of the rapids had soaked her ears with white noise until the surrounding sounds blended into one droning roar.

Ace sat higher and studied the riverbanks, which had given way to gentle sloping woods instead of the twenty-foot stone cliffs along the first part of the trip. "Like a thunderstorm."

Clara squinted against the early afternoon sun. A few high clouds had invaded the morning's perfect sky, but they were white and wispy, not the type to harbor ill weather. All fine, but sometimes Ace saw things beyond the sky.

"Something ain't right."

"Ain't right" was Ace's sixth sense, the preternatural alarm that went off whenever danger was near. She believed it was this gift that had so far allowed him to elude capture. Of course, Ace thought such things were messages from the Lord, sometimes beamed right into his brain from heaven above. Compared to the armchair radicals and garden-variety crackpots Clara had met during her first two years of college, Ace came off as practically a messiah. Charming in a crude way. Sincere, as only a zealot could be.

"Maybe more FBI agents," Clara said, raising her voice, sibilants lost in the splashing. "If they really thought you were here, wouldn't they send in a bunch of people?"

"They ain't that smart, or they wouldn't be walking haircuts with dicks made of liver mush. No, it's something up yonder." He nodded downriver.

"Why don't we take a break, then? Think about it some?"

"If I told you once, I told you a thousand times, you don't run from the Lord's will, you jump in with both feet and a prayer and a gun."

If that were the case, Clara wondered why Ace had been evading capture for eighteen months instead of staring down those who wanted him dead or alive. After all, if the mission was for the glory of the Lord, God would deliver him in his dark hours. Thanks to a half-dozen university-level courses in philosophy and religion (and the extracurricular, sensory-challenging research that went along with them), Clara decided that God would pick and choose depending on the situation and followed no set rules Himself, though His believers labored under a rigid and archaic moral code. All fine and dandy for the faithful, but that didn't ease the ache in her back and shoulders and belly.

Her belly. She touched it. Sick, that was all. Bad diet, too many canned meats and energy bars, maybe some contaminated water. The morning's purge hadn't totally eliminated the nausea, and the roiling of the canoe didn't help matters any.

She stopped paddling. "I'm going to be sick again."

Ace beat the water with his oar, sending spray across her already soaked clothes. "All right, goddamn it, just quit your bitching for a minute."

He guided the canoe to the shore and the thunder swelled in intensity. Ace, watching for rocks off the bow, didn't see it looming downstream, but Clara already had her paddle in the water, noticing the current had picked up steam.

"Waterfall!" she screamed.

Ace didn't hear her, or didn't understand her, because he still wore the pissed-off scowl. Clara leaned forward and grabbed him by the shoulder. "Look!"

Ace muttered something that probably was "Shit fire," one of his favorite expressions, but the words were lost amid his flailing maneuvers with the paddle. The canoe spun until they were heading downstream sideways. The smooth lip of the waterfall loomed ahead, the river channeling to a spout about fifty feet in width. Clara couldn't tell the height of the falls, but judging from the bit of rocky river she could see downstream, the drop seemed plenty long enough to smash them and the canoe to pieces and put paid to Ace's holy work.

Calm descended upon her, though she was aware that her arms now worked in frantic rhythm with Ace's, dipping into the water and shoving the canoe toward shore. She had no death wish after all, she discovered, at least not here in this cold and lost river with a cold and lost man. Sure, she loved the danger and the thrills, but she didn't like the ending. It was pain that attracted her, not the absence of feeling.

"Fuck it," Ace shouted, letting his oar slide into the water. He stood, grabbed his backpack from the middle of the canoe where it lay in a thin skin of water, and jumped overboard. Clara watched, giving three more useless strokes before she realized Ace had actually abandoned her.

The bastard.

It should have deserved an exclamation point, but Ace had been a bastard for at least two weeks.

With time off for good behavior.

No surprises anymore, just another man grabbing in desperation. No higher power, no real threat where it mattered, nothing to offer except a strange, glowing thing deep inside her stomach, a thing that made her both sick and suspicious.

Ace bobbed off the stern, five feet nearer to shore than the canoe. He stroked with one arm, trailing the buoyant backpack behind him. Not looking back. Leaving Clara—

and the thing inside

—behind.

Ace didn't understand trailer trash summers, where kids jumped off the bridge into water that had collected the raw sewage runoff and livestock spills and cast a greasy rainbow stain in the current. Clara could swim. She was a survivor, at least so far.

She rolled out of the canoe, kicking it away from her,

recalling some distant lesson in science about bodies in motion. Bodies in motion didn't mean molecules and atoms and quarks and stuff you couldn't see. It meant moving, staying alive, dodging the worst. Getting by.

She gulped cool air and her face hit cooler water; she raised her arms in a butterfly stroke and plunged, awake, belly tingling, nipples tightening, toes wriggling around the thong of her sandals.

Her hand slid across a rock, skinning her knuckles, then her feet hit bottom. She skated on the algae-slick stones for a moment and gained purchase on a sandy shoal. Wading ashore, she realized she had beaten Ace to high ground. He crawled out of the water, spitting and wheezing, the backpack hooked around his elbow, his camo trousers soaked.

"We made it," Clara said.

Ace pounded the backpack into the shallow water, splashing both their faces. "What you trying to do, kill me?"

"I'm trying to save us. All of us."

"That's the Lord's job."

Clara was so tired, she just wanted to lie in the sand and take a nap. But the sun had gone cold, hidden behind clouds that resembled a flock of dirty sheep. She wrapped her arms across her chest, shivering. "What now?"

Ace, knee-deep in the current, watched as the canoe swept over the edge of the world and into the thundering spray far below.

"Wait for the next ride," he said, and Clara decided that was the story of her life.

CHAPTER TWENTY-SIX

Jim Castle walked a quarter of a mile along the riverbank, occasionally getting his feet wet, sometimes climbing along the mossy and root-rich lips of soil where the river had carved its path. The Rook hadn't invaded his thoughts since he'd encountered the couple on the shore, and Castle believed himself cured of whatever temporary syndrome had afflicted him.

You mean, "Short-term post-traumatic stress disorder."

The Rook was back and better than ever.

"No, I mean, I can't decide whether you're dead or I'm crazy."

Go for both. It's the most reasonable explanation.

"Since when have you ever been reasonable?"

Look, you're the one thinking all this up.

"Except you make me think things I don't understand."

Join the club. It's a big one, and at last count included six and a half billion other bald monkeys. Plus those things. You know ....

"Flying, man-eating creatures that don't exist. Yeah, I know."

Castle concentrated on his respiration, the roar in his ears mirroring the rush of white water. *Sympatico* with the river, both of them heading downhill toward the lowest common denominator, the final crush of time and tide.

Deeeeeep, partner. Like the river. Extended metaphors. Not the kind of thing you expect from a crew-cut type.

"Don't look now, but we've got company."

Company?

Maybe when you were dead, or just the figment of some cracked cop's imagination, you couldn't see the two inflated rafts bobbing on the river, rows of white helmets glinting in the afternoon light. They bounced over a series of whitecaps and reached an eddy that pulled both rafts in a slow circle. There were three people in each raft, all wearing life vests. One, a muscular man in a tank top with dark, curly hair, shook a triumphant fist at Castle, who waved back. He fought an urge to lift one thumb in the universal sign of the hitchhiker.

Instead, Castle waved his badge and gun. The nearest raft headed toward shore, two of the occupants paddling while the one in front slumped as if deciding whether to make a dash downstream, away from the threat of the gun. As if Castle would actually use the weapon, as if they could outrun his bullets if he did.

"Hey," Castle shouted, as the raft scooted ashore and grounded on the muddy, debris-wracked shore. The man in the middle looked pale and ill, eyes focused miles downstream. The man in front, in some type of wet suit, appeared to be the leader. At least, he stuck his chin out in a defiant gesture.

Castle felt stupid holding the badge out for the man's inspection. Protocol was protocol, though.

By the book, right, partner? Straight down the line, all the way.

"All the way?" Castle answered aloud.

"What did you say?" the man in the raft said.

"Nothing."

Tell them it's the only way to fly.

"It's the only way to fly," Castle said.

The three men in the raft stared at him as if he'd just dropped from the sky.

CHAPTER TWENTY-SEVEN

Expect the unexpected.

ProVentures had adopted the oxymoronic cliché as a slogan for its line of climbing gear. Bowie Whitlock had to admit the phrase was perfectly crafted to catch the attention of hurried, harried Earth children and the overachieving stoners who were the biggest consumers of outdoor adventure equipment. But the phrase was just as appropriate to being flagged down by a man waving a badge and a gun, as if the rafts had broken the speed limit and the man was playing backwoods traffic cop.

Though Bowie figured the group might encounter hikers, fishermen, and possibly kayakers and canoeists along the way, he hadn't imagined interacting with them. Bowie, in the lead raft, had intended to simply wave and do the bit about relaxing and floating downstream John Lennon had encouraged in the drug-drenched Beatles tune "Tomorrow Never Knows." The badge had been barely recognizable when viewed from mid-river simply because it was so unexpected. But there was no mistaking the gun, especially when the man made menacing gestures toward them.

"What is it?" Lane asked behind him.

"I'm not sure." He gestured to McKay, indicating that he should stop paddling. The second raft was about a hundred feet upstream, too far away to see the man's gun.

Apparently Raintree had lost some of his determined edge.

"He thinks he's Kojak or something?" McKay said.

"Might be a park ranger."

The current had eased since the group had launched after the noon break, and even if Bowie had been tempted to float past the man and ignore him, a competent marksman could have easily picked them off like ducks in a kiddie pool. Even if he missed, bullets piercing the rafts would have grounded the whole enterprise. Bowie figured the man must have been a law enforcement officer or he wouldn't have bothered flashing the badge.

Whether the man was really a ranger or merely imitating one, Bowie felt he had little choice. He stroked the raft toward the dank stretch of shore. When he could see the glittering stones of the bottom, he went over the stern into thigh-deep water and guided the boat with the grab loop. Twenty feet away, and the man said, "All the way?"

"What did you say?" Bowie asked him, one eye on the handgun.

"Nothing."

From that distance, the badge looked real. Bowie disregarded the obvious question, the one about why a ranger should be standing by a river in the middle of nowhere with a gun in his hand. "U.S. Forest Service?"

The ranger cocked his head as if listening to something in the distance. After a moment, he said, "It's the only way to fly."

As a kid, Bowie had been a big fan of *Serpico*, both the television series and the titular movie. Bowie especially loved the movie version of the experiences of the realistic cop, portrayed by Al Pacino, one of the greatest actors of the last century. *Serpico* had shaped Bowie's perception of all officers, because his own biggest criminal offense had been an expired inspection sticker. He tried to picture Serpico flagging down a raft, but couldn't. This trip had long ago passed the point of reason. This was already Alice's journey down the rabbit hole, and ten miles of crazy river still lay ahead.

"Sorry to scare you," the man said. "Special Agent Jim Castle with the FBI. I'm afraid I need to commandeer this boat on behalf of the U.S. government."

"FBI?" Bowie said.

"You can't be serious," Lane said.

"Do I look like I'm joking?" Castle said. The guy looked liked he'd eaten a bucket of brass tacks for breakfast and was getting ready to shit brass knuckles. His eyes held a clouded, elusive quality, as if they'd seen something they hadn't quite believed. He lowered the handgun to his hip, pointing it at the mud. A little comforted, Bowie glanced at Dove's raft. She gave him a look, one he knew too well and despised.

"We're on a commercial enterprise," Lane said to Castle. "ProVentures. We secured all the proper permits."

"I need the boat."

"Assignment or vacation?" Bowie asked.

"Government business, like I said."

"Top secret, no doubt," McKay said. "Like the hunt for Bin Laden."

"Not really. I don't know enough yet to know what's secret and what's obvious."

Castle's tone was deep and gruff, though more uncertain than other cops Bowie had known. Not a bit like Serpico. Maybe FBI agents were different, removed from public interaction and television cameras.

"I'm in charge of this trip," Bowie said, feeling Dove's eyes boring him the way they did when she expected something of him. "I'm responsible for these people. I can't just let you abandon us out here."

Castle looked past him to the second raft, which was making its way to shore. Farrengalli greeted the stranger as if he were an old frat brother whose name was lost in a hundred keg parties. "Yo, Otter Face, what's the deal?"

"I only need one boat," Castle said.

"Nothing personal, but I'm not sure you have the authority to seize private property. There's a little matter of the Fourth Amendment."

"I'm invoking special powers as granted by my superiors."

Superiors. Bowie loathed that word. Or maybe he was just in denial and had never truly learned humility, even after causing the death of his wife.

No, you didn't cause her death. That's second-hand and passive. You were active. You killed her as surely as if you had laced her coffee with arsenic.

This wasn't a time for dwelling on her death. No time was.

"Are you after a terrorist?" Bowie asked. In the early twenty-first century, the umbrella of terrorism had given broad powers to a range of government agencies, from the National Security Agency's secret wiretapping down to small-town cops whose uniforms had taken a turn toward the paramilitary with black jumpsuits and jackboots.

"Could be," Castle said. "But you're wasting my time."

"Look, if you leave us here, we're at risk of exposure and of running out of supplies. It's a three-day hike to the closest road, assuming we don't get lost."

Castle looked toward the sloping forest above, speculative, as if expecting a helicopter to swoop over the horizon. "You'll be okay."

"Do you know how to handle white water?"

Castle eyed the craft, which bobbed in the current. "Maybe."

Bowie's primary responsibility was for the safety of the crew. He'd failed his wife, and he'd come close to failing himself, but he considered this his last big adventure run. He wouldn't let it end this way. Especially with Dove giving him the look. "We're experienced. We can get you there faster, safer, and drier than if you take the raft by yourself."

Lane, catching on and no doubt calculating the publicity advantages of assisting an "unsung hero," added, "The ProVentures Muskrat is capable of solo maneuvering, but it's designed as a tandem craft. We'll be pushing the weight capacity, but I'm sure the engineers fudged it a little to the low side. You know how engineers are."

"No," Castle said. "Not really."

Lane gave a nervous grin. "Neither do I."

Raintree, Farrengalli, and Dove Krueger eased their raft beside the one Bowie held. Farrengalli folded his arms and leaned back as if soaking up a sun that had hidden away. "The hell," he said. "You're dicking with my bonus."

"The bonus applies to everyone," Lane said. "We all have the same timetable."

"If Agent Castle here wants to join us, I guarantee we'll make Babel Tower by sundown," Bowie said. To Castle: "Where are you headed, anyway?"

"Don't know yet."

"Fucking fantastic," Farrengalli said as Castle waded

into the water and stepped into Bowie's craft. Bowie looked at Dove. Her eyes were black pools, full of deep, cold water.

Yeah. We'll make it. And I don't love you, okay?

He didn't need to speak. She knew him better than he himself did.

Castle settled behind Bowie, who hollered, "Wagons, ho!" as he dipped his paddle into the water, turning the raft so it pointed downstream toward where all rivers collided into a great sea.

CHAPTER TWENTY-EIGHT

"There's one of them wrong angels," Ace said, pointing a thumb at the sky.

Clara shivered in her damp bra and panties, her clothes spread on a rock to dry. She looked up to where the clouds had thickened and spread, gray mayonnaise smeared over the red and ochre treetops of the high cliffs.

"I don't see anything," she said, wondering if that was the correct response. Perhaps Ace was having one of his visions, or maybe he was getting ready to launch into one of his fits.

"Up there," he said, leaning back. He had stripped completely, his skin as pale as the belly of a trout. The cool autumn air didn't seem to affect him, though his penis was shriveled and beet-purple. She touched her stomach, wondering about the thing he had passed into her. But that was a wonder best left for later. Right now, she wanted to get away from the river, and eventually away from Ace. Maybe.

She squinted against the filtered sun. Nothing, not even a bird. Too cold for mosquitoes. Dead air, except for the soft, whisking wind from the northwest.

"Why did you leave me?" she said. "In the canoe?"

Ace blinked and continued to stare at the sky. "It was in the Lord's hands."

"The Lord wanted you to swim and me to sink?"

"It ain't that easy. You need to read more of the Good Book. Some of it's plain, but other things you got to figure out. Sometimes good looks like evil, and sometimes words mean something else besides what they say."

She had once thought such pronouncements were the insight of an idiot savant, one who had been given the secret decoder ring for truth and spirituality. Now they sounded like the blather of a man who was desperately trying to make sense of a world that was beyond his comprehension. When she thought of the violent losers she had dated (her retroactive word for S & M encounters), even the ones who had thrilled her beyond measure, in the end they were all attempting to destroy the things they couldn't understand. Often, she now realized, the main thing they couldn't understand had been *her*.

Funny how getting nearly killed, really killed, had opened her eyes.

Or was it something else? Some creeping change at the cellular level, a biological signal that forced her to get past her selfish and self-destructive nihilism?

The thing Ace had planted in her belly.

"Reckon the Lord has a different plan now," Ace said.

Like what, drop down a golden ladder and let us climb? "I'm hungry."

"We'll be all right, with the angels watching over us." Ace rummaged in the backpack and pulled out its contents. Some type of explosive he'd double-packed in Ziploc bags, along with an electronic detonator. His gun. A soggy bag of cereal. A dented apple. His King James Bible, ragged around the edges, pages stuck together, little more than a papier-mâché brick.

"Here." He handed her the apple.

She bit into the mealy flesh of the fruit, wondering if she'd be able to keep it down. Who would have thought pregnancy would arouse hunger and nausea at the same time?

Ace ran a hand over her breast. "The cold's making your nipples hard."

"That hurts." Her breasts had swollen over the past few weeks. Ace hadn't commented, but she could feel the difference. They were heavy and tender and strained against her dirty bra.

"You like it hurt," Ace said, putting his stubbled cheek against her chest and rasping her skin.

Clara couldn't explain that she had changed. Maybe she hadn't. Maybe whatever consumed Ace, the insanity, the delusions, the sheer blind fervor, had squirted through him and into her and she was now as crazed as he was. Maybe.

Either way, Ace wasn't stopping, hands busy, going lower. The head of his penis emerged from the wrinkled sheath of skin like a snake from a winter den.

"I don't feel like it," she said, the apple bitter in her throat. She tried to move back on the rock, away from him, but he held her in place and eased her down on her back. Her skin chafed against the gritty surface, the rock's weak warmth providing no comfort. Ace yanked aside one leg of her panties, tearing the elastic.

"The Bible says a woman submits," Ace said, climbing on top of her, crushing her against the stone, pressing his cruel hardness against her. He didn't care if she was ready or not, had never once bothered to attend to her needs, and though maybe she had changed—*maybe, baby, maybe*—no way in Hell had Ace. He rammed inside her, rough and dry, and she had no choice but to submit like always.

She wrapped her arms around him, gripping the apple so hard her fingernails pierced its skin. His breath smelled of mud and reptiles, algae scum and raw meat.

She gasped. "Oh, my God."

Ace gave her a rotten-toothed grin. "Good, huh?"

Clara couldn't answer, because past his shoulder and high in the sky soared three of Ace's angels.

CHAPTER TWENTY-NINE

"Test weight is good to one thousand pounds," Travis Lane repeated, as if to hone his ProVentures sales pitch.

"We're close, then," Bowie said. The raft was crowded, with Castle jammed up behind Bowie. Lane had completely given up on paddling due to the lack of elbow room. The waterline was within a foot of the bow, and each buck of the rapids tossed a few more tablespoons of water into the craft.

The current had eased, and Bowie remembered this middle leg as one of the gentlest stretches of the river. In autumn, the river was generally at its lowest anyway, far removed from the torrential rains of summer and the snowmelt of early spring. But even the gentlest stretches had their occasional hair runs, moments when a lack of concentration could result in another spill or worse. And Castle had no PFD to float him to safety.

"So they have you working alone?" Bowie shouted over his shoulder.

"Yeah," Castle said.

"There's a lot of territory to cover out here," Bowie said. He didn't believe the agent, but accepted that the FBI had probably instilled some weird code of honor in Castle's head. Loose lips sink ships, and all that. Still, Bowie felt it was fair to be forewarned of any potential danger. An armed federal agent in the middle of nowhere probably signaled "manhunt."

As a devout recluse, Bowie had willfully avoided newspapers and magazines, and his Montana property had been too isolated for cable television. He could have set up wireless Internet service and satellite TV, but it seemed counterproductive to let unwanted information into his cabin while he had spent so much energy keeping the real world at bay. Bowie couldn't recall any sensational cases that might have triggered a serious federal manhunt, but he was sure not every crime was as high-profile as the 9/11 attacks, the Green River Killer, or the Unabomber case.

McKay, at the rear of the raft, spoke up. "I saw on the news that abortion clinic bomber was supposed to be hiding out in the mountains of North Carolina. Is that the guy you're after?"

Bowie, focused on the upcoming swells, couldn't see Jim Castle's face, but he was willing to bet the man's jaws were clenched. The agent hadn't immediately responded, which hinted that McKay was close to the mark. Bowie hadn't heard of the case, but figured some nut job was on the loose somewhere. Plenty of them to go around. But if this bomber was hiding in the Unegama Wilderness Area, it would take an army to smoke him out.

"Yeah, the Bama Bomber," Lane said. "Some kind of redneck mass murderer, right?"

"Technically, he is both a mass murderer and a serial killer, if that is who I'm after," Castle said.

Cop-speak riddles. No wonder people got away with murder. But the best killers could move in different worlds, disguise themselves as plumbers, politicians, or pet shop owners.

"He's from North Dakota," McKay called from the rear.

"They just call him the Bama Bomber because it fit the headlines better."

"Mr. Castle, I need to know if my group will be in any danger," Bowie said.

"I promise you'll be the first to know. If and when."

"I'll just assume he's considered armed and dangerous, then."

"Isn't everybody these days?" Lane said.

A budding J. Edgar Hoover or an explosive-packing member of the moron militia might be the least of their problems, Bowie thought. Clouds had pushed in and coalesced into a rumpled and smothering blanket. Bowie had studied the weather reports for the two weeks prior to the trip, and a warm front was predicted to push precipitation across the central states and possibly into the Northeast and Canada, completely dodging the South.

From Bowie's previous experience running the gorge, though, he knew weather in the mountains could change dramatically, the escarpment playing with wind patterns and sometimes swinging temperatures thirty degrees within a few hours.

The Unegama River, with stretches ranked between Class III and Class VI when the river was at its safest, could quickly become a torrential storm drain. If the rain was more than just a passing shower, Bowie would have to decide between taking the rafts out and losing precious hours, or even a day, or sticking to schedule and ramping up the risk factor. With one raft already overloaded, he might have to ditch a couple of crew members.

Farrengalli, maybe. The thought brought a smile to his lips. But Dove might volunteer to keep him company, reasoning that she had more hiking experience than the others. The smile tightened. He knew well what happened when Dove kept a man company in the woods.

"How far do you expect to ride?" Bowie asked Castle.

"As far as it takes."

Bowie glanced upriver, saw Dove working the paddle, and admired her strong but slender arms. He should have put her in the raft with him, but he had been determined to interact with her as little as possible. This morning had been a mistake, though the memory of it caused a warm and pleasant swelling in the crotch of his SealSkinz.

"Your clothes are wet," Lane said to the agent. "You're in danger of exposure."

"I've been exposed before," he said.

Every time Bowie glanced at Castle, the man's eyes were scanning the sky as if expecting a strafing run from a formation of jet fighters. Though the eyes never stayed fixed on anything for more than three seconds (nothing like Serpico when played by Pacino, who could beat a mirror in a staring contest), Bowie had seen enough to wonder if the man might just possibly be some kind of nut job himself. What if Castle was the suspect and had somehow obtained a federal badge, possibly from one of his victims?

Bowie guided the lead raft to the right, into the shallow shoals, so the other raft could catch up. He was about to ram his paddle into the sandy bottom when the piercing shriek erupted from above and fell like a meteor.

CHAPTER THIRTY

Castle recognized the shriek instantly.

It was the same sound that had accompanied the swooping attack on The Rook. One of *them*, the flying things, monsters that had once lived under his bed but now inhabited the granite cliffs above the Unegama. The high-pitched noise was the combination of a bat's squeak, a dying woman's wail, and the death gargle of a hanging victim.

The sound swelled and then the raft rocked. Lane, the man behind him, slammed into his back, causing him to topple like a fleshy domino, and likewise he bumped into Bowie. The sudden impact was accompanied by a wet spray as the raft was pushed into the water by the force of the blow.

At the rear of the raft, the blond man screamed.

"What the fuck?" Farrengalli shouted from the other raft.

"Bowie!" the lone woman in the group shouted.

Castle turned to see the creature latched onto the blond man's back, bony fingers grappling against the man's dry suit. Unlike the one that had carried off The Rook, this one had a gray, leathery hide and thin arms that bore the suggestion of loose skin. The face was humanoid, but the bald, blunt dome of skull descended to a sharp, bony chin. The eyes were large and milky, with no pupils, as if the creature had no use for vision.

All those features made only fleeting impressions on Castle, because his attention was drawn to the two glistening incisors that dug into the blonde's neck above the collar of his life jacket.

Castle struggled for his Glock, trying to push Lane out of the way. Lane crawled onto the inflated bulge of the bow, arms flailing, moaning as if he were the one being attacked. "Oh, Jesus, dear sweet oh-my-Christ Jesus, dear goddamned Jesus," he muttered in a loose and profane litany.

Bowie jumped out of the raft and let it glide past him; then he raised his paddle and swung the end against the creature. The flat end of the paddle thwacked against the creature's hunched back, but it didn't pause in its assault. It lifted its head, and twin drops of blood dangled at the end of the incisors. The lips were parted in a frenzied sneer. Castle raised the Glock, but with the rocking of the boat and the blonde's jerking attempts to throw the thing off his back, he couldn't get a clear shot.

"Get it off me," McKay shouted, reaching behind to grab at the oblate, wizened head. No doubt he hadn't seen his attacker, or he would have been even more frantic to escape.

Lane was now sprawled fully across the bow, his legs in the air, and Castle tipped him face-first into the river to get him out of the line of fire. Bowie chopped again with the paddle, and the vinyl blade broke against the creature's neck. It turned its head in Bowie's direction and sniffed the air with cavernous nostrils.

It can't see. Castle tried once more to draw a bead on the creature, figuring the kill shot would have to go to the skull, because its limbs were entwined around the blonde's body as if they were fiercely fornicating lovers.

The raft spun slowly, leaving a drenched Lane splashing upstream. Bowie waded after the raft, jabbing the broken end of his paddle at the creature, penetrating a few inches through the wrinkled flesh. The creature's mouth opened, but no sound issued forth, only the strained rasp of its flapping tongue.

Its head swiveled wildly, as if not understanding the source of its pain—*if it even* felt *pain*, Castle thought—but then its lips settled once more onto the wound in the man's neck. Blood spotted the front of the blonde's life jacket.

Castle decided the safest shot would be from a stationary position. "Grab the line," he shouted at Bowie before rolling over the bow into the river.

He kept the Glock above water. The river was colder than he'd realized, the chill shocking him and causing his breath to hesitate in his lungs. The water was knee-deep in the shoals, which allowed him to quickly regain his balance. Bowie gripped the thin nylon rope that girdled the raft's bow, holding it in place, though it still bobbed up and down with the current.

"Shoot the fucker," Farrengalli yelled as the second raft hurried toward the carnage.

Bowie lifted his paddle handle like a Zulu warrior chucking a spear. The jagged tip was covered with a viscous substance the color of used motor oil, the same liquid that oozed from the gash in the creature's back.

Give 'em hell, cowboy. Castle wasn't sure whether the man in the raft had yelled the words or whether The Rook was still indulging in his Brokeback Mountain fantasies from beyond the grave.

"Hold still," Castle shouted, his words meant for the blond. However, Bowie also froze, the line clenched in his right fist, his back arched as he fought to hold the raft in place.

This is for you, Rook. Castle leveled his arms in a two-handed grip, sighting down the barrel. The blond's head slumped forward, the man either unconscious or dead. The movement gave Castle the moment of opportunity and he gently squeezed the trigger. The top of the creature's gray skull exploded in a shower of ochre bone, black grue, and bits of ash-gray meat that might have been the thing's brain.

The roar of ignited powder raced up the gorge and echoed off the cliffs, the sound like a cannon volley in the otherwise hushed wilderness.

Bowie released the raft, and it floated a few silent feet before bumping against a fallen tree. The boat gave a slow, full turn, and the two tangled bodies appeared unaffected at first. The creature's mouth was still locked on the blonde's neck. The blonde's head lolled forward, his eyes closed, mouth parted in an unvoiced scream.

Castle was readying for a second shot when the thing's fingers—*claws*, Castle thought, though he wasn't sure whether the observation was his or the disembodied Rook's—slackened and released their grip on its victim's life jacket.

The creature's arms dropped and it fell backward into the river, leaking a greasy, dark chum across the silvery surface of the river.

The blond pitched forward. The raft wheeled along the length of the half-submerged tree before the grab line caught on gnarled, exposed roots.

Bowie hurried past Castle, who checked the sky and listened past the gentle and constant wash of running water for a descending, primitive shriek.

"McKay!" Bowie shouted, flopping onto the raft and lifting the man's head. The injured man's face was pale and bloodless, but his eyes blinked. He was still alive, though he appeared to be in shock.

Twenty feet away, the river erupted in thrashing foam. The gray, skeletal creature lifted from the shallows, beads of water cascading from its flesh. The ivory rim of its skull was jagged, still oozing a putrid fluid.

You should be dead, Castle thought. *You don't have a goddamned* brain *anymore.*

But, like the creature under the bed that never went away even when the sun was out, this thing was stubborn.

The creature twitched and whirled in crazy loops like a kite in a hurricane. The circuits of its airborne path became more erratic. Then it steadied in mid-flight, like a wingless hummingbird. It hung weightless for a moment, and then made a beeline for the forest, crashing into the high pine branches.

CHAPTER THIRTY-ONE

"Downriver's the best bet," Bowie said, addressing the group on a sandy stretch of shore. *Expect the unexpected* was a lame little cliché, but it sure beat the alternative: *Gray creatures will drop from the sky and suck your blood.* "We could rig a makeshift stretcher, but it would take two days to hike out from here."

"I want to know what the hell that thing was," Farrengalli said. He jabbed a thumb toward Castle. "He blew its head off but it didn't die."

"The worst thing we can do is panic," Bowie said. "Let's just all calm down and talk it out."

"This ain't no self-help circle jerk," Farrengalli said. "This is totally fucked. Look at Golden Boy."

McKay was wrapped in blankets, shivering, cheeks pallid. Dove attended to him with her usual precision, the same bedside manner that had soothed Bowie's brow on more than a few troubled nights. The difference being that Bowie hadn't suffered bite marks to his chest, except those passionate little nibbles she sometimes left.

"He's in shock," Dove said. "Blood pressure dropping, breathing shallow. He won't make it if we don't do something fast."

"We can't do anything fast out here," Bowie said. "It's not like we can dial 9-1-1."

"I should have insisted on a more thorough first aid

kit," Lane said. "I was expecting some scrapes and bruises, maybe a broken bone. Certainly nothing like this."

"The hell you were," Farrengalli said. "You wanted somebody to die. Like you told me, there's no such thing as bad publicity."

Lane could barely suppress a grin. "This will cause our liability insurance to take a big hit. Though I suppose we can wiggle out under the 'Act of God' clause."

"Like a bat-faced bloodsucker dropping from heaven is an act of God?"

"One thing I want to know," Bowie said to Castle, who stood watch as if he were in the 1940s South Pacific and Japanese kamikaze pilots could drop from the clouds at any minute. "We didn't know what hit us, but you reacted like you *expected* something like this."

"Training," Castle said.

"There's no training for a wild animal attack."

"That wasn't an animal."

I know it's not an animal. But I'll be damned if I'll be the first to admit what we saw. Or that it took a .357 caliber bullet to the head and flew away like a butterfly at a church picnic.

"I saw one," Raintree said. "During the last stop. I thought it was some kind of bird, then I thought it wasn't, then I didn't know what to think."

"You been smoking that shit in your medicine bag?" Farrengalli said.

"My people had legends about this place, about the Raven Mocker, an evil spirit that could change forms."

"Don't give us that redskin voodoo shit," Farrengalli said.

"What do you think it is, then?" Dove asked, taunting him. "Count Dracula?"

"Vampires ain't real," Farrengalli answered, though his eyes flicked upward. "Even if they were, they're all European poofs, fags who wear sunglasses at night."

"What about it, Mr. FBI?" Bowie asked. "Did the Boys Upstairs brief you on those things?"

"Need-to-know basis," Castle said, his eyes cold, the Glock tucked into his exposed shoulder holster, unstrapped and at the ready.

Though Castle outweighed him by thirty pounds, Bowie fought an urge to grab the man by the front of his shirt and snap his head back and forth. Better to be calm. The others were looking to him for guidance, and he couldn't fail them now. He'd done enough of that. "Maybe we do need to know."

Castle glanced at McKay, whose lips were parted like those of a beached trout. He walked to the water's edge and examined the high granite cliffs. The darkening sky brought out the striations of the veins, revealing tons of Earth that had been peeled away over millennia by the ceaseless rub of the river.

"Okay," Castle said, turning back to the group. "I saw one of those things last night. It—" Castle looked at the wet tips of his hiking boots—"It carried off my partner."

"Whoa, whoa, whoa," Farrengalli said. "Hold on just a doo-dah-fucking-minute. You're saying there's more than *one*? And you didn't care to mention such a fact?"

"Look," Castle said. "I thought I was seeing things. The monsters under the bed...."

"I don't see no beds around here, do you?"

"Take it easy," Bowie said, though his blood was probably boiling as hot as the Italian's. "Tell us what happened."

"We were closing in on the suspect," Castle said, his words fast and fluid. "The Bama Bomber was camped upriver on the ridge, just above where I flagged you guys down. He must have set some kind of booby trap around his camp, because one of us triggered an explosion and started a landslide. My partner was trying to help me out of a hole when one of those things swooped down and carried him off."

"Are you sure it wasn't the same one?" Bowie asked.

"It was bigger than the one we just saw."

Bowie traded looks with Dove, whose face registered disbelief. She mopped McKay's forehead with a wet cloth. "Chupacabra," she said. "First reported recently in Puerto Rico, then all over the Southeast. Doglike creatures that supposedly suck the blood from cows and goats."

"Urban legends out here in the sticks?" Lane said.

"I think they were in the hole," Castle said. "Like maybe they were living underground, maybe sealed off for years, maybe even decades or centuries, before the bomb set them free."

"Then who knows how many of them are flying around up there?" Farrengalli said. "Could be dozens, for all we know."

"I only saw one," Raintree said.

"Might be the one that attacked us," Bowie reasoned. "You saw its eyes. Blind, like it was nocturnal."

"Looks like a fucked-up bat-creature to me," Farrengalli said. "Unless it's what Raintree called it—

"Raven Mocker."

"Yeah, and it changes forms."

"I don't buy it," Bowie said. "There has to be some sort of explanation."

"None that will do him any good," Dove said, pressing her fingertips to McKay's jugular. "He's dead."

CHAPTER THIRTY-TWO

"Sin's a funny thing," Ace said. He'd been thinking about it for a while, since they had nothing else to do.

"What's so funny about it?" It was the first time Clara had spoken since they'd finished making love.

Women. Who could figure 'em? Blab your ear off one minute, then sink into a long sulk.

"It's almost like the better it feels to do something, the higher the price ought to be. Take killing, for instance. It didn't bother me one bit to blow up a few baby-butchers. And I know I'll get rewarded for it come Judgment Day. But if I really had to kill somebody, look them in the eye and make their heart stop, why, that would be plumb awful."

"What's that got to do with feeling good about it?" She had put her clothes back on, though the day was still warm despite the gathering clouds. Truth be told, she was putting on a little weight in the gut, despite not eating much. Just proved what he'd always heard, once a woman thought she had you hooked, she let her body go all to hell.

He rummaged in the sealed Ziploc and pulled out a Camel. "Shit. Only three smokes left."

"Don't you feel bad for killing those innocent bystanders who happened to be in the wrong place at the wrong time?" she asked.

Ace lit the cigarette and watched the smoke curl into the

sky. "First off, nobody's innocent. The women who went to the clinics to get their babies sucked out of their bellies sure ain't innocent. That plumber who died in the bathroom had hands as red as any of them, because he was roundabout helping commit murder."

"So it's murder when they do it, but not when you do it?"

Ace didn't like the way the clouds were mashing together and ruffling up in a slow boil. His clothes were just about dry, and he was starting to feel exposed. Like maybe the angels would frown on his nakedness. "I ain't the one ordering the killing. I'm just the Lord's instrument."

"You know when we first got together, when I said a woman didn't have the right to make a choice about her baby?"

Ace bit down hard on the Camel's filter. "Yeah," he grunted.

"And life is sacred, and all that?"

"Yeah."

She'd get to the point eventually, but it would probably be some highfalutin horseshit she'd learned in college, morality and religion dressed up in a suit and tie. Hell, religion was just another layer that kept you from God. He knew it was horseshit, and *she* knew he knew, but it made his gut tight all the same. Another reminder that she came from money and fine society while he fought, fucked, and fast-talked his way out of a Southern trailer park to Dakota.

"Maybe it's different when you actually make a baby out of love. Maybe it really is a gift from God."

Ace cackled like a rooster with a sore throat. "What the hell you think I been telling you?"

"I don't mean like that. I mean, like, it's something you

own. Something you owe. Something you have a duty to care for."

"Don't be getting uppity. It's God's will that makes them, and it's God's instruments that plant them, and it's God's whores that spread their legs and squirt them out. A woman's just there to serve. That's the only reason it's set up that way."

"I could never kill a baby."

"Me, neither."

"But you *did* kill one. In Birmingham. That pregnant woman who died."

"That's different. The baby wasn't born yet."

"So it was just another innocent bystander?"

"Ain't nobody innocent. I told you that already." Ace was getting a headache. He wished his instrument would get hard so he could shut her up with another round of loving, but the cigarette tasted like mud and his toes were cold and it was going to rain before long and the Feds were closing in and they wouldn't take him alive, which meant this might be all he had left so he'd better make it matter.

"Well, if I ever got pregnant, I'd consider it a blessing."

"It's gonna rain."

"What are we going to do, Ace?"

"Get up under them big trees, I reckon."

"No. I mean, what are we going to *do*?"

The angels were nowhere in sight. Maybe they were off helping other servants in need. "We're already doing it," he said.

CHAPTER THIRTY-THREE

Raven Mocker.

Robert Raintree couldn't believe he'd even mentioned the legend. Raised in the Qualla Boundary, less than two hundred miles from the Unegama Wilderness Area, he knew better. The Cherokee reservation had been the home of alcoholism, violence, and poverty during his childhood, until his grandfather had whisked him off to Oklahoma. In Qualla, the best job you could hope for was to pose in ceremonial headdress and buckskins beside a stuffed, moth-eaten black bear while sweaty white people took your picture. Or, if you had patience, you might work your way into a cashier's job at a shop that sold rubber tomahawks and Confederate license plates.

All that changed with the coming of Harrah's Casino, federally approved gambling that offered belated reparations for the White Man's long-ago massacre. A tiny portion of the profits were distributed to anyone who was at least one-sixteenth Cherokee. Not a bad deal, all the way around. The U.S. government shed the public's collective guilt, and the average Qualla resident graduated from drinking Boone's Farm Kountry Kwencher to Crown Royal, though white people ran the casino and managed to gain a majority interest in nearby hotels and restaurants.

Raintree invested his gambling proceeds in his fitness gyms, and now he was a partner in another White Man project. One that now had a body on its hands. He wasn't sure he liked the way Bowie had ordered them to haul it to the edge of the woods and cover it with stones.

It wasn't an it. It was a person. C.A. McKay was a celebrity to some people, those who followed cycling. A man was dead, torn up by a creature that wasn't a vision and wasn't a Raven Mocker because the Cherokee spirits were too weak—

"What you thinking, Chief?" Farrengalli called from the rear of the raft.

He was thinking of the painkiller he'd taken while on burial duty, and how it was seeping softly through his bloodstream. Raintree made a powerful dip with his paddle, sending the raft shooting ahead of Bowie's. A drop of rain hammered off his nose. "I think we're going to get wet."

Dove touched his shoulder, her fingers gentle and warm. The first warmth he'd felt in a long time. "You have to talk to him."

Him. Raintree wasn't in any position to challenge Bowie Whitlock. Though Raintree had a formal business relationship with ProVentures, his contract for the Muskrat run was clear: He was only along for promotional considerations.

He assumed the others had received the same contract, though he had no doubt the payments varied, depending. Bowie would earn the most, probably twice what the others made. Travis Lane, already on the payroll, would probably get a bonus and maybe some stock benefits, while Vincent Farrengalli had probably signed for minimum wage and a date with a hair stylist.

But nowhere had the contract covered the possibility of being ripped to shreds by bloodsucking creatures.

"We finish the mission," Raintree told Dove. It was the sort of thing Bowie would say. What she would expect to hear.

"Did you see that fucker?" Farrengalli said, working his paddle at a feverish pace, dipping off starboard and hurrying back to port, arms not resting. "I mean, I know I don't have no imagination, so I couldn't dream up nothing like that. Fucking doo-dah-day."

"I wish I had photographed it," Dove said.

"Did you see it fly off and leave its brains behind?"

"Maybe we should have collected some of the flesh," Raintree said. "For later analysis."

"Would you touch that shit?" Farrengalli was talking even faster than usual. "No telling what kind of alien AIDS that thing carried. You saw the way it ripped into Golden Boy's neck."

"A search team will have to come back for his body," Dove said.

"Let the FBI worry about it," Raintree said. "Castle acts like he's seen it all before."

"He seems a little unstable to me," she replied, her voice barely audible over the incessant wash of the river.

"You kidding? He's a goddamned nutter," Farrengalli said. "Talking to himself all the time. I can't believe none of us brought a gun."

"Why would we need a gun?" Raintree asked. "Nobody expected something like this to happen, even ProVentures."

"Expect the unexpected, dude. Isn't that what Bowie Boy says?"

"That's not helping any," Dove said. "Bowie knows this gorge better than any of us. Maybe better than anybody."

"Yeah, well, he didn't know about the bat-freak

fuckers."

The reminder of the horror they had witnessed chilled Raintree even more than the dampness that had seeped beneath his SealSkinz. He took his attention from the river and scanned the sky overhead. A drop of rain hit him in the eye, causing him to blink. The cloud ceiling had descended, and he wondered if they'd have time to react if another of the creatures swooped down to attack.

As if sharing an unspoken dread, the three of them paddled with urgency. The falls Bowie had warned them about were somewhere ahead, and below that was the fabled Attacoa, the high, flat stone peak where the Cherokee had held sacred rituals and where shamans asked the Great Spirits for signs and portents.

The white settlers had named the peak Babel Tower in tribute to the Biblical edifice that was built so high into the clouds that the workers lost their ability to communicate with one another. Raintree saw little metaphorical connection between a man-made construct and a natural wonder, but the white names for many things often stripped away their inherent magic.

"We should wait for Bowie's raft to catch up," Dove said.

"Fuck that." Farrengalli worked the paddle like a whip-driven galley slave, grunting with each word. "Let's put some distance between us and those bloodsuckers."

A soft fog rose from the river, the sun filtered by the gray gauze overhead. The rain was steady but not yet heavy, and drops ticked off the sides of the raft. An inch of water had collected in the bottom of the boat, but it hadn't affected navigation. This slow stretch of the river was deeper than the previous runs, posing little danger of grounding the watercraft. But the current was picking up speed, the rocky banks narrowing.

In the distance, Raintree imagined he could make out Attacoa, though the fog limited visibility to less than a half mile. He strained his ears for the thundering gush of the falls, but all he could hear was the lapping water and the thrashing made by the three paddles.

Dove touched his shoulder again, on the soft skin just beyond the collar of his life jacket. He enjoyed her touch, though it made him shiver.

She rasped in a half whisper. "If anything happens to Bowie—"

"What's the big secret?" Farrengalli bellowed. "This isn't no 'Don't ask, don't tell' operation. Leave that to the Fed."

"Farrengalli?" Raintree didn't like saying the man's name. Everything about him was disgusting, from his hairy forearms to his two-day growth of stubble to his oily black hair. And the way his eyes roamed over Dove's body, as if he'd like to club her over the head and drag her off to a dark cave somewhere—

"Yeah, Chief?"

"When we get out of here, I've got a job for you."

"Serious?"

"I need a spokesman for my fitness gyms. I'm ready to get out of the spotlight."

"I'll be on TV?"

"Regional cable. Probably a hundred thousand households."

"Fuck-a-reeno, my friend. I'm you're guy."

"So let's make sure we get out of here alive."

Raintree didn't need to turn his head to know

Farrengalli had cast a worried glance at the mottled, bruised, and leaking sky.

That will shut him up for a few minutes.

And a few minutes might be all he needed, because the first eternal rumble of the falls sounded ahead.

CHAPTER THIRTY-FOUR

The rain began as a soft, subtle invasion from above. The first drops were barely more than coagulated mist, settling on Clara's skin with a gentle tickle. The water was warmer than that of the river, though cooler than air temperature. Her clothes were still a little moist from jumping out of the canoe, but she no longer wanted to be naked in front of Ace.

The lust and sick pride of ownership she'd enjoyed in his gaze (first seen by the dashboard lights of his pickup, later by campfire, cheap motel fluorescents, and, once, by candlelight when they'd spent the night with one of Ace's militia buddies, the men taking turns with her) now disgusted her more than flattered her. She figured he was breaking several of the commandments Moses had brought down from Mount Sinai, but Ace said those rules only applied to kikes, yet another of his intellectual contradictions.

She guessed it was somewhere between three and six o'clock, though time had lost most of its meaning as the sky had settled into a persistent twilight. Ace had stretched a thin, tattered vinyl canopy over a rhododendron stand, and they huddled among the tangled branches and long, waxy leaves, waiting. Waiting for what, she wasn't sure, and she was pretty sure Ace didn't know, either. She was afraid to ask.

Actually, she knew his answer already: *Waiting for the Lord to give us a sign.*

They were slightly above the Unegama, and massive hemlocks grew all the way down to the water, their roots hugging the thick black soil where the current lapped at them. The branches were brown halfway up their trunks, afflicted with blight or pest infestation. Higher up the slopes on this side of the river, hardwoods dominated the forest, though the undergrowth was thick with laurel, briars, stunted pines, and crippled dogwood. Hiking through the greenery would be like tackling a boot camp obstacle course.

The opposite shore was an unforgiving tumble of rocks that time had taken from the high cliffs. The rocks were a mixture of square, chalky slabs and rounded granite, evidence of the different geologic layers that had facilitated the erosion. Clara would have found the scientific puzzle fascinating if she had been here camping with one of her college lovers, smoking dope, drinking wine, and laughing about God's seemingly random ditch. Since Ace, God was no longer a laughing matter.

Neither were the angels.

Ace was curled in a fetal position, turned away from her, lying on his side on the leafy loam. He wore only a filthy tank top. She couldn't tell if he was asleep.

"Are we going to stay here all night?"

He snorted, his sinuses thick as if he were catching a cold. She chalked it up to congestion from smoking.

"You asleep?" she ventured.

"I was until you started up."

"Tell me about the angels."

"What about them?"

"They don't look like the angel pictures they showed us in Sunday school. Your angels are gray and nasty-looking. Those Sunday school angels were blond and white, I mean pure white, not pink like white people, and they had big, feathery wings and wore robes and appeared in golden light–"

"Them Sunday school angels were on paper. Who you going to believe, something on paper or something you see with your own eyes?"

"Angels shouldn't look nasty."

Ace rolled over with a suddenness that surprised her. She flinched away and lifted her forearms, but the blow didn't come. She wondered if the constant clench of her stomach would hurt the thing inside her.

"That's the trouble with people like you," Ace said. "You don't got no faith. The Lord lays it out plain as day and you don't see it, because you think you know so much. Well, all you uppity smart people don't know a goddamned thing. You don't believe in miracles, you don't accept that the Lord works in everybody, you don't allow that there's a higher law. You got to dream up a reason for things."

"Ace, I–"

"You don't see no magic. That's why smart women think it's okay to flush a baby out of their cunts. To them, it's just a mess of cells thrown together, a little accident of nature. Something they got to control. See, that's the real problem with people. Control. They don't know how to give it up to the Lord."

Ace knew all about control. She'd seen that firsthand. When she ran away from the campsite, after the FBI agents had appeared, she had expected him to kill her if he managed to escape. She wasn't even sure why she had fled. Maybe it was the thing inside her, as if for the first time in her life, she had something to live for.

Ace wouldn't kill her. Perhaps he needed a vessel for his anger. Out here in the wilderness, there were no abortion clinics. The bombs he'd planted with trip wires around the camp might have killed the two agents, but Ace wasn't a mindless killing machine. After all, he'd spared the New Jersey couple, taking only their canoe and leaving them with their money, jewelry, and lives.

"It's raining," she said. The drops were heavier now, ticking off the dry leaves.

Ace sat up. "I had a vision."

She cupped a hand over her eyes, scanning the breaks in the canopy for the angels.

"No, not up there," he said. "In my head."

Clara expected him to cite book, chapter, and verse. "Did it show you the way to the Promised Land?"

He looked at her as if gauging the length between his hand and her cheek. "No," he said, nodding down the slope to the long, plunging falls that had caused them to ditch the canoe. "It showed me *that*."

Through the gray gauze of the rain and the mist that was beginning to rise over the river, she saw the raft above the falls, making for shore. Three occupants. They reached the shallows, apparently forewarned of the falls and able to avoid the insistent pull of the main channel.

The person in front, wearing an orange life vest, rubber-looking suit, and blue helmet, jumped out of the raft and towed it to the muddy bank. The other two got out when it ran aground. Unlike the couple with the canoe, these boaters looked experienced and confident.

"They're going to carry the raft around the falls," Ace said. "Smart."

"Should we catch a ride?"

Ace reached for his pants. "That's what the vision told me to do."

"Maybe we should wait. If they give us the raft now, we'll have to carry it ourselves. But if we wait until they reach that sandy beach at the bottom of the waterfall, we can get in the water and put some distance between them and us."

Ace twisted his mouth to one side, chewing the inside of his lip. "It'll take them at least twenty minutes to get around those rocks on foot."

"They might even be setting up a camp." The vision of a dry tent appealed to her, but she didn't want to think about Ace marching the three people into the woods and pumping them full of bullets. Killing was okay when it happened off somewhere in another state, or if it was cops or something, but people you looked in the eye were another matter.

The man Ace had killed in Atlanta was trying to stop them from stealing his car. That murder made sense. It had a purpose. She understood that one, and knew God would forgive it. But these people were innocent.

The three had hoisted the raft over their heads, which provided protection from the rain as well as allowing easy balance. The raft was the inflatable kind, so it probably wasn't that heavy, but Clara didn't see how they could carry it that way over either the steep, rocky drop or the dense and twisted vegetation. But instead of walking the raft along the shore, they carried it to a sparse stand of trees, where they set it down and stood talking to each other, the tallest one making wild gestures with his arms.

"What are they waiting for?" she asked Ace, who was now rolling his damp socks up his pale, knobby ankles.

Ace reached for the backpack and pulled it to him, drawing out the pistol. He pointed it upriver, well above the falls. "Them."

Another raft. Three more passengers. Three more victims. The one in the rear wore no helmet or life vest.

"And them." Ace poked a thumb toward the sky.

As if determined to be a permanent fixture in Ace's visions, the angels circled high overhead, mixing with the roiling clouds.

CHAPTER THIRTY-FIVE

Bowie dragged the raft up the bank where Dove and the others waited under the trees. After giving McKay a shallow burial, Bowie had warned the group about the upcoming falls, a severe and impassable drop known as Little Flush to white-water enthusiasts, though on the official maps the stretch was called Echota.

Bowie no longer fully trusted his memory of the river's twists and turns because Hurricanes Katrina and Ivan had flooded the gorge and altered the channels. However, Little Flush was still just as severe as ever, and probably had been since the dinosaurs had died out. The only way down it was *around* it.

"What took so long?" Farrengalli asked, the trace of a taunt in his voice.

"The important thing is getting here safely," Bowie said, not mentioning that he'd slowed down so Castle could maintain surveillance against the flying nightmare. Or nightmares, if there were more than one, and Bowie was willing to bet there were. After all, God had commanded Noah to carry two of every species on the ark. "This rain will make the river even more dangerous."

"Should we make portage down to the bottom and then look for a campsite, or do the best with what we have here?" Dove asked him, in obvious deference as if to show the others that the decision was Bowie's alone.

"We need to push on," Jim Castle said. The rain and river moisture hadn't affected his hair a bit. The crew cut bristled up like the business end of a wire brush. "The suspects might be just ahead. They had to get out and walk, too, or else went over the brink and got smashed up."

"They mighta gotten munched." Farrengalli squinted into the rain.

"We haven't seen any sign of the creature," Bowie said. The word "creature" sounded odd on his tongue, as if naming it gave it more credence. He still wasn't quite willing to accept what he'd seen. He'd assimilated it as just another danger, a natural hazard that could be handled with proper preparation and caution. Like the rain and the rising rapids.

"I'm exhausted," Lane said. "I think we should break here."

"This isn't a democracy," Bowie said. "ProVentures carries weight in the boardroom, but out here I call the shots."

"I say we move on," Castle said.

Bowie wondered if the agent would force them ahead with his gun. Or worse, split them up. He decided to exaggerate the potential danger in order to sway the doubters. It wasn't much of a stretch.

"Remember how I explained how the Unegama ranged from Class III to Class VI waters, with VI meaning there's a risk of death? Well, when it's raining like this, you can bump it up to Class VII."

"There is no Class VII," Lane said.

"That's what I mean."

"I don't want to wait around here and get my ass chewed off by a flying thing with no brains," Farrengalli said.

Bowie looked at Raintree, who, as usual, stood off to the side, meditative and stolid, almost spaced out. "What do you think, Raintree?"

"Shit, why you always got to ask the redskin?" Farrengalli complained. "Like the rest of us don't matter. Or do you just make a point of including minorities?"

"Because he knows how to listen."

"Listen?" Farrengalli put his hand to his ear and made a theatrical tilt of his head. "Me hear-um call of nature. Oh, wait, that corn fart. You call it 'maize.'"

Raintree didn't blink. The rain fell harder, the staccato fusillade rivaling the sound of the river. Bowie realized the others, even Farrengalli, were waiting for Raintree's opinion. He didn't know whether it was Raintree's stony equanimity or his people's ancestral link to the area that gave his opinion added weight.

"What do you think of a compromise?" Like Dove, Raintree directed his remarks to Bowie, who was relieved to have at least two allies in case the dispute came down to a war of wills. Both Castle and Farrengalli appeared on the point of rebellion. "I think we all could use a rest. Maybe we could break until we see whether the rain keeps up, then make the trek to the bottom of the falls and set up camp for the night."

"Makes sense," Lane said. "We couldn't run her in this rain anyway, even though the Muskrat is designed to handle heavy swells."

"Just say maybe," Farrengalli said, mocking the company's slogan. Apparently, he had lost some of his loyalty when faced with the threat of attack by unidentified flying nightmares.

Vampires. Chupacabra. Raven Mocker. The Appalachians are the land of legends, not fairy tales.

"I can't let you do that," Castle said. "The subject is getting away. If we stop now, he'll have a full day's head start. Don't forget, nobody else knows he's here, so they won't send backup."

"Don't your higher-ups expect you to check in?" Dove asked.

"We knew we couldn't get a cell phone signal out here, and handheld radios don't have the range to reach the field office in Asheville. We could have used shortwave radio or a satellite phone system, but the extra weight of the equipment was prohibitive. And, to be honest, nobody really expected Goodall and his partner to be here."

"Yeah," Farrengalli said. "And you didn't expect bloodsucking, bat-freak fuckers to drop from the sky, neither."

They listened to the rain for a moment, the walls of the gorge slowly becoming encased in fog. They were all aware the reduced visibility meant they wouldn't be able to see the creatures descend for an attack.

"Maybe we left them behind," Dove said. "Maybe they're territorial."

"Maybe," Lane said. "But, assuming these things are an undiscovered, carnivorous species, they would need large game like bears, wolves, and deer. They would have to eat a lot of small animals to survive. And, of course, we have no idea how many of them there are."

"You saw its eyes," Bowie said to Lane and Castle. "It was blind. Maybe it's a subterranean species and it works like a bat, using radar or echolocation to find its prey."

"I told you about the bombs Goodall set off," Castle

said, his hand on the pistol holstered under his arm. "But it's hard to believe these things have been hidden in a cave for who knows how many years without needing food."

"They would have attacked somebody before now," Dove said. "The Unegama Wilderness Area is remote, but campers, hikers, and kayakers use it all the time."

"Maybe they have," Raintree said. "The Cherokee told stories of those who got lost here. We have a legend about a man who was found so pale that at first he was believed to be a white man, back before even Daniel Boone walked these hills. The tribe was frightened, so they buried him under a pile of rocks at Attacoa, the high, sacred mountain above the river. When a young brave took his vision quest there, he found the rocks had been moved and the body was gone."

"Is this like the Raven Mocker bullshit?" Farrengalli said.

Bowie noticed the group had drawn closer together under the trees, as if instinctively banding for protection against an unknown threat. "People go missing here all the time," he said. "I don't know if I'm ready to buy into any supernatural legends, but the gorge claims about one victim a year. You can drown, fall off a cliff in the dark, wander in circles until you starve to death. A couple of years ago, a man drove five hundred miles, walked the trails until he came to a campsite, and hacked a young couple to death with a hatchet. He didn't know them, or even know why he came to the gorge. He later told police he just had to kill somebody."

Lane blinked into the encroaching mist. "Okay, I'm rested. What do you say we get the hell out of here?"

Bowie checked his waterproof watch. "Six o'clock.

Sunset is a quarter after seven but, with this cloud cover, it'll be dark by the time we reach the base. Let's deflate the rafts and get moving. I'm sure we'll all feel better if we can get a fire going."

Raintree and Farrengalli hurried to the task, while Dove took her Nikon camera out of its protective case. She angled a long lens up the length of the gorge, where the mist, the river, and the slick rocks made a soft study in gray. "Creepy but beautiful," she said.

"If we get out of here alive, nobody's going to give two shits about the Muskrat expedition," Farrengalli said. "They're going to want to know all about the bat-freak fuckers. Nightly news coverage, book and movie deals, chicks." He sounded cheered by the prospect. "Hey, Dove, take a picture of *me*."

Bowie noticed she focused instead on Raintree. The wrestler was much more photogenic, projected a quiet dignity, and no doubt his dark coloring triggered some sort of primal tingle inside her.

Let him have her, Bowie thought. *After all this is over, I'm heading back to Montana by myself anyway.*

Somehow, the thought of being alone in his cabin, except for whatever unknown creatures might be lurking in the mountains at the head of the Missouri Breaks, no longer offered security. "Safety in numbers" had never held much appeal to him, because "numbers" meant other people, and that meant responsibility. This trip had been plenty enough of a reminder that he no longer cared to have other people's lives depending on him.

Besides, security was a psychological state, not a physical state, and after witnessing what Farrengalli had coined "the bat-freak fucker" rip into McKay's neck, Bowie couldn't imagine a night when the creature wouldn't swoop down from the high shadows of his dreams.

Emitting that unforgettable, keening shriek that froze the blood and—

SkeeEEEEeeek.

It emerged from the mist at treetop altitude, a gray blur of sinewy limbs, ears peeled back, the glistening teeth in stark ivory contrast to the blackness of its open mouth.

CHAPTER THIRTY-SIX

When the unearthly banshee wail split the sky, Castle reached toward his armpit for his Glock. At Quantico, he'd been one of the fastest on the draw at those after-hours, impromptu contests at the shooting range, where even the few female agents had to prove their prowess. Those parodies of Wild West street showdowns were a test of skill that no one thought would ever make a difference in the field. While quick reflexes might win you a beer in a bet, you never expected your life to depend on the split-second reach from holster to trigger.

Now, when it counted, Castle's arm was a hundred-pound tube of soggy sausage, lifting in slow motion, fingers numb and bloated. He wasn't even halfway into his draw when the creature burst from the mist. It was a flurry of wiry limbs, its bald head and pointy ears just as alien and chilling as those of the first two creatures he'd seen.

This was larger than the one that had taken The Rook, and still had the top of its skull intact, so it wasn't the same one that killed C.A. McKay and then rose from the river in a resurrection that would have made Lazarus jealous.

Castle's fingers touched the cool plastic of the Glock's handle just as the creature struck Travis Lane at full speed, knocking him sideways into the middle of the group. Lane's helmet flew free and bounced off Farrengalli, the loudmouth, who, like the others, was stunned into a deep freeze by the suddenness of the attack.

The nightmarish beast was a little smaller than Lane, squatting atop his body as Lane struggled on his belly, trying to rise and crawl away. Bowie was the first to react, swinging his backpack at the creature. The blow was ineffective, but the creature turned to Bowie and flashed a vicious mockery of a human grin, sharp incisors slick with saliva, the dark tongue flapping against the roof of its mouth as it gave a rattlesnake hiss.

See what got me? The Rook's voice filled Castle's head, unbidden, unwanted, causing him to lose his grip on the Glock before he could pull it free from the holster.

The creature reached out a long, stringy arm toward Lane's head, and Castle saw the creature had only two fingers and a stunted thumb that ended in sharp, tapered nails.

"Hey!" Raintree shouted, clapping his hands from where he knelt by the deflated raft.

Castle wasn't sure whether the Cherokee was trying to divert the creature's attention or snap the others out of their collective daze. He accomplished both. The creature paused, its menacing fingers poised and trembling inches from Lane's flesh. Farrengalli stooped to grab one of the paddles, Dove perhaps instinctively raised her camera and twisted the lens into focus, Bowie yanked the backpack over his head for another blow, and Castle finally had the pistol free.

"Get away," Castle yelled at the group.

The creature appeared confused by the eruption of movement around it. The ears twitched as the leathery head swiveled, the milky eyes blinking, Lane screaming like a rabbit in a hawk's claws, Castle's index finger caressing the groove of the trigger even before he brought the weapon to bear.

Head shot, The Rook commanded. *You have to take out the brain. The hypothalamus. Basic hunger drive.*

"Been there, done that," Castle said. He was scared, not because a beast from beyond reason had invaded his world, but because he had no idea what a hypothalamus was, and could no longer tell himself that The Rook's voice was a figment of his imagination.

A hurried and scared shot was a bad shot, he knew.

He tried to brace his shooting hand by grabbing the wrist with his left hand, but his left hand was quivering just as wildly. Rain on his eyelashes blurred his vision.

Lane slid forward a few feet, upsetting the creature's perch. Now it straddled him, and Castle saw the creature had three toes that mimicked the structure of its hands, though the nails were blunt.

Quit with the catalog and get on with it, cowboy, The Rook said.

But this was the thing from under the bed, the sleep-killing nightmare that clicked the hardwood floor, that teased the fabric at the bottom of the mattress, that tugged the hem of the top sheet. It had stayed hidden for three decades, but all buried things eventually crawled into the light and demanded attention.

The Rook could shrink him around the clock, chalk up the monster to childhood insecurities, a distant father, a recurring fever, the remnant of a late-night horror movie glimpsed from the obscurity of a parted door. In the high holy church of psychology, everything had an explanation and a root cause.

But explanations didn't make the monster less real.

The creature stood on unsteady legs that bowed backward like those of a bird. No, not a bird. Like a bat.

If the monster under the bed could exist, why couldn't a vampire?

If it was a vampire, you'd be hog-tied, pardner, The Rook said. *You don't have any crosses, garlic, silver bullets, or AIDS-contaminated blood. Throw out the comic-book bullshit and just pump the son-of-a-whore's head full of bullets. No mouth equals no biting.*

Pump it full. Castle took aim. Fired.

A hurried shot is a bad shot.

Lane, who had scrambled to his hands and knees beneath the creature and was posed absurdly like the bottom in a gay porn flick, let out a grunt. His left forearm spouted a geyser of blood and he moaned and collapsed onto his side. The creature must have smelled the fresh blood, because it dipped its head toward the wound, tongue hanging out like a filthy bag of baby snakes.

"Damn you," Bowie shouted, and Castle didn't know whether the words were directed at him or the monster.

The creature must have had no concept of firearms, because it ignored the threat of the pistol. Its radar—or whatever orientation system it used—was no doubt unable to detect the path of the whizzing bullet. Its tongue flicked at Lane's gushing sauce of blood. Castle tried to steady for another shot, but he was afraid of hitting Lane again.

Another notch in your gun, pardner. First me, and now Lane. With a little more bad luck, you can be a mass murderer like Robert Wayne Goodall.

Bowie again swung the backpack at the creature and it made no attempt at evasion. Instead, without turning its head, it flicked a wrist, grabbed the backpack, and tugged.

Bowie, holding onto a shoulder strap, was yanked off balance. The creature swiped at Bowie with filthy claws, but Bowie dodged his head back just in time.

Dove rushed forward, wielding a stippled tree branch. She chopped at the creature, hitting it across the shoulder blades. "Run, Bowie," she shouted.

Now Castle had to worry about hitting Lane and the woman both. He should have emptied the clip at the first sign of the creature.

Indecision? What will the brass make of that? No soft inspector's chair for you. No headlines, no citations of merit, no handshake from the President.

"Get the hell out of my head," Castle said, locking down on the trigger. The Glock spat a bullet that ripped through the backpack the creature still clutched. He plucked the semiautomatic again, this time striking the creature's chest and ripping a ragged hole.

Gray pus oozed from the entry wound, but the creature didn't slow down. Castle had no sense of aiming as he squeezed off another round. The third bullet hit the creature's sinewy thigh, causing another sewage-colored leak.

Lane gave a twist, crawling from the creature's legs. The Indian, who had been tending the raft before the attack, circled the creature and took the branch from Dove, swinging it wildly. The wood bounced off the creature's skull with a dull *thwack*. It twirled, unaffected by its wounds, but apparently confused by the chaotic movement around it.

If it relied on echolocation rather than sight, it wouldn't know where the next assault was coming from. But radar wasn't the only sense that guided it; it lurched forward toward the scrabbling Lane and grabbed him by the shoulders, rearing back and then driving its open mouth toward the soft flesh of Lane's neck.

Lane's scream was muted by the falling rain, but it was no less horrifying in the otherwise-quiet wilderness. The barrel of Castle's pistol veered unsteadily.

Shoot, urged The Rook, that invisible tormentor inside his head. *It may be a private hell, but it's the only hell you've got.*

But whatever hell Castle was enduring, it couldn't compare with Lane's. The man's scream descended into a low gargle as the creature's fangs punctured his neck. Bowie grabbed Lane's legs and tried to tug him free, but the creature had a headlock on Lane, its lips working as it dug into Lane's flesh and took his blood.

Unlike the creature that had killed the bicyclist, this one worked with intensity and purpose, as if its hunger had been roused by the battle.

A head shot, The Rook had said. Lane was in agony, eyes wide and staring beyond the world, his mouth a silent O of darkness. His throat was too torn to draw air for a scream.

Castle fired. Lane's forehead exploded. Dove shouted, or maybe it was Bowie.

The creature lifted its mouth from Lane's neck as if sensing the heart would pump no more blood. The blunt head swiveled in a mockery of indignant anger, lips peeled back in a sneer, a rivulet of Lane's blood running down the pointed chin.

Castle fired again and the bullet hit the creature between its milky eyes. It went down without a sound, the miasma of its skull cavity spraying onto the wet leaves.

Nice shot, pard, The Rook said.

"Screw you," Castle replied.

Bowie, kneeling by Lane, looked up from the body and said, "You killed him."

"A mercy shot."

Bowie sprang up from the ground, fist curled in rage. Castle pointed the Glock at him.

CHAPTER THIRTY-SEVEN

Robert Raintree, who still held the branch in a two-handed grip as if it were a baseball bat, nudged the hideous thing that lay on the ground like a knotted lump of wet rope. A dark, putrid fluid oozed from the holes in its leathery skin. The FBI agent's final shot had blown out the back of the creature's skull, but the oversize, wrinkled ears still twitched.

"Forget it," Castle said to Bowie.

Dove went to Bowie's side, gripped his arm, and pulled him away.

"Look at this," Raintree said.

Farrengalli, who had fled into the woods when the shriek had first rattled the dying leaves, was now standing amid the group as if he'd been there all along. "The fucker's fingers are still moving."

Castle still held the pistol in business position, making Raintree uncomfortable. The agent's eyes rolled around the perimeter of the surrounding treetops as if expecting more of the creatures to drop from the fog. But Raintree was afraid Castle was as likely to shoot humans as he was the creatures. He'd blurted out several nonsense phrases during the attack, as if he'd lost connection with reality.

Maybe they all had. As Farrengalli had noted, the long, knobby fingers hooked and then relaxed. The creature's head was in ruins, and its nervous system must have been demolished. If it even had a nervous system. Raintree recalled how the one that had killed McKay had risen from the river with most of its head gone.

Raven Mocker. A shapeshifter, a harbinger of death. Something supernatural that could only be defeated with powerful magic. Raintree touched the soft suede of his medicine bag.

Wishing doesn't make it so.

As a beginning wrestler in high school, competing in the 128-pound weight class, he'd dreamed of beating out Eddie Cucumber, conference champ the year before. In the week leading up to their face-off in the tournament, the freshman Raintree had practiced "positive visualization," imagining himself on top of Cucumber, pressing his opponent's shoulders to the mat as the ref slapped out a three count. Each night, he pictured Cucumber's straining, panicked face and imagined the weighty brass of the championship trophy in his hands.

Cucumber beat him in a walk, 11 to 2, with Raintree's only points coming on a spin move and reversal as he was about to be pinned. At least he lasted the full three rounds. Positive visualization had failed him then, but it was the last match he lost until college.

Now he faced a different kind of test, one that maybe his ancestors had faced before. If these creatures had existed for centuries, then the Cherokee must have encountered them at one time or another. Considering this was sacred territory, the land of vision quests, then who knows how many nightmares were brought back to camp by the young warriors who had ventured out in search of their spirit guides? And who knows how many had not returned at all, but instead had followed these demons back into whatever hell had coughed them out?

"Fucker's going to get up and fly away like the other one," Farrengalli said.

"No," Bowie said. "It's changing."

Raintree poked it again with the tree branch. Bowie was right, the creature was quivering and trembling, its skin tone lightening. Curled in a fetal position, it shook like a rat in a paper sack.

"Stand back," Castle said, leveling the Glock. He gave the strange head tilt again, attuned to something beyond the river and the rain. Maybe another creature?

Raintree held his breath and listened for the telltale shriek. Only water, ticking, rushing, splashing, giggling.

At his feet, the creature's body shifted and swelled, as if soaking up water and taking on muscle mass. The skin was waxy, wrinkled, like something submerged in the river. Instead of ash-gray, the corpse was now as pink as a mouse's ear.

"Cletus Christ on a clothesline," Farrengalli said.

"It's a person," Dove said, an observation that was suggested by the evidence but by no means obvious.

"No dice," Farrengalli said, stepping over Travis Lane's cooling body and grabbing his backpack. "Bonus or not, I'm getting out of here."

"Wait," Bowie said. "We stick together."

Farrengalli cradled one of the deflated rafts to his chest. "You want to stay here and get your head chewed off by these freaks, fine with me." He glanced around the faces of the group, and then fixed on Dove. "You with me, babe? You and me, we get out of here alive, we'll both be rich and famous."

"You're forgetting something," Castle said, waving the

pistol in the rain. "You're the property of the federal government at the moment, by authority of the National Security Agency's prime directive on terrorism."

"I never heard of no prime directive."

"Of course not. Top secret. But it gives me the power to requisition all available resources in order to do my duty. That means any equipment or personnel."

"Bowie," Farrengalli said. "Is he making this shit up?"

"He's the one with the gun."

The knotty-limbed, vicious creature that had swooped out of the mist and torn Travis Lane's neck to shreds was now little more than a pile of slick cheese, its skeletal frame plainly visible beneath, the fibrous wings dissolving. The face might have been humanoid, but it had collapsed upon itself, the clabbered effluence draining down into the mouth and nasal cavities.

In the yawning gap of skull, the remnants of the brain oozed out like Jell-O from a broken bowl. Where drops of rain hit the body, a nacreous substance spattered into the air. The corpse now lay in a puddle of muddy cream soup.

Its legs moved.

"I'm out of here," Farrengalli said. To Castle, he said, "Go ahead, shoot me in the back."

Dove, who was snapping off some photos as the creature decomposed, said, "I don't want to be around when this thing does whatever it's going to do."

"If it stands up," Bowie said, "the meat's going to slide right off its bones."

It wasn't hard to imagine that twisted, long-fingered skeleton flying through the air like some kind of Halloween lawn decoration strung from a tree. Raintree threw down the branch and retrieved the other raft. "Bowie?"

"Let's go," Bowie said. "We'll make camp at the foot of the waterfall."

"And crawl into our sleeping bags like nothing ever happened?" Farrengalli said. "I don't know if I'll sleep another wink as long as I live."

"With the water up, it's too risky to raft, and it's going to be dark soon."

"Aren't you going to bury him?" Dove asked. Raintree wasn't sure whether she meant the creature or Travis Lane.

"We'd better get away as fast as we can," Bowie said. "We don't know what kind of communication system those things employ. They could work off their olfactory sense as well as echolocation. And if they smell the blood ... "

They. No one doubted there were more of the creatures, lurking somewhere in the high cliffs or hovering in the mists. Maybe a flock.

"Leave him," Castle said. "It might slow them down if they stop to feed on his corpse."

Raintree noted how the quality of the group's mercy had become strained as the nightmare shifted deeper and deeper into reality. At this rate, it wouldn't be long before Castle was leaving behind live bait. As if these deadly creatures were somehow a less significant threat than a single paranoid bomber.

Bowie had already headed down a narrow trail between two looming, mossy stones, Farrengalli right behind him. Castle, apparently intending to keep a close eye on his "resources," lagged behind, watching as the creature tried to rise. The head, now little more than a curved and broken plate of bone with patches of rot attached to it, rotated as if trying to orient itself.

Raintree helped Dove slide her backpack into position.

"Don't worry," he said. "I'll watch out for you."

Wet tendrils of hair framed her tired smile. "I think from here on out it's every man for himself. Even for the women."

Castle leveled his Glock at the thing as if debating a final round. But he must have decided there was no kill shot for something too stubborn to die.

"Yeah, Rook," Castle said. "All pigeons eventually come home to roost."

Raintree gave Dove a knowing look and slung the deflated raft over his shoulder. They followed the path blazed by Bowie, Castle bringing up the rear and whistling an off-key tune.

Raintree, holding Dove's arm as she nearly slipped on the slick rocks, recognized the song: "Singing in the Rain." Among the threats they were facing, the river, the bomber, and the beasts, Raintree was beginning to believe the worst enemy might be walking not in their shadows, but in their footsteps.

CHAPTER THIRTY-EIGHT

"Halle-fucking-lu-*yah!*" Ace couldn't help shouting toward heaven.

God had sent more than a sign this time; He'd sent an angel to the rescue. Watching the gray creature flit out of the fog and launch itself into the group of rafters, Ace knew God was doing one of those mystery moves that kept the believers strong and made the doubters wonder.

Though the angel appeared down for the count, nothing lasted forever, and Ace knew the creature would be back at Rapture, when the forces of good and evil would stage the final battle. The only battle that mattered. For now, it had served God's purpose.

The group gathered its equipment and the two deflated rafts and the people now scurried down the slick rocks beside the waterfall. The rain killed visibility, but the blaze orange of the five life vests moved across the landscape like bugs in a computer game.

Ace scooped their supplies into the backpack. Clara was sluggish and sleepy under the makeshift vinyl shelter. Figured. Whenever a man was ready to do great works, a woman was along to slow him down.

He slung the backpack over one shoulder, gripping his pistol. "Come on. This is our ticket out of here."

"You said that last time, with the canoe."

"That was just luck. This is a blessing."

"What's the difference?"

Getting more and more uppity each goddamned day. Once we get out of these woods, I'm going to have to set the bitch straight about the facts of life.

"Stay here if you want." He set off through the undergrowth, his damp clothes taking on more water until they were soaked and sagging around his body. He'd be dry soon enough, once they made it to the lake. Clara could hang around at the gas station, beg for money by saying their car had broken down. If that failed, he could always let her screw for money. Fifty bucks a pop, and she'd probably enjoy it. Either way, they'd soon have bus fare for Kentucky.

In Kentucky, a man known among militia groups only as "Dredder" had extended a personal invitation for Ace to stay in his cabin as long as necessary. Dredder lived somewhere beyond the depleted coal mines of Whitesville. He had no street address, but instead had sent a strange, coded set of directions. Ace had set them to memory and burned the piece of paper Dredder had mailed general delivery, care of "Ted Rudolph," to a Birmingham post office.

Ace himself had chosen the name in tribute to the Unabomber and his most recent role model, Eric Rudolph, who had eluded capture in the remote mountains of North Carolina for nearly three years despite a nationwide manhunt.

"Ace! Wait!"

Ace smiled and slowed only slightly. His boots slid in the leaves, carving up long scars of black dirt. Among the taller trees, he'd lost sight of the group, but there was only one point from which they could emerge: the flat stretch of sand at the base of the falls.

"Ace!"

She sounded a little panicky, the exhaustion gone. *Just goes to show every woman needs a little nudge. You don't challenge her, she thinks* she's *the one with control.*

Control. God was the one in control, but all the rest of the world was fair game for Ace's special brand of chaos. God knew the winning numbers, but let human beings roll the dice. Shit fire, that was half the fun. They made their own choices, followed their own roads to salvation or eternal hellfire.

And she was choosing to follow him.

Just as she'd chosen to get into his truck on that dark emergency lane in Georgia. Just as she'd chosen to submit to him and take his seed. Just as she'd chosen to run when the FBI showed up. Just as she had chosen to be found again.

As he scrambled down the mossy embankment, through ferns, briars, and the twisted limbs of rhododendron and laurel, the sky cleared a little. The chimney of boulders, stacked like fat, mottled-gray pancakes, was visible, a few stunted pines bristling from cracks in the rock. Under other circumstances, it would have made a great sniper's post, where he could have held off a hundred cops. But he lacked the ordnance. He was down to a handful of plastic explosives and the Colt Python.

He moved faster, the footing treacherous. The roar of the falls swelled louder, like the pissed-off sigh of God. A branch snagged his arm, running a shallow furrow in his skin. He shook free and skidded down a slanted, leaf-covered rock face, and he was on the sandy shore.

Ace eased back into the concealment of the undergrowth, wondering if Clara had gotten lost. He wanted to take the group by surprise. Since the rafters had been attacked by the angel, they were on edge. But they'd be looking to the sky, not the woods.

Though Ace was pretty sure they wouldn't understand the meaning of it all. Even most religious people, who claimed to believe that God worked among them each day, were quick to deny the real miracles in their own lives.

"Ace!"

Damn. She was faster than he'd figured. He smiled. She must really love him.

But she'd best shut her apple-biting, back-talking mouth or she'd give away the game.

No big deal. The rumble of the river would muffle her voice. And it would take the group at least ten more minutes to make it down the embankment along the falls.

The pistol felt good in his hand, the rod and the staff that comforted. An instrument of God. Like the detonators he'd wired for the clinic bombs.

All it took was a steady hand and a little faith.

If only the rain would stop.

He lifted his face to the sky, precipitation on his cheeks like cold tears. The rain turned red. It fell from the bruised and beaten clouds like pellets of hellfire. A glow arose from the water, shimmering in waves of yellow and orange. The river was molten lava, sluicing between the rocks and pounding down the stony channel, burning its way deeper into the earth. Here and there among the flowing heat, creatures poked pathetic, singed limbs above the surface, attempting to crawl from the fluid damnation.

Creatures with scarred human faces, charred lips peeled

back in eternal, soundless screams.

Ace smiled.

This vision was sweet. He was one lucky son of a bitch.

"Hey," he shouted at Clara. "You should come see this."

Like it was a blooper on *America's Funniest Home Videos*. As if she'd be able to see it, or understand its significance.

"Ace? Where are you."

Right where the Lord put me. Where I'm supposed to be. Like always.

He leaned against a tree, oblivious to the water tickling down the back of his neck. The show was about to begin.

CHAPTER THIRTY-NINE

Bowie led the group down the portage trail, one he had traversed a couple of times in his early career as a white-water guide. However, like the river, which had been shifted and rerouted by floods, the trail had changed in the years since Bowie's last visit to the Unegama. Moss grew on the boulders, ferns and mushrooms sprouted from the rotten brown leaves, and a thicket of laurel huddled at the base of looming hemlock trees. The landscape had changed, the trail branching off into narrow animal traces before coming together again in a steep, muddy thread.

There were plenty of other differences since Bowie's last jaunt. For instance, bloodsucking freaks, an armed FBI agent, and a mass murderer. A woman he'd once almost loved. And lots more money waiting at the end of the run.

But the biggest change was in Bowie himself. He could hardly remember the muscular, confident young man who had given orders with the sharpness of a drill sergeant while at the same time commanding the respect usually reserved for preachers and sages. Too much had happened. The weight of failure and isolation colored him, and he labored in the shadow of a death he'd been running from for five years.

Now he had two more deaths in his ledger.

"Are we going to make it, Bowie?" Dove had slipped up behind him while he was lost in thought. He shuddered because he should have been planning ahead, watching out for attacks from above, expecting the unexpected. Instead, his head was firmly up the sphincter of Bowie Whitlock, the tightening ring cutting off the oxygen to his brain.

"Sure."

In the semi-darkness, she caught up with him, leaned her head against his shoulder, and took his hand. Her damp hair tickled the skin of his upper arm. "I didn't mean to say those things this morning."

"That was this morning. Forget it."

"I was being mean."

"Well, you learned it from me."

"Do you think we have a chance?"

"Sure. All we have to do is make it to the foot of the falls, raft eight miles in Class VI rapids in the dark, and avoid getting our necks ripped open by creatures that have no right to walk the face of the Earth."

"No, I mean you and me."

"Oh. That."

Behind them, back in the trees, Farrengalli was bellowing something, probably harassing Raintree, who had paused in the woods to attend to some private matter. Castle had fallen to the rear, whether from some misguided notion of protecting the group, or because he figured numbers would be more likely to draw the attention of the creatures. If the beasts worked on radar and smell, as Bowie theorized, then they'd be more likely to detect humans if they were traveling in a pack.

Which made Dove's company even more dangerous than usual.

"Do you think we're safe here in the trees?" Dove's grip on his hand tightened. He couldn't tell if she was scared or just pretending. Maybe it made no difference.

"They like to attack from above. So far, they've hit us when we were out in the open. But remember, if we accept them as some undiscovered species, then this is their natural habitat. They would have adapted to the terrain."

"Unless they usually hunt on the river."

Bowie pushed away a wet rhododendron branch and let Dove pass. After he ducked beneath it, the branch slapped his helmet as it swung back into place. "Some choice," he said. "We risk walking out of here, on terrain that's nearly as rough as the rapids, or we make a blind run with the rafts. And we don't know enough about those things to make the best decision."

"We trust you, Bowie."

He winced. Trust. Like he needed a reminder. "You like Raintree, don't you?"

She let go of his hand and adjusted her backpack. "Robert? He's okay. A little on the quiet side."

Built pretty well, too, Bowie wanted to add, but he discovered he wasn't jealous. Dove was like a roomful of chocolate. You couldn't wait to eat your way through the door, but once inside, you were in danger of getting suffocated by her sweetness and your own appetite.

"If anything happens to me, then he's the one you should count on," Bowie said.

"Nothing's going to happen to us. Besides, I wasn't counting on you, anyway. I know better."

"Smart girl."

The rain had slackened a bit, but was like icy snakes as trickles of it worked down his neck and under his PFD. Leaves rattled and he thought the rain was picking up again.

SkeeEEEEeeek.

"Bogie at twelve o'clock," Farrengalli shouted.

Bowie turned, cursing his lack of a firearm. He held his paddle out before him like a *jujitsu bo* stick, the sound of wet leaves rattling overhead as branches snapped.

Forget the safe-under-the-trees theory. Forget the safe-anywhere theory.

Farther up the trail, Raintree had ducked under the relative cover of a swooning pine tree. Castle was out of sight, his pistol not able to provide any immediate help. But, as they had learned, bullets didn't necessarily make much of a difference.

Farrengalli raced down the path, the deflated raft in his arms, which were folded like an offensive tackle's blocking for an end sweep. He bulled his way between Bowie and Dove, knocking Dove to her knees in the mud. Bowie regained his amateur *jujitsu* pose as the overhead menace swept nearer.

The rain hampered his ability to trace the sound, and it was only when he realized branches were now snapping fifty feet to his right that he realized something else was approaching behind him and to his left. Bansheelike shrieks of two different frequencies ripped the forest.

"Stay down!" he yelled at Dove, knowing the instruction was stupid, that the creatures had already exhibited a deadly tenacity and suddenness. But instinct kicked in, one born of primordial fear and the desire to survive despite the odds.

The first creature broke through the canopy with its arms extended, following its gleaming talons toward its prey. The red-rimmed eyes, though sightless, glimmered with a luminescence that seemed to bore twin holes into

Bowie's flesh. He knelt and braced himself for the assault when a blur of movement caught his eye just in front of him. His initial thought was that it was a third creature, and he knew he would never be able to fight off such a multipronged attack.

Then another shriek ripped the foggy sky. Not a monstrous shriek of the high pitch emitted by the creatures, but the wail of an attacking warrior. Raintree raced headlong, carrying a long, sharpened stake before him as if he were a medieval jouster.

His scream wasn't like those of the dehumanized villains in Westerns, where the cool-eyed white men picked off their hapless, poorly armed attackers one by one. No, this scream was fueled by rage and hearkened back to a primitive era when perhaps his ancestors had fought these same creatures.

The beast spun in midair, graceless, as if unused to maneuvering in the tight quarters between trees. Raintree's sudden movement had confused the thing's radar. It hovered for a moment, ten feet off the ground, its ragged, vestigial wings quivering in a mockery of avian flight. Bowie, realizing the creature was homing in on Raintree, swung his paddle in the air and smacked the shaft against a tree.

The creature turned its dead eyes toward the sound, lips parting to reveal slick teeth and two curving incisors.

Dove, catching on to Bowie's plan of overloading the creature's perception, rolled off the path and grabbed a stone from the mud. She hurled it at the creature, and though it missed by several feet, the creature's head tracked the stone's trajectory.

Raintree seized the opportunity to leap forward and

plunge the point of his makeshift spear into the creature's chest.

The creature's expression curdled into what might have passed for anger on a human's face. Elephantine skin collapsed around its eyes and the long tongue rolled out in a soundless hiss. Raintree knelt and balanced beneath the creature as a pole vaulter might prepare to hurdle a high bar. The creature slid down the length of the spear, and Raintree released it just before the unwholesome flesh of the nightmare reached his hands.

The second shriek signaled the attack of the other beast, and Bowie wondered if they had learned that their prey could fight back and had thus changed their strategy. The thought that these deadly monsters, already cursed with claws, fangs, and a seeming invincibility, could develop complex tactics and coordinate their attacks filled Bowie with deep, sick dread.

He swung the paddle around just as the creature exploded from the trees. The shriek rose in intensity as it accelerated straight for Bowie. Dove had collected another rock and hurled it toward the creature, but it ignored whatever stimulus the missile had aroused. This one, larger than the first, appeared hell bent to take out Bowie, like a heat-seeking missile targeting an artillery post. Bowie slapped with the paddle, but the creature grabbed the shaft with one hand, wiry fingers ripping it from Bowie's grasp.

The thing plowed into Bowie, striking him in the chest, and he went down hard, lungs dead for air.

The creature crawled along his torso, claws making painful tracks up his arms, the PFD ripping like a toilet-paper kite in a hurricane.

Up close, its eyes gave off a strange radiance, as if deep

in the back of the orbs, muted kaleidoscopes spun and glimmered.

But the eyes didn't get much of Bowie's attention, because the teeth were closing in on his throat, and his arms were pinned to the ground. Though no wind of breath issued from the gaping mouth, a putrid stench rose from the thing's inner workings.

Bowie bucked, trying to toss off the writhing burden like Raintree had once thrown his wrestling opponents. The creature was only half of Bowie's weight, but clung with a desperation born of unholy hunger.

Failure.

The final one.

Bowie was about to close his eyes so he wouldn't see the red proof of his own futility when, over the creature's shoulder, he saw Dove, face straining, arms quivering, a large, jagged rock raised over her head. She brought the blunt point of the rock against the creature's head just as it was countering Bowie's evasive maneuver.

The contact made a moist *sloosh*, like the dropping of a watermelon on pavement.

This time, Bowie did close his eyes as gore squirted from the top of the wizened, bald skull. The viscid juice splattered across his face, mixing with the rain. The creature didn't immediately release its grip, but gave a startled turn of its head. Bowie opened his eyes, hoping the obscene blood wasn't infectious. Dove was lifting the rock for another blow, a thin strand of gray fluid stringing from its tip. Bowie saw the shattered back of the creature's head, and the bloated, larva-like meat of its primitive brain.

Though the crenulated brain was violated with deep wounds, the creature's physical responses were still quick and strong.

Because it thinks with its mouth.

And its thinking had turned from hunger to self-defense, because its talons slid from Bowie's arms and, monkey-quick, it lifted toward Dove. Bowie flinched, waiting for the latest death of someone he loved.

The creature never reached her, because Raintree skewered it in midair. He must have retrieved his spear from the body of the first creature.

Raintree bore his full weight against the creature, twisting the spear and nailing the squirming form to the ground. It raked its claws at him, but Raintree stepped back and lowered his shoulders, a study in combat leverage. Dove moved within striking distance and slammed the rock down once more, this time full on the creature's forehead. It quivered, more of its foul, gray blood leaking from the deadly mouth.

Bowie rolled to his feet, planning to join the attack, when he was hit by a wave of dizziness and nausea. By the time the mental fog lifted, the creature lay still, though its open eyes appeared to glare at Bowie with a smirk of victory. As if it knew the battle was just beginning, and it would somehow return.

In the heat of his near death, Bowie had forgotten all about Dove, Raintree, the trip, the long nightmare that lay ahead, and the two victims decaying upstream. His universe had been reduced to mud and fear, a primordial combination that had spawned the birth of the world and would no doubt be its ultimate, eternal condition.

CHAPTER FORTY

"Take Haircut's gun," Ace Goodall said to the girl.

"That's not a good idea," Castle replied, wondering how fast he could pull his weapon. This wasn't Quantico, where the quickest draw would win a beer, or a Western where the actors were firing blanks.

The short, unkempt man with the wild eyes had crept from the forest as the group reached the bottom of the falls. Castle, busy scanning the sky, noticed too late. He'd been listening for The Rook and his prey had found him instead. Another balls-up boondoggle.

"I don't mind killing," Goodall said. "I done it before." He eyed each member of the group as if counting them, apparently not noticing Farrengalli's absence. "Where's your sidekick? Did my trip wire get him?"

"No, something else. That's why you'd better let me keep my gun."

Goodall laughed. "The angels, you mean?"

Total schism, The Rook said in his head. *Goodall has lost all touch with reality. Delusions of religious grandeur. It fits the assessment.*

The Rook hadn't spoken in nearly an hour, long enough that Castle had thought it had all been in his head. *In your head? Ha, that's funny. Never figured you for a sense of humor.*

"You've seen these creatures, too?" Bowie said.

"You the leader of this group?" Goodall asked.

"Looks like *you* are."

"Smart-asses all up and down this river, I swear."

"I don't know how much you know, but those things have already killed two people."

"Maybe more," Castle added, remembering the New Jersey couple he'd sent into the woods.

Castle thought Goodall's companion looked almost young enough to be his daughter, but her body was mature enough to be on its own. Though her face was etched with misery, she wasn't being held against her will. If she had wanted, no doubt the night forest had afforded her many opportunities to flee.

Except, where could she go? Maybe she knew about the creatures, too, and figured Ace Goodall could protect her. After all, better the devil you knew.

Jim Castle didn't blink as she approached him and lifted his Glock from its holster. She held the gun between two fingers as if it were a snake as she carried it back to Goodall, who took it from her with his left hand and stuffed it into the waistband of his dirty camouflage pants.

Goodall waved his gun, a little cocky now. "Who's going to blow up this raft?"

"You're the one with the explosives," Castle said.

"Ha-ha," Goodall said with a sour grin. "You want to put your lips on the valve, or you got a better way?"

"We have a portable air pump," Bowie said.

"Fill 'er up, then. What the hell you waiting for? Judgment Day?"

Raintree, standing beside Dove, hadn't moved a muscle, as implacable as a stone pillar. Dove stooped for his backpack, but he stopped her, grabbing for it himself. He was unzipping a side pocket when Goodall said, "Easy there, Tonto. Don't make no sudden moves."

Castle eyed the distance between him and Goodall. Chances were a lot less than fifty-fifty. Maybe one in a hundred. But without a gun and without a raft, their chances were near zero anyway, assuming more of those creatures came pouring from the sky. At least the rain had let up a little, though the visibility was still poor. And getting worse as darkness set down its tent pegs.

As Raintree inflated the raft, Goodall appeared to consider something. His cold, reptilian eyes narrowed. "Clara, did you count how many there was up at the top of the falls? When the angel flew down and scattered them?"

Clara, arms folded, shivering a little, spoke for the first time. "I don't remember. It was so foggy–"

"Five," he said. "They was five, not counting the one that got took down." He swung the pistol barrel back toward Castle. "You said your partner was dead?"

I'm not dead anymore. I'm UNdead. Castle was disturbed by the distant, alien tone. The Rook should know this wasn't a time for joking around.

"The vampires got him," Castle said. "He's one of them now."

"Vampires? The fuck you talking about? This ain't no video game."

"The creatures," Bowie said. "We think they're vampires."

Ace laughed so hard, he leaned over with his fists on his knees. "Holy Christ, Clara. Did you hear that? These dickheads must think we're some kind of gravy-sopping, redneck morons."

"I heard," Clara said. "Let's get out of here, Ace."

"You, too? I told you ya got to have faith. Have those

angels harmed a hair on our heads? Nary a one. And has the Lord provided, every time we needed a lift or a hideout or a bite to eat? Damn right He has."

Clara didn't look convinced. With her saturated, stringy hair trailing across her shoulders, she was as miserable as a drowned rat.

"What about you?" Goodall said to Dove. "You and Tonto must be the brains of the bunch, since you ain't talked much. You think they're vampires?"

"I think they're a missing link," she said. "An undiscovered species. When the world finds out, it'll make Bigfoot and the Loch Ness Monster look like something out of the Goosebumps books."

"Big words," Goodall said to Clara. "She must have gone to college, too."

"Angels don't rip open the necks of humans and drink their blood," Raintree said.

"What do you think it is, Tonto? Some kind of Evil Spirit?"

"Whatever they are, they're dangerous, and they could attack any second," Bowie said.

"Take off your life jacket," Goodall ordered. Bowie frowned and undid the plastic snaps that held the nylon restraints in place. Goodall shook the pistol at Dove and Raintree. "You, too. Throw them on the ground."

Clara retrieved them, giving one to Goodall, who slid one arm in, switched the pistol to his left hand, and shrugged into the other armhole. Clara put on the other one, and Ace tossed the other two into the river, where they squirted away. "All right," he said to Bowie. "Let's get this love boat heading downstream."

Castle wondered if Bowie would warn them the water

was too treacherous. More likely, he was in a hurry to send them on their way. With nightfall coming on, Goodall and the girl would be lucky to make it a half mile before the raft was swamped or they got pitched out by the rocking rapids.

"What about food?" Clara said.

"Load up all the backpacks, Tonto. We'll need all of it sooner or later." Goodall opened one, rummaged, and brought out a magnesium flashlight. He gave it to Dove. "Rig this to your helmet."

He put another of the Maglites in his pocket.

"You're going to leave us here, unarmed and without supplies, to face the vampires?" Bowie said. "*Angels*, I mean?"

"Not all of you," Goodall said to him. "You're coming with us."

Dove stepped forward. "You'll need another experienced paddler to make it through the water. It's risen at least a foot."

"Sorry, good-looking," Goodall said. "Might get a little too crowded, and it's hard to keep a watch on two people."

"I'm a better paddler than Bowie."

"Yeah, I'm sure. But I got my hands full with Clara here. Be hard for me to keep two women satisfied."

"Asshole."

Goodall swung the gun from Castle to Dove. Raintree stepped in front of Dove.

Hmm, Castle thought. *He's sweet on her. Or maybe he has some kind of stupid code of honor. A code of honor like I used have, back when I gave a damn.*

Because Castle realized now was the best opportunity to charge Goodall, knock the gun from his hand, throw a right punch into his crooked sneer. But like the quick-draw fantasy, this was the empty, scripted imagery from an action movie. His feet were as heavy as boulders, the rain in his eyes as warm as tears.

So much for the courageous F-uh-bee-eye Man, taunted The Rook. *You're still four years old, pissing in bed because you're too scared to put your feet on the floor and walk to the bathroom. Scared of what's under there, down in the dark.*

"Nice move, Tonto," Goodall said. "Now, load those backpacks in the raft and drag it over to the river."

Raintree didn't move.

"Get going or I'll blow a hole right through you and into your squaw."

"You'd better listen to him," Castle heard himself saying. "He's got a half-dozen notches in his gun, and a couple more won't matter. He'll face a death sentence anyway."

"Wrong, G-man," Goodall said. "I don't face death. I face eternal life in the bosom of the Lord."

Raintree gave Dove a look, then collected the four backpacks and dropped them in the swollen raft, along with three of the doubled-headed paddles. Dove helped him pull the raft to the water's edge.

Castle watched Goodall's eyes. The bomber was distracted, watching the churning river as if expecting it to calm down, or maybe for the waters to part. The Rook had made a big deal about Goodall's religious mania, a textbook case of schizophrenia. Except Goodall had shown a rational cunning in planning his bomb attacks and eluding pursuit. This wasn't the work of a guy who had scrambled eggs in place of brains.

So maybe God is on his side, The Rook chimed in. *And the* angels really are angels.

"And they carried you off to heaven?" Castle said aloud.

Goodall brought the pistol to bear on Castle. "What did you say, Haircut?"

Castle folded his arms. Maybe *he* was the textbook case. Voices in his head, the childhood memories of claws tracking the bed frame, an inability to act despite the best law enforcement training on the planet. He was little more than a bag of blood, waiting to be tapped by Ace's angels. "Nothing."

"A lot of words to say nothing," Goodall said. "Come on, babe, it's bon voyage time. You—what's your name? Bowie?—get it in the water and hold in place till we're in. You up front. I'll be riding shotgun in the back."

"Have either of you ever done any white-water rafting?" Bowie asked them.

"No, but we took a canoe ride," Goodall said. "I'd guess the canoe is two miles downstream by now."

"I need a second paddler, then."

"No can do, Chief."

"I need a PFD."

"A life jacket? No, I don't want you to get any ideas about jumping ship."

"It's suicide to set out on this water. I know this gorge. Lots of tributaries and gullies. A flash food could come tearing down on us like a tidal wave."

"It won't be suicide," Goodall said. "'Mercy killing' is more like it. You ought to have a little faith."

"Faith was great for Noah and his family," Castle said. "But it sucked for the rest of the world."

Goodall ignored him. "Get on, big man," he said to

Bowie.

Bowie scooted the raft in the water, holding it by the grab loop. It caught the current immediately and bounced against the rocks along the shore. Bowie, knee-deep in the water, strained against the obvious force of the fast-moving Unegama. The girl, Clara, rolled up her pants legs, though they were already soaked, before she waded to the raft and boarded, nearly tipping it over.

Goodall took a last look around, as if counting again. "Shit fire," he said. "I lost count of you folks, but I know you had *two* rafts at the top of the falls. Where's the other one?"

Raintree, shielding Dove again, said, "We busted it."

"Thing looks pretty sturdy to me."

"You want to know the truth?" Castle said. "I shot two holes in it. I didn't want these people slowing me down."

"Hey, G-man, don't be filling me full of bull. We both know it's not that easy to walk out of here. Take two or three days if you're lucky, and that's not counting the rain and my little flying friends. You'd have to be crazy to do something like that."

"He *is* crazy," Raintree said. "He's been talking to himself."

Goodall looked around, then checked the sky. The precipitation had eased, but the sky was still a writhing mass of oily rags. Castle figured full dark was a half hour away. He wondered if the creatures, like the monsters that had lived under his bed, would become more active at night.

"What do you think, Clara?" Goodall asked.

"I don't want to wait around. I'm scared."

"Jesus, babe. You're as bad as the rest. I told you the

Lord would deliver, and He brought this raft right to us, gave us a bunch of food and other goodies, probably some nice tents in those backpacks. This group is outfitted to beat the band. And He gave us a guide." Goodall grinned, showing stained and chipped enamel. "The Lord wandered in the wilderness himself, but it was all just a test. Did Jesus give in to the devil even if it would have made His life easier?"

Textbook, The Rook whispered.

"We can't do anything about the other raft," Clara said.

"Reckon you're right for a change."

Castle waited until Goodall took a precarious step onto a mossy stone. The killer's gun was held out at shoulder level as he established his balance on the raft. He was swinging his other leg forward when Castle took a running leap. Three quick steps and then he was airborne, he was flying, flying like a goddamned vampire angel, soaring toward his target and–

The left side of his body burned as if splashed with a bucket of hellfire and he crashed down on the sand, a dead, soggy leaf sticking to his cheek as he sucked in a lungful of broken glass and rusty nails.

CHAPTER FORTY-ONE

Holy fuck, he shot the son of a bitch.

Not that Farrengalli gave a damn about the Fed, or any cop for that matter. He'd never learned respect for law and order, ever since he'd been pinched for stealing a Nirvana CD in the fourth grade.

In high school, he'd pulled thirty days for breaking and entering, which led him to flunk out and graduate to serious small-time crime: boosting cars, peddling hot TVs and computers, and turning over the occasional kilo of Mexican grass. For most of his life, cops of any kind were the Enemy. And Special Agent Jim Castle had come on two doughnuts shy of a sackful, closer to Hannibal Lector than Clarice Starling.

But as he watched from the woods while the Fed took a bullet from the scrawny Charles Manson wannabe, Farrengalli's gut was a block of ice. He'd felt no desire to interfere, and he figured the guy with the gun was the Bama Bomber, which would make his story worth even more money once he got out of this bad horror movie of a river trip.

All he had to do was dodge the vampires, survive the river, avoid getting shot, and collect his money from ProVentures. The survival of the rest of the group, or the ever-expanding list of extras and bit players, was not his concern.

He wouldn't mind bringing Dove along with him, though. After all, she had the camera and the publishing contacts, plus she was hot enough to scorch an Eskimo's dick. He could probably work her for a tumble if he could get her away from the redskin. At least that prick Bowie was apparently getting kidnapped, which was just fine with him.

Dove went straight to the Fed, playing nurse like she had the whole trip. The Bama Bomber looked ready to take down Dove and the redskin, too. Hell, if the nut shot Raintree, then Farrengalli could bring the raft out of the woods and play "Moonlight River" with Dove. Except it didn't look like the night would offer up a moon, and he wasn't sure he'd be able to handle the raft without some help.

The Bama Bomber climbed into the raft with Bowie and the girl and shoved off. Bowie shouted something that was drowned out by the river's rush. The raft spun, undulated like a fat larva, and entered the heart of the current. It slipped downstream and was quickly lost in the mist.

Farrengalli shouldered the second raft and headed out from the relative shelter of the high evergreen trees. By the time he reached the group, Castle was propped against a boulder, his shirt open, rain carrying rivulets of blood down his belly. The agent was conscious, but his eyelids fluttered as if he were focusing on something beyond the wall of mist.

"Man, oh, man," Farrengalli said. "Guess we need a new trail boss."

"Where the hell were you?" Dove said.

"Never mind that now," Raintree said. "We've got to patch him up."

"The first-aid kit was in my backpack," Dove said.

Raintree unzipped his SealSkinz and peeled it down his torso. Underneath was a white T-shirt that advertised his fitness gyms. He yanked the shirt up and over his head, showing a muscular chest. Farrengalli figured him for a show-off, but Dove was too busy tending Castle to get an eyeful.

Raintree ripped the T-shirt into several large swathes of cotton and handed them to Dove. She used one to wipe at the wound, then wrapped two around Castle's upper abdomen and tied them tightly. Castle winced and moaned. *Some tough guy*, Farrengalli thought.

"The bullet didn't seem to pierce any major organs," Dove said. "It may have broken a rib, but I think it went below the lung and above his liver and kidney. Looks like it just hit meat."

"Thank God for all those doughnuts," Farrengalli said.

Ignoring him, Raintree rummaged in the little leather pouch that was tied to his belt. He pulled out an orange vial, rolled a couple of pills into his palm, and held them to Castle's mouth. "Here," Raintree said. "This will help the pain."

"What are those?" Dove asked.

"Oxycodone."

"Oxy." Farrengalli said. "Where did you get those?"

"From my medicine bag," Raintree said.

Smart-ass redskin. If Dove wasn't here, I'd mash those government-subsidized teeth straight down your throat.

Castle swallowed the pills with effort. Dove removed her helmet, carried it to the river, and scooped up some water. "Guess a little diarrhea is the least of his worries," she said as he sipped the water. "With the rain, it's probably cleaner than usual."

"Well, Chief," Farrengalli said to Raintree. "What's the plan?" Maybe he should have asked Dove, too, but the way she was making horny-squaw eyes at the Cherokee, she would go along with whatever he decided.

Castle cleared his throat. "Guess this is the part where I tell you to go on without me. I'm dead weight and I'll just slow you down."

"The painkillers will kick in soon," Raintree said. "Hang on."

"He's right," Farrengalli said, as if Castle weren't there. "He's vampire bait. Let's get on down the river."

"No way," Dove said.

Castle sat up a little. The makeshift bandages were stained with a crimson blossom, but the bleeding appeared to have slowed. He reached inside his shirt. "There's one other option."

"Shit, he's got another gun tucked in there," Farrengalli said. "I knew it. Like something out of *Wild, Wild West*."

Instead, Castle brought out a small silver object the size of his palm. He flipped it open. "No bars."

"You can't get a cell phone signal down in the gorge," Dove said. "Surely you tried it before."

"Not down here by the river," Castle said. "I mean up there."

He pointed above the tree line, to the stack of stone that rose like an edifice out of the mist.

"Babel Tower," Dove said.

"Attacoa," Raintree said.

"High ground," Farrengalli said.

Castle coughed, a gurgling in his throat as he spoke. His words were slurring, and Farrengalli figured the redskin's happy pills must be doing the job. "Our plan–me and my partner's–was to climb the peak and see if we could pick up a tower. Though this area's remote, you might get a line-of-sight connection even if the transmitter's fifty miles away."

"It would take a half day to reach the top," Dove said. "I've seen the trail maps. There are stretches where you'd have to climb instead of hike. Hard climbing, with fingertips and toeholds. No can do in weather like this, when the rocks are slick, even if darkness wasn't falling."

Farrengalli thought about it. Babel Tower looked like something out of *The Lord of the Rings*, a precarious and treacherous natural turret. Except it wouldn't be orcs and trolls that would crawl out of the shadows to attack them; it would be bloodsucking bat-beasts.

But if they made it to the top and put in a successful call, then a helicopter would swoop down, pluck them–well, those that survived the climb, anyway–off the stony, flat peak, and carry them off to a date with *CBS Evening News*. He didn't know shit about cell phones, he'd always been too broke to buy one and the calling plans were confusing as hell, but Castle's idea sounded fine to him. Especially because both Dove and Raintree were frowning.

"I like it," Farrengalli said.

"We don't have much climbing gear," Dove said.

Farrengalli shook his backpack. "Ropes, pitons, and a couple them funny hammers."

"Which of us would make the climb?"

"Well, I figure you and me," Farrengalli said to her. "You got the experience and I got the stubbornness. But Raintree's the one in charge now, so I guess it's up to him."

Farrengalli gave his best shit-eating grin, hoping his gleaming, television-ready teeth were visible in the fading light.

CHAPTER FORTY-TWO

"Grab my hand!" Raintree released the safety line and reached down from the narrow cleft of rock where he lay on his belly.

Dove dangled fifty feet above the river, which was nearly lost in the gathering mist and darkness below. She swung suspended on the primary belaying line.

"I can't reach you," she shouted. Her eyes were wide in the faint light, but not from fright. Or maybe that was wishful thinking. Raintree had endured too much wishful thinking about her.

Raintree cursed under his breath because he hadn't taken the time to properly set the anchor for the safety line. Instead of driving it into the granite with the blunt end of the lightweight climber's pick (the ProVentures ProPik, patent pending), he had jammed the anchor into a crevice, figuring the tension would be plenty good enough for backup.

Dove reached toward him, dangling like a clock's pendulum on eight feet of rope. Raintree hooked the tip of one boot around a stub of rock, then eased out another six inches. He wrapped the primary belay around his wrist, another no-no, but this was a night for no-nos.

"Hold on," he yelled, though she had little choice, since a carabiner linked her belt to the belay.

He waited for her to bump into the sheer rock face

below, and then steadied the rope until she was still. "Okay," he said, gathering his breath. "On the count of three, pretend you're Spiderman and grab everything you can while I pull you up."

The rope girding his wrist bore most of her weight. Though she was barely over a hundred pounds, his fingers were tingling, their first stop on the way to numbness. And numb fingers to a lead climber were like broken wings on a bird.

Raintree shifted from his belly to his left side, allowing room to swing his right arm. His left hand gripped the safety line, the one with the weak anchor. If that line gave way, and he slid over the ledge, he wasn't sure the primary line would hold their combined weight.

Even if the line held, they'd have to rappel down to the last secure anchor and start from there, losing precious time in the race against full dark.

"One...."

Their ascent had been to the left of the tower, up a series of natural steppes. They'd free-climbed that stretch, but then the handholds had given way to tiny chinks, where strong fingers were required. Their hiking boots hadn't helped, because they were steel-toed and not designed for climbing. They were on the third pitch of the climb, Raintree taking lead and setting the anchors, when Dove lost her position and swung free on the primary line.

"Two...."

Though Babel Tower had been climbed before, no permanent safety bolts had been drilled into the granite, and no mapped routes existed. Because the Unegama Gorge was a designated wilderness area, such damage to natural resources was a federal crime. Climbers were already considered undesirable by the U.S. Park Service because of alleged destruction of rare lichen and other plant species at popular climbing destinations.

Raintree didn't give a damn about federal regulations at the moment. All he cared about was pulling Dove within reach of the ledge.

"*Three!*"

He tugged with all his strength, his biceps screaming and his wrist burning, feeling the give in the safety line and knowing it wouldn't hold if he really needed it.

But then her fingers were sliding up the length of the belay where it encircled his wrist, then her hand slid up the slick, sweating length of his forearm, and finally, her face appeared over the crag.

Her eyes were still wide, not in fear, not in excitement, but in search of information. A photographer's eyes, clicking at a high shutter speed, capturing the most important visual clues.

Like where to grab.

That tiny ridge of rock, one that only an experienced climber would appreciate. She had it, her fingers hooked like an eagle's beak.

He could smell her breath, the faint smell of chamomile shampoo beneath the sweat, the salamander odor of the miles-long muddy river.

She wedged her torso over, the shoulders of her damp khaki blouse covered with sand and tiny rocks. Using the rope, she gained another few inches, repositioned, and launched her elbow against the rock. With a little leverage at last, she worked until her trunk was on the ledge, as Raintree murmured encouragement while blocking out the fiery agony in his wrist.

He could deal with the pain later. He had plenty of cures for pain.

Medicine bag speak with forked tongue.

Then Dove had both the primary rope and the safety rope, distributing part of her weight between them, working a knee over the ledge and onto solid rock. Wriggling forward, she fell onto Raintree, and despite his relief over her safety and the release of the constriction of his wrist, he couldn't ignore the press of her soft breasts against his body as she moved across him to the rear of the rock shelf.

"Close one," he said. *Too damned close. Not the fall. Her.*

"You saved my ass that time. I owe you."

"Hey, good climbers use the buddy system." Raintree sat up and carefully unraveled the rope from his forearm, then shook blood back into his fingers.

"Looks like the rain's easing up."

"We'll be able to make better time."

"You were right," Dove said, still panting from exertion.

Raintree took his eyes from the slight heaving of her breasts. He leaned out a little and squinted against the drizzle, gauging the gray, quartz-veined cliff face. From below, he had mapped a likely route in his mind. But now, nearly midway, he was disoriented. The stuff in his system wasn't helping.

He'd need an extra oxycodone tablet, what he had taken to calling "Limbaugh lemon drops" after the drug-abusing conservative radio personality. And he'd definitely need to sharpen the edges of that buzz with an amphetamine.

And don't forget me, said one of his other round friends from the bottom of his medicine bag.

Of course he wouldn't. How could he ever forget that

one?

"You were right," Dove said. "Down there. We should have waited."

"We'll turn out okay."

In rock climbing, patience, caution, and precision were the buzzwords, but they had time for none of those. Climbing in the dark was nearly impossible, and Raintree had argued the climb should wait until the morning.

Castle and Dove believed they wouldn't *live* until morning. And Farrengalli had shrugged and said, "Whatever you think, Chief."

So Raintree thought he should make the climb by himself, but Dove put forth the reasonable argument that the climb would be safer with two people. The buddy system. They'd discussed the route, the dark triangular wedge halfway up that suggested a cave should they need cover, the method of working the ropes, with Raintree leading and setting the anchors. He'd tried to talk her out of coming along, but part of him, that sick part of him ruled by pills and bottomless hunger, wanted her off alone.

Despite the danger.

But danger was everywhere now, even by the river. The winged creatures could swoop down at any moment. Age-old demons from ancient visions, bad dreams brought to life. Bad medicine.

The others probably thought Raintree was calm and fearless, even during the animal attacks, due to some sort of native spiritual makeup, an ancestral chemical that pumped through his genes that allowed him to switch from reflective shaman to blood-crazed warrior in an instant. Genetics could claim no credit, and neither could Raintree. His system pumped enough illicit prescription medications to stagger an elephant or stimulate a sloth.

But he was balanced now, ready for action. Ready for anything.

He bent to coil the primary line. It straightened and grew taut.

"Hey, you guys, wait up," shouted Farrengalli from below.

CHAPTER FORTY-THREE

Derek Samford dreamed.

He was weightless, hollow, but felt powerful despite it. The licking, nibbling, and sucking had ended some time ago. In this timeless dark vault, it might have been hours or centuries. The noises had faded, that soft scurrying like nails on stone. As he lay there in his strange half sleep, he dreamed his body was lifting in the darkness.

Levitating a moment, he found he could perceive the boundaries of this prison. He couldn't explain it. All psychological knowledge had left him, years of training and study washed down an invisible drain along with his soul. He didn't need to explain it.

He could hear the slanted walls, the rubble strewn on the subterranean cavern floor, stalagtites dangling overhead like icicles frozen in the slow melt of eons. Hear in a way he had never known, with a deeper and more basic understanding of his surroundings. At Quantico, he'd practiced with infrared goggles and thermal imaging systems, and those advanced technologies offered a fresh and bizarre perspective. This backward evolutionary step had enriched him far more deeply than anything found in the federal armory.

Samford, for the first time since his capture, realized he could move. Perhaps it was merely the freedom of dreaming. It didn't matter. To his drained flesh and poisoned brain, movement meant flight.

He could escape.

While pursuing his master's degree in behavioral psychology, he had encountered a theory suggesting the brain played tricks at the moment of death. Perhaps as a protective mechanism, certain portions of the brain took over, suppressing the frontal lobe, giving way to more primitive, reptilian emotions. Other electrical impulses created the illusion commonly referred to as "going toward the light" by those who had been pulled back from death's door. According to the theory, this cushioning was nature's way of easing the inevitable.

Suspended in pitch blackness, flexing his thin fingers, Samford crafted a rival theory, one drenched in the morass of nightmares and ignited by the lightning that had sparked the zoological soup.

Death was okay.

Death felt goddamned *good*.

But just as energy could be neither created nor destroyed, every natural transition had its price.

The price of death, of newfound freedom, was hunger.

He licked his lips and found he was no longer grinning. The persistent erection had lost its blood, along with the rest of his body, and his new sensory perception detected its flaccid wiggle between his naked legs. He spun like an acrobat on stunt rings, though he needed no safety net. In this new state of being, safety no longer mattered.

All that mattered was instinct and the lulling whisper of the night.

Not the night he now smelled seeping from a far crack in the cavern's walls, but the truer night, the ultimate dark that feasted on the universe and would one day finish its meal, yet still suffer an endless ache for more.

Samford shook his wiry, withered limbs, and despite his dearth of blood, a mockery of feeling returned. He stroked the air like a beginning swimmer in shallow water, tentative. After flailing in place for long moments, wasting a precious stretch of night, he finally relaxed, letting his body do its own bidding.

He moved through the air, ragged wings fluttering behind him.

He realized why he'd heard no more scratching sounds and endured no more bites.

The others were gone, prowling for prey, sick with the same hunger he now endured.

He wouldn't be hungry for long.

Beyond the opening in the mountain lay a world where Samford and his new kind had never really belonged. A world that had forgotten them, though the creatures themselves harbored an ancestral memory stronger than those who had thrived and populated the planet during their time of captivity.

Samford drifted toward the fresh air that was rich with the smell of the river, teeming with movement, ripe with red possibilities.

CHAPTER FORTY-FOUR

Damned redskin thought he'd leave me in the dust and steal my thunder.

Farrengalli worked his way up the rope. He was glad he'd reached the bottom of it before Raintree reeled it in. The first part of the climb had been easy, but a day of fast water and an afternoon of dodging bloodsucking Stephen King nightmares had worn him down a little. He was running on pure adrenaline now, and wondered what kinds of smells the creatures picked up on.

Probably fear. Or blood. Wonder if Dove's on the rag?

One thing for certain. When they put the call in and the cavalry came swooping over the ridge in their black helicopters, Vincent Stefano Farrengalli was going to be in the spotlight taking credit. He'd propped Castle up in a nice little niche, a place where two boulders had fallen against each other. Castle was alert and seemed recovered from shock. In fact, he'd tried to talk Farrengalli into taking the raft, just the two of them.

Farrengalli had half the same idea: He'd take the raft by himself. But he'd already seen the power of the flooded river, and he knew he couldn't handle the raft by himself. If any of the bloodsuckers attacked, he wouldn't be able to fend them off while keeping the raft on course. Castle would be useless, except as ballast. Even if Farrengalli completed the solo run, odds were better that Chief and the

Babe would strike pay dirt with their little cell phone trick, leaving Farrengalli in the drink when the reporters started their feeding frenzy.

"What the hell do you think you're doing?" Raintree said, peering over the ledge.

"The Bat-climb," Farrengalli said, bracing himself to rest his forearms. "You know, in the *Batman* TV show, when him and Robin would walk up the side of the building. Except, really, they just turned the camera sideways, because you can see the wires tugging their capes straight out."

"I ought to cut this rope and let you fall."

"You might need me. What if those things attack while you guys are playing bondage with your ropes?"

"Where's Castle?"

"I went to get some firewood, figured it would help him get comfortable. And the son of a bitch stole the raft while I was gone. Can you believe that? A fucking federal agent."

Farrengalli renewed his assault on the slope, his sheer strength and size compensating where Dove had failed. He didn't want to count on Raintree's helping hand, as she had. He wasn't sure how helpful it would be this time around.

"Did he inflate the raft while you were gone?"

Shit. Farrengalli hated being caught in a lie. It had always made him angry, but he also enjoyed the challenge. Honesty was for dumb-asses. Liars were smart, because they had to remember all their lies, whereas smart people only had to remember what really happened.

"Well, he ordered me to pump it up. Wanted the two of us to make a run for it."

"*Ordered* you? Without a gun?" Dove said, her head

now poking over the ledge beside Raintree's. In the growing darkness, he could barely make out the teeth inside her grimace.

"He's got a badge. What did you want me to do?"

"I thought we decided—oh, screw it." Raintree tossed down a second line. "Here's a backup if you need it."

"Preesh, my man." Though Farrengalli had no intention of putting his weight on any line that Raintree hadn't tried first. Besides, eight more feet of busting his balls and he'd be within reach of the ledge. Raintree wouldn't try anything funny in front of Dove.

He'd slid the carabiner through his belt, the way they'd taught him on the reality show. But it felt a little bit faggy, like some gooty body jewelry or something. Safety was for sissies, anyway. What was the point of looking both ways to cross the street when God was probably dropping a player piano on your ass?

Faith, man, that's the ticket. You got to believe in your own fucking self.

He propelled forward, hand over hand, water squirting from the rope as he gripped it. Dove and Raintree barely had time to move away before he launched himself up and over the rock edge. The ledge was about ten feet wide, with a few scrub pines and patches of moss clinging where dirt had collected over the centuries.

Farrengalli managed to disguise his exertion. "So, you guys going to have a picnic, or should we get our candy asses up sugar mountain?"

"What really happened down there?" Dove said. Chief stood a few feet away, arms folded. One good shove away from a fifty-foot drop. But that could wait for later. Right now, he needed Raintree to help get them to the top. Like he'd needed Bowie at first. And he needed Dove for the photographs, the promise of fame stored on negatives, in the backpack he'd left with Castle along with the words "Guard this with your life."

"Like I said, he stole the raft."

"He was wounded and in shock."

"You know how those Feds are. They're messed up in the head. All this duty and courage and toughness bullshit."

"I think we're the ones getting the bullshit," Raintree said.

The red bastard's forearms were pretty big. Farrengalli would have to be careful getting rid of this one. "He had this cockamamie idea that he still could catch the Bama Bomber. Said he owed it to his partner."

"We're losing daylight," Dove said. "We can sort this out later."

Not a whole lot of daylight left to lose. "All I know is we're all here and, on this little piece of rock, we're like deviled eggs on a plate for whenever those bloodsuckers get hungry."

"Okay," Raintree said, working on threading the safety line through its anchor. "I'm lead. I'll go up a little bit, set the lines, and drop one down."

Dove put a hand on Raintree's forearm. "Let me go first this time."

Farrengalli had to choke down a laugh. *Touchy-feely P.C. horse crap. And Raintree will have to say —*

"I'm more experienced."

"Now *you're* the one that's bullshitting. We both saw how your safety anchor wasn't secure."

"Remember when you said I'd have to be the leader if

anything happened to Bowie?"

Farrengalli's ears pricked up. Not at this little tidbit of revelation, but because of the banshee wails bouncing off the walls of the gorge a couple of miles downstream.

CHAPTER FORTY-FIVE

"It's getting dark," Clara shouted over the churning water. She knew she was stating the obvious, just as she knew Ace would ignore the obvious.

Ace, behind her in the aft position, worked the paddle from side to side, splashing her shoulders with each stroke. She no longer felt the chill; her body had passed into a numbness that matched the deadening of her spirit.

The only warm spot was in the center of her belly, where a sick miracle of biology was taking place, cells divided and growing, mass forming.

Maybe she'd name it Wayne. It was boy, she knew. She'd always heard "A woman knows," and she'd always thought it was bullshit, same as "Jesus loves the little children" and "You can trust the government." But now that she had a cluster of living cells squirming inside her, she thought it was magic of the highest order. The connection went beyond mere extrasensory perception. She now had a religion, a nest egg, and a deepest fear all rolled into one.

"It's darkest nigh on before dawn," Ace said, as if offering up some bit of Biblical wisdom.

"You think that cop is dead?"

"Don't matter none. He had it coming, sooner or later."

Somehow, his shooting of the FBI agent was more horrifying than the abortion clinic bombings. She certainly had no special place in her heart for cops, mostly because the guys she'd dated thought of them as The Establishment. She'd never dealt with them much; despite the drugs and the violent boyfriends, she had a clean record. Now, her jacket was pretty crowded, assuming she ever got caught.

She didn't want to think about how that would affect Wayne Jr.'s future.

"How much farther?" Ace shouted over her shoulder to Bowie, who bent over the front of the raft, body tense as he fended off rocks and guided by the graying plumes of foam. The beam of the flashlight on her helmet cut blue lines across his back, failing to illuminate their path. Clara noticed for the first time that his shirt was ripped. His arms were marked by a series of long, shallow wounds.

"Depends on how much longer you want to live," the haggard guide said.

"Eternal life is already mine," Ace said, his voice booming like a tent evangelist's.

"In that case," Bowie said, pausing to spear his paddle against an outcropping of rocks, "there's not much incentive in sticking to calm water."

"He leadeth me to lay down by still waters," Ace said, mangling one of the psalms. "Though I walk through the shadow of the valley of evil, I will fear no death."

Valley of evil. Clara thought the dividing line between good and evil was nearly invisible, and probably depended on which side of the line you were standing. Ace's angels had already killed people, yet Ace had been spared. So far. Maybe the Lord really was on his side.

But what about Clara, and the formative soul inside her? Would God show the same mercy to them?

The raft lurched, skidding up onto a shelf of rock that

must have been lurking inches beneath the surface. A side current skirled against the port side, throwing the three occupants against the inflated bow. Clara clung desperately to the grab loop as Ace lost his balance and plunged forward against Bowie. The tour guide recovered and swung his paddle hard, catching Ace on the back of the neck.

Ace sprawled, semiconscious, his eyelids fluttering. One of his guns popped free of his belt and bounced around in the bottom of the raft, coming to a stop at Clara's feet.

She picked it up.

All she knew about guns was what she'd seen in the movies. And in the movies, women always got it wrong. They either had tiny pistols that were as effective as a mosquito, or they were dames with mustaches who used their guns as surrogate dicks. Which told her nothing.

She pointed it.

The raft bucked and swayed, Ace and Bowie tangled liked clothed lovers, both looking at her. The flashlight's dots glinted in their eyes.

"Shoot the son of a bitch," Ace shouted, his words squeaky because of Bowie's grip on his neck.

Which one is the son of a bitch?

She figured the pistol's safety switch, if it had one, was off. Ace liked to walk locked and loaded. Half-cocked. In more ways than one.

She could be a heroine. She could get her name in the papers, probably be forgiven for her past crimes. All she had to do was pull the trigger. She could blame it all on him.

It was his fault. Of course it was. He was the man. What judge or jury would ever blame her?

Shoot him, and she was free, no matter how the journey ended. And if she were free, life would be easier for little Bobbie Wayne in her womb. With luck, she might even get a little money out of the deal. Go on *Oprah* or *Montel* or *Jerry Springer*.

All those guys who'd banged her at Radford would see her and remember. All the pain she had sought and endured would disappear–however briefly.

She held a loaded gun. At this moment, for the first time in years, she was at the delivery end of pain instead of the receiving end. And it felt damned good.

CHAPTER FORTY-SIX

Jim Castle was groggy, his side like a small volcano spouting red heat. The woman, Dove, had done a fine job of trussing him up. The mistake had been in leaving Farrengalli behind as his bodyguard. The loudmouth was obviously scared, hiding in the woods as Ace Goodall hijacked the rafting expedition, running at the first warning shriek of vampire attack.

Not that Castle had much room for criticism. He'd failed The Rook, and maybe his getting shot was some sort of cosmic payback. The final joke in God's pet little passion play.

Except the wound didn't seem imminently fatal. Castle couldn't even check out as another agent lost in the line of duty, to be forever enshrined with a bronze plaque at headquarters in DC.

After Farrengalli tucked him between the two leaning stones, positioned in a natural teepee, the idiot had abandoned him with a "Catch you on the flip side, Mulder." Castle wasn't sure where Farrengalli was headed, but he'd left the raft behind, along with some of the other dead weight from his backpack. He'd taken only the rations, some rope, and climbing gear.

Castle had no means of defense, and as darkness fell, he wasn't sure he wanted to spend the night without rations or a weapon, even though the stones provided decent shelter. Mostly, he couldn't bear being alone with his thoughts, feeling inept and useless. He'd lost a pint of blood and was a little woozy. He sipped at the dented tin cup of silty river water Farrengalli had left for him.

"Hey, Rook, what do you think?" he asked aloud through chapped lips. "Should I ride it out here? Or go for the glory one more time?"

He listened, and heard nothing but the rising hum of crickets and katydids, the croaking of early frogs, the ticking of droplets off the leaves, the incessant swish of the Unegama. So he'd been imagining Derek Samford's voice all along. The thoughts had been his own. Not sure what was worse, the fact that he was cracking up or that even afterlife ESP had failed him, he decided he couldn't bear the night alone. The blackness would press in and suffocate him.

Wait it out, he told himself, mentally mimicking The Rook's voice. *The climbers might reach the top of the cliff and call for help. You might be on a helicopter to Bethesda by midnight.*

He didn't believe it. He'd been an FBI agent too long to buy that type of rosy, bullshit happy ending.

Plus, he'd heard the shrieks. What had sounded like at least two of the preternatural killing machines, though the echoes off the gorge walls made them sound like an army. The woman and the Cherokee were probably dead by now. Waiting wasn't the wise choice.

Which left him *no* choice.

With a groan he didn't try to suppress, he raised from his sitting position, his side throbbing like a cavity in an oversize molar, each beat of his heart pulsing the pain through his entire body. He rolled onto his good side and crawled out of the opening onto the rock-strewn shore. The rain had stopped, though the mist was nearly thick enough to count as precipitation.

Castle crawled on his hands and knees to the place where Farrengalli had dumped the pack. He retrieved the air pump and crawled to the deflated raft, which lay over a low, dense bush. The metal pump clacked as he put weight on it, but he was determined now. Twenty feet had never seemed so far, and his wounded side felt slick and wet, as if the hole had resumed leaking.

He finally reached the raft, flipped open the primary valve stem, and attached the hand-operated pump. There were two valves on the raft, and Castle didn't understand its construction, but figured he'd only need to inflate one section since he would be the sole passenger. He didn't think he had the strength to finish even one. His ribs ached as he worked the lever, air hissing into the raft.

Castle checked the luminescent readout on his watch. 7:22. About 15 or 20 minutes away from sundown. He wasn't sure how much darker the gorge could get. The absence of electric lights, the veil of mist and clouds that would obscure the stars, and his own amped-up fear would combine to create the longest night of the millennium.

The rush of the river was a constant reminder of passing time, the slow leak of his blood, the utter smallness of a man in the grand scheme of nature. He'd never been lonely. FBI agents almost always worked as partners, as teams, as cogs in a well-oiled but still-human machine. He'd had his share of wives and women, sometimes both at the same time. He'd socialized with U.S. senators, been interviewed by the *Washington Post*, and had even swung a brief guest segment on *America's Most Wanted*.

But here, in the churning bowels of the world's oldest mountain range, he couldn't lie to himself about his helplessness.

But he wasn't ready to quit.

With the raft half inflated, he tugged it from its perch on the bush and dragged it toward the river. The raft made a sloughing sound as it trailed behind him like a giant used condom. Farrengalli hadn't left a paddle, or if he did, it was tossed in the woods somewhere. Once Castle launched, he'd be at the mercy of the swollen river.

At the mercy of nature.

Maybe he had been at nature's mercy from the moment he set foot in the Unegama Wilderness Area, sent off on a wild goose chase so he wouldn't mess up the "real investigation" elsewhere. And to top it off, nature had rained down a flock of bloodsucking, predatory nightmares.

Castle used the elbow on his good side to ease his body over the smooth rocks, sand, and mud. His ragged side, the one sporting the Lincoln Tunnel of a flesh wound, bore the task of holding onto the raft. His feet, cold and tingling from poor circulation, contributed what they could, but they seemed so far away, Castle wasn't sure his brain's commands were reaching them.

Exhausted, barely halfway to the river, he rolled onto his back and opened his mouth, allowing drizzle to collect on his parched tongue.

We'll have to work up a new assessment.

"Rook?" He said it aloud, maybe, though he wasn't sure his tongue moved.

You might say that.

"You sound different. But I'm glad you're back. I was

getting ... "

It's okay, my friend and partner. You can talk to me. I'm trained, remember?

"I was getting...."

Trust me. I've been here for you, even after you let me down. Brothers in arms. To the end. And beyond.

Castle thought The Rook wasn't sounding quite like The Rook anymore. He was talking less like a Behavioral Sciences guy and more like a host on a cheesy late-night horror series. Nevertheless, the relief flooding through Castle almost flushed out the pain and dread. He could say it.

"I'm scared." He swallowed, the last word as wet and cold and stinking as a river rock.

Nothing to fear, my friend. I'll deliver you.

"Partners can always count on each other, right?"

Pause.

About that new assessment ...

Something moved by the edge of the forest, though in the murk Castle couldn't tell if it was just a shiver of leaves in the wind. Even after three weeks in the gorge, he'd never noticed how full and teeming the wilderness was. A world apart, oblivious of the civilized and sane place ruled by phone lines, computers, television, and highways. This was a universe that made its own rules.

And sometimes breaks *its own rules.*

The Rook's voice in his head sounded louder, colder, the words taking on more reverberation, as if spoken from a deep cave.

"Help me," Castle whispered.

Derek Samford emerged from the undergrowth, trying his new wings, licking lips that had grown swollen.

He experimented with his throat: *skeeee*.

The two fangs were a little awkward, but Samford-thing thought he could make them work. With a little practice. And he planned on getting *lots* of practice.

CHAPTER FORTY-SEVEN

The cut-throat, backstabbing bitch!
Ace was tied up in human knots by the raft guide, Bowie. Ace was used to kicking ass, but he'd always picked his victims with care. He didn't have size, so he counted on the element of surprise. Out of a dark alley with a tire iron, up from the backseat with a cheap pocketknife, in the middle of the night with a time bomb.

Right now, with the raft pitching and the drizzle seeping down, the fog closing in and the dumb cunt pointing the FBI agent's Glock at both of them, with Bowie flexing muscles and rage, Ace wasn't sure whether he wanted her to shoot or not.

First off, if she pulled the trigger, odds were even she'd miss and plug a nickel-sized hole in his guts. Second, she was such an uppity, highfalutin, educated bitch that she probably couldn't kill somebody in hot blood, even when that somebody could take the gun away from her, hold them both as prisoners, and turn them over to the cops.

Third, she could miss them both, knock a slow hole in the raft, and they'd wallow down into the churning water, knocking against rocks and sucking for air.

Fourth (and Ace wasn't sure he could count much higher, because the Bowie ass-wipe was squeezing off the oxygen to his brain), Clara's eyes had gone a little cold and distant, kind of like his own mother's eyes had looked the first time she'd caught him stealing coins from her purse.

Like she wasn't sure.

Just like an uppity bitch, a woman, an eater of the devil's apples.

All this smart talk about feelings and caring and even that cuntfest word "love," a word the Bible didn't really have all that much use for except that part in John 3:16 where the Big Love went down.

Sacrifice. That was what it was all about, and he didn't think Clara had seen the light yet.

Fucking bitch.

He kicked upward, hoping to knee Bowie in the nuts, but the dude was too fast. Bowie brought a fist down hard against Ace's ear, ringing tiny sleigh bells in his head.

"Shoot!" He didn't recognize his own voice. The air from his lungs flung needles up the length of his throat.

The fading whine of the bells mingled with the constant wash of the rushing river. White noise, white might, and might always made right.

"I can't do it," Clara shouted, clinging to the grab loop with her left hand.

Bowie, his weight pressed on top of Ace, ripping the top buttons off his shirt, turned to Clara. "Give me the gun."

As Bowie reached his hand toward her, Ace twisted to the side, a move he'd learned when his father had kicked the living shit out of him for dropping a carton of milk. Bowie was nothing like Daddy, because Bowie was fighting for survival and Daddy had delivered the goods just for the sheer hell of it. Daddy was a lot more desperate, a lot better at the game.

Ace lifted and rolled, and now had Bowie on his hip. The tour guide, off balance because of reaching for the gun, bounced against the swollen side of the raft. Ace sprang from his knees and hit Bowie with his shoulder, knocking the ornery son of a bitch overboard.

Bowie caught the grab loop as he went into the river, rocking the raft up on its side. As Ace and Clara tumbled in the direction of the tilt, the angle grew more severe. Two of the backpacks bounced out of the raft and into the rapids, swept away in the swift, dark froth.

Ace's belly flopped onto the same side of the raft to which Bowie clung. The man's hand was inches away, fingers clenched around the nylon rope. Ace did the first thing that popped into his head: He opened his mouth and sank his teeth into the taut hand.

Ace's teeth were no marvels of modern dentistry. He still had his molars, though they were cracked from his love of hard candy. From the age of seven, he had chewed tobacco, first sneaking pinches from his dad's plug of Beechnut, soon escalating to swiping entire pouches of tobacco at the local gas station.

Several years spent camping in the remote peaks of Dakota, where he'd met up with fellow survivalists, militants, Klansmen, and the occasional Charles Manson worshipper, had stripped him of any remaining hygiene habits. Those seeking to tear down society, to bring about the destruction of order viewed through their distorted lenses as oppression, weren't much interested in brushing their teeth.

But the broken and chipped bits of enamel that stippled Ace's gums were plenty good enough for this job.

Bowie's flesh was salty from sweat and tasted like old fish, but the man's blood was sweet—probably a pure-breed, from good English stock, true white meat.

So this is what them wrong angels get all worked up about. Getting washed in the blood, hallelujah.

Clara leaned against the tilt of the raft, losing her grip on the Glock, the flashlight momentarily blinding Ace. The gun plopped into the pool of water that had collected in the bottom of the raft. Ace jerked his head back, bringing a shred of Bowie's skin with him. Blood ran from the gaping gash in the back of his hand, but the dude held on.

Ace could almost respect him. Almost. But it was God's job to judge, not Ace's.

He reached along the waistband of his camo trousers, feeling blind along the soggy seams for the cold grip of the Python. He'd have a hell of time navigating the raft downstream with only Clara's help, but no way could he trust the dude now.

But maybe he didn't need to be in such a big hurry, since Crew-cut was down for the count, maybe dead, which would all but seal Ace's death sentence if he were to stand trial.

But his judgment, like that of Bowie's, would come later, in front of the Big Throne, and all his actions now would serve as proof of his faith. Because he still had plenty of the Lord's work to do, and a few of the guilty would have to die so that many innocents might live.

The raft flopped again, riding up a white, curling swell of water. Bowie flung his other arm out of the water and grappled for the rope, but his fingers slid off the rubberized nylon. Bowie was stretched out behind the raft, bodysurfing, the Unegama battering his body as he clung to the grab loop with one bloody hand.

Just as Ace clutched the Python, the raft bounced against a protruding boulder, tossing Clara against him. He shoved her away. "Watch yourself, damn it."

Ace yanked the pistol free. Clara wrapped her arms around him.

"Don't shoot him," she shouted.

"Whose side are you on, bitch?" He shoved her away.

Bowie, with only his head and one arm out of the water, opened his mouth to speak, but a spurt of storm-stained water splashed into his face and drowned his words.

Ace settled on his knees in the raft, which had taken on nearly a foot of water now. He figured another foot or so and the boat would swamp. That was okay, though, assuming the backpacks he'd swiped from the rafting group contained food and a means of lighting a fire. But there were only three of the backpacks left, including his.

He pointed the Python at Bowie. Feed the fishes or feed the angels, it was all the same to Ace.

"Let go," he said.

"We need him," Clara yelled, getting tossed against the side of the raft again. Ace held on with one hand gripping the rope, trying to steady the pistol. Along the riverbanks, large rocks, strips of vegetation, and the dark bones of giant trees sped by in a blur. The mist capped the top of the forest, obscuring the high walls of the gorge, but Ace could feel their weight, millions of years of God-stacked stone.

"You stupid bitch," Ace yelled, letting go of the rope to wipe the drizzle from his eyes. No good, his sleeve was soaked. "We can't trust him now. You seen whose side he's on."

"We can't make it down the river without him."

As if to second her words, the raft made a sudden spin, as if hung up on a submerged log. Bowie winced as his body slammed against something underwater. The raft jostled along a ribbed run of water, then reached the relative calm of an eddy. Here, with the roar of the river suppressed, Ace could concentrate on a clean shot.

Not that he cared if Bowie died bloody and ugly, drowning before his heart pumped out the last of its blood. No, he still had pride. The Dakota Sons of Freedom had trained him well, even if they'd eventually kicked him out for his radical views.

Well, screw them, too. They didn't have the guts to piss out the blood of tyrants and patriots alike, the way the Good White Man Thomas Jefferson had said. Revolution wasn't a fixed event in American history. It was a constant turning of the wheel, with God pouring the gas. Some took it personally, others were just too damned gutless.

And bigger than the fight to keep America free was the war to keep God's way.

The river divided into three channels, with dense, low growth clinging to the islands. A pebbly sandbar lay to the right, but without anyone working a paddle, they were at the mercy of the current. The raft skirled along a bladelike wave, pushing toward slower water.

Bowie, now able to touch bottom, said, "I guess you have to shoot me, because I'm not letting go."

"The captain goes down with the ship, huh?"

"Ace?"

The bitch's whining was getting on his nerves. Once they made it to the lake, he'd get rid of her. He wouldn't have any trouble, once he stole a car, to find another starry-eyed cunt who wanted to rub against greatness. The next one probably wouldn't be as good-looking or young (Clara was one of those precious gifts God granted him once in a while, the way a fat man might occasionally leave a bit of meat on the bone he tossed to his dog). But she'd have a warm, wet hole when he needed it and, most important, she'd be there to take the pain.

"Maybe I ought to just leave both of you here and take the raft myself," Ace said to her.

Bowie rose higher out of the water. It was to his waist now. In the deepening darkness, he might have been a ghost formed from the surrounding mist.

"Ace, you can't leave me," she said. "Ever."

Bowie was almost close enough to reach for the Python. Ace, in the calmer water, sighted down the barrel at the pale, river-drenched brow, right between the fire-filled eyes.

"See your ass on Judgment Day, except I'm figuring you'll have a seat way in back," he said to Bowie.

Clara leaped from the flooded bowels of the raft just as Ace squeezed the trigger. She didn't knock his arm away, the way it happened in movies, because she wasn't that fast. Still, the movement of the raft was enough to send the shot high and wide, its report booming up the river and reverberating between the slopes of the gorge.

As the shot died away, an even louder thunder sounded. "I'm pregnant," she said.

Ace was trying those words in his head when the tail end of the gunshot's echo changed pitch and gained altitude.

No, it wasn't a final echo.

It was the trumpet blast of the angels, hidden somewhere high in the twilight mist.

CHAPTER FORTY-EIGHT

"This is getting way past old," Farrengalli said, but Raintree was already launching himself against the slick cliff wall.

"The cave," Raintree shouted. The lead rope, which he'd reeled up, lay in a coil around his shoulder, limiting his movements. But he scrambled like a monkey on an electric fence, moving to his right, taking him away from the planned route. But plans changed.

The keening wail came from above and below simultaneously, and Raintree thought the sonic phenomenon was caused by the reverberant cliffs. Then he realized two of the creatures were swooping, one from above and one below.

No time to set an anchor and drop a rope to the others. He'd be lucky to reach the cave. And he had no way to defend his back, because both hands were occupied with holding on for dear life.

"Bad news," Dove said from the ledge below, as if she also realized what the dual attack meant. The creatures were growing smarter, learning about their prey.

Raintree wondered if he'd made a mistake, if they should have waited on the ledge with the others and tried to defend themselves with their backs to the wall. Too late to second-guess, because he was midway between the ledge and the cave, grabbing for the next handhold before he'd fully tested the most recent.

The twin shrieks changed pitch, became lower and more guttural. If the creatures had discussed strategy through whatever strange means in which they communicated, then they'd want to separate their prey, culling out the weakest first.

In this case, because he was by himself and exposed, Raintree was the evening's choice entree.

Both attackers went silent, which was even more disconcerting than their bloodcurdling sirens had been. Raintree knew from the previous encounters that silence meant they were preparing for touchdown, most likely with talons extended for his exposed back. He froze in place, attempting to merge with the granite, to become rock.

"Find something to throw," Dove yelled at Farrengalli.

Raintree felt the whisper of air as the creature swept past. He didn't know if the creature had lost track of his location or had merely been making a test run to size him up.

Gripping an outcropping with one hand, the toes of his boots jammed into separate crevices, he fumbled toward his belt. His fingers touched the leather pouch and a hunger shot through him. If only he had taken that second amphetamine, he'd already have reached the cave. Of course, oxycodone wasn't exactly known for its clarity-inducing powers, so there was more fog going on than just the stuff rising from the river.

He might have time to chew and swallow a handful of oxy before the creature struck, but no way would the massive dose of pharmaceuticals beat the pain it was designed to suppress.

He forced his fingers away from the pouch.

To the cool, wet steel of the piton in his belt.

The ProVentures Pocket Rocket, eighty millimeters of slender steel, was designed to be driven into rock or ice and left as a permanent climbing fixture. An eye at the broad end was used for attaching a carabiner or for threading a belay, and the piton tapered to a stiletto tip.

Raintree hooked two fingers in the eye and gripped it like a serial killer, one who insisted on the ritualistic downward thrust made famous in Alfred Hitchcock's *Psycho*. Raintree wasn't sure he could get leverage for any style of thrust, much less one that could deliver a killing blow.

"What the hell, are you some kind of cowgirl?" Farrengalli said.

Raintree risked a downward glance and saw that Dove had the safety rope, shortened and doubled, and was swinging it overhead like a convoluted lasso. He understood her motive, even if Farrengalli was too thick. She was attempting to confuse the creatures' radar.

The first pass had been barely ten seconds ago, and that initial assailant was likely preparing for round two. Even if Raintree remained motionless, the odor of his sweat and fear would give him away.

But where is the other one?

As the first creature reached the apex of its arc, it let loose with the high-pitched cry again. The tonal quality had changed, this time suggesting not hunger but rage. Raintree was refreshing his handhold when Dove shouted a warning from below.

Raintree flattened belly-first against the cliff, extended his right arm, and let the piton protrude like a sharpened coat hook. The second creature, who must have ridden in on the draft of the first, met the steel tip, slamming Raintree's hand against granite.

The fingers hooked in the eye kept him from dropping the Pocket Rocket as the creature winged past, screeching in what might have passed for complaint.

A sudden shower erupted, cold as the river, and Raintree thought the storm had returned in force.

He looked at his hand, at the piton jutting from it, and the slimy gray entrails that dangled from his wrist. The creature was cold blooded. Nearly ice blooded. If he could even call that stuff "blood."

He took advantage of the reprieve to scoot another five feet up the slope. The cave lay another eight feet above and to his left. Using the three free fingers of his right hand, he grabbed the trunk of a scraggly jack pine that sprouted from the wall of stone. It held, and he hooked a leg over it.

Estimating the speed of the creature's flight, and its cry from the top of its arc, and the subsequent lapse into silence, Raintree figured he had three seconds before–

It slammed into him, knocking the breath from his lungs and clacking his teeth together. Though the creature was barely the size of a large dog, it packed the weight of gravity and momentum behind the element of surprise.

He was helpless, because he couldn't let go or he'd fall. With no safety rope, and the ledge far to the left, the plunge would break every bone in his body and he'd probably burst open like a balloon full of soup.

If there was any consolation in such a defeat, at least he'd be leaving little behind for the creatures to drink.

Ears roaring with concussion, Raintree brought the piton around as claws raked his neck and face. The creature's cold breath played over the base of his skull. Shouts sounded from a distance. Dove? He couldn't tell. Counting on the jack pine to hold their combined weight, he locked his leg, reached back with his free hand, and grabbed at the creature. Its skin was rough but slick, like the chamois cloth rock collectors used to polish stones. The thing's teeth nicked his neck, flaring double streaks of hurt. He felt along the creature's bald head for its eyes.

Here's looking at ya, Count Chocula.

He stabbed the piton over his shoulder, going for a point just above the bridge of the nose.

Raintree had made more than a handful of serious climbs, and had hammered in his share of pitons and anchors, but none had ever felt as satisfying as this one. The steel tip found the center of the beast's forehead. It entered the skull with a *thwick.*

The creature's cold tongue stopped wriggling and lay against his neck like a damp sock.

He gave the piton a twist. Grue oozed from the wound like liver mush from a sausage grinder.

The trunk of the jack pine cracked and sagged.

Raintree tried to shrug the creature off his back, but whatever state it had entered upon death, it still clung to its victim with a fierce tenacity. Raintree was afraid to shake too hard. The jack pine might give way completely. He slid the piton from its gruesome sheath and worked it back into his belt, then jammed his fingertips into a slim crevice.

Once he had a decent grip, he lifted, distributing his weight so he wouldn't fall if the tree no longer supported him. With his left hand, he scrabbled for the creature's neck, then up the bulge of the skull. He found one of the leathery, peaked ears and yanked it as if trying to pull a rabbit out of a hat.

The thing's head lolled backward, though its talons still hooked his flesh.

Raintree wondered how deeply his wounds ran. The oxycodone dulled the worst of the pain, but it merely masked symptoms and didn't address the real damage.

"Christ on a crutch," Farrengalli shouted from the ledge below. "Get it *off* me."

Raintree shoved upward, sliding his knee to the base of the pine, then jabbing the tip of his boot into the nest of roots. Using the extra purchase, he tossed his shoulders and arched his back, and the creature slid down, its sharp claws snagging on his fanny pack. The creature's weight was going to rip the pack free, taking the cell phone and their best hope of rescue with it.

It dangled for a moment, his belt tightening, squeezing his guts.

If the belt snapped, he would not only lose the cell phone.

The medicine bag was attached to it.

The bag that spoke with many tongues, that whispered its sweet, poisonous promises, that delivered what his hollow soul craved.

The lifeline.

His fingers lost their tenuous perch.

CHAPTER FORTY-NINE

SkeeEEEEeeek.

Bowie released the grab loop when he heard the shriek, diving into the shallow water. Even though the current was weak, it pushed him downstream. He didn't fight it, but instead let his body go limp, exhaling so he didn't float immediately to the surface, grateful now that he wasn't wearing a PFD.

The choice between getting shot and being eaten alive had been no choice at all. Like most choices in his life, the real decision had been yanked out of his grasp. Or so he'd always believed.

This time, as the actor Ed Harris once said, failure was not an option.

Which is odd, he thought, as his lungs burned with emptiness. *Because there's nobody left for me to fail. They're all either dead or abandoned.*

Maybe this time, he was kicking for himself.

Bowie scraped his elbow on a rock, igniting one of the wounds he'd suffered in the earlier attack. The pain allowed him a little extra stamina, as if fear wasn't enough. Fear had never been enough. Bowie had swallowed it and swallowed it over the years, and instead of getting fat, he'd wasted away. On the inside. No chance to break the diet now, but maybe he'd sample the wares a little before the buffet table closed.

He broke surface thirty feet downstream from the raft, rising from the water just in time to see the creature swooping toward Clara. The Bama Bomber stood transfixed, in ankle-deep water, his gun held out like a lollipop he was offering a child.

Bowie should have shouted a warning, but the creature's clarion call had done the job. Clara ran for the cover of the dense vegetation that sprouted from the black mud of the island. *But she was too slow.*

Any human would be too slow. You can't outrun bad luck.

And you can't beat fear.

Bowie should have dived back into the water, hit the deeper current, and allowed himself to be swept downstream. The turgid water, if it didn't kill him, would carry him to safety. If safety existed anywhere in these raw, remote mountains.

But that would mean failing another person. Even if she probably deserved it. And he still harbored some shred of chivalry, despite his casual abuse of Dove's affection.

He fought his way back toward shore, the dark water lapping and licking at him, wanting to swallow him. His boot slipped once, and he was almost gone to the safety he'd considered, but then he was knee-deep and thrashing, then on sandy soil and rocks, then in the island mud.

As he ran, the gray creature flew past the stock-still Ace.

Why didn't it attack him? What sort of predator passes up easy prey?

Maybe one that enjoyed the hunt.

Bowie didn't like that idea, so as his legs worked and his lungs pumped, water falling from his head and shoulders, he latched onto a more soothing one: Because Ace had not moved, the creature's primary sense hadn't detected him. No doubt it could smell and taste and hear, as the flared nostrils, long tongue, and oversize, peaked ears would indicate, but it seemed to mostly operate by radar.

Theory confirmed, for all the good it would do them.

The creature was forty feet from the woman, and Bowie was twenty. The creature was three times as fast.

Just before it struck, the woman reached a bristle of rhododendron, fighting her way through the slick, reptilian branches.

Bowie remembered Dove's trick from earlier. He stooped, slowing only a little, and came up with a rock the size of a cantaloupe. He hurled it through the air, not taking time to get his feet set for an accurate throw. He didn't care if he hit the creature. He just wanted to distract it.

The rock did better than distract it. The creature changed course in midair, gliding toward the rock as if it were fast-moving prey. It closed on the rock, raising its claws as if to seize it and drag it to the ground for feeding; then other senses must have kicked in and warned the creature away.

By the time it wheeled and homed in again on the woman, she was nestled inside the protective branches. Bowie couldn't see her in the gloom, only the thin beacon of her Maglite, but knew the creature would be able to smell her if it came near. Though she'd stopped moving, the rattling, rain-dripping leaves gave away her position. The creature lifted its head, ears standing erect, and sniffed.

"Shit fire," Ace said. "I reckon she wasn't good enough after all."

The creature turned its ugly head in Ace's direction, but didn't attack.

Bowie, who thought the turbulent water might help disguise his scent and movements, crept along the shoreline toward Ace. He wanted to tell the crazed bomber to shoot the thing, but figured Ace would rather shoot *him* than a beast he thought was a messenger of God.

The creature rose in the half light, slick-scaled body repelling the soft rain. It hovered over the rhododendron thicket as if searching for a way through the tangled canopy. To her credit, Clara hadn't screamed since the initial attack. Or maybe she was so frightened that the only sound she could make was mouselike squeaks.

Ace was mesmerized by the creature. His revolver dangled from one limp arm, touching his hip.

Stooped low to avoid the creature's echolocation, Bowie eased toward the killer. No doubt Ace had seen him come out of the river, but he seemed to have lost interest.

The raft.

Ace must have released it after Bowie submerged. Bowie's spirits fell. Even if he somehow managed to subdue Ace and take his gun away, kill or ward off the creature, and rescue Clara, they'd have no real means of escape. They'd either have to hike out or hole up and wait for rescue.

First things first.

The creature swooped over the thicket, nostrils flaring as it sought its prey. Bowie wondered why it was focused on the woman while two other pieces of warm-blooded meat were readily available. Maybe the creatures had senses beyond those near-supernatural ones the group had already attributed to them.

Or maybe the creatures functioned on a plane that was above that of simple feeding machines.

Maybe they were the product of intelligent design, the spawns of higher or lower powers.

Bullshit. If God existed, Connie would still be alive. So would McKay and Lane. And Dove ...

He tried not to think about the fate of those left upstream, the ones for whom he bore responsibility.

Just as Agent Jim Castle had become single-minded in his pursuit of his subjects, just as the creature was intent on sucking the life from Clara, Bowie was determined to kill Ace.

Kill.

As he eased along the licking, lapping, muddy river, he collected a couple of fist-sized stones.

"You wasn't good enough, Clara," Ace shouted. "Not in the eyes of Him who sees all!"

Keep preaching, you son of a bitch. Bowie was within ten feet of the target now, but he didn't want to throw the stones. Not because he feared missing and getting shot, but because he wanted his revenge warm and raw and red. He wanted to feel the pulse of Ace Goodall's carotid artery fade beneath his fingers.

He wanted—

Skeeeeeeeeeeeeeeeeeeeeeek.

The shriek came from above, in the shroud of mist. Another creature plummeted from the heavens.

CHAPTER FIFTY

The babe can dish it out, Farrengalli noted with admiration. Chief up there, stuck to the side of the mountain with one of the bloodsuckers on his back, didn't have half the balls of Dove Krueger.

Come to think of it, she was probably a dyke. Going around without a bra in the middle of a pack of men. Only a rug-muncher would tease them like that.

Lesbian or not, she could bring it. And right now she was bringing it against the head of the second bloodsucker. It had its arms around Farrengalli's legs, trying to climb him like a monkey up a coconut tree. Its teeth ripped the fabric of his jeans, and he was glad he'd changed out of the SealSkinz before the climb, or he'd be catching vampire herpes and whatever other shit the things carried.

Farrengalli reached for the Buck knife in his thigh holster, but the thing's ugly mouth was closing in. Farrengalli had avoided contact with the creatures so far, through luck and cunning, but now that the thing was staring him in the face (it was blind, but those balls of sour milk had a hypnotizing power all the same).

It was butt-fucking-ugly, the nostrils flared, nose and forehead wrinkled, deep pouches of loose skin around the sightless eyes. The lips were a parody of those sported by geezer rock star Mick Jagger, bloated and sneering, punctuated by two long, slightly curving, and yellowed fangs.

The mouth was open, filled with blackness deeper than any night, and Farrengalli could imagine the bottomless void beyond, a belly that housed an endless hunger. *But damned if you're chomping into this Italian white boy.*

He raised a boot and drove its rubber heel into the creature's face. Something gave, bone or cartilage or whatever hid beneath that lizardlike skin. Dove whipped the doubled rope across its back, striking several times in quick succession. The creature didn't seem to acknowledge the blows. Instead, its Jaggeresque lips, now drooling a slick strand of gray fluid, worked along Farrengalli's thigh.

"Get it off me," he yelled again. The thin but corded arms wrapped around his legs again. He couldn't kick free.

The falling darkness, the rising mist, the stink of the river, all combined to confuse him. *This is a hell of a way to get a book deal, but keep your eyes on the prize.*

Dove gave the doubled rope some slack until there was a loop at the end. Then she flipped it over the bat-beast's head, yanking back as it dropped below the pointy chin.

She gave a violent lift of her arms, tightening the makeshift noose around the thing's throat. Planting a knee in its back, she arched, straightening until she applied pressure with all her weight. Farrengalli expected the bat-beast to start bucking like a rodeo bronco, with Dove holding on for the ride of her life.

Wait a sec. Those fuckers don't breathe. *So you sure can't choke one to death.*

He'd heard Lane's, Bowie Whitlock's, and Dove's theories on the nature of the beasts. Chupacabra, the goat-suckers. A lost species. A mutant strain of oversize bats. Even the Chief, who currently looked to be locked in a wrestling match tougher than anything the Olympics had thrown at him, had come up with the out-the-ass theory of the Raven Mocker.

The dumb redskin. These things didn't have any feathers at all.

While Dove wrangled with the creature, Farrengalli freed his knife. He slashed sideways, opening a seam beneath the creature's left eye. Soft drops of gray snot leaked out. The gray fluid spattered his jeans, and he wondered if skin contact would cause infection.

No time to worry about that now, because the creature went nuts. It flailed its claws at Farrengalli, coming way too close to his crotch, shredding his jeans down to the white threads. One of the thin, spindly fingertips broke through the cloth and jabbed him like a ten-penny nail.

"Hey, asshole, that *hurt*."

"The head," Dove said. "You have to mess with its motor controls."

Farrengalli imagined some sort of radar equipment in the thing's brain, tucked away in a chamber like the command helm of a submarine. Cut off the head, the body dies, someone had once said. Or maybe it went, "A fish rots from the head first."

Either way, Farrengalli was ready to roll with it.

He swept the knife forward, the eight-inch blade digging into the creature's eye socket. The eyeball *plopped*, oozing rancid buttermilk.

"The brain," Dove said between clenched teeth. "Get the brain."

Farrengalli didn't think the bat-beasts had any brains. He'd watched the vampire movies, same as everybody, and to kill a vampire you drove a stake in its heart. Zombies were the things you killed with head wounds.

But Farrengalli figured he might as well play the odds and do both. As Dove held the skewered skull in place, he rammed forward until the Buck knife was buried to the hilt. He figured the thing deserved a good frontal lobotomy just for ruining his jeans. He twisted the knife handle back and forth, gouging.

The Jagger lips flapped, and Farrengalli wouldn't have been surprised to hear "(Can't Get No) Satisfaction" coming from them.

Its limbs slackened and it flopped forward, limp, across Farrengalli's waist. He crab-crawled out from under it, giving it another kick for good measure. Dove whiplashed the rope, pulling it from the thing's neck like floss from the tight gap in two rotted teeth.

Farrengalli went to his knees, raised the gory blade, and plunged it where he guessed the thing's heart would be.

Tired, his limbs shaking, he shoved the creature to the edge of the rock shelf with his boot. With one last kick, the thing tumbled off and into the thick mist below. He didn't hear it hit.

He turned to Dove. "That will teach those sons of–"

A wet, flexing snake brushed his shoulder and he dropped the knife, squealing in surprise.

"Don't fill your drawers," Dove said, snatching out with her hand. "It's a rope."

"Hurry up," Raintree shouted from the dark notch above. "Before more of them come."

CHAPTER FIFTY-ONE

"Better save the batteries," Dove said.

Raintree, crouching at the lip of the cave, checked the bars on the cell phone again. Nothing. It was an inept tool, an artifact from an alien world that wouldn't function in such a primitive environment. He felt silly holding it, like a Neanderthal pointing a laser weapon at a mastodon.

They had divided up the pitons, two each, as their only weapons. Farrengalli took the penlight, saying he wanted to explore the cave. Raintree hadn't argued, even though, strategically, the group should stay together in case of another attack. In truth, he wanted to be alone with Dove.

"I'm not sure it will work even if we get to the top," Raintree said, looking out over the dark valley. Though the rain had stopped, the clouds hung low and heavy over the gorge. The hidden moon provided some filtered backlight, but the sky was almost as black as the cave's interior. The river was completely obscured by mist, and the drop might as well have been bottomless.

"The FBI agent believed it would."

"Him. I think he was cracking up. Didn't you hear him blurting out random sentences, like he was talking to somebody who wasn't there?"

She glanced behind her, and then lowered her voice. She was close enough that he could feel her breath on his ear. "What do you think happened down there, with him and Farrengalli?"

"Who knows? I don't trust either of them. I can see the agent pulling rank and taking the raft. Like I said, he's going nuts."

"He was hurt pretty badly."

"Crazy people sometimes ignore their bodies." *And I'm star witness for the prosecution in that trial.*

He tilted the cell phone for a moment, casting the green glow of its screen on her face. Her cheeks were dirty, hair tangled and greasy, and a long scratch stitched her forehead. But her brown eyes were unfazed, wide and beautiful and hopeful, pupils large in the darkness.

"Well, we're here now. What choice do we have?" she asked.

"Two choices. Go up or go down."

"Or stay here."

"For how long? Even if the Bama Bomber makes it out of here, do you really think he's going to send a rescue team? Do you think he'll let Bowie live once they make it to the lake?"

He caught her sharp intake of breath, the wince of inner pain.

"Sorry," he said. "We just have to be realistic. We have to keep it together if we want to get out of here alive."

Like you're one to talk about getting it together. Already, he was starting to itch, to feel the crab-crawl of addiction across his skin. The night was the worst, for some reason, as if his body didn't want to shut down and his brain craved fuel and sedation at the same time.

"We should have already been dead," Dove said. "You saved us."

"We all saved us. I just got lucky."

Luck, hell. He wanted to tell her how close he had come to falling after losing his grip. About that moment of desperation, the rush of fear that even modern pharmaceuticals couldn't suppress. Not fear for his life, but fear of facing survival without his medicine bag. But the pine branch had held, the brain-skewered creature's corpse dropped away, and he'd scrambled to the cave, set an anchor, and swung the line down to the ledge.

"We're going to need a lot more luck." She reached out and touched his hand. Though her fingers were calloused and ragged from the climb, they moved with a smooth, reptilian grace, up along his thumb. Raintree focused all his attention on the sensation, and he wasn't sure whether it was the painkillers, the speed, or the tranquilizer, but something was pumping through his bloodstream with a full load of electricity. She hesitated a moment, squeezing his hand gently until the cell phone closed. "Better save the batteries."

Her mouth was close to his cheek, her breath sweet despite the long day's trauma. Raintree turned, wondering if their lips would meet, either accidentally or on purpose. As if there were ever any difference.

But she was already gone. She had eased back into the concealing ink of the cave.

Raintree looked out across the valley once more. Even in the dim, filtered light, he would be able to see the creatures if they made an aerial attack. He believed, based on their habits, that they wouldn't attack unless the prey—*odd to think of ourselves as such*—was out in the open. He recognized, on a deeper, intellectual level where the drugs swam with lazy strokes, that he knew nothing about these creatures, and didn't think they could ever be understood, even if the finest scientists on the planet had a crack at them.

He decided he and his companions should at least wait until morning, when they'd have a better chance of fending off attack. A little rest would help. They could take turns, one keeping watch while the other two slept. He thought of lying in the dark next to Dove, the two of them drawing close to one another for heat. He was letting his mind wander when the pinprick of light danced deep in the cave's guts.

The light grew larger, brighter, and then cast a cone of bluish white that revealed Farrengalli's arm. He joined them at the mouth of the cave, then flicked off the light. They stood there, silhouettes barely visible. "Nothing back thataway," he said.

"How far did you go?" Dove asked.

"Hard to say. All looks the same after a while. Two hundred feet, maybe. Started branching off in places and I was afraid I'd get lost."

"This changes things," Raintree said.

"How so, Chief?"

"I thought we should rest for a while, try to get some sleep, and keep one person on watch at the mouth of the cave. But you heard what the FBI guy said. They had been trapped in a cave when an explosion set them free."

"You think they live in caves, then? Like this one?"

"Who knows? The point is, we don't know. So we'd have to keep two guards, one up front and one deeper in the cave."

"Cletus Christ," Farrengalli said. "You let me go in there knowing vampires might be waiting?"

"We don't know anything," Dove said. "He's just trying

to think ahead, consider all the options. Maybe if you kept your mouth shut once in a while, you'd think of something, too."

They all fell silent for a moment. Somewhere below, an owl hooted. Such an ordinary, natural sound took on a plaintive note because it was from a sane, normal world they would never again experience. Their lives had been changed, and whether they lived another fifteen minutes or fifty years, they would never outrun the nightmares that would forever stay one step behind their dreams.

"Okay," Raintree said. "I'll watch the back end first shift. Give me the light."

Farrengalli handed it to him without protest. "Guess that means I got to be a goddamned gentleman and let Dove sleep."

"Here," Dove said, unbuckling the band of her wristwatch and passing it to Raintree. "Two-hour shifts. In six hours, we can catch the dawn's early light."

Raintree pressed the button on the timepiece, and the tiny LED showed it was after 11 o'clock. Time flew when you were scared shitless.

"Okay." He played the light inside the cave until he found a spot where eons of sand and grit had swept into a passable mattress. "Here's a bed," he said. "Wish I had a midnight snack and a pillow to go with it."

Dove sat on the sand and curled into a ball on her side. Two coils of rope lay beside her, along with a small pile of carabiners.

"Hell, if you're going to play hero, I might as well mind my manners," Farrengalli said, unbuttoning his shirt. He took off the garment and draped it over Dove, his sweaty muscles glinting in the weak light. Then he moved to the lip of the cave and sat on a large rock, looking over the valley like Rodin's Thinker with a hangover.

Raintree aimed the thin beam of light in front of him and entered his own private hell.

CHAPTER FIFTY-TWO

She could hear Ace's angels above her, their flicking wings and occasional high-pitched whistles reminding her how close they were.

Clara had worked her way into the rhododendron thicket, where the dense leaves blocked the last shreds of dying daylight. Each time she rubbed against a knobby, scaly branch, she thought it was the arm of one of the creatures. Her hair tangled in a forked branch, and she ripped the damp strands free. She wanted to collapse, throw her face into the rotted leaves and loam of the forest floor, and surrender.

The old Clara, the one who sought pain and danger, the suicidal coward, would have given up long ago. That Clara wouldn't have had the courage to run from Ace when the trip wire triggered the bombs. That Clara wouldn't have stuck with him later, when he continued his cruel, abusive ways.

But she also wasn't strong enough to make it on her own. Ace wasn't her savior, and she realized she had shifted her dependence to Bowie. Which is why, in the raft, she had hesitated when Ace asked for the pistol.

She wished she had the pistol now.

Because, for the first time, she had something to defend, a reason to live beyond the hedonistic pursuit of slow or fast death.

Ace talked about the angels as allies, but Clara didn't see them as something God would send to Earth. She'd been willingly screwed and tortured by some of the finest nihilists and atheists in the business, and had endured a wild six-week fling with a Satanist, whose smoke and mirrors and candles and chants just grew completely corny after a while. She'd sensed no evil in that self-proclaimed "Dark Acolyte," just as she sensed no evil in these angels.

Like all the other things that were claimed to be "evil," when you looked right into the heart of them, they were just single-mindedly stupid.

Leaves rattled above, sending down a shower of drops. One of the creatures was trying to penetrate the canopy.

"She wasn't good enough," she heard Ace say for the third time, as if talking to some invisible higher power.

Maybe she wasn't worth a damn, but she was getting smarter by the second. The creatures worked on radar and smell. Which meant if she kept perfectly still, they couldn't locate her. Maybe the serpentine branches would confuse them. Would they be able to smell her with all the odors rising from the river mud?

The bigger question: Why weren't they attacking Ace and Bowie? Especially Ace, who had stood and watched while the creature flew past his face and chased her.

She shivered. Maybe Ace really was protected by God, as he believed.

The light. She'd forgotten about the flashlight attached to her helmet. Were the creatures blind? She reached up an unsteady hand and flicked it off.

Something rattled just above her head. She ducked lower. It couldn't hear her. Not with all the noise it was making, thrashing the wet leaves.

But it could smell her. Smell something that made her far more appealing than the two men.

She could only think of two things. Either her hormonal glands, her vaginal scent, had brought them sniffing the way she had attracted the juvenile-delinquent boys in Ohio.

Or else, through some strange sense she couldn't begin to understand, they knew she carried a young, tender bud in her womb. Something they might find a rare delicacy, a bloody treat. Or maybe to be used for another purpose.

You're not getting him. One way or another.

Claws raked her hair, closed, yanked some strands out by the roots. She endured the attack without a whimper. She'd been hurt harder by better.

But the arm behind the claws, though she couldn't see it, thrust with renewed ferocity, and she could tell from the snapping branches that it had detected her position. That meant the other one would be right behind it.

And she'd closed herself in, rolled the dice all or nothing on the rhododendrons. She had no weapon, and she didn't think she'd be able to slip past the Gordian knot of branches to make a run for it.

"This way," she heard somebody hiss, where she believed the thicket gave way to the greater forest. Bowie.

Did she trust yet another man?

Did it matter?

She rolled away from the sweeping claw, thumping her head against a protruding root. The loam was slick and smelled like mushrooms. She kept her face close to it as she wriggled forward like an inchworm.

The claw snaked around her ankle and tightened. Her leg was yanked hard enough to nearly tear it from its socket. Then she was being lifted off the ground.

Impossible. She'd seen the size of the creatures. She was twice as heavy as they were.

But she couldn't deny the weightless moment. She grabbed blindly for branches as her body rose upside down in the stinking, moist darkness, rhododendron tearing her clothes, water or blood trailing under her arms.

Her fingers closed over the slippery cable of a branch, and for a moment the upward movement stopped. Then she was ripped free, spinning in dizzy circles, and below, in the gloaming of a fantasy-land mist, she made out Ace's slim form, his pale face looking up at her without expression.

Fifty feet up in the air, now hanging high above the river, she arched her neck and looked at the thing that was carrying her. She had been wrong: it wasn't an arm that held her ankle, it was a foot. Her skin chafed beneath the powerful grip, but she kicked anyway, believing a drop to her death was better than whatever fate the creature might have in store for her.

And the thing inside her....

Little Robert Wayne.

She couldn't let them have him.

But she couldn't curl her body enough to grab at and attack the creature, whose deformed wings seemed barely to ripple on the night current. Its grip on her was too strong to escape.

She let her neck relax and rolled her eyes to look down at the wide ribbon of the Unegama River. In the scant light, the wet rocks of the gorge walls glistened like jewels.

Ace said the creatures came down from heaven. She wondered if this one were returning there, or if God's orders had been misinterpreted and twisted, or just plain forgotten altogether.

Clara Bannister closed her eyes and folded her hands across her belly. She'd never had a choice between heaven or hell, and she saw no reason for things to change now.

CHAPTER FIFTY-THREE

Bowie should have made a run for it. The woods were waiting, dark and dense enough to allow him to evade the creatures. Two full days of hiking, as long as he kept in one direction, and he'd eventually reach a highway, a house, or someone with a motorized camper. Springs would provide water, and some late berries were probably in season.

He'd find safety, give directions, and wait until the whole chaotic mess died down, the government agencies and police and rescue squads sated, the creatures eradicated in the type of wide-scale military sweep that would rival the invasion of a small, troublesome dictatorship.

When the last bullet was fired and the last corpse collected, Bowie would be allowed to slink away to the Missouri Breaks, to a lone, thick-walled cabin in the hills, where he could add this freshest failure to his menagerie of memories. With exercise and a proper diet, he'd live another fifty years. Over eighteen thousand nights in which to lay his head down and endure its swirling stew of accusations and guilt. Nights when dreams, as they rose like rats from sewer holes, would pick at the torn meat and nibble down the long list that no longer had Connie alone at the top.

Yes, failure was an option. It had always been an option. And he recognized that revenge against Ace Goodall, no matter how sweet, was not as spiritually fulfilling as saving Clara would be. And, since Clara was pregnant, maybe he'd get a two-fer in the eyes of God, wipe the slate clean for the loss of Connie and Dove, if not the rest of his group who had been slaughtered. So he'd bypassed the mesmerized and dazed Ace, who could have easily shot him in the back, and dashed toward the rhododendron, yelling and waving his arms, hoping to draw the attention of the two creatures. They ignored him, just as they had ignored Ace.

When Clara had been ripped from the thicket and carried across the night sky, Bowie had emerged from the woods and approached Ace. Bowie, the legendary tour guide, wasn't even fit for prey, wasn't good enough to serve as monster meat. A clean death would be a happy ending.

"They took my baby," Ace said.

"Shoot me, you ugly son of a bitch."

Ace lifted the Colt almost as an afterthought, the action of an absentminded mass murderer and serial killer. "I thought they was going to eat her."

Bowie was calm. It would probably hurt like the Devil's hot sauce for a split second, but the peace that followed would more than make amends. "A bullet, please."

"God sent His angels, and they took *her*. Not me."

"Maybe God left you here for a purpose. Maybe God needs you to kill me. Listen to Him."

Ace actually cocked his head and put a hand to his ear, in what would have been considered a display of overacting if a movie camera had been rolling. "I don't hear nothing. He used to talk to me, but now I don't hear nothing."

The clouds had thinned a little and the rain had stopped. The moonlight spread across the night sky in melodramatic purple wadding. The barrel of the pistol glinted, and its dark round eye looked into Bowie's heart.

"He led me down by the still waters and left me there." Ace glanced above, exposing the stubbly knot of his Adam's apple.

"The waters don't seem all that still to me," Bowie said. "Class VI plus."

"They took my baby. God took my baby."

Ace, who had taken half-a-dozen lives without showing a shred of regret, and who had just lost his lover to an unknown and possibly supernatural species, harbored no room for self-reflection. It confirmed what Bowie had always heard about the most successful killers: They were sociopathic, lacking morality, possessing loose wires and corroded contacts where the higher-order brain housed its sense of right and wrong.

So, one more wouldn't hurt, right? God wouldn't hold it against his special little agent. If God were truly fair and merciful, Ace Goodall would even get an additional reward for eradicating one more cockroach in the Great Big Bug Motel. Maybe an extra string on the harp, or a golden-cross tattoo on one wing.

"Maybe God knows something we don't," Bowie said, stepping toward Ace, goading him.

Ace nodded as if Bowie had served up a sage's helping of spiritual smoke. "Him that has the plan."

"Right."

Bowie was three feet away now, instinctively flinching in anticipation of the .32-caliber bullet. But Ace let him come, until Bowie wrapped his hand around the pistol's barrel and pulled it from Ace's limp fingers.

Shit. What now?

"We got to save her," Ace said.

"She's probably dead by now."

Ace dropped to his knees and grabbed his head, squeezing it between his hands like a rotten melon he was trying to smash.

"She ain't *dead*," he shouted, voice breaking and rising to an unsettling, keening pitch that roared back and forth across the gorge, so loud even the lapping, churning river couldn't suppress it. Then he flopped forward in a quivering seizure, limbs twitching, fingers clawing at the coarse sand of the riverbank. The schizophrenic killer vomited a staccato rant of strange syllables.

Bowie could only stare transfixed, the Colt Python as heavy as a dead snake in his hand, as Ace spoke in tongues.

CHAPTER FIFTY-FOUR

Nice.

In the temperate bowels of the cave, Raintree had perched the penlight on a rock shelf. Here, the cave angled down and the walls were worn smooth, as if the channel had once carried water. The rock contained striations of crystal that caught and reflected the battery-powered light. Other layers in the granite revealed sandstone, a crumbling, chalk-white rock, and even a vein of coal. But Raintree wasn't here for a geology class. He'd already taken that one in college, the easy three-hour credit known around campus as "Rocks for Jocks."

He'd gone at least a hundred yards, at one point squeezing through a narrow crevice that had filled him with claustrophobia. But now he was alone to seek the Spirit Guide.

Raintree thought the inner search should be conducted in the forest, at the primal moment of first light, when the nocturnal creatures shut their eyes and gave way to the day shift. But that was cheating. Many species of animals could be found in the forest, and it would be difficult to know which one was the chosen spirit. Raintree's vision quest would follow a hard path, so that when the good medicine came, he would know it for what it was.

But first things first.

He rummaged in the medicine bag and came out with

three vials. The oxycodone was half gone, but he still had a good palmful left. Enough to put a damper on his central nervous system, though probably not enough to kill him.

He had four amphetamines left, Black Beauties, strong enough to make his dark hair stand on end. The third vial contained diazepam, better known under the trade name Valium. About a dozen of those were left if he really needed sleep and tranquility.

Under perfect conditions, he would time his medication so he would ease between moods. Oxy in the morning to numb the edges, then a Black Beauty for a midday pick-me-up, then Valium to blend the afternoon into a smooth concoction. From there, the choices were nearly limitless. Well, actually, they were quite limited, but the choice between a balls-tingling, eyelid-quivering speed buzz and a thick-tongued ride down the Oxy Highway seemed like a no-lose opportunity.

But this was a special circumstance. The painkillers kept his muscles from screaming at their overtaxed state, and the Valium allowed his mind to entertain images of the Raven Mockers without succumbing to a fit of fear. He'd held off on the speed, figuring he'd need it in the morning to make it to the top of Attacoa, the stone chimney the white settlers called Babel Tower. But there was one special ingredient that spiced the stew of his vision quest.

He pinched down into the medicine bag and came up with a piece of tinfoil. Some Southwestern tribes had used peyote, belladonna, jimson weed, tobacco, or hemp blossoms in their spiritual ceremonies.

Raintree figured the Cherokee vision quest needed a serious upgrade. He pulled out the one-thousand-microgram dose of Mr. Natural LSD, concocted in a

Berkeley lab by a bald, bearded professor. The acid manufacturer had been a client in one of Raintree's fitness gyms, and when the man had pulled a muscle doing dead lifts, Raintree offered him half an oxycodone tablet. The man traded for four, giving up an eighth of an ounce of sensimilla bud in return. A lasting and mutually rewarding friendship was born, with Raintree having a dozen doctors writing pill prescriptions and the professor cranking out an alphabet soup of illegal substances.

A tiny, sane part of Raintree's mind, the one where the pills hadn't shorted out the circuits, knew this was no time for an acid trip. But it was shouted down by the other part, the seeking part, the unhappy and selfish part. The part that had wanted this trip in the first place.

He wished the cave harbored an underground spring, because the speed, the climb, and the assault had made him thirsty. But the cave, at least this far down into the mountain, was only moist, where water seeped between layers of stone and didn't collect enough for drinking.

He unwrapped the foil and raised the dose of acid to his mouth. He paused, wondering what sort of ritual was required. A tribal chant, an improvised parody of old ghost dances, or maybe a paean to the buffalo spirit.

The Cherokee, who lived in houses and had a written language at the time of their forced removal from the Southern Appalachians, would have been better off as savages. All the written word had done was allow contracts between the tribe and the U.S. government. Those promises were as broken as their spirits on a thousand-mile walk where disease, famine, and exhaustion took them by the hundreds. No wonder many of the Cherokee had abandoned their Great Spirit, left it behind in the territory now owned by the White Man. They deserved each other.

In the thin shaft of the flashlight's beam, he examined the scratches and runnels on his forearms. Even now, some sort of infection or contamination could be racing through his system, poisoning his brain. Raintree wanted his own brand of poison.

The acid was soaked into a tiny square of paper, waiting to form a mushroom cloud in the user's head. Lysergic acid diethylamide was known to scramble serotonin levels, distort perception, and confound the DEA. Raintree wasn't a chronic acid head. After a brief love affair with the drug, like most space cadets, he'd found the experience was best when saved for a special occasion.

Like a date with his spirit guide.

He put the dose to his tongue and swallowed. He wouldn't sleep tonight, though he could probably ramp down on the amphetamine doses and turn up the volume on the Valium. For the next twelve hours, he wouldn't be able to fully trust his senses. The discipline and self-control that had made him a wrestling champion would be given up to uncertainty, confusion, and a golden, illuminated doorway to the Other.

On an intellectual level, he knew any encounter with a spirit guide would be a hallucination. The goal of a vision quest, as least in the original form, was to push yourself to the limits of endurance, exhaustion, and hunger, then fall into a stupor of delirium. In the twenty-first century, vision quests were chartered field trips run by corporations that provided satellite television, refrigeration, and catered dinners so the customers could experience their inner selves in comfort and style.

Raintree switched off the light and listened. A low

moan ran through the dark beyond. The wind. The night breeze finding cracks in the ancient stone.

He was well aware that he might die while tripping. Some LSD users flipped out, developed schizophrenic delusions, and went into psychotic fugues. In such a state, Raintree would be helpless against the attacking creatures. He touched the pitons in his belt and smiled.

Somehow, he didn't figure it that way.

He recalled the surge of fear, the struggle on the cliff wall, the creature clinging to his back. And his thrusting of the steel spike into the creature's head.

That was power. That was a vision worth pursuing and celebrating.

The trip of life and death.

Did God have bones?

The wind changed pitch and became a whale's submarine song.

Salamanders became oil in these mountains.

He wasn't sure how long he sat in the dark. The blackness pressed against him, snug as SealSkinz. He checked the watch. A quarter after twelve. Half an hour had passed since ingestion. His feet were balloons, his hands were sand. They seeped toward the flashlight.

He flicked it on. He couldn't tell which way to go. Both directions looked the same, and either could be the throat of Hell.

He sat for another ten minutes. Ten minutes according to the watch. In real time, as marked by his malfeasant synapses, he was still in the Now.

Shit. Maybe tripping wasn't such a good idea. Vision quests were for the birds, man.

He giggled. Hawks, falcons, and other birds of prey

were popular manifestations of the warrior spirit. But since authentic vision quests had been the domain of aspiring warriors, that wasn't surprising. What Cherokee brave wanted to slink back into camp and report seeing the bluebird of happiness?

That brought another giggle, and his voice sounded much too loud in the stifling space. Echoes were like footsteps on the gritty cavern floor. Like footsteps ...

He thumbed the piton and slid it from his belt.

The footsteps were in tune with his breathing, with the beating of his pulse in his ears. His skin itched. He cut the light and listened to the oceanic roar of his lungs. Listened.

In the dark, the Great Spirit came to him. Not as a predator, not as a bat, not as an animal long extinct in the Southern Appalachians, like an elk or red wolf.

No, this was a rabbit. It came up from the cold, clammy darkness with its own luminescence, eyes casting a green, milky light. The thing was blind, because it kept bumping into stones. It paused near Raintree's feet, sniffing the air with its ears laid back against its neck. Then it parted its lips—showing two sharpened incisors. The bunny faded to gray, then to black, its eyes dousing themselves. The teeth were the last to disappear.

Then Raintree realized he'd been staring at the LED readout on the watch.

The numbers were upside down, disembodied characters floating in the ether. He took a Valium, chewing it so it would race through his stomach lining unencumbered. He checked the watch again. Nearly one o'clock. His shift would be over in less than an hour. He'd let Farrengalli sleep, and then he and Dove could—

What if Farrengalli had fallen asleep already?

What if the creatures had come into the cave and taken Dove?

He stood, swiveling his head, looking for the lesser darkness that would indicate the mouth of the cave.

That way. Fifty-fifty chance.

He cut the light, but kept it in his left hand, a piton in the right. Ready for anything. Bending, tiptoeing, ears alert for any rustle of wings. A Bugs Bunny cartoon came to mind, the classic episode where Elmer Fudd stopped in his sneaking and told the viewing audience, "Shhh. We-ah hunting wabbits." Raintree didn't laugh.

"Follow the light," preached the New Age sages, those who sold remote control crystal power for a limited time only, $19.95 plus shipping and handling.

Raintree followed the light, the bluish thread that seemed so small against the oppressive onyx. He expected the beam to be snuffed out at any moment. Behind him, hopping, hopping, hopping. Whiskers whispering. Wabbits walking.

Must be going the wrong way.

He checked the watch again. He'd only been walking for two minutes.

The beam reflected a silver flash on the floor of the cave. Raintree retrieved the wrapper of a granola bar, a ProVentures Plenty, containing whole wheat, oats, and "pure dehydrated cane juice." The fancy, feel-good name for sugar. Farrengalli was holding out on them. He must have taken all the rations they'd left by the river for the wounded FBI agent.

Raintree played the light behind him, saw no fierce lepine fangs, no menacing, erect ears. He rushed on, sweat breaking out under his arms, soaking his bare chest and shoulders. Even his sense of smell was distorted. The stink of his body resembled rotted roses.

Harsh breathing, whimpers of pain, suppressed grunts. He heard them before he reached the wider opening of the cave's mouth.

They had been attacked.

While Raintree was on his goofy trip, searching for a Great Spirit who had packed his travois and headed West long ago. He broke into a run, stumbled, fell to his knees, touched the medicine bag as if it were a Catholic's rosary beads.

Rising, he plunged forward, tossing the light aside, gripping the piton so hard his fingers ached.

He braced himself. If he had wanted a vision, a hell of an opportunity awaited: He imagined the red, ripped flesh, the creatures perched on the bodies of his traveling companions while their heat faded and their blood filled unnatural cavities. He would kill them all, make them pay, use revenge as the Higher Power that had never been strong enough to pull him from the well of addiction. Rage would be his new drug.

Not that he gave a damn about Farrengalli, but Dove didn't deserve—

As he entered the gray spill of leaking moonlight, it took his acid-drenched cerebrum a long second, a big stretch of Now, to make sense of what he was seeing.

No creatures.

Farrengalli, half-naked, sweating, and grunting, toiling over the struggling, whimpering Dove, pinning her back against the rock and tearing at her clothes.

Raintree gave a war whoop and went for the kill.

CHAPTER FIFTY-FIVE

Red.

The river running red, cliffs on fire, sky filled with flickering orange.

Trumpets and screams, lava gouging a rut deep into the Earth, hot electricity sparking in the air.

Ace's belly boiled, his head clanged with the din of Armageddon. This was Revelation's promise made good, the seventh seal broken, the whore of Babylon rising.

The intensity of the vision sliced at him like knives at an altar, torturing a sacrificial lamb in anger over its innocence.

God was delivering. He that sat on high was dishing it out big-time.

And Ace, His servant, His vessel, His holy antenna on the mortal plane, could only accept and endure, and let the message pass through him. Coarse sand clung to his lips as he spewed forth words in a thousand lost languages. He didn't know what they meant, and he didn't care.

He couldn't crawl away from the thundering liquid blaze behind him. All he could do was wait for the storm to pass, or to engulf and swallow him, as God saw fit. And, oh, the red raw glory of Rapture. Praise be to Jesus, our Father who art in heaven, who laid me down by still waters, in sickness and in health—

"Get up."

Ace's tongue pressed against his jagged teeth. Blood. He'd bitten his lip.

Ace lifted his head. Red had gone to dark, though tiny streaks of lightning cracked the edges of the black shell above. The river was no longer in flames. It churned and whispered and hissed, a snake without end, sliding over the world in search of the hole that led to Hell.

"Get up."

This wasn't God's voice. God had a deep, cruel, demanding voice—almost like that of his real father, the mortal man who had shot angry jism into a throwaway slut three decades before. God wasn't talking to Ace. Not at the moment, but he'd told Ace plenty enough already.

Ace blinked. *I've gone blind. The lion tore out my eyes.*

He rose to his knees, running a gritty hand over his cheeks. Blood. Goddamned blood. He wiped, blinked again, hung between panic and surrender.

Then he saw that it was night, and he remembered the gorge, the raft, and the angels. Clara. And his baby in her belly.

And Bowie, who held Ace's pistol. "Get up," Bowie said a third time.

"They took her," Ace said.

"They took other people, too. Some of them because of you."

"You don't know." Ace stood, his knees weak and wobbly. "You don't know what they're going to do. But I saw it."

"I saw it, too. She's dead by now."

"No, she's not dead. I tell you, I *saw* it." For just a moment, Bowie's silhouette rippled and transformed, became tall and brick red, scaly, eyes smoldering with the moon's dead and buried light.

"Doesn't matter anymore. You didn't kill me, and I don't really feel like killing you."

"They took her to the cave. Lots of bones there. Put her on the rock."

"The rock?"

"The Changing Rock."

"You can tell the forensic psychologist all about it when you stand trial."

Ace laughed, from so deep in his gut that it hurt. "You think you can *arrest* me? Like God cares about this cops-and-robbers horseshit? There's only one law and one order and it don't matter shit for you and what you want."

"Right now, I have the gun, so I'm the law." Bowie, speaking just loudly enough to be heard over the river, his head held erect and his glare fixed on Ace like the mean teacher he'd had in sixth grade. Even in the bad light, there was no mistaking those eyes.

Jesus, the fucker means business. Forgive him, for he knows not what the hell he doeth, but the river-rat bastard is dead serious.

"They're going to put her on the Changing Rock. They're going to take my baby. Make it one of *them*."

"They're animals. Vicious, cunning animals. Call them what you want, make up some comic-book legend, it doesn't change anything."

"We got to hurry," Ace said. He began walking away from the gun, and then broke into a crippled jog.

"Stop or I'll shoot, you son of a bitch," Bowie shouted behind him. "God knows, I've earned the right."

"Go ahead," Ace shouted back. "You can't kill me. You can only make me deader."

He ran along the river, knees and lungs on fire, blood sweet in his mouth. God had showed him where to go. God didn't show the whole picture, because it had never been that way. Part of the mystery and beauty of the visions was that God gave him a few pieces to the puzzle and Ace had to sort out the rest. He only wished it didn't make his head hurt so damned much.

CHAPTER FIFTY-SIX

Farrengalli was close to nailing her when he heard the shriek.

She was so hot, and had been such a teasing bitch the entire trip, that he didn't give a damn that he might get clawed, bitten, and bagged for a trophy at any moment. This was his first chance at her alone, and she was going to love it or else.

It wasn't easy to get the Big Boy Boomeroo up when fear was doing a shrivel number, but he intended to bag a trophy of his own. She clawed at his face, drawing blood, and he liked a little fight in a woman. But Dove was putting up more than a little fight—she slammed a knee into his thigh, nearly crushing his testicles, but the pain only made him more determined.

His turgid length thrust forward like a snake seeking heat. Once the big boy got rolling, it liked to finish the ride. It was only fucking natural.

But even the Boomeroo couldn't withstand the effects of a balls-clenching shriek from the throat of a bloodsucking animal. And the monster had come out of nowhere, because the sky over the gorge had been quiet, only the occasional red wink of a distant jet to mar the clouds, stars, and smudge of moon.

Farrengalli barely had time to turn his head from Dove's angry hisses when the creature struck him, flying sideways to ram into his shoulder. As Farrengalli was knocked across the rocky terrain, the slow-motion tumble knocked some thoughts together:

...Dove didn't want this as bad as he figured...

...the Boomeroo was flopping like a bobble-head doll, right out in the open where the creature could rip it away like a monkey plucking a banana ...

...the creature had attacked not from the sky, but from the rear of the cave ...

...meaning the redskin had let them down, not covered their asses, sold them down the river...

Then he was rolling away from the mangling grip of the beast, trying to get up and run, hoping it would attack Dove instead, but it tackled him around the ankles, and this one was *huge*, not chimp-sized like the others. And the son of a bitch was strong.

"You goddamned rapist!" the creature yelled, and Farrengalli elbowed the thing in the head before the words registered.

The redskin.

Gone off the deep end. Grinding his shoulder into Farrengalli's gut, lifting him and slamming him onto his back. Raintree did some kind of homo wrestling move, then had Farrengalli pinned on his belly, his arms tucked under Farrengalli's armpits, hands locked behind Farrengalli's skull, applying enough pressure to nearly snap his neck.

Farrengalli tried to roll away, but the man knew his stuff. Farrengalli's knees were scraped and raw, and he couldn't twist free. He remembered something he'd seen on World Wrestling Federation broadcasts, and though the matches were staged, the violent intent seemed real enough.

Farrengalli jerked his head back hard, smashing it into the broad cartilage of Raintree's nose. The full-nelson headlock loosened, and Farrengalli drove backward with his elbow again, causing the breath to *whooosh* out of his opponent. Twisting, he managed to work a knee into the Cherokee's crotch.

The man may have been an Olympic wrestler, but he didn't know shit about fighting dirty.

Farrengalli kicked again, breaking free, crab-crawling away. "Hold on, Chief!"

In the muted moonlight, Raintree looked like something out of a Frederick Remington painting, savage, primitive, deadly. The Injun was on the warpath. He pulled the piton from his belt and closed in.

Farrengalli backed up to the lip of the cave, holding his hands apart. "Easy, fellow," he said, as if Raintree were a rabid, growling dog.

His pupils are HUGE.

Raintree hunched, tensing his body as if preparing to leap. If he did, his momentum would knock them both into the gorge. Farrengalli could try to step aside, like they did in the movies, but he wasn't a stunt man and there was no safety net below.

"She wanted it!" Farrengalli yelled. "She begged me for it!"

He was aware of the Boomeroo in its now-flaccid state, exposed and dangling, where one blow with the crude blade of the piton would leave it laying in the dirt like a half-eaten, ketchup-drenched hot dog at a Labor Day cookout.

Raintree eased two steps closer, the tension in his muscles almost palpable. The distant whisper of the river fought for attention in Farrengalli's roaring eardrums.

"Robert!" Dove called from the cave.

Raintree's pupils were black holes. Farrengalli looked left, then right, for a rock or something he could throw. He'd had a piton lying beside him while taking care of bidness with the fox, but the suddenness and ferocity of Raintree's assault had caught him off guard.

"Robert," Dove said, her voice calmer now.

"Listen to her," Farrengalli said. "She'll tell you." He licked his lips. He shouldn't have eaten all those granola bars. The water bottle he'd kept secret from the others was hidden in a crevice inside the cave. River water, but water nonetheless. If he got out of this mess alive, he'd drink nothing but Canadian beer for a solid week.

Raintree hesitated, though his eyes remained just as wild, his biceps twitching. He finally spoke. "Does white man speak with forked tongue?"

"What the fuck?" Farrengalli said.

Raintree raised the piton, letting its tapered steel catch the moonlight. "Does he speak the truth, Dove?"

"Come here," she said.

Raintree stood poised like a cigar store Indian, in a mockery of nobility that was all the more preposterous because it so closely resembled the real thing.

Mocker. Raven Mocker. Is that what Chief called the Cherokees' evil spirit?

Farrengalli was starting to think Raintree was more evil than the vampire suckers. They were just hungry and stupid. Raintree was civilized, an American success story, buying into the whole corporate thing. But when pushed just a little, the veneer fell away and he stripped down to the same meat-eating monster as his ancestors.

For all Farrengalli knew, the vampire suckers *were* Raintree's ancestors.

"She was loving it, brother," Farrengalli said. "Hell, she's just getting warmed up. Go ahead and take your turn."

Cigar-store Indian.

Then Farrengalli realized Raintree wasn't looking *at* him, but *past* him.

He turned, the cool night air shrinking the Boomeroo even further, until it was hidden in the nest of his pubic hair.

A flock of the creatures flew silently up the valley, stunted wings barely moving. Three came out of the mist, following the river. A few more emerged. Then more, spilling forth like shaved rats from a storm grate. Farrengalli couldn't count them all.

Their silence was more unsettling than their shrieks had been, and they soared with an eerie determination. Farrengalli stepped back into the cave, risking Raintree's piton, but the creatures didn't detect them.

Or, Farrengalli thought, *they know we're here but they just don't care. Like they got bigger fish to fry.*

One of them flew close, not altering course below them. Farrengalli's breath caught.

Doo-dah-fucking-day. That one looked like McKay!

The creature had no hair, like the others, but its face wasn't quite as wrinkled and it had the same arched brow as the dead bicyclist. A tattered piece of fabric, the same color as McKay's royal blue SealSkinz, trailed from its neck like the cape of a deformed superhero, flapping in the wind.

Being dead ain't good enough. Being dead doesn't mean you

get out of this cluster fuck.

All the more reason to keep from being dead.

Farrengalli was about to suggest they all hide deep in the cave for a while, but the words never got a chance to leave his vocal chords. Raintree rammed into him from behind, knocking them both over the ledge and into the great gulf of space.

CHAPTER FIFTY-SEVEN

Ace knew exactly where they had taken Clara.

God had shone a thin, golden beam through the clouds, casting its pure light on a dark cleft in the granite. The opening was only about thirty feet above the river, and probably back in the days of Noah, it had been deep underground. But the Unegama had bitched and moaned, as persistent as a psychotic woman, until it cut deep into God's green Earth and first released these underground demons.

Why had God played such a trick? He'd let Ace think they were angels, in a nasty piece of bait and switch, and that they had been sent from above to assist in the holy work.

It all came down to a test of faith. Why, God had tested the faith of Adam, Abraham, Jonah, Daniel, Job, pretty much every big name in the Good Book. He'd even tested his own worldly son, Jesus. So Ace should never have expected any different.

Besides, God was still on his side, as promised by the guiding light.

"Wait up," Bowie rasped from behind him.

Ace, beating his way through the scrub vegetation, had no reason to wait. This was his mission, even if Bowie now held the gun. Ace had something even more valuable: the C-4 in his knapsack, rigged with a touchy detonator.

The river guide was maybe fifty feet behind him, and though Ace was exhausted, an inner fire kindled deep in his gut and warmed him. God may have tested him, but it also meant Ace was up there with the big names, that maybe one day an extra testament would be added and preachers would be reciting from the Book of Goodall.

Ace had never been much for schooling, but he aimed to pass this test with flying colors.

He scrambled along the base of the cliff wall, following a natural shelf toward the opening. A geologist might have explained erosion patterns and the different properties of various rock layers, but to Ace, the shelf was God's version of the straight and narrow.

Though he could use a vision right about now to give him a clue. In school, before he dropped out, he'd been able to bully other kids into cheating for him, or else just wrote the answers on the back of his hand. Except he always wrote down the wrong answers, or they always asked the wrong questions. Tricks. Always tricks.

God, though I walk through the valley of death by the still waters, may I cast no shadow. And if it be Thy will, deliver me unto evil so that I might show you I'm worthy.

And, just as simple as that, the demons came out of the misty night and winged toward the opening. Ace had guessed right. They were all gathering inside, gray, blind pigeons come home to roost.

He paused, moving aside a branch to watch them enter. They were silent, except for the soft stirring of their wings and tongues.

Three made a beeline for the rock cleft, slowing a little and angling sideways as they entered.

Then came another batch.

Feeding time.

Except Ace knew they were after a different, darker kind of nourishment. They had passed up Bowie to go after Clara. They needed the thing in her belly.

And goddamned if they were going to take his blood kin without a fight. A baby was a baby, and life was life. Worth fighting for, worth killing for, and worth dying for.

Bowie caught up, breathing hard right behind him. "Jesus," the rafting guide whispered.

"Not exactly," Ace said. He was calm, his pulse and hands as steady as they had been when he'd planted the clinic bombs. Some of his fellow patriots were hot-blooded, ranting about revenge and revolution, but Ace approached his duty with patience and humility. He was a servant. Rewards would surely follow, but not on this mortal plane.

"How many of them are there?"

"They are legion. Don't you read the Good Book?"

"Not lately."

"You ought to. Lot of wisdom in them pages."

"Any instructions on this kind of thing?"

Ace watched another small flock of the creatures descend and swerve into the cave, their gray flesh making them look like glass ravens in the moonlight. "There's one of yours," he said, pointing.

"Shit. Can't be."

"Proof that he wasn't worthy. I expect your other people will be along shortly."

"Vampires. Farrengalli was right."

"Call them whatever you want. They're unfit. Cast into eternal darkness."

"She's already dead, you know."

Ace shook his head as the stream of demons slowed and

the gorge again fell hushed except for the riffing melody of the river. "Don't matter none. Being dead don't get you off the hook. And they ain't getting' my baby. Dead or alive."

Ace stepped from the low, concealing trees and walked toward the light.

CHAPTER FIFTY-EIGHT

Raintree heard Dove call his name as he took Farrengalli over the edge and into space. Or maybe he imagined it, because the loud *smack* as he and Farrengalli slammed into the side of the cliff was followed by exploding fireworks inside his skull.

The intensity of the headache was rivaled by the orange strip of napalm in his leg. He was dimly aware of the naked man hanging onto him with a passion Farrengalli had probably never shared with a lover.

He opened his eyes, and the river was above him, its rapids pale in the light of the grounded moon.

Farrengalli's arms were wrapped around his waist, hooked in his belt. The two of them were swaying, and Raintree understood.

Amateur technique. Poor awareness. The kind of thing you'd expect from a pill-head.

He'd left the safety rope secured in its anchor, coiled loosely at the edge of the cave. His foot had tangled and aborted his kamikaze attack. Hanging upside down, his leg broken and the tendons separating further by the second, blood pouring from his scalp and nose, he could only imagine how silly he must look. A red puppet on a yo-yo string. He laughed.

Farrengalli planted his toes on Raintree's chin, launching himself upward, grabbing for the rope. Raintree was too weak to hold onto him, the Olympic grip now impotent. His back was pinned to the mat, the ref counting down.

Farrengalli skinned up Raintree's devastated leg like a summer camper climbing a greased pole for a watermelon. Just before abandoning him and scaling the rope, Farrengalli reached for the belt, tugging at the fanny pack that held the cell phone.

Raintree closed his eyes, focused the LSD chaos into a gleaming beacon of purpose, and jabbed his thumb into the back of Farrengalli's hand. Farrengalli yelped and let go of the belt. Raintree laughed again.

Two points for a reversal, but the ref was still counting him down and out.

The rope wiggled, sending electric fire though his body. The oxy was letting him down when he needed it most.

Letting him down.

When he was all hung up.

He laughed again, as Farrengalli's weight was lifted from him. Then he heard Dove's voice again.

"Robert!"

Robert. She said his name with affection and urgency. The way she might if they had made love—

"Help me pull the rope up," she shouted.

"Hell, no! The crazy redskin tried to scalp my ass."

"Help me. I'm not strong enough—"

"Sorry, babe. You're a good lay and all that, but you're on your own. Don't you get it? We've all been on our own all along."

Odd, Raintree thought, blood pooling in his head and making him dizzy even as it leaked down the granite wall. *The river should be falling out of the sky any minute now.*

He thought of the two of them below him, naked as Adam and Eve, sharing the apple and the worm.

"Help me, you bastard!"

Raintree felt a dull, distant tugging on the rope. Dove was strong, but not strong enough. Just as well. Raintree's only regret was that his fingers were too numb to dig into the medicine bag. A few Valiums would be the perfect topper for this bum trip.

Bum trip. Skipping rope. Amateur technique.

He stared out across the Unegama Gorge, dangling from the heights of Attacoa, the place his Cherokee forefathers had ascended in search of wisdom. He had come up short, that was all.

The rain started again, though the moon still cut though the clouds enough to throw a strange gleam on the sacred stack of stones.

One of the Raven Mockers flew from the cooling mists above, lost and late. It paused in the air, its hueless skin slick from rain or an unwholesome sweat. Then it altered course as if receiving a silent telegraph.

Toward Raintree.

As it closed the distance, Raintree realized this was what he had sought. This hideous, gray, knotty-limbed creature, this ancient evil spirit, was his animal guide.

This was his totem, his medicine.

The object of his vision quest.

The Raven Mocker drew near, uncertain, as if sizing up a possible adversary. Or else having no idea where to sink its curved, yellow teeth.

Good acid, Robert Raintree thought, as the flicker of stunted wings cast a soft, ill wind across his rain-spattered skin. *Because my spirit guide is a white man gone gray. It has*

Jim Castle's face.

CHAPTER FIFTY-NINE

Clara awoke in utter darkness, or maybe she wasn't awake and this wasn't darkness, but a new state of being.

Maybe she hadn't slept at all. Or maybe she'd always been asleep and the dream merely changed phases.

Hands crawled the length of her belly, and she wondered if it was Ace, wanting some hurried, empty, dry intercourse. She slapped at the hands, though her arms felt heavy, full of sand. The grogginess of dreams infected her and slowed her movements. She felt as she had one night at Radford, when the philosophy professor had drugged her with Rohypnol, the date-rape drug, despite her being a willing partner in perversity. The drug had not been used to ease her pain, for the good doctor knew they both enjoyed the sensations too much to dull any of its sharp edges.

No, the drug's sole purpose had been to erase her subsequent memory of the event. To this day, she had never been certain of the doc's exploits, only that she'd bled from her vagina and rectum for a week, bruises mottled her breasts, and her back and buttocks had been covered with welts. The doctor called a few weeks later and asked if she had enjoyed it. She answered in the affirmative, and even saw him on several other occasions, though the doctor must have used up his entire bag of tricks, because she quickly grew bored with him.

Perhaps because he knew the limits and had observed them. Not just his own limits, whether moral or physical or legal. No, he'd been reined in by a social order that promised freedom, shouted it as a slogan, and sold it like a commodity, but when real freedom opened up the possibilities before its believers, they turned their cowardly faces away.

She had known limits. Ace's cold, slick hands could fondle and penetrate her, but they would never *touch* her. None of them had ever touched her, not even those who had punished her the most deeply or hit her the hardest.

"Don't, Ace, I'm sleepy." Her tongue was thick, and the words slurred.

Ace wasn't giving up. You had to give it to the human cockroach, he was persistent. The Bama Bomber had a "never say die" attitude, a "can do" spirit, a "kill them all and let God sort them out" mentality.

Even if he was a lousy lay.

The hands moved over her belly, up to her swollen nipples. They pinched gently, and she felt her nipples grow larger. Shit. Ace had hit her weak points. She moaned, despite her discomfort.

She was on her back, lying on something hard. She recalled Ace's quick screw by the river, just before they'd hijacked the rafting expedition, how he'd derived pleasure in the slap of her bare flesh against unyielding granite.

She laughed. She'd been hit harder by better. Her new motto.

The hands–*Jeez, had he grown an extra pair in the night?*– now went along her legs, caressing the insides of her thighs. Gentle, soothing, arousing, the sharp fingernails tracing along her flesh, applying just enough pressure to mark the skin.

As if Ace had found an instructional manual on foreplay.

She moaned again, and Ace's tongue flicked across her lips. Then at her belly button, then both at the same time.

Two tongues?

If not Ace, then who?

The group of rafters?

No, they were probably all dead by now.

Dead by now ...

As full memory and awareness came flooding back, she tried to sit up, but the hands confined her. Besides, she was languid and exhausted. The hands were gentle, soothing.

Not hands ... *claws.*

She remembered glimpse she'd had of their gray, knotty power, as one of them carried her into darkness. She was in their lair.

She cringed, waiting for the hands to squeeze her, the teeth to sink in, the blood to flow.

No.

These creatures weren't going to kill her, or they would have already done so.

They wanted something.

She fought for control, pushed at the claws that felt along her belly.

They wanted Little Ace.

A liquid flush erupted from deep in the bowels of the lair. The claws hesitated, and unseen wings flicked uneasily. The fluid rumble sounded again, and the stone vibrated beneath Clara's back. Something heavy fell, followed by a splash.

Splash?

Another rumble, and the claws left her, the air filled with rustling and stirring, leathery tongues licking parched, swollen lips. She could feel the wind of their wings, and the air of the confined space had taken on a damp quality. The flushing sound was rivaled by a rushing hiss far away.

Rain. Outside. Wherever "outside" was.

She let her arm flop over the side of the stone. Her hand dipped into frigid liquid.

The water was rising. The lair, or cave, or hole in the ground, wherever they had taken her, must be connected to the river. The creatures had gone to high ground like rats.

Well, not like rats, because they're flying.

And when the waters receded, they would return and take her baby.

With all the control she could muster, summoning back all the parts of her soul she had given up over the last few years, she raised her arms and reached for her head.

The helmet. She tugged at the restraint strap with fingers like cold snakes.

Once the helmet was free, she laid it beside her on the stone. The air was alive with rustling wings and the *skee, skee, skee* of creatures soaring above her. She shifted and wriggled her sodden sandbag flesh until she was at the rim of the stone. She fumbled for the flashlight switch, flicked it on, and rolled off the stone and face-first into the shocking swirl of water.

The chill revived her, shaking the lethargy inflicted by the creatures' infectious hands and tongues. She drew air and submerged, her skin tightening, her limbs aching to the bone. But a golden warmth emanated from her center, in the place where promise was born.

Ace was right. Unborn life was life after all, and still

sacred.

Maybe not worth killing for, but worth living for.

Clara gripped the large stone, letting her feet dangle until they touched bottom. She lifted her head from the water, expecting one of the creatures to yank her out by the hair. The flashlight, its bulb weak, revealed little about the space, and offered only the slightest shifting of shadows above. She didn't know in which direction to swim.

Okay, Ace Jr., Mom's going to have to pick a horse and ride it. Eeny-meeny-miney–

"Clara," Ace called, causing the creatures to scurry in frantic arcs overhead.

CHAPTER SIXTY

Bowie checked the bullets in the revolver. Four left.

Two for the creatures and, when worse came to worst, one for Clara. And one for himself.

That would be okay. Finishing on a high note, the perfect ending to an American success story.

Going out with a bang, all sins redeemed, all failures washed away in blood.

Ace could fend for himself. Maybe God would reach a soft white hand down from heaven and scoop up the sociopathic killer. Sit the Bama Bomber on the left side of the golden throne, where they could laugh together about good times and share murderous memories until Kingdom Come.

He followed Ace into the cave, hand sweating around the butt of the Python. He had to admit, religious mania had its good points. Ace had a cocksure strut, as if walking into the lion's den was a stroll in the park. Ace held the backpack to his chest, a sacrament carried into a high temple. Bowie was pretty sure the man didn't have an extra pistol stashed away. Maybe he'd finally gone off the deep end, thinking he was entering the hall of angels.

The cave was inky black, the air damp and stifling, but Bowie could swear a glow emanated from the depths, like a match head flaring at the bottom of a rank well. Behind him, the sky drummed a million silver bullets into the world.

He ducked low, though he doubted subterfuge would provide any deception against creatures whose senses had been honed in this sightless, cramped environment. Besides, Ace was giving away the game, marching with heavy feet, onward Christian soldier, hallelujah.

Best-case scenario: the dozens of creatures swooping down on Ace and surrounding him like sharks hitting a chum slick, while Bowie danced in like Fred Astaire on steroids, located Clara in the dark, and carried her to safety.

Well, *relative* safety. Once out of the cave, they'd still be exposed and vulnerable, sirloin on the hoof, walking bags of V-8.

Plan A and Plan B were both a little melodramatic. He wished there were a Plan C, but the stink of the cave disrupted his concentration. He kicked over a clattering stack of something, knelt, and felt the roughened knobs and smooth lengths.

Bones.

Whether they had belonged to people or to animals, he couldn't tell in the smothering darkness.

Probably not people. They wouldn't be so lucky.

He shuddered, recalling the wizened, altered form of C.A. McKay floating, flocking, as mindless in its flight as the others. Just another creature. Now *other*, the beast inside finally revealed.

Maybe they were all monsters inside.

All that had risen from the cosmic spark that spawned this world, from bacteria to bugs to flippered fish determined to taste the mud.

That's crazy thinking. Leave those sorts of delusions to Ace.

But Bowie wasn't sure there was any kind of way to

think *except* crazily. He was walking into a vampires' den with the tactical equivalent of a squirt gun. He didn't even have any holy water or garlic, much less a stake or silver cross. Hell, he couldn't even cobble together a decent prayer.

"Clara." Ace said it with clear conviction, a command, the word echoing in the enclosure.

Bowie flinched, expecting a flurry of fang and wing and claw.

Instead, he heard only a soft rustling deeper in the cave. And a gurgle. Maybe his stomach was churning from fear.

The glow deepened, and he saw it was coming from a point barely twenty feet in front of him. The blackness had distorted his depth perception. The cavern floor appeared to slope downward. Clara's rafting helmet lay on a flat stone shelf, its attached Maglite dim from low batteries. Her clothes lay like rumpled pelts beside her.

They must have killed her already. Would she be coming out of the darkness, back from the dead like McKay?

He recalled what Ace had said about the demons wanting the baby. *Why?*

The creatures had exhibited signs of intelligent behavior, a basic social order, a survival instinct that belied their fierce aggression. Were they smart enough to set a trap, expecting Ace and Bowie to walk right in and hop into the frying pan?

No. The creatures could have easily taken both of them by the river. Something else was at work here.

And I hope to hell it isn't God. Not the God who killed Connie, who failed those who prayed to him, who put my people on a river and plucked them one by one like daisy petals in a sick game of they-love-me, they-love-me-not.

A rumbling arouse from the hidden depths, a liquid burp. The cavern floor vibrated beneath Bowie's feet.

"I got one for you," Ace said. "I got one for the baby-killers. Don't you morons read the papers?"

Movement in the shadows beyond the orange globe of the flashlight.

Bowie lifted the Python, not knowing in which direction to point it. They were probably behind him now, cutting off their escape route. If he even managed to find Clara, the best he could hope for would be a clean mercy shot.

Being dead don't get you off the hook. A bit of Ace wisdom that made sense. Even if Bowie killed Clara and then turned the gun on himself, they would both end up shriveled and transformed, infected with whatever craving possessed these creatures. Whether of natural or supernatural origin, in the end there was no difference. Bottom line, being a vampire would suck.

"Come on out and play," Ace said. "I won't bite."

More scurrying. Restless sighs, moist flutters.

"I walked through the valley and, lo, it was righteous," Ace said. He was near the flat stone now, and in the weak pumpkin-colored glow, Bowie could see him unzipping the knapsack. "Deliver us from evil, for Thine is the kingdom."

He pulled out a jangled heap of wires, cylinders, and shiny metal. It looked like an orgy of alarm clocks and telephone cable.

"Clara, reckon your time ain't come yet," Ace said, calm, moving deeper into the cave and standing at the head of the flat stone. Like a heathen priest at an altar.

Clara rose from darkness behind the stone, her hair wet. The dying light made an orange fright mask of her face.

"This way," Bowie whispered, throat dry. The cave was as cold as the river had been, as if the darkness and the thundering water sprang from the same source.

"They want the baby, Ace. *Our* baby." Clara's voice was small and frightened. Bowie hadn't realized just how young she was. Just a dumb kid making a bad choice. Bowie knew all about bad choices.

"I know, honey," Ace said, dropping the knapsack. "They don't understand the mysterious ways of God. They got cast down from heaven way too early, and never learned about blood sacrifice. About getting washed free."

Bowie didn't know why the creatures were waiting to strike. Maybe Ace really was a messenger. An untouchable. Whatever the reason, Bowie didn't see any advantage in waiting. He burst from the concealing shadows, tripped over a hidden wedge of stone, and fell to his knees as the gun bounced away from him. He scrabbled for the Python, felt its cold, smooth barrel, and came up just as the air erupted with a cacophony of shrieks and movement.

Clara dove into the darkness with a splash.

Splash?

Bowie fired once, blindly, the muzzle flashing blue-white. The bullet whizzed and made a meaty smack, but he couldn't tell what it hit. A knobby tendon brushed his shoulder, and he threw out a panicked fist. The creature was already gone, joining its brethren.

At the head of the table, where dinner was served.

Ace.

"Deliver us from evil," Ace shouted as the creatures swarmed him.

Bowie ran toward the place where he'd last seen Clara. The water surprised him, rising fast to his knees. She swam into him with panicked strokes. He yanked her to her feet and dragged the dripping, dazed woman toward the entrance. Water swirled around his feet, and he understood why the creatures had held back. They sensed the rising floodwaters, had probably dodged them countless times over the eons.

Bowie was afraid he'd lost direction, but the drilling hiss of the rain outside provided a compass point. One of the creatures clawed him, running a line of fiery red stripes down his neck, but Bowie didn't slow down or fight back.

He ran—

Connie!—

—toward the roaring avalanche, into the blinding whiteness, and this time in the dream he reached her, pulled her to safety—

And they rolled together under the wet, cleansing rain as the cave screamed and vomited a geyser of fire and sulfuric smoke and steam, as the Earth rumbled, as boulders spun down from the hidden heights and crashed around them. Bowie tugged Clara toward the river, not because the churning rapids offered rescue, but because they offered a swifter escape, even if escape meant a suffocating death.

At least, if God had any mercy at all, their corpses would be washed far from this gate of Hell.

Bowie had Clara's hand, dragging her as the rocks tumbled down from the cliffs above. He lost his grip, reached again, and made contact in the darkness. Daggers raked his forearm and the white noise of the deafening blast gave way to a piercing

Skeek skeek skeek.

One of *them*, free of the cave, or else late to Ace's party.

Its foul, blood-drenched mouth was near his ear, seeking his jugular, and beneath that corrupt odor was a soft and familiar trace of chamomile and mint.

Dove.

Except the earthiness of her scent had given way to the sepulcher stench of grave dirt. And she wanted him more fiercely than she had the previous morning. He ran his hand along her body, which was slick and nude, limbs twining against him in a mockery of their lovemaking. Any kiss she would plant now would be final. No more good-byes.

"Run!" he shouted at Clara, realizing Fate had provided him yet one more chance to fail. A stone the size of his fist bounced off the Dove-creature's shoulder.

In the blackness and thick precipitation, Bowie couldn't make out the creature's face, but his mind painted it in vivid and sordid shades. And he pictured the teeth that wanted to punch their way into him and drink from the fountain of his heart.

The creature's demonic strength pinned him back against a long, moist sheet of rock. He ran his left hand along her hips, looking for a crevice to attack. He rammed his fist between her legs but Dove was no longer a woman. He was drawing back for another blow when his fingers touched the rope coiled around its leg. He yanked the slack line, hearing a metallic clatter against stone. Thrusting his elbow under the creature's chin, Bowie felt gray pressure rising against the back of his eyelids. He was losing consciousness.

Another shriek erupted, and Bowie thought a second creature had joined the attack. At least the end would be quick.

Instead, the Dove-creature shook, its oily, wet hair slapping against Bowie's cheek. "Go back to Hell!" Clara screamed, banging a stone against the creature's head.

Bowie couldn't see Clara, but judging by the location of her voice, she had launched herself onto the creature's back and slowed its assault. Bowie pulled the rope until his fingers felt the knot, then the piton. He rammed upward with all his strength, spearing his former lover in the gut. A viscous substance colder than the rain oozed over his fist.

He withdrew the steel spike and rammed again, this time toward the leathery lips that nipped at his cheek. The metal shattered teeth and bone.

Skeeeeeeeeeeeeeeee.

The thing that had loved him in human form now wailed in the agony of a second death. The talons lost their grip on Bowie and went toward the source of the wound, the sinister throat emitting a sick, deflating wind.

Bowie ran his hands along the creature's repulsive hide until he touched Clara's skin. He grabbed the woman and pulled her free.

"That was no angel," Clara shouted against the downpour.

"Nobody's perfect," he replied.

He wrapped one arm around Clara's slick, naked body and slid into the edge of the frothing current. The rain was so thick, he could barely tell where it ended and the river began.

CHAPTER SIXTY-ONE

Morning had never looked so beautiful.

Farrengalli peeked out of the cave at the pink clouds that rimmed the horizon. The storm had been awesome, so intense that he was afraid he wouldn't be able to hear the creatures if they attacked. He'd seen the Jim Castle thing chomp on Raintree while the Chief dangled like a squirming worm on a hook. Proof that Farrengalli had been right: Those things *were* vampires, goddamn it.

Too bad there was nobody around for him to gloat, "I told you so."

Dove, the dumb babe, had tried to rescue the redskin, climbed down the rope naked, without a weapon. Castle had made munch meat out of her, too. Farrengalli wondered how long it would take them to come back to life and go looking for some spicy Italian salami.

He didn't intend to be around long enough to find out.

He finished the last granola bar, washed it down with river water, and played the extra rope (not the one that had entangled Raintree—no, he couldn't bear to touch *that* one) down the side of the cliff. He gazed out over the gorge. The flood had carved new routes in the rocks, torn trees out by their roots, pushed up beaches of fine grit. Though the rain had stopped a couple of hours before sunrise, the river was still thick and brown, a rush of mottled chocolate milk.

Farrengalli eased his way down the rope, taking care not to look at Raintree's raw, red corpse. He imagined, or told himself he'd *only* imagined, the dead Chief twitching and quivering in obscene animation. He thought of retrieving the cell phone, but couldn't summon the courage to touch the body. He accelerated his descent, burning grooves in his palms. The rope was only fifty feet long, but it enabled him to reach a craggy, less severe slope, which he then carefully navigated, expecting to come across Dove's body at any moment.

Come across her body. Heh. My buddies will never believe I scored with a dyke.

By the time he reached the bottom, the sun was above the cliff-top trees. The storm had knocked most of the leaves off them, and their gray bones stippled the edges of the gorge.

He found the rocky stretch of shore where he'd left Castle. *Should have cut off his head or something. Or put a stake through his heart. Well, live and learn.*

In the forest, above the flood line, he found the backpack that held Dove's camera. Good as gold. With her pictures, and his first-person account (sold to the highest bidder, film rights separate), Vincent Farrengalli was going to be puffing nothing but twenty-dollar Cubans for the rest of his days. Along with the occasional Grade-A Thai stick, that was.

The grab loop of the half-inflated raft had snagged on a willow sapling, and the raft bounced like a rubber ball banded to a wooden paddle. He waded into the water, wary of being exposed to the vampires—*but, hell, they don't come out in the sunshine, do they?*—and brought the boat back to the shore. Travis Lane and ProVentures could be proud of the Muskrat, and he'd be sure to strike up an endorsement deal with them, assuming the offer was solid.

He sat, unscrewed the outer valve, and wrapped his lips around the stem.

Breathe in through nose, then out through mouth.

In, out.

Eyes on the prize.

He had the raft nearly to an air pressure he thought was good enough to get him to the lake when he heard them. At first, he thought they were vampires, and he lost a good dozen huffs worth of oxygen. They splashed in the shallow water, walking slowly, Bowie bare-chested, his shirt worn by the girl. It reached the tops of her thighs. Farrengalli figured, if she sat behind him, he'd get a pretty good view as they worked their way downstream.

"Hey, folks," he said. "Some night, huh?"

Hell, he might even let her share the media coverage. Bowie would probably go back to Oregon or Saskatchawan or wherever the hell they said he hid out. No threat there. No fight for the spotlight. So he might as well be part of the team for now.

Besides, if some vampires did come along, it probably wouldn't be that hard to shove the suckers overboard.

The *human* suckers, that was.

He smiled.

It was only fucking natural.

Bowie's eyes widened as he pointed in the sky behind Farrengalli's head, Clara scrambling to duck down into the water as if to hide.

He wants the raft. Oldest trick in the book. I turn and he knocks me in the head. Even a dummy like me wouldn't fall for—

SKEEEEEEEK.

THE END

OTHER BOOKS BY SCOTT NICHOLSON

Next #1: Afterburn
Next #2: Earth Zero
Next #3: Radiophobia
Next #4: Directive 17
Next #5: Crucible
Next #6: Half Life
After #1: The Shock
After #2: The Echo
After #3: Milepost 291
After #4: Whiteout
After #5: Red Scare
After #6: Dying Light
Zapheads #1: Bone and Cinder
Zapheads #2: Scars and Ashes
Zapheads #3: Blood and Frost
Solom #1: The Scarecrow
Solom #2: The Narrow Gate
Solom #3: The Preacher
Liquid Fear
Chronic Fear
Disintegration
The Red Church
Drummer Boy
McFall
Kiss Me or Die
Speed Dating with the Dead
The Skull Ring
The Home

Creative Spirit
October Girls
Monster's Ink
Thank You for the Flowers
Dirt
Grave Conditions